kinship
theory

kinship theory

A Novel

Hester Kaplan

Little, Brown and Company

Boston   New York   London

First Edition

The characters and events in this book are fictitious.
Any similarity to real persons, living or dead, is
coincidental and not intended by the author.

Library of Congress Cataloging-in-Publication Data

Kaplan, Hester.
Kinship theory : a novel / Hester Kaplan. — 1st ed.
p.   cm.
ISBN 0-316-48211-0
1. Mothers and daughters — Fiction.   2. Surrogate mothers — Fiction.
3. Pregnant women — Fiction.   I. Title.
PS3561.A5577 K56 2001
813'.54 — dc21   00-034812

10 9 8 7 6 5 4 3 2 1

Q-FF

Book design by JAM design

Printed in the United States of America

For Tobias and Alexander

antepartum

1

MAGGIE Crown was pregnant with her daughter's baby, and she was alone. Her imagination insisted on veering toward peril during the long pacing minutes and the solitary wait in the chill of an ultrasound examination room. She was a scientist, and so at first her mind presented her with clinically detailed pictures of a baby with missing limbs, its organs gnarled as walnuts, its skull filled with dishwater. She was a mother as well though, and next saw a narrow-eyed fetus (vaguely resembling her ex-husband) hugging his knees and smirking at her. But women who are going to have babies always feel a little undone by fear; she wasn't alone in envisioning the worst. Awake, they dream of their children born with the ears and tails of dogs, of their mothers, of their past, of disappointing lovers, of the things in life that break your heart.

Nervous sweat iced Maggie's face and her nausea rose so fast she thought she might be sick in the metal sink. Why wasn't Dale there with her now? She had counted on her daughter's company and calm to assure her that everything would be fine, that the day would reveal something wonderful. But Dale had said on the phone the night before that she wouldn't be able to pick her mother up, they would have to meet at the appointment instead — and now, oddly, she was late. The music in Dale's apartment had been playing too loudly when they talked, so that her voice had only the thinnest edge of intention.

To distract herself, Maggie moved through the room and opened drawers jumbled with tubes of jellies, flat-ended wooden prodders, scrapers, a hundred sharp implements. Rubber gloves in a cardboard box slithered and sighed when she poked at them. On the counter, diaphragms were lined up like dishes in a doll-house plate rack. Women came in different sizes, like men, but she found it funny that no one ever talked about this or what it might imply. She'd have to bring it up with Doris. Her closest friend might be embarrassed at first in her vaguely prissy way, but would be eager enough to get into it later. Through the thin, female-colored walls, Maggie heard the murmur of professionally pleasant voices and the amplified sound of a fetal heart beating.

Soon, a hazy picture of the baby would appear on the screen of the ultrasound machine; but such technology, she knew from years of her own work in the eye lab, was cold, heartless in its goals, unconcerned with outcomes. In the end, it would send people back to Ouija boards, to hand-holding, and silent prayers at night. She distrusted it not only for what it might reveal later, but more for what it could never divine and make sense of, that she was forty-eight, and that this baby she was growing was not hers at all — not genetically, biologically, or legally — but Dale's. The list flowed through her mind in a well-practiced, rational way. The machine might detect fetal abnormalities or not, but it could never know that this baby was the product of a request, a promise between mother and daughter, a cautious pact between warm body and cool technology, the emotional, the bloodless, the oldest and the newest forces in the world in edgy, untested alliance. It could not know this baby was for her to love, but not to keep.

*   *   *

"SORRY, sorry, sorry," Dale repeated when she finally arrived, her hands up and open, as though she'd just let loose a bird. A telephone call and a traffic jam on Beacon Street formed the tangle of her excuse. Maggie half listened and watched the way her daughter's fingers strained through her hair, how they twisted the rings she wore on both forefingers.

The white-coated technician came in and instructed Maggie to lie back on the table. A line of gel was spread across her belly. The lights were turned off, and the monitor was turned on, casting a silver glow through the room. Dale sat on a stool, leaned forward studiously, elbows to knees, chin in hand, ready to be instructed rather than delighted. There was a recent immovability about Dale, a holding back and keeping in, that Maggie didn't like to think about.

"No, exhale, please," the technician told Maggie, and tapped her hand.

"Breathe normally," Dale urged. "You're way too tense."

But Maggie could not take a full inhale either — her lungs were already filled with something as sodden as a premonition — and she sucked in tiny clots of air. When she turned to look at the screen she saw nothing but white dust in an overcrowded night sky, and she immediately thought of disaster, a planet exploded inside her womb. She imagined airplanes vaporizing in midair, bodies returned to their original, wet, red state. A line of panic began to crawl across her chest: there was no baby here. Maggie forced herself to look again, to acknowledge the scampering of cells inside her womb, and now a picture began to fall into place, like distant forms appearing in a fog. She saw the curve of a head turned diffidently away, a bubble of a heart fluttering like a whip of ribbon in the wind, its shades of black and gray already in training for the endless highs and lows of life. A whooshing, watery sound filled the room.

For a stunning moment, Maggie and the baby lived at the center of the world. They were a single, twisted filament around which everything else scattered and sizzled, grew and then disappeared. The blood rushed in her ears, pounded at her fingertips and deep between her legs. There was no form to her body at all now, no barrier between outside and inside, no age or hour. She knew this was the single transforming sensation of a lifetime, unlike anything else.

Maggie turned excitedly to her daughter, but Dale was frozen and silent, staring at the monitor, her legs coiled tightly around the base of the stool, her back rigid. It seemed that in her stillness, Dale understood she was missing something essential at that moment but was unable to do anything about it. Sadly, Maggie recalled that when she'd been pregnant with Dale twenty-five years earlier, she too had missed something like this, had felt nothing like what she'd just experienced. The room in its dimness took on the hollow, sorrowful air of a cave.

"Do you see the baby?" Maggie asked Dale. The technician's rolling wand ground painfully against her belly like a fist.

"No, not yet." Dale tilted her body closer to the screen. "Give me a second. All I see is snow. Lots of snow."

Dale had never been good at the game of finding shapes in the clouds, or describing the face on the moon either, so the technician used the wrong end of a ballpoint pen to trace the outline of the baby. The sound of plastic on glass was like teeth against teeth, cold and deathly, and Maggie didn't want to hear it, or see Dale struggle. Dr. Gauld came in then, smooth with the assurance that everything looked good, her mouth set in an overworked complexion.

"Okay, *there* it is. Finally, I see it now," Dale said pragmatically, and sat back as though she'd just solved a problem. "It's not so easy when you don't know what you're looking for."

Was that all her daughter would say? Where was her elation, her amazement? The technician continued to probe Maggie's insides, one hand on her wand, the other at the controls, her eyes on the screen. It's like she's playing a video game in a dark arcade, Maggie thought, and told the woman to stop, she'd had enough.

"I'm not done, Mrs. Crown. Lie back."

"But I am," Maggie said fiercely.

"Why don't you let her finish," Dale suggested, and glanced at Dr. Gauld behind her, who was bent writing under a tiny light. "It's probably almost done and then we'll be out of here. You should see your face, all twisted up and tight. What? Why are you looking at me like that?"

"This is your baby, Dale, and you've been staring at it. How do you feel? My God, at least say something."

Her daughter hesitated, and then there was a flutter at her lips, as though the words passing out were too uncertain to be spoken. It's not that she is unmoved, Maggie suddenly realized, but all she sees is a throb on the screen, the suggestion of a shape, and Dale has always needed real evidence of love, of hope. Maggie wiped the sticky gel off her skin, took her daughter's hand, and placed it on her belly.

"Touch it," she said, and felt the most tentative dots of pressure from her daughter's fingers. "Press down here."

"You know it's much too small. You know I can't possibly feel anything."

Dale's tone was measured, but with a hint of defensiveness, and she withdrew her hand quickly. In the gray of the examining room, her expression was as unreadable as the surface of cold water, and it chilled Maggie.

HOURS later, Maggie got off the train at Newton Centre and walked home. From the end of the block, she was able to see her house from a slight distance; somewhat neglected, streaked with fresh tears of rain, wood swollen but still proud. Cushioned in the bed of uncut jade grass that was her lawn, the place looked to her as if it were about to float away. She imagined it might drift through the evening over the hazy Boston skyline with her in it, and tomorrow offer lush, exotic views from its windows, landscapes that were nothing like today's.

Suddenly, though, she saw broken gray coastlines instead, violent, sooty cities, and gaping canyons painted in human colors below, and it was as if she hadn't risen at all to some great adventure — it was the earth that had fallen away from beneath her. She thought of Dale's curious dispassion that morning, and knew that this was a vision of a lonely orbit, her home — and all the life she had lived in it — without foundation now, its familiar light scattered, its rooms whisked clean of attachments.

When she won the unspectacular cape on Benton Road in her divorce battle nine years earlier, it was still the unblemished white it was intended to be. The shutters had all their slats, like mouths full of perfect teeth, and the lawn was snipped to an even buzz. Such caretaking had been Gordon's fussy work; her ex-husband was the kind of man who took a broom to the front walk, who bent at the knees to pinch a leaf that angled out of line, picked up toys left outside, and pulled weeds in the near dark, collecting them in his smooth hands.

Gordon had warned her that she would be better off bleeding him for money every month than she would be keeping the place. Maggie knew even then, at the saddest moment of disassembly of her sixteen-year marriage, that he was right — houses ate people, and she'd have a hard time not being devoured by this one. Every year it gulped down greater quantities of care and money, but she still left the windows open during storms because she loved the spray urging through the screens more than she loved being practical and thoughtful all the time. Puddles of milky water sat for days on the windowsills doing silent damage, but the rooms smelled of fruit and nature, of places much farther from the city, and of Dale, who'd grown up there. Sometimes Maggie told herself she was too attached to the place; the house was only an imperfect *thing*, a tilting, needy construction. It was the life inside that you were supposed to love.

Maggie unlocked the front door and breathed the hallway's cooler air. The unsettling events of the morning, now this dizzying apparition of herself aloft and alone, and July humidity so thick you could pack it into a jar, had left her sticky and agitated. Sweat silked the spaces behind her knees, under her arms and breasts. Her body was not changing gracefully in pregnancy, even at eighteen weeks, and she had developed a habit of pulling at her skin so that she was covered with faint red spots, like faded kisses. She put down her bag, which bulged with work she'd brought home from the lab. Then she stepped out of her low-heeled sandals and let her flowered skirt drop around her ankles like sea foam, then her pale underpants. Finally Maggie unbuttoned her white blouse and took off her bra so she stood naked except for the necklace of gold beads she always wore. She waited for even the thinnest breeze to wrap itself around her.

She thought of her daughter again, and how she had looked so uneasy that morning in the doctor's office. Dale was sleek as usual in her black clothes and silver jewelry, her skin still luminescent. But she seemed oddly askew, as though she'd had to push her way through an unyielding crowd to get to her mother and baby, and then wasn't sure she wanted to be there at all.

Maggie ate a dinner of fruit and listened to the news on the radio, to the drag and scratch of heat-softened noise on the street. Her eyes lingered on the textures around her — the back door's brass knob mottled green and black, her neighbor's porch light already on in the bright evening, scattered by dirty, diamond-patterned glass, her own short fingernails darkened by peach pulp. Her mouth explored the sodden honeydew and the cool, happy watermelon, the ripe nectarine. Details gave depth to a flatness she was feeling at the moment — or was it, she wondered, an unexpected pinch of longing for her daughter? Had Dale been in the kitchen then, she would have directed her mother to sit at the table. She would have offered a dinner full of the right, baby-healthy elements, and a glass of milk, instead of the wine Maggie kept eyeing. Her diligence, her attentiveness, would have tightened the air, which felt droopier with indirection by the minute. Maggie's naked solitude would also have made Dale concerned enough — there were times she wished her daughter weren't quite so scrutinizing — to wonder out loud about it. The man announcing the news on the radio was only a deep voice, she'd point out, not a lover or friend in real conversation, and in any case, his news was all bad. (And would she also mention the webs of spidery veins on Maggie's upper thighs, and the few startling tendrils of gray pubic hair?)

But Dale wasn't there in the kitchen, hadn't even called, and she had not really been so self-assured or even so attentive in a while, not since Maggie had gotten pregnant. The morning was clear enough evidence of how things had changed. Dale's unsettling and impassive mood at the doctor's office struck Maggie again now like the muddy off-taste of the overripe plum she leaned over to spit out into the sink.

For a few minutes Maggie paced the kitchen, then the hall, until she stopped and stared into her living room. She didn't know why or when it had become the one place she avoided so assiduously, but decided it was time to start over. Her first targets were the erect blue armchairs Gordon had chosen years earlier because they were sensible and appropriate — two of his favorite attributes for people and things. After years, they had finally begun to sag in gentle resignation like old military men and to fade to a softer, less serious blue. She moved them toward the window facing each other. Each time she bent over, blood rushed to her nipples like tiny cautionary headaches, and she held her breasts and slowed for a minute. She gathered up the endless piles of magazines, papers, and books that covered every surface, and dumped them in a back closet off the kitchen. Maggie knew she grew attached to too much, a fault that weighed her down and crowded rooms and her life. Dot and Isabel, her two ancient cats, walked bitchily across the tops of things until they found a place to settle together and observe her.

By the time Maggie finished she was trembly enough to have worried herself, and she sat down in one of the blue chairs by the window. She placed her hands over the swell of her stomach, which felt bruised, as though the ultrasound had actually burned its way through layers of pink tissue and the elastic wall of her muscles. She took one last look out the window for some shadow of Dale coming to talk to her, or the unexpected, uncomplicated pleasure of fireflies or fireworks or a friend. The yellow curtains were only half drawn, exposing her to the world. Maggie didn't need her flushed and pregnant nakedness under the lamp to give the neighbors one more thing to wonder about, so she reached up to pull the curtains closed. Moths continued to bang optimistically against the screen, as though their persistence would change her mind and she'd open up to warm them again.

MAGGIE tuned the radio to *Eric in the Evening*, the jazz show she liked mostly for the man's liquid voice, and retrieved copies of *Ophthalmology* and the *American Journal of Ophthalmology* from her bag and brought them back to the chair by the window. Her work had always been a powerful distraction for her, a passion, sometimes a frustration, but this evening the smooth white pages fanning across her belly felt like a reassuring caress. Flipping ahead, she turned to a glossy photo spread of scarred and ruined eyes, some burned by chemicals, others by illness or bad genes, lined up like a montage of repulsive most-wanted posters. She was not immune to their lure, the way they seduced the healthy to stay a little longer, take one more sideways glance, to feel pretty lucky.

Dale at six had been fascinated by Maggie's clinical textbooks and journals, which were shelved in the tiny upstairs room Gordon had claimed as his home office. She would sit on the floor with the colorful pictorial atlases of infection and deformation open on her lap, run her hands over the photographs of people with sore and scabby gazes, babies with absurdly crossed eyes. Maggie had watched her daughter study the collection of disaster as another child might study her mother's jewelry in a heart-shaped box on a dresser, or her father's ties hanging in the closet. She thought then — mistakenly, she later realized — that her daughter was like her in that way: curious, drawn to curing the afflictions in life, a little dreamy.

Looking down at Dale one night, Gordon had declared his daughter's interest in the pictures unhealthy; they'd become a kind of creepy narcotic. Always full of doubt as a mother, Maggie didn't disagree when he took the books away and instead gave

Dale *Stuart Little* and *Little House on the Prairie*, though she couldn't quite read yet. Later, he moved Maggie's books to the attic. She'd watched the muscles on his back rise and lengthen as he climbed the ladder to put them away, unmoved in any way, or anymore, by his body. She wished he would never descend. The books were still up there nearly two decades later, dusty stacks of her derailed ambitions.

Maggie bent over and let her breasts rest on her thighs. She smelled herself, salty and somewhat unfamiliar, and felt the erotic pulse of her body. It made her laugh to wonder who would make love to her now, in this ridiculous state. She wanted to be admired, but didn't always think she was admirable; she wanted proximity, but couldn't stand to be crowded. She wanted confirmation, but knew she'd always doubt it. Such longing and impossibility were an inseparable pair in her life, forever jammed together and fighting, like an old married couple on a slow, hot bus. In this way, Maggie told herself, she and Dale were very much alike; her daughter would never be able to have a baby — that was the broadest fact of her life, it was the real, physical truth — and so she wanted one more than anything else.

It was the single story of the past three years, a series of unsuccessful attempts by Dale and her husband, Nate, to adopt a child. A seventeen-year-old girl named Blossom had changed her mind at the last minute and kept the baby she'd promised them. Adoption agencies and lawyers entered their names on mythically long lists, others confidently pointed them down blind leads to bitter ends. Each failure brought a little greater grief, so that when Dale cried about it, her tears were slow and golden with condensed pain. Every time she was told no, turned down, beaten out by someone else, Dale became more convinced that she would never have a child. There was something about her that people could sense, she confessed to her mother, though she didn't know exactly what it was. At Dale's lowest point, Maggie allowed herself to wonder if this were true, there *was* something about her; maybe it was Dale's composure that made people step back, or her infallible, effortless beauty, which she seemed unaware of.

Maybe it was simply that she was too young, just twenty-two when her quest began, and Nate only thirty, to be so zealously single-minded. Perhaps they *could* sense a deep neediness in Dale that made them stop, fiddle, and evade — or was it only Maggie who saw this so clearly?

On the weekends, when she and Dale walked by the Charles River or around Jamaica Pond, as they had done forever, Maggie longed for the time before baby-need and baby-disappointment was the only topic and the sole desire that seemed to drive her daughter's life. She did not entirely understand it, or where this obsession had sprung from. Maggie had gotten pregnant with Dale by accident, had not wanted a child at all, and so her longings had always been of a very different sort. Sometimes she stopped listening to her daughter altogether and looked out onto the placid urban waters as though real talk — even with its predictability, repetitions, and irritations — had drowned there. When they stayed in and watched the cooking shows on television that Dale was addicted to, she saw how her daughter became mesmerized by spoons stirring and the inevitable, slow rise of bread. Momentarily, her hunger seemed sated, as though cream sauces and melted butter filled her childless void. Maggie's stomach sometimes turned at the richness, the lushness of her daughter's descriptions of the food.

Once a week they still ate breakfast together at the S & S restaurant in Inman Square. Over the years the place had gone from an awkwardly angled pair of rooms, heavy with the smell of bacon grease and cigarettes, to an overly-bright, air-filtered space with all the charm of an airport hotel. The transformation depressed Maggie — it didn't seem to be at all in the right direction — but she supposed it reflected the ways in which she and Dale had also changed in less than wonderful ways. Where conversation had once bobbed between them, ever since Dale's baby fixation a heavy deliberateness had come to sit there instead. Maggie sometimes imagined leaping up from the table so she wouldn't have to see Dale's expectant face turned to her waiting for an answer or a solution she didn't have. Her daughter's fierce attachment, her ceaseless longing, was sometimes stifling, and was painful evidence to Maggie that she'd been an unsure, aloof mother. But wasn't this always the way between mothers and daughters? she wondered. Wasn't this the truth of herself as a daughter, too?

And then a year ago in Maggie's kitchen, they had read in the *Sunday Globe* about a forty-seven-year-old school librarian in Hollywood, Florida, who was having a baby for her daughter, who, like Dale, had been born without a uterus. They had bent over the picture of the woman, their fingers tapping the big belly taut against a sweatshirt, the shag haircut, with the odd feeling that they were looking at themselves. The woman was watering a philodendron that had gone crazy and crept up walls streaked with flowered paper.

"You done?" Dale had asked Maggie before she turned to page 23, where the article continued. The newspaper had already softened under her hands.

The daughter looked like her mother, same leafy haircut, an upturned nose, elbows two sharp points on a clean kitchen table. It had all seemed so otherworldly to Maggie, as distant as sedated pain, and it made her think how far Hollywood, Florida, was from Newton, Massachusetts. Out the window in Florida was an orange tree heavy with fruit, while on the wall to the right of the daughter was a set of pot holders and a calendar showing a covered bridge and a man in boots trekking through deep snow, a pine branch held in front of him like a divining rod. The picture was so aggressively winter in New England that Maggie's first and most lasting thought was, these parts don't fit, this is not as simple or benevolent as it looks.

Later Maggie would recognize her quick dismissal as panic, but at the time, she had simply said, "This is very strange science," and gone back to cutting vegetables for minestrone soup. Behind her, Dale flipped back to the beginning of the article, and said that it was actually very amazing science if you thought about it. She read the piece again, a few lines out loud. A little later, when she'd left to have dinner with Nate and her father and his wife, May,

Dale's eyes were rimmed red; not, Maggie knew, from the onions she had chopped so fine they'd floated off the cutting board on their own stinging juice.

Maggie understood only later that a shift had occurred that day in the kitchen. At the time, it was enough to see that her daughter no longer cried or asked to be soothed quite so often. She didn't question it, but simply welcomed the reprieve a little selfishly and hoped it would last. Dale was finally thinking of things other than disappointment — her marriage, her job, her friends, her life. At work, she had a new position as promotions director at an Internet company, and appeared happy enough to be sucked into the screen's life for hours.

And then, three months later, she and Dale had stood in a snowed-in parking lot outside the S & S, where they'd just finished eating, and watched a plow lazily work its way around the cars.

"I guess we're not going anywhere for a few minutes," Dale said, and zipped up her pillowy coat. Steel gray, it made her look like a rain cloud. Dale had hovered too close that morning; at one point, she'd leaned far over the table and toppled the tower of tiny plastic cream containers Maggie had erected. She told her mother not to play with her food.

"I'm not sure why we live here and put up with this weather at all," Maggie said, and added that now she'd be late to the lab. Already she felt the damp seeping into her shoes. "It says something basically masochistic about all of us."

"Yes, but you love it. Admit it — all this weather, good, bad, and destructive, is your favorite thing. I'm not sure why exactly." Dale wiped the snow off Maggie's hair. "Do you remember the woman in Florida we read about in the paper?"

"Of course I do." When Maggie had heard that Hollywood was a town always on the edge of a Miami riot, she'd pictured the librarian, pregnant with her own grandchild, cowering in the corner of her shag-carpeted bedroom, eyeing the gun stashed in the bedside table. "But Florida's much worse than this. Its range is only hot and hotter. And anyway, that's where my mother lives, so forget it. I'd rather get frostbite."

"I really wasn't suggesting we move there." Dale hesitated. "I saw the woman on the news last night."

Maggie sucked in the damp air. It was what she needed suddenly, like glass after glass of cold water. In front of her the cars were as glossy as gumballs in the wet snow, and traffic had stopped on Cambridge Street. Some people looked unhappy at the prospect of missing work, but many more, she noticed, looked as though this were their first lucky break in years. She felt tension radiating from Dale beside her, and her own mind jumbled with urgency: she'd left the stove on, there was a crisis at work, cancer was invading her breast that second. There was something she'd forgotten to do but she couldn't remember what it was. She really had to leave, to run.

"Maybe we can maneuver around the plow. Or I'll stand out here and direct you." Maggie looked at her watch. "I have a new group for the eye study coming in half an hour. I really have to go."

"Plenty of time — look, he's almost done. It's called gestational surrogacy," Dale said in a factual way that made Maggie think of Gordon. "In case you were wondering."

"Thanks. I know what it's called."

The plow finished and backed out of the lot. Dale unlocked the door of her tiny Honda, scratched and dented with evidence of her driving habits. "The daughter's eggs, the husband's sperm, the mother's uterus. It's remarkable that it can be done at all — but in a way it also makes absolutely perfect sense. Are you getting in?"

"Why is that?"

"Who better than the mother to do it? Really, what is the difference between the mother and daughter when you think about it. It's just reversing the natural order a bit, but the ingredients stay the same."

Instead of looking over the roof of the car at her daughter, who was expecting a response even as snow landed on her eyelashes, Maggie stared down at her feet in their chapped brown flats. Always the wrong shoe for the wrong day, that's what kind of person I am, she thought, out of step, off-kilter. She knew that if she stood there long enough, and the snow kept falling, when she finally moved the shape of her shoes would remain, like the outline of an accident, the place where someone had been hit and fell.

"This might actually be a blizzard," Maggie mumbled. "Did you know about this? Where have I been that I didn't?"

"They've only been talking about it for days on the news. Were you listening at all?" Dale shifted from foot to foot.

"I thought I was. Look, maybe I should just take the subway this morning, save you the drive. The roads are awful already."

"I meant were you listening to *me*. Anyway, I want to drive you," Dale said firmly. "I want to talk to you. But I'm getting really cold, so can we get in now, please, or is there some reason we need to stand out here in the snow?"

Maggie reluctantly opened the door and slid onto the seat. Nate's basketball sat between her feet like a dog, and the car was littered with his students' work. At The Willows, the year-round residential school where he taught, his students produced sad confessions scribbled in journals by the armload. Maggie had read some of them once, with Nate hanging over her shoulder eager for her reaction, but she had soon felt too pummeled by the litany of missteps and sorrows to keep going. They made her feel old and out of things. Maggie turned around and saw a shovel resting on the back seat. She knew Nate would have made sure Dale had what she needed before she left the house. He might have placed a hat on her head too, if he thought she'd be cold, rubbed her lips with protective balm, asked what he should make her for dinner.

Dale put a stick of Dentyne into her mouth and threw the wrapper on the dashboard, where a small collection gathered like dried flowers. "She's having twins. I heard that on the news, too."

"Give me a piece of that."

Dale handed the gum to Maggie, who softened the pink block between her fingers and finally turned to her daughter. The smell of sweet cinnamon was strong. "I know what you're thinking, Dale, but it's completely impossible. I'm too old, so don't even ask. You can drive now. Go ahead. It's clear."

"Actually, not impossible at all," Dale persisted. "The woman in Florida is your age. Did you know *that?*"

"Yes, I know that. Listen, Dale, I live alone, I work too hard, spend too many hours in the lab. I talk to myself, I never eat the right things. I drink too much coffee, too much wine, eat too much fat, no fiber. I don't know when snowstorms are coming."

"You're healthy," her daughter countered. "You're beautiful. You walk miles every day. You have good bones."

Maggie laughed. "Good bones? I inhale chemicals, I'm exposed to nasty stuff all the time. I can't handle money. Ask your father." Maggie talked frantically, competing with the fall of snow. "I hate doctors, they scare me, cancer and heart disease run in my family. The house is probably filled with lead paint. I'm indecisive, I'm impulsive, I'm clumsy. I'm crazy at times."

"And you're also smart and incredibly good at what you do. You just like to imagine you're a mess, but you're not."

Maggie wouldn't add that she sometimes slept with men she didn't like very much, men whose hairs she'd find on her pillow, whose condoms were stuck to the bottom of the wastebasket the next morning, or that she could be cruel and too critical, even to Dale, in ways that surprised her. She wouldn't add that there were too many other things she wanted to do instead of this, that she'd have to stay too still to have a baby, that it would age her too fast. That her body had made a terrible mistake the first time around with Dale, and to do it twice would just be asking for it. Or that she wasn't sure Dale was up to the job of motherhood at the moment, despite the intensity of her longings — or maybe simply because of them. What did Dale understand at all about being a mother? And wasn't a woman supposed to want something more for herself first before giving it all away?

If I'd had the choice, Maggie thought incompletely. The notion of some different life was as pale now as a match lit on a bright beach.

"There are options you and Nate haven't explored," she told Dale, aware of how tight and scolding her tone had become. "Ones you haven't even considered. You're inside your computer all day, but that's not real life at all. There's too much speed and the gratifications are flimsy, and then tomorrow everything's different again. You have no idea what waiting is for."

Dale leaned over to fix the collar on Maggie's coat, and Maggie thought how much other women, Doris in particular, envied Dale's closeness to her. They were too close probably, the break never completely made even given so many opportunities and reasons, and this the very best evidence. Dale still wanted everything from her — this desire to possess her!— and she pulled away with an abruptness she quickly regretted. The cold window pressed against the back of her head like a fast-approaching headache.

"I stay up all night and go around naked. The neighbors want to burn me out of my house — which needs a lot of work, by the way. I never finish anything, I'm flighty. I still forget to lock the front door most of the time. I'm lazy and have bad thoughts. Jesus, I have menopause lurking around the corner. I have phobias, my ups and downs and moods you don't even know about. I live with cats. There are days I want to dump everything and go away forever. That can't be good." Maggie hesitated. "And I wasn't such a stellar mother to you. My God, what did you ever learn from me?"

"But I'll be the mother, not you."

Maggie smelled a sour, anxious odor rise from under her layers of clothing. "Okay then, I think it's wrong, Dale. Really wrong."

"No, it's fine, it's safe, totally," her daughter insisted. "I've talked to lots of people, I've done a ton of research this past month, yes, on the web, too, inside my computer, as you say. Nate and I have talked to doctors at the IVF clinic at Mass General. There are procedures and drugs and some precautions, but they say we'd all be good candidates. You wouldn't be the first woman to do this. It's hardly experimental at this point."

"But *I've* never done it before. For me it would be entirely experimental. There's only so much you can trick your body into believing. Maybe some things just shouldn't happen, some things shouldn't be forced. Women having babies at forty-eight, women having babies for other women. It's too complicated, it does terrible things to their heads, to them. What will happen to them later on? What will it do to us, Dale?" Her words hung in the air as frozen mist.

"But I'm not another woman, and neither are you, and nothing will happen to us now or later. This baby would be my baby and Nate's, not someone else's. And I'm asking you today, because if we wait, we'll lose the chance. You really will be too old then."

"But look what I did to you. I gave you a body that couldn't have babies," Maggie said desperately. Her daughter's lack was the greatest sorrow of her life, but she understood it was also what bound them so closely to each other. "I already fucked up once. It would be completely crazy to do it again, to test what we're made of."

"It wasn't your fault, and the likelihood is just . . . Well, it won't happen again, that's all. It would be like getting struck by lightning or winning the Megabucks."

Maggie shook her head. "You're so confident, Dale. So convinced by statistics and probabilities. I just don't know how you can be, or what you do with all the parts of life that don't make sense, that don't fall the way you expect them to." She sighed. "You can love a child that isn't genetically yours, you know. People do it every day."

"Yes, I know they do, but if you had a choice, wouldn't you want this more? Wouldn't you want to know what your child was made of?"

"You can't control the future any better that way," Maggie said. She turned away from her daughter to watch the city disappear behind a gauze of steady snow. She believed in the force of spirit — she knew hers to be like her daughter's, particularly willful and not always so thoughtful — but she *knew* the determination of the body was stronger. It aged when you didn't want it to, it allowed itself dangerous pleasures without pause or caution, it loved what and when it wasn't supposed to. It could turn on you. There was no way to explain how she, young and healthy, had borne a daughter without a uterus. Freak occurrence, bad luck, even a clinical name for it was no explanation for *why* it happened, and it didn't ease her guilt or regret.

"All I know is that the thing I want most is the thing I can't have," Dale said. She lifted her hands and Maggie saw that her palms were pink, as though stained. "I want a baby so much I can't stand it, I ache all over. Sometimes I feel like I might die over this." Snow had blanketed the windshield, and Dale's voice had a glassy sharpness to it. "You've always done everything for me. I know what I'm asking now, I know how huge it is. I have thought about it. Will you lend your body to me for nine months? Have *my* baby for me because I can't do it for myself?"

Maggie accepted how *much* Dale wanted a baby, that after everything, this was not a reckless request, an indulgence. It was, Dale had said, an ache, deep down and impossible to extract or examine. Still, as completely as she knew her daughter, she did not understand the *why* of it entirely, when it was so painfully different from what she'd wanted. Maggie had always envisioned a boundless, unfettered life for herself in science first, and maybe a child later, but it hadn't happened that way at all.

Dale had explained over and over that she wasn't going to feel differently about this; she wasn't going to wake up one day and discover she'd grown a uterus. It wasn't a matter of patience or good behavior. She had a husband she loved, and work was not her life — it never would be — so why wait? And for what? Why not want this now instead of later? Wasn't motherhood, in fact, the best, truest thing? she'd asked.

"You don't know what it feels like to have no one follow you," Dale said softly. "The cold is always at my back. It's like someone left a window open and I can't shut it. I just want to be warm. I don't think you'll ever know what that's like. I mean, I'm always right here next to you and I always will be."

*   *   *

IN the weeks after Dale's request, before she made her decision, Maggie sometimes went out of her way to drive by the family planning clinic on Brookline Avenue. Stopped at the light, she tracked slim-backed women making their hunched way inside. The men who went with them caught her eye — a boy in a Boston University sweatshirt, a husband, a tired father fingering the quarters he'd collected for the parking meter. It seemed to Maggie that connections were being missed all over the place, and she would whack the steering wheel for such waste. These women didn't want a baby, but Dale did, and Maggie was tempted to rush out of the car in her lithe and furious way and make a deal for her helpless daughter, this for that, that for this — what do *you* want in your life more than anything? But she knew it was not so simple (though she believed it should be), that people had all sorts of inexplicable reasons for doing what they didn't believe in, for not doing what they thought was right. And on these days, she knew she couldn't change the world, but maybe only herself, to ease her daughter's losses.

A month later, on the subway on her way to work, Maggie had been caught in a heavy rain that made the morning as dirty as night. The train rocked as it pulled itself across the Salt and Pepper Bridge, and she felt herself slipping away and into herself under the weight of the decision. The puckered ribbon of the Charles River was revealed window by window, as though life were slowing down to give her time to view every piece of it.

There was a sudden wet sizzle, followed by a flash of blue, and the train stopped on the highest arc of the bridge span. The lights went out. In the dark, in an instant, anything could happen, Maggie realized. She could hear the man next to her breathing through his mouth. Maggie remembered how Dale, at ten, had once been caught on a Ferris wheel at the very top when it had stopped for some unknown reason. From down below, Maggie looked up and saw her daughter's head move like a panicked moon rising too fast in the sky. "Sit down!" Maggie had screamed.

"Sit down! Just wait. It will go in a minute." Dale had only leaned farther over, straining to hear what her mother was saying. Maggie knew she was making things worse by screaming, but she couldn't stop herself from pleading as she realized how easily Dale could tip out of the bright red box and come soaring down in her yellow dress. And then the wheel had started turning again, and her daughter passed by at the lowest point, her face now blurred with delight, her fear immediately forgotten. Those are the ups and downs of motherhood, Maggie had told herself; her heart had clenched and sighed, and always would.

The lights went on and the trolley began to scratch its way forward. Maggie remembered how the woman in Hollywood had said her sole motive for having a baby for her daughter was love. Her heart too must have clenched and sighed over the years for her daughter. But love was not the only motive, it couldn't be, it was never so uncomplicated or oblivious of its surroundings or its history. Hate — hating yourself for saying no — Maggie decided, was probably a sharper, more defining sentiment. And sometimes you said yes because to not do so would be worse.

She had always carried around a burden of maternal guilt, but she could not ever say motherhood had been wrong for her. She recalled times of despair with Dale, a baby not wanted, conceived through carelessness with a man she wasn't sure she loved. She felt she had been a failure at the toughest moments with her child; she was full of self-indictment for her impatience and selfishness, and later for the hard fact of Dale's deficit. She remembered the endless worries of motherhood, the long hours of boredom, the desire to escape and do something else, the weight of responsibility, the huge wound of indecipherable resentment she thought might never heal. But amidst this, she also easily recalled the astonishing pleasure she'd found in Dale from the moment she was born, in how she moved, how she smelled, what she felt like naked, how the child loved her completely, how even the moments of sorrow could be beautiful. She loved her daughter fiercely, still. Look what you have given me and taken away, Maggie would think, look how you are the center of my life.

The newspaper had called the woman in Florida an altruist, and maybe she was. But there was joy in giving, too, and sometimes hope for the giver, and at that moment, Maggie knew she would say yes to Dale. It's what she would give her daughter.

Maggie sat up, startled by the doorbell. Its whispered static hinted at a loose wire somewhere deep in the house, and warned of the possibility of fire, and of the need to escape rather than repair. It brought to mind once more Dale's mood that morning, and Maggie's own incendiary doubts. Despite Dale's calling to her from the other side of the door, Maggie thought how much their closeness felt like distance these days. She didn't understand what her daughter was doing at all, why she was acting this way. Look what I have given you, she whispered, and look how you're miles away from me now. Look how I don't really know you anymore.

As she stood there clutching the red plastic raincoat closed at her chest, Dale and Nate looked at her and then back at each other, as though confirming some ancient private joke. When the doorbell rang, Maggie had put on the first thing her hand found in the closet, a coat that had belonged to Dale and reached only inches down her thighs. The heat from her body released the coat's ancient scent of cheap high-school perfume and sex, of her daughter's bumpy past.

"Such an attractive outfit," Dale teased, and raised her eyebrows, as the humid air pushed past her and into the house. She peered down the hall at the artistic attempts of her mother's two most recent lovers, both painters in their off-hours. Dale called it the Wall of Flame, as though the pictures — or the men — were trophies of a sort, framed and mounted, of much better use to her mother inert. She turned back to Maggie, her head tilted curiously. "What exactly were you doing?"

"Some reading for work. It was so hot in here, I —" Maggie stopped. She didn't have to explain herself in her own house. "Catching up on things."

"You're working too hard, as usual. You look like Little Red Riding Hood, porno version," Nate said, and pulled at his T-shirt to cool himself. He was tall — elongated was what Maggie thought — his body like one endless, languid stretch. He wore faded cargo shorts that hung far below his knees. "Who's here with you?"

"No one. It's just the radio." Behind them, across Benton Road, which still glinted a little in the evening heat, Maggie saw Dr. Riesen, a tight-faced gastroenterologist, inch his front door open. In a string of recent neighborhood break-ins, his house had been hit first; hers was as yet untouched, a fact she knew her neighbors found not only illogical but unfair. A laptop computer and a gun from a bedside table drawer, the two standards of modern life, had been stolen. She could not imagine Hugh Riesen taking aim at anything. Since the robbery, he confused vigilance with disapproval and now glared at her suspiciously.

At first Maggie had blended into the neighborhood, with her ambitious and friendly lawyer husband, her young child in braids and jumpers, her appearances at barbecues and sidewalk chats under the full, sticky maples. But these days — or years, more precisely — she was out of place, a single, unpredictable woman on a married street. Her grass was uncut and her garden untended, her cats prowled at night, and her house was dark when it should be lit up, blazing when she should be asleep. Strange cars sometimes spent the night parked in her driveway, and on those occasions she was sure the sounds of sex, but never love, romped out of her bedroom window. Her recycling bin revealed her penchant for anchovies and marinated artichokes, hearts of palm, mandarin oranges in heavy syrup, white wine. Other people were more discreet about their tastes, she knew, stashing bottles and cans under neatly bound stacks of last week's newspapers.

She looked down at her thin knees now jutting out from under the plastic hem of the raincoat, like a little girl's. The intervening years seemed suddenly as solid and small as a pebble in her hand.

"Riesen's becoming completely paranoid," she said, and waved a single, scolding finger at him before closing the door. "He told me he bought another gun because even the suburbs are rotten these days, and then he suggested I should get one too. Can you imagine? What would *I* do with a gun?"

"You? That's a pretty scary thought," Nate said, and then his face became soft with distraction. The year before, a student at The Willows had shot herself in the basement of her dorm, and he had cried when he talked about it. As Nate had rested his blond head on Maggie's table among the uncleared plates that day, she had realized that her son-in-law was a rare man of long and large emotions, when she'd once believed he was capricious. He was, she'd told friends, the kind of boy who majored in Frisbee in college. Now he leaned over to kiss her on the cheek, an afterthought. "I guess this means you forgot about tonight then," he said, "given the outfit."

"Tonight?" Maggie turned to Dale. She knew it was entirely possible to have blocked out some plan they'd made.

"He's joking," Dale said, and gave Nate a flat-handed push on the arm. "We just wanted to see how you're doing."

Earlier, Maggie had wished Dale would come by; now she didn't feel up to this visit or the jocularity and simply wanted to be alone. Before she could say anything, Nate placed both hands on the rise of her belly. Since she'd become pregnant he did this without hesitation or permission, and through the plastic, his touch was startling but not unpleasant. She'd seen pictures of healers with their hands splayed like his, their faces set in concentration.

"I swear I can tell it's bigger," he said, his hands still on Maggie. "Dale, come here and feel this. Tell me I'm wrong."

Dale glanced uneasily at her mother, and turned to look at the living room instead. Nate gave Maggie an apologetic shrug; he was patient with Dale in a way she wasn't.

"No, you did not walk into the wrong house, if that's what you're thinking," Maggie said, and walked into the middle of the room to place herself as a landmark. She held her arms out and the raincoat fell open. As she grabbed it closed she wondered if Nate had seen the blooming, the fullness of her breasts, a rounding everywhere, a dark line of pubic hair, in such a quick flash. What did he make of his seed inside her from sterile technology, all glass and stainless steel, but conception and nakedness nonetheless? What did anyone make of all this? Nate pulled at his shirt again.

"What do you think?" Maggie asked, turning to Dale. "I'm not sure if I'm done yet, if this is how I'll leave it finally. I need to see it in the daylight first."

Dale held up her hands. She had always been skeptical of the impulses that seized her mother, as though they were causes for concern, when she was much more considered about things, like her father. She walked around the room in her slow, sleek way, dragging her fingers over the backs of chairs, across the sleeping cats. Maggie was often amazed by her daughter's elegance and the anesthetic effect it had on people, on Nate, who watched her now. She suddenly realized how tired she was, how much she just wanted to be in bed.

"I think it looks great." Nate flopped down like a dropped sail, all sighs and folds, in one of the blue chairs and smacked the arm for emphasis. He rested his sneakered feet on the opposite chair and looked over at his wife. "We should try moving some stuff around in our place, Dale. See what happens."

"Happens?" she asked. "Like magic?"

Maggie pictured their apartment in Cambridge, everything, though not much of anything, sharply angled and neat. It was full of white, too, as though parts of it had been erased. Maggie was restless when she was there, and sometimes felt a tingling of sensory deprivation that made her want to talk loudly and disturb the order. She always opened windows, even in winter, and more than once at dinner she spilled, she toppled, she burned something. Nate often seemed uncomfortable in his own home, too; he dodged pieces of furniture at the last second as though they were legless men parked in the middle of the sidewalk. He shut the door of the refrigerator gingerly, when she knew he'd grown up in a house full of boys who kicked it closed with their heels.

"These days, every time I come over you've changed something," Dale said. "What is this need you have for it to be different all the time? It would drive me crazy. Enough changes, without having to do anything with the furniture. If I got up in the middle of the night I'd think I was in the wrong place."

"That's sort of the idea," Maggie said.

"To be confused?"

"No, not finding myself in the wrong place exactly, but finding myself in a different place without having to leave," she said.

Dale looked unconvinced as she sat on the arm of Nate's chair. "Isn't there some disease where people can't throw anything away? They collect, they're psychologically unable to get rid of anything?"

"Oh God, Mrs. Dobkin," Maggie moaned.

"Yes, Mrs. Dobkin." Dale nodded and looked up at the ceiling.

"Who?" Nate asked.

"A woman who lived down the street," Maggie told him. "She had it: obsessional neurosis. I looked it up once."

Mrs. Dobkin (everyone had assumed the Mr. was a phantom spouse) had lived at the end of Benton Road in a house that was only slightly remarkable for how far back it sat on its lot. One Memorial Day, the old lady was buried under an avalanche of magazines she'd been plucking out of other people's trash cans for years. Neighbors were shocked to see their names and addresses on the covers, implicating them in her death. Mrs. Dobkin also stored garbage in her bathtub and peed behind the couch so that the floor rotted through to the basement.

Maggie remembered how seven-year-old Dale had cried as the paramedics removed the lady in her shit-stained, cherry-red satin bathrobe that early morning. Dale's heart had pounded away under her pudgy chest, and Maggie knew what a sensitive, easily disturbed girl her daughter was, but she couldn't turn away from the sight. What weird and terrible things happen on this quiet street, among all this normal-seeming life, Maggie had decided then as she'd looked up at the sky, which was so painterly that day. Even the old lady had the beatific look of the dead in portraits, her attendants stoic and strong-jawed. Maggie did not know then how a woman like Mrs. Dobkin could fall so out of step. Now, disturbingly, it wasn't such a stretch to imagine; you start by eating only one kind of food, talking to birds, refusing to cut your toenails, hiding money in rinsed-out soup cans, doing strange things to your body. Talking to yourself. These were the tics and turns that could lead a life astray.

"Mrs. Dobkin ate cat food," Dale said, snagged on the same memory. She paced the room again. "I just don't know about all this, though. It's not the way I think of the house. You have a picture in your mind of the way things are and what you can expect, and when you get there, it doesn't match up." She passed one hand quickly across the other with a cool, whisking sound. "That's what's throwing me off."

But it wasn't as though the past had been something so wonderful it was worth enshrining, Maggie told herself. Earlier, as she'd pushed furniture across the floor, she had a sense that memories were being reassigned too, and when she'd tried to conjure herself, Gordon, and Dale in happy, requisite poses, she couldn't.

"Sometimes I can hardly remember what the house I grew up in was like," Maggie said. "My mother had her parakeets in the corner of the bedroom, and I remember the newspaper on the floor to catch their droppings. I remember the Contac paper on the bathroom window, but I have no idea where my father liked to sit or where I did my homework." Memory is full of holes, she decided; we'd never move — or move on — if it weren't. "Do you think of this house a lot?"

"The thing is," Dale admitted, "I still think of this house as mine in a way."

"But it hasn't really been how you remember it for a long time, not since your father left, at least," Maggie said, and was tempted to add that *she* was different as well now, and so was Dale, and all her daughter really had to do was look. Be patient with her, Doris had urged. When Dale looks at your belly, she said, what can she possibly see? Maggie was hot under the plastic, which had begun to stick to her skin, and she was irritated by the meandering conversation. Maggie wished Dale and Nate would go home, but when they made no sign of leaving, she went upstairs to change.

At the stair landing on her way back down, Maggie saw Nate and Dale embracing in the living room. It was a strange scene, in stranger surroundings, and Maggie imagined she could have been the one to walk into the wrong house. Dale's short black skirt was gathered at her waist, revealing bright red underpants and the shocking paleness of her thighs. Her arms were around Nate's waist, while his hands rested on her back. The two of them were pressed in a rough kiss, and a kind of erotic urgency invaded Maggie at that moment. It had been too long since she'd had sex, too long since she'd felt the hairs on a man's arms, or been kissed on the eyelids or the neck. That this was her daughter she was watching somehow made her desire both disquieting and intense.

When they pulled apart slightly, Nate began to pat Dale's back. There was something unsettling in his movement, its weightlessness, its attempt to console rather than seduce. It was how you might touch a person whose fears are real but tedious, a person you've taken a step away from. Maggie knew she tended to watch too much, too closely, that she recklessly concocted scenarios out of inadvertent gestures. But she was more often right than wrong about things, and this, she knew, was not the way a man touched the woman he was in love with.

In the past it had sometimes irked Maggie how easily Dale handed over the most private details of her life with Nate — how he liked to make love to her on the nights when one of his students slept on the other side of their bedroom wall, how there were weeks when they had sex twice every day, how he liked to smoke a joint to slow himself down. Dale seemed undeterred by Maggie's failure to tell her own stories and divulge intimacies, or by the look on her face that said, There are some things I really don't want to know, things that should not be shared with your mother. But now Maggie realized how long it had been, certainly not since the mania of conception began, that Dale had told her anything private. A hot wind of worry blew in her face.

Maggie retreated into the kitchen and opened the refrigerator. Four years ago, when she and Nate had danced at his wedding, his hand had felt huge on her, paw-like. He was a smooth and fluid dancer, in control without effort. It was his years of prep school, he'd told her when she'd asked, all the dancing lessons he'd shown up high to. In the woods behind the gym, he'd smoked dope until he thought he heard the trees telling him to follow the music. He was so high, in fact, he'd called dancing lessons floating lessons, and could barely stop himself from bending over to press his lips to the breasts of his box-step partners.

He'd been the one, suddenly, in this benign and delightful wedding-day conversation, to talk about the fact that Dale couldn't have children, and how it didn't matter to him. He loved Dale so much, he said — and it was obvious he did — that something would work out. Maggie had stared at her feet gliding across the polished floor of the Parker House (Gordon's predictably traditional choice) and thought, this problem with Dale will not work itself out. Nate is lying, though he doesn't know it yet, and how long will this dreaminess last? She'd looked over at Dale, radiant and without any terror, wrapped in a vapor of white gown, wrapped in Gordon's glow. Gordon's new wife, May, smiled broadly, her hair the color of good pearls. Nate is setting Dale up, Maggie had decided, and of course, she'll fail — and after that? A man could never fully understand; having a baby was never expected of him.

And then because Nate had decided such seriousness had no place at his wedding, he'd laughed, said Maggie's name, and crushed her to his chest. It was barely a year later that Dale and Nate began talking about kids. Other people's marriages were a mystery, and Maggie was grateful for her daughter's happiness, but she wondered about this rush. Remarkably, by their first anniversary, Dale and Nate had found the girl named Blossom, seventeen and seven months pregnant, who promised to give her baby to them, and remarkably, it seemed as if life was going to work out perfectly.

Maggie closed the refrigerator and poured three glasses of wine. She quickly drank from the one with the most in it — she would even them out, a habit from childhood — though she would have liked to drain them all. She felt the alcohol pleasantly take the edge off her uneasiness.

"Come have something to drink with me," she yelled into the other room. She heard their whispers, and then Dale's light step across the brittle wood. Maggie wished she'd washed the dishes from breakfast, straightened up a little, wiped the surfaces. The room had a distracted look to it, and she turned off the radio.

"Have you eaten yet?" Dale asked as she came into the kitchen. Maggie heard Nate pull the squeaking bathroom door shut. "We want you to come out with us. We're meeting some friends at a place in Somerville. One of Nate's students just started as a bus-boy there." Dale shrugged at her husband's passion for his kids. It was not hard to see why, she'd once told Maggie, Nate was the most popular teacher.

"You should have called first," Maggie said. "I already ate. I can't wait these days, you know. I get too hungry, too shaky if I don't have something immediately. It's a little scary."

Dale eyed the sticky peach pits on the counter. "I did call. I've been calling for hours, actually. I finally figured out that you probably unplugged the phone again. I don't understand why you don't just let the machine pick it up."

"Because I hate that thing. The blinking red light is like some-one nagging me, and who wants that? But you're right, the phone was off since last night. I couldn't sleep." Maggie paused. "Well, you should have come earlier, then."

"You're always saying you don't like it when people come over without calling first."

"Maybe, but that was never about you, Dale."

There were times though when she *had* meant Dale; the times her daughter let herself into the house, full of a story, news, or affection, and shattered Maggie's solitude; the early mornings she appeared with a melon and a bag of bagels to greet her mother, who was still woozy from a dream. Such intimate trespass. How could a person not push it away and yet want it at the same time?

Dale lifted the hair off the back of her neck. "We took a long walk after we got home from work. I guess I didn't realize how late it was." She smiled apologetically. "It's such a beautiful night, so steamy, everyone's just wandering around waiting for it to rain and break this humidity."

Maggie heard water running in the bathroom, and then a screech and shiver of pipes as the toilet flushed. She gulped the wine.

"Dale, this morning, when I saw the baby on the screen at the doctor's, I was so ecstatic I thought I was going to float off the table," she began, and took a step toward her daughter. "I want to tell you what it was like, so that you —"

"Mom —"

Maggie refused now to let Dale say it wasn't miraculous, and she put a hand up to stop her. She wanted to talk about the deep currents and vibrations running through her body, the sensation of floating, but she hugged Dale instead, arching her back slightly so that the rise of her belly pressed into the hollow between Dale's hips. "Switch bodies for a moment so you understand what I'm talking about," she urged. "You be me, I'll be you."

"I don't think you'd like that," Dale said, her voice flat. She was alarmingly limp in Maggie's hold. "I can't believe you're drinking."

Maggie released her daughter and took a step back, deflated. She looked down at the empty glass on the table. "Damnit, don't change the subject. And I am not drunk."

"I didn't say you were drunk. I mean you're not supposed to be drinking at all. I know you think these prohibitions are so much crap, but I just don't think you should push it."

"When I was pregnant with you, I had a glass of wine practically every day. Please don't tell me what I should do now," Maggie said sharply.

Back then, she'd been to cocktail parties full of other pregnant women in tent dresses. Wives of young lawyers-on-the-rise, they gathered in apartment kitchens the color of sunflowers and avocados, sipped sweet cocktails and talked about the bigger places, in-ground pools and all the kids they'd have. She wondered where those women were now. Could they imagine her like this today? — and arguing about a single glass of wine?

When she'd been pregnant with Dale, Maggie had also grabbed Gordon's cigarettes when he put them down still lit. She'd eaten steak tartare with raw, oozing eggs, quivering, salty oysters when someone else was paying the bill, felt much too much like a child having a child to take it all so seriously, too young to imagine that her body was anything but invincible. She would have pointed out to Dale that everything had turned out okay without those horse pill vitamins she gagged on every morning, without the endless lists and lectures given to her by the ice-cold Dr. Gauld. There was such a thing as too much science, after all. But she stopped when she saw Dale's sensitivity glowing in dangerous dark reds and hot pinks. Everything did not turn out okay, she told herself, which is why we're here now. Maggie slipped her hands into the broad sleeves of her faded bathrobe and cradled her elbows, rough as cats' tongues.

She softened. "You're right, I shouldn't be drinking. I won't do anything stupid, okay? It was just a little glass."

"I know." Dale's eyes looked withdrawn, as though a sharp light had suddenly come on. "If it were me . . . Well, I just wouldn't, that's all. You can live for a few months without it."

Nate came into the kitchen wiping his wet hands down the front of his pants. "Sounds like someone's choking to death when you flush. I'm going to come over and work on those pipes for you this weekend. I promise." He stopped when he felt the lines of tension crisscrossing the room. "Probably an air bubble or something."

Maggie turned her plants on the sill, which were bent like drooping arrows into the room. "Or just old age," she said, suddenly defeated by the whole evening. "You learn to live with it. I don't even hear it much anymore."

Dale let out a sharp breath. "Look, you just can't expect me to feel everything you do, because I don't, I can't, we're not the same person."

"Then what do you feel?"

"Whatever I say isn't going to satisfy you. It will always be too much or too little or too different from what you want to hear. Like this morning. You should have written a script for me. Look, you have to give me some room, that's all."

The reversal stunned her. Hadn't it always been the other way around? Maggie asked herself, Dale standing so close, waiting for me to respond in just the right way. She watched Dale pinch an edge of toast off a plate and eat it. It was a sad motion, one she'd seen her daughter make so many times, a furtive feeding, her hand in front of her mouth, crumbs like fallen stars on her front.

"I still need *something* from you, Dale."

"But I'm not living this like you are," Dale insisted. "You feel the baby, you're going through some transformation. I can see it in you already, the way you look and act these days, like you know something, like you've gone somewhere else."

"Sometimes it feels like that," Maggie said.

"But what do *I* feel, what do *I* know?" Dale shook her head. She fingered another piece of toast, and her face was heavy with disappointment. "I'm not the pregnant one, not a mother. I'm still exactly the same, and I'm still right here."

Nate stared at the floor, his arms across his chest. Outside, on Maggie's small fenced-in yard with its crabby grass, chain-link fence, yellow supermarket lawn chairs, the plastic pool she filled with water and stuck her feet in on the hottest days, the rain began. It was gentle at first, but the downpour quickly filled the room with the hard sound of its insistence.

3

ON the telephone in her office the next morning, Maggie persuaded a nurse at Dr. Gauld's to fax over a copy of an ultrasound picture; she hadn't taken any with her the day before. Minutes later the machine spit one out, curling it toward the floor. Maggie half expected to feel a surge of elation again, but instead felt a slight doubt that the black-and-white image had anything at all to do with what was inside her. The picture seemed to recoil in the glare of the fluorescent lights.

Later, in a shaded patch of the park, she watched Ben Wakem, her boss and friend, study the picture intently, his fingers so tight at the corners that the paper threatened to rip under his scrutiny. He ignored her hand waiting to take it back. From the first moment she'd been his graduate student, Maggie had admired Ben's focus, but now it made her worry that he'd caught something others had missed. More invested than the technician, less linear and cautious than the doctor, cooler than Maggie, Ben would see the baby's genetic aberrancy or its predisposition to violence, bad decisions, or nastiness, its determination to bring heartache.

"Immaculate reception," Maggie said to distract him, but he didn't respond. She held her hand out again and snapped her fingers. "Okay, give it back now. Your time's up. You're making me nervous."

"Just a minute, Mags. What are you so antsy about? I'm still looking."

Ben was always slow and studious about things; she knew she probably shouldn't take this scrutiny to be something ominous. She'd seen him read a street map the same way, as though the final destination was almost incidental — it was how you got there, the unexplored way, that mattered.

In the small triangle of urban green squeezed between the university's School of Dentistry, with its acid-pocked marble steps, and the shadowy School of Public Health, the leaves on even the youngest trees were heavy and thick, signs to Maggie that an oppressive July was going to be followed by an equally oppressive August. She would have liked a week on the Cape to look forward to, but with little time and less money, it wasn't going to happen. She'd get her usual handful of invitations to be a weekend guest at various friends' houses, but even with the special dispensations made for single women, she found the prospects unappealing. She wasn't a good houseguest, wasn't much good at doing things anyone else's way. There was always her back yard and her plastic pool; if she coiled like a rope, she might be able to fit into it.

Maggie lifted the damp hair off her neck and felt the black soot of buses passing on Longwood Avenue settle on her skin like toxic powder. Ben, without comment or verdict, floated the picture onto her lap. She knew it might be a while before he said anything. They both stretched their legs out, their heels balanced points on the concrete. Maggie looked at her calves, still unswelled by pregnancy, long, though she wasn't tall, at her ankles, feet, and Achilles tendons. She wiggled her toes, and the toenails Dale had painted the pink of shells caught the sun. Ben's proximity, his lazy pose and assured, relaxed body often made her feel more graceful than she knew she was. His skin was bright white where his khaki pants frayed at the hems and drifted above the tops of his running shoes. Lab legs, Maggie called them; the man is afraid of the sun. Ben peered inside the bag that held his lunch.

"You going to eat?" he asked. "Or do I have to do it alone?"

Maggie shook her head, suddenly queasy at his lack of comment on the picture. Was he trying to avoid the subject? She heard him pop a grape in his mouth, and then another: small, icy detonations. Restless in the hot present, Maggie's memory took a long and unexpected leap and landed in the cooler artificial wave pool at Pearl Gardens in Florida, eleven years earlier. It was a depressing place, where the trucked-in sand was half dust that settled on your scalp, and the hotel towels were so full of bleach they burned your nose. She had worn a new red bathing suit that was exactly like the one she'd bought for Dale on an impulse that was completely foreign to her; she wasn't a matching outfit kind of mother. Dale had taken one look at the suit and declared she wouldn't even put it on. Gordon had pointed out to Maggie, within earshot of his daughter, that no self-respecting, plump thirteen-year-old would wear twin outfits with her sleek mother.

Maggie remembered the way a wall of water had moved toward her small but still intact family standing on the fake beach, a load of temperature-controlled waves pushed their way. No whitecap was bigger or smaller than the next, so that it seemed to her as she stared at the false horizon, marred by the rusty guts and gears of the wave-making apparatus poking up here and there, that even she was becoming part of the artificial scene; mother-wife in a cute red number about to plunge in. Just like Gordon, she'd thought at the time, to pick some Disneyish nightmare, a place so unreal that she with her intense emotions and odd enthusiasms would have to fit in — or not, as it turned out. The vacation was about taking sides and getting ready for the big split. Already she was losing soundly. But it was too easy, she'd learned, to blame Gordon for a marriage that was never much good to begin with, and now she sighed, as though defeat were still riding the false, tepid waves toward her.

"You okay?" Ben said, looking over at her.

"Just hot. I was imaging I was somewhere cooler. Sometimes it works."

Ben held up a bunch of green grapes, sparkling with condensation. He threw one into the air, opened his mouth, and missed. The next time, he caught the fruit and halved it between his front teeth. "Have some, do me a favor, please. I don't even like grapes. I don't know why Doris gives them to me all the time," he said, then added, "like I'll change my mind if I eat enough of them."

Doris still packed lunch for Ben every day, though recently he more often gulped down a hot dog from one of the carts or went for something in the cafeteria. His mouth shiny with forbidden nitrates and grease, he would offer his untouched, homemade lunch to a grateful grad student. In all the years Maggie had known Ben and Doris, she had never completely understood everything that was packed into that brown paper bag. She knew Doris, and knew that it had nothing to do with wifely duty, servitude and devotion sealed under Saran Wrap. A long marriage like theirs was full of pacts and silent understandings, far, far beyond her. She took two grapes and bit down.

"You're just like Dale," she said, startled at the fruit's sourness, which made her face pinch. "Speechless. Withholding. You like to torture me."

"Me?" Ben asked. His eyes were slightly hooded and slanted down at the corners, a clear silver-blue. His hair was cut very close and mostly gray. A circle of sun moved to hit the top of his head, and Ben's hand flew to cover himself. He was the most self-contained man she'd ever known. "You probably shouldn't care so much what I think. It's not healthy."

"Well, you know I do, I can't help it. So tell me."

"Adorable is not the word that comes to mind. Not cute, either. They're so scorpion-like at this stage. Like alien insects." With his eyes growing more animated, the radiating lines deepening, he turned to her, excited. "It's incredible, though, that you can see the fetus at this stage. It's what, this big?" He indicated the smallest space between his thumb and forefinger. "The technology is overevolved; it's really too sensitive for what we use it for. But that you're pregnant at all is something in itself. I'm still getting used to the idea."

Maggie laughed. "So am I."

"You really should eat something, you know."

Maggie lifted the lid of her plastic container and sniffed at the two-day-old vegetable curry. Her appetite had disappeared, swallowed up by a low-level nausea, but she knew it would come slamming back later, sending her down to the basement vending machine for two Mars Bars. She'd have finished one before she'd even left the room, the sweetness choking at her throat and making her eyes tear.

Maggie stood up and pulled at her dress, which had twisted around her. Considering something in the distance, Ben held out a roll of LifeSavers to her. She took one and clicked the candy against her front teeth. When she reached her arms up over her head, the weight of her belly was like ballast.

"God," she moaned, "I feel like some experiment gone wrong. What's wrong with this picture?" Maggie even smelled different now, and noticed it first thing in the morning, as if she'd woken up with someone unfamiliar. "Look at me. I'm a freak. I'm like an eighty-year-old man with a gold chain and white shoes. I'm like a seven-year-old girl in lipstick and falsies."

"Sit down!" Ben's snap was so unexpected, Maggie froze. "Did you know you say the same idiotic thing every day? Yes, look at you. You look beautiful, your skin is great, you've finally put on some weight, your breasts are —" Ben stopped, and his mouth tightened. "Forget it. Just don't do that anymore."

"My breasts? We're talking about my breasts now?" Maggie said, and touched herself. She was not prepared for the pleasure of her own hands or his words. Ben saw this and looked away.

Maggie suddenly didn't recognize this man anymore, the one she knew as perfectly as possible. When she asked for another Life-Saver because she didn't know what else to do, he handed over the entire roll.

Ben spoke without looking at her this time, his tone oddly defensive. "I see the way you admire yourself. Just now for instance, the way you looked at your legs. You move in a different way, you're confident; you know you're no freak, you're lovely, so why do you pretend otherwise? What's the point?"

"I'm not pretending, Ben. It's really how I feel. Like a freak."

A girl in white spandex shorts and a sports bra, hair flying behind her like a sheet, Rollerbladed through the triangle, past benches and overflowing trash cans, and cut directly toward them. As she worked her powerful legs to gain speed, she made a noise like a zipper being tugged up and down.

"I really hope she can stop," Maggie muttered, recognizing the girl as a graduate student who worked in Jackmeir's lab, one floor down from Ben's.

"Hey, Dr. Wakem," the girl panted as she came up to them. With the back of her hand, she wiped away the sweat from above her upper lip. She lifted her arms to collect her hair into a pony-tail, revealing perfectly hairless and glistening armpits and elbows that ended in smooth points. She looked like she was made entirely of wax, pliable and mindless.

"Shelby. That looks like a great workout," Ben said, and stood. His head bobbed a little in pace with her breathing. "Maybe I should try it sometime instead of running. Less stress, probably, on the bones. But don't people smash their knees into dust on those things?"

Shelby laughed. "You sound like my father. Anyway, that only happens if you don't know what you're doing."

"Like everything else, I guess," Ben said, and hiked up his pants.

Maggie wasn't sure she'd ever seen so many perfect white teeth in one mouth. The terrain of the girl's breasts pressed against her damp bra. Even the indent of her belly button was clear, deep, like a finger pressed into dough. A man would want to put his tongue there, Maggie thought, a man should put his tongue on *me*. She sighed shakily, so that Ben turned to her.

"Do you know Maggie Crown?" he asked the girl.

"I know *who* she is," Shelby said. "You're the woman having a baby for her daughter. People around here talk about you all the time. The surrogacy thing might be a little weird, but it's pretty cool. I believe in it, basically."

"Basically," Maggie repeated. Getting pregnant had been the easiest part, shockingly so, the doctors agreed. She was flattered when they pronounced her insides photogenic, proud when they called her an excellent candidate. But having to explain who was who, and who did what, was generally a useless exercise, she'd found. Most people had already made up their minds about surrogacy; they didn't want details or arguments. Shelby's nose twitched, and Maggie decided she was like a big sexy rabbit on wheels. Soft, fluffy, pink. Something that probably should be caged at night.

"Basically, I am Lady Bountiful," Maggie pronounced, heard the bitterness in her voice, and turned to Ben. "You know we have a meeting at two? We should get back."

"Is it that late already?" Shelby asked. "I have to go."

"Sure, see you," Ben said, raised his hand as she rolled out of sight, and then bent to touch his toes. At fifty-four, Ben was tall, with a chest expanded from years of running. He let out a little groan and kicked a stray soda can, which flew onto the grass opposite them.

"Nice outfit on Madame Curie back there," Maggie said as they walked back to the lab. She struggled to keep up with his wide, slightly bowlegged stride. Today he was like a coil of energy, ready to spring at any moment, dodging the flashes of sun that broke through between the trees.

"Maggie, she said I sounded like her father. That hurts a little. It probably should hurt a lot."

"That's called flirting. How did you get to be so clueless? Shelby has a crush on you. She did the hair thing."

It amused Doris that the man she was married to had such an alluring effect on people, men and women alike, and didn't even notice. Sometimes Maggie wondered how Ben could not be turned on by his own turning on.

"The hair thing?" Ben asked. His hands played in his loose pockets. "Lady Bountiful. Where did you find that one?"

"I'm not sure. Sounds like a cruise ship, *The Lady Bountiful.* Or a strip club."

"Do I really sound that old?" he asked. "I don't think of myself as old at all. Anyway, Shelby's a great student, one of the best we've seen in years. Too bad she's in Jackmeir's lab. The guy's a complete asshole. But I hear he's lost some of his funding, so I mentioned to Shelby that we might have a position for her. What do you think? Maybe she can start when you're out," Ben mused. "She can do some of your work at first, maybe move into the eye study later, take over some of the interviewing. I think she'd be good at that. She has an easy manner with people."

"An easy manner? Is that what you call it? Forget it, Ben. The interviewing is mine and so is the study. I really don't need any help," Maggie said, alarmed. She wouldn't even let the girl sit in her chair now, if she could help it. "Give me a week after the baby is born. That's it, then I'll be back. This was not supposed to derail me. That already happened once."

Ben nodded, but it was a vague gesture of his that often had nothing to do with what he'd heard, only with what he was think-ing. "Shelby has one of those rare instinctive minds," he said, and looked at Maggie. "Really, she does. Why are you so skeptical?"

"Maybe because you said that about me once, too, and how many rare, instinctive minds can there actually be? It loses the ring of authenticity after a while."

It had thrilled her then, as a young graduate student, to hear those words coming from a rising star, and it had confirmed for her what she'd always suspected about herself. (Odd was what her mother had always called her, a wonk, get a date, be a girl and not an egghead.) It was okay to finally stand out, because standing out was what it was all about in science. It's what got you where you wanted to be. She'd dreamed of her own lab, publications by the armful, brilliant discoveries and cures. She had been in love with Ben, too.

It all seemed a little beside the point now though, when she was essentially a lab manager, grant coordinator, researcher, interviewer, whose brain sometimes felt as slack and as dense as a fat man's middle. From the time Dale was born, Maggie's job had been made possible by Ben's magic ability to win grants, to include her always as a write-in, an add-on, a soft-money purchase for his research on cataracts and blindness. His work was dependent not on her mind, or her instinct, as he called it, but on her help, her clarity, her organization and competence. The hours were too long, the gratifications slow in coming and at heart not hers to always feel gratified by, the money steady but not great. She wasn't doing science most of the time, she was only making sure it got done, which was a very different thing.

An unplanned pregnancy, motherhood, then inertia, the ups and downs of life, divorce, money — facts even she couldn't ignore — had kept her there, always thinking of a time she might go back to school and get back on track, or even get out entirely, do something different but entirely hers. So many women her age, her friends, felt this way, and they struggled to justify the choices they'd made, or the ones made for them, even as they adored their children. The fact was that life set women back — it happened to them — in ways it never touched men. And here she was, she reminded herself, pregnant all over again, as though she'd made no progress, as though she'd been sent back to Go. And now Ben was talking so blithely about giving away her job.

"Well," he said a little wistfully, "it was true then, about your instincts, and it's still true now. You have a particularly incisive way of formulating problems. Your analytic thinking is very sophisticated. You're a lateral thinker, always working outside the box. I've never seen anything like it, to tell you the truth."

"But where does that leave me?" There was no point in wondering how her life might have worked out differently. "Just don't replace me, okay?"

Ben shook his head. "I know you don't always believe it, Maggie, you can be so thick sometimes, but I couldn't have done this work without you or gotten where I am." Sticky sap from the linden trees made their shoes suck the sidewalk like kisses. "Things may not have worked out exactly as you wanted them to, but this is as much your work as mine and it really can't happen without you. I'm not about to cut you out, so don't get nuts on me."

As they continued down the shady side of Longwood toward the lab, she noted how much their conversation that day sounded like the end of something.

"What do you mean I'm just like Dale?" Ben asked when they arrived at the steps of the Bain Building. He might appear not to be listening, but in fact he always was. As usual, Ben indicated he didn't have his keys by patting his empty pockets. One day, Maggie decided, she'd forget hers too just to see what he would do.

She rooted around in the dark jumble of her bag, her head bent. "Dale didn't react at all when we saw the baby on the ultrasound. It was really strange, Ben, as if she wasn't there, or I wasn't there to talk to. She always tells me everything."

"Which you aren't always thrilled about."

"But this is different. I want to hear it all now."

Ben glanced at her, and for a moment she thought he might touch her face; she wanted him to. But he leaned back to look at the white sky, thick with hot haze, and his voice sounded tight when he spoke. "Wouldn't you like to go somewhere, drive out to Walden Pond for a swim right about now, forget all this and everything we have to do? Fifteen minutes floating on your back, swimming underwater. How nice would that be?"

It was a game they played together sometimes — there were fantasies of sledding, of driving to Newport for lobster, of sailing on the Charles — but one that never went further than words because Ben never left work. For him, the imagining was enough, while increasingly for her, it wasn't. She started to tell him that a swim would be nice, though the beach would be better — she intended this as a dare — but he was staring at her again with a look she couldn't name, and she stopped herself.

Inside the building the foyer was dark and smelled of chalk, and the highly polished floor caught their reflection. Maggie saw herself and wondered if it really was time to cut her hair as Dale kept urging her to do; it hung heavily, and too familiarly, around her face. The breeze from a huge fan roaring at the end of the hall suddenly lifted her hair, and she saw a younger picture of herself.

"Have you ever had an affair with a student?" she asked.

"I wasn't expecting *that* question," Ben said, amused, when they'd reached the stairwell. "Why? You thinking of doing it?"

"Yes, with Shelby. She's just my type." As Maggie pressed her back against the wall she felt coolness radiating from the pale, glazed tiles. "No, I'm just curious, really. I was thinking about all the years we've been here, and how it is that when you get so used to something you wouldn't even recognize change if it happened. I can ask you, can't I?" Her voice traveled up the stairs. Somewhere above, a door eased shut with a sigh.

Ben cleared his throat. "Sure. Okay. Maggie?"

"Yes?"

"Once."

Maggie felt a surprising flood of disappointment — for Doris, for herself for not knowing before, for a thrill that she herself hadn't had — and also a tic of excitement. "When? Who?"

"Maggie," Ben said, and held on to the strap of her bag so she couldn't move. He put his face near hers. His lips looked pale and very soft. "Remember?"

"What are you talking about?" She could almost taste his mouth so close to hers. This was Ben, her best friend's husband, and her desire left her hollow and confused. She closed her eyes.

"Us."

"Oh, come on," she said, and pushed him away. Her hand was gentle on him, but she felt the cleave of his chest bone, her fingertips brushing his skin at the open collar of his shirt, the buttons imprinting themselves on her palm. "That was so long ago, before Doris, Gordon, the kids. It doesn't count. Christ, *this* lifetime, I meant."

Ben used his finger to wipe away the drops of sweat collected on her upper lip. "We men," he said, and tapped his chest in a way that made Maggie laugh, "we count everything. It certainly counts in my book." He paused. "I *really* loved you, Maggie, so it absolutely counts."

They climbed the stairs. Ben made his way through the lab, greeting the few people in the room, who looked up as he passed. The lab was his fertile garden, full of fumes and exotic constructions, rubber tubing snaking like vines, and Caution signs blooming everywhere you looked. She knew the purpose of things, she knew their hot or cold touch and the metallic glare of machines, the quiet hum of it all. But where was her garden? She supposed for most women, it was their children; for her it had to be Dale. Ben slipped into his office, but what he'd said stayed with her.

On the night she had ended their affair many years ago, they had sat on one of the squeaky black plastic sofas in the student lounge long past the time everyone else had gone home. Ben had gotten word that week of an enormous grant which would carry him for years, and he was still elated and talking fast. Maggie told him that she'd slept with another man. Ben cried, she had thought, only because the affair itself was over and she'd cheated on him, and not because he actually loved her, though he insisted he did and kept reaching for her, his hands tucking into the low waist of her blue jeans. Despite the fervor with which they'd come together — and they were both a little new when it came to such passion, making love in a lab, or on a couch, not even a bed most of the time — she had known it was right to break up with him. Their involvement had taken her by surprise; there wasn't room in the lab for both work and love.

Within two years Ben was married to Doris, a woman whose directness was a complement to his dreaminess. Eventually Maggie married Gordon, because she thought she should, given her enormous attraction to him. In the end, of course, it was Ben's marriage that had stood so steadily and not hers, since, as it turned out, she wasn't suited to marriage — or to Gordon — at all. She'd always been in love with Ben, and that was all right. It had settled into Maggie, muted, softened, and absorbed, a fact about herself like a taste for chocolate or long walks. Her lovers appeared like bright flashes to take away some of the dingy spots of life, but they were always easily, and never regrettably, forgotten.

The other time she had seen Ben cry was last winter, after his youngest son, Aaron, had met him for lunch downtown and told him that the skin cancer he'd had removed when he was seventeen was back, less than two inches from the beautiful sunburst scar on his shoulder. Maggie had held Ben in the men's room at work while he vomited up the few bites of food he'd eaten. He told her how Aaron had kept touching the bad spot on his shoulder and cracking ice between his teeth, and how he'd wanted to scream at him to stop; the sound made him picture slit wrists and snapped necks, boys running through glass doors.

"You just don't think of your children dying and dead," he'd told her, "just as you don't think of your baby as your last."

"But you don't know that he's going to die from this," she'd insisted. "He said the spot was thin, right? That they were going to remove it?" Ben had waved her away furiously.

Ben always carried around something he'd been given by his boys: a piece of knobby quartz from Peter, an inkless fountain pen from Aaron he never refilled. He touched the reminders of them like men jiggle money in their pockets, like women twirl their rings. Still, with Aaron he'd always felt something inexplicably different and bigger from the moment he was born. That afternoon, he'd asked Maggie if it was terrible to love one child best. Disease doesn't happen that way, Maggie had said, not entirely convinced; it doesn't come to take away what you love the most.

She had driven Ben home to Doris, who wordlessly wrapped him to her chest. She already knew about Aaron and had done her day's crying. Maggie wanted to be wrapped in there too — she'd known the boy forever — but it was their marriage, their family, and their sorrow. In another life, it could have been hers. In the worst moments, she'd thought then, life reveals itself, unbidden, in other scenarios.

4

MAGGIE looked at herself one last time in the mirror before she left the house. The late afternoon dimness made it hard to see distinctly, but the blind dates Doris set up for her every so often were usually indistinct too, so she didn't feel the need for better light. Most of the time she, or the man, lacked the interest, the energy, the initiative, to take the relationship any further. It was all pleasantness, but not much more, their only common bond being that they'd found themselves at the same place at the same time. Maggie had a hard time saying no to Doris's machinations, though she often thought with some irritation that her friend didn't believe her when she said she didn't need to be fixed up. Maggie could find a man by herself; Doris invariably decided he was the *wrong* man. At fifty-three, Doris claimed she had developed a pretty accurate sense about these things and about what people needed but didn't always know themselves.

What Maggie knew from Doris about Milt Weinstock was that he was a recent widower, that his wife had had a heart attack while doing her laps in the Jewish Community Center pool. He was lonely, of course, Doris explained; he didn't get out much, though oddly, he'd taken up swimming lessons. To Maggie, this particular setup — he, the grieving man fighting his water fears and sorrows, she, the five-months-pregnant woman — seemed a little desperate.

"I like your outfit, very multicultural," Milt said stiffly as he held open the door of the car, where Ben and Doris waited in the front seat. Though she could tell he was trying not to look, Milt's eyes kept drifting down toward the round strain against her Chinese silk blouse. "I guess that's the thing these days. We all want to look like we came from somewhere more exciting than Teaneck, New Jersey."

"Hershey, Pennsylvania," Maggie said.

"Her father was in chocolate," Doris said, and twisted around in the front seat. The bright red lipstick, the pale, perfect skin, the hair that swept off her smooth forehead in a single high wave, gave Doris the glamorous look of an earlier time.

"Is that right?" Milt asked. His gaze swept over Maggie's front again, bounced off the row of covered buttons bisecting her, and ended at the mandarin collar just under her chin.

Ben had not yet turned around, and his neck looked painfully rigid. "My father was a food chemist," she explained. "He invented kids' cereals, mostly." Maggie felt her dead father's lumbering presence in the car and wondered what he would make of her now, when he had never talked to her about the future. It wasn't that he was disinterested, it was that he was a man remarkably empty of words. "I grew up eating the stuff, but most of the cereals aren't around anymore, banned because they made kids psychotic from the sugar overload."

"And ruined their teeth," Doris added, "and stained their insides all sorts of fruity colors. Personally, I miss them."

Ben suddenly pulled away from the curb, and Maggie could not help but slide into Milt as they sped to make a light.

"Seat belts," Milt said, and reached under himself. He raised his eyebrows at Maggie.

"There aren't any back there," Ben told them. "You're on your own."

Doris spoke sharply. "Hey, Ben, what exactly is your hurry, anyway? Slow down."

"It's simple. I want to miss the traffic, and I don't want to miss the movie. I know exactly what I need to do, so just let me do it. If not, then you drive."

There wasn't really any traffic to speak of, just people out in the early evening, walking, running, following dogs and children, and Maggie knew that Doris, always so organized and precise, would have left plenty of time to get to Cleveland Circle. She assumed they'd been fighting again; their voices were soaked with animosity and Doris's nose was tensely flared. Until recently there had always been a placidity and predictability to Ben and Doris's marriage, which Maggie often found mind-numbing. (Watching them these days, she recalled their discomfort when she and Gordon had picked at each other, also their discomfort when she and Gordon had groped each other, their hands sliding up each other's shirts.) Now an unpredictable storm sometimes blew in — Ben described it as turning a corner and suddenly being hit in the face by gale force winds — and at its eye was a sick son and an uncertain future of grief. At its fringe was often Tina, the troubled seven-year-old Cambodian girl in one of Doris's art therapy classes whom she was becoming increasingly involved with. Privately, Maggie sometimes wondered about the intensity and timing of Doris's attachment to the girl. There had always been a silent competitiveness between friends, and here was a maternal drama to match her own.

Milt grasped the door handle. To steady himself over a bumpy stretch on Beacon Street he opened his legs, and they spread across the back seat like his doughy optimism. From time to time he pulled at the waist of his chinos, fiddled with the buttons of his white shirt. He was clearly uncomfortable with Ben's driving, though he kept a small, gracious smile on his face as Doris talked. He glanced at Maggie often, as though he somehow found solace in knowing he wasn't doomed alone. At one point he turned around to gaze out the back window, and she imagined him as a child being driven away from someone he didn't want to leave. Milt was neither attractive nor unattractive but just himself, familiar, though she'd never met him before, not surprising in any way, probably a real comfort to some people. Possibly to her, if she would allow it. There were dog hairs on his pants.

"This reminds me of driving around with my parents, who argued — not that you two are arguing — about whether to stop at the IHOP or Howard Johnson's," Milt said, and began a story about traveling the length of Texas in a station wagon. One of his sisters had peed in a snow-cone cup, which dribbled onto the seat. They were all restless and whining. It seemed, he said, to take weeks to cross the state.

Maggie had never been to Texas, but the deep golden glow from the reservoir on her left seemed fitting for his story, which had the soothing lilt of exaggeration and the aim of distraction, the tones of myth. What I don't know about this man, she thought as she settled into his words, he could make up, and what he doesn't know about me, I could invent, I could revise and reshape. It was not an unappealing idea. But as they arced around the reservoir, a harsh orange glare suddenly spiked off the water and through the trees. It was like being slapped across the eyes, and Maggie drew back. The heavy activity at Cleveland Circle blinked light and black up ahead.

Maggie saw something race toward the car from the left side and she knew that whatever it was would hit them. Ben saw it as well, but too late, and slammed on the brakes. A man, loose-jointed, like a worn-out rag doll, flew over the hood of the car. Maggie saw each point of contact — one shoulder, a bare expanse of flat stomach, a foot with a white sneaker on it, a hand with thin fingers — and heard each distinct thump, wet and heavy, on the metal.

"My God," Milt said, his voice like an old woman's, both scolding and frightened. "What was that?"

The man unfolded himself from the pavement. He trembled as he leaned into the car through Doris's window and blew out a breath that smelled of wheat. His eyes were almond shaped, the whites slightly yellowed. His hair, closely cut, showed a few strands of gray on white scalp, but his bare chest was hairless and shiny with sweat. It was impossible to tell how old he was. For a moment he stared, and they stared back. On the sidewalk behind him, people waited, rocked baby carriages, reined in dogs. The trees were still, holding their breeze.

"Are you all right?" Ben rasped. He cleared his throat and asked again. "Do you need to go to the hospital?"

"I'm here, right?" the man said. He ran his hands up and down his thin chest, then over the contour of his rib cage, and pulled his elbow, where there was the tiniest dotting of blood, toward him. Like a swarm of aphids, Maggie thought. "I'm alive, right? Nothing broken."

"I didn't see you," Ben said.

"No," he panted. "I was running. Too fast. But, you know, I'm in training. The light . . . you had the green . . . and I didn't see you, either. My fault totally. The sun was in my eyes."

Maggie leaned over Milt toward the man. "We should take you to the hospital anyway. Sometimes you can't tell if you're hurt or not. Sometimes you don't know until much later. You should just get checked out, to be safe."

"Oh, *I* can tell," he said. The man bent down — collapsed? dead?— and when he stood again he smiled at their anxious expressions, but his face had taken on the pallor of crumbling cement. "Relax. My shoe was untied is all," he said, and walked away, not quite limping but not quite balanced either.

"Don't you think we should take him? Make him come with us?" Maggie asked. She was already picturing a steady, undetected flow of blood, an internal drowning, the man alone on the cold kitchen floor where he'd collapsed at midnight. "Do something?"

"If he says he's fine, what else can we do?" Ben said. "You can't force him, Maggie."

The movie theater was just to the right of them, the marquee graceless in the evening sky, up a small hill and over the trolley tracks, but the distance and the obstacles seemed daunting now. Ben drove slowly, two hands on the steering wheel.

"That was the strangest thing I've ever seen," he said after he'd pulled the car into the lot. People moving around them made a muffled, cartoonish sound, as though they were walking under water. The evening's heat urged itself against the car and slipped through the cracks. "What an odd guy."

"He was obviously in shock," Maggie said. "He talked like he was drugged, like he was in a dream."

"Well, and you have to wonder what he's in training for, don't you?" Milt asked.

Doris, who hadn't spoken, was focused on Ben. "You could have killed him," she said, so fiercely that Maggie knew she was thinking of other sins and other accidents. Her voice filled the car like a panicked bird. "It's going to happen one of these days, and it's going to be bad. Where is your head, Ben? What the hell were you thinking about?" She got out and slammed the door, leaving the others in hot silence.

Inside the theater, Ben and Maggie watched a huge man bend to the candy, his shorts straining at the seams, his stubby hands pressing longingly against the glass, where he left greasy whirls of fingerprints. A line of people had collected impatiently behind him.

"Doris and Milt," Maggie said. "They both seem to have disappeared. Did you notice?"

"Bathroom. Small bladders. Maybe they ditched us."

"I don't know, Ben. Maybe the movies isn't what we should be doing now. Pretending nothing happened, when maybe something terrible did."

"What can we do?" He turned to her. "Really, another second and a different angle, and I would have killed that guy, run him right over like a paper cup." Ben slapped his hands together. "Was it my fault? I have no idea what I was thinking when it happened. Was I not paying attention?"

"No, the man came out of nowhere, and like he said, he ran against the light," Maggie assured him. "There was nothing else you could have done. You reacted pretty fast, actually."

"But you saw him, Maggie. I heard you gasp behind me. I know you put your hand up to your mouth right before he hit us. I heard it. That much I do remember."

She didn't know if it was the accident replayed, or the sickening smell of sweet butter floating on the overcooled air, or Ben's being tuned in to even her smallest movements that hardened in her stomach. She sat down on a low bench by the video machines, the bangs and bells blocking out the echo of the man tumbling over the car hood. A few feet away, Ben gaped at a movie poster while crowds parted around him and his hand moved mechanically from the popcorn bag to his mouth.

Since their lunch in the park almost a month earlier, when she'd shown Ben the ultrasound picture, they'd barely talked. At times, Maggie found him skittering around corners, his head down to avoid her, and she recalled with a touch of excited uneasiness their conversation in the stairwell. Other times, when she caught him watching her, his eyes half closed but still locked on her, she teased him by making a moronic face back at him, but he turned away awkwardly, almost angrily. She'd thought of mentioning it to Doris the week before when they had been walking around Fresh Pond, but she'd stopped herself. What would she say? *I think your husband might be in love with me?* In any case, Doris had been talking about Tina and hadn't noticed Maggie's faltering.

Across the lobby now, Maggie saw Milt come out of the bathroom. One hand fiddled with the zipper of his fly and the other dabbed at the drops on his pants. Maggie could tell he had never imagined he would be without his wife, and now he probably felt as though he were living in a foreign country, and not by choice. What he really wants, Maggie decided, and felt a surprising gentleness toward him in the garish light of the theater lobby, is to go back home and have his wife there, to not have to do this sort of thing, not have this sort of very troubling evening out, in the midst of troubled lives. She imagined carpets without fuzz, a sink without dishes, a marriage without argument, no loose ends, a quiet night of gazing at each other across the cleared and wiped table. Milt had that kind of placid, low-level look. The world was probably too violent, a much too ugly and deceitful place for him. No man had ever tumbled over the hood of his car and walked away like a zombie, no wife of his had ever been as fierce and accusing as Doris.

"Ready?" Doris said, appearing in front of Maggie from another direction. "We should go in, get good seats."

"Are you okay?" Maggie asked. Her friend looked unperturbed, but her good-naturedness seemed a little too glossy.

"I'm fine, why?" Doris scowled quickly into the dark room of noisy machines and then back at Maggie. "But you look pale. I bet you didn't eat anything again. That's not too smart."

"I can't stop thinking about the man we hit."

Doris hesitated, and leaned closer to Maggie. "Can you believe Ben?"

"It wasn't his fault," Maggie said. It was surprisingly difficult to stand up all of a sudden, and she put out her hand for Doris to pull.

"Of course it was his fault. He wasn't paying attention, as usual. He can't drive like that, he can't *act* like that."

"Act like what?"

"Like what goes on inside his head is more important than what goes on outside it. That only his world matters. You know him, Maggie, you see the way he is, how sometimes he's not even there. It's not out of his control, it's self-indulgent, it's easy. It's weak."

Milt came over and placed a damp hand on Maggie's elbow, guiding her in to the movie so that she would sit next to him. He needed the aisle, he said, for his long legs. In the dark Maggie watched Ben on the other side of Doris. The whites of his eyes were lit up by the screen, and reminded her of a childhood game of sparking LifeSavers in the pitch-black coat closet. Pieces of popcorn glowed on Doris's black leggings where he'd dropped them. Milt's breath enveloped Maggie, and she discovered he was the kind of man who takes the entire armrest and doesn't notice.

But if anyone were to say anything about it, he would be horrified to think he'd been anything less than considerate, horrified to imagine that his breath was just the slightest bit stale. He would bring her a present the next time to make up for it, to show what an infinitely expandable heart he had.

AFTER the movie, in a red plastic booth at the Moon Palace, Milt showed Maggie how to twirl a chopstick like a baton. He ate most of his meals out alone these days, so he'd found ways to amuse himself, he told her. He'd never been able to read and eat without getting food all over the pages or on the front of his shirt, but he could make a balloon out of a paper napkin. Milt struggled to lift the pall that had settled stubbornly over the table, and batted the balloon to Maggie. The waiter who took their order leaned one hip against the table and looked impatiently at her, a white woman in a Chinese restaurant in a real Chinese blouse, bouncing a folded napkin on the palm of her hand.

When the waiter left, Doris peered around the restaurant. "Dale said she might meet us here. Did I tell you already?" she asked Maggie, and then turned to Milt. "Dale's her daughter."

"No you didn't, and neither did she," Maggie said. "God, you'd think she'd have something more exciting to do than hang out with us."

Dale and Doris had always had their own friendship, but their closeness never failed to sting, just as it did now. If she didn't know what Dale was up to though, or didn't know as much as Doris, it was only half her fault — they hadn't spoken since breakfast together almost a week earlier, and even then, not much had been said. Dale had seemed not morose exactly, but uncomfortable and evasive. "I mean," Maggie added, "shouldn't she want to play with people her own age?"

"Nate had something to do at school tonight, and she didn't seem to have any other plans, so I asked her."

"Dale always has plans," Maggie countered. Her daughter was scrupulous about her social life, the kind of friend who complimented, called, and always remembered birthdays. She accepted less in return with great equanimity.

"Well, not tonight. I thought it would be fun, and she could meet Milt." Doris's words were oddly measured.

"Maybe she just doesn't trust you out alone," Ben said to Maggie. He planted his elbows on either side of his plate, his chin in his hands, and looked at Milt. "What did you think of those special effects in the movie? I have to say I have no idea how they were made."

Milt hesitated for a second; he knew he was being offered a challenge. Earlier, Maggie had heard him call Ben "Professor."

"Hey, I'm just a traffic engineer. Ask me about the Big Dig, or stoplight patterns and staggered feed-ins." He laughed. He held up both hands — as though he's a crossing guard, it occurred to Maggie — before he gave an answer that went on much too long. She glanced at Doris, who looked away. Milt's voice was like a ticking school clock that marched painfully on, even as the food was brought to the table. She wished he would shut up.

"Now there's a real insight," Ben said when Milt finished. "I guess I was hoping for something a little more enlightening than what I could read myself in *Parade* magazine. But, okay."

"Since when have you been so interested in special effects anyway? You didn't even want to see that movie, as I recall," Doris said to Ben. "Let's eat already." She pushed a plate of food toward her husband and shrugged, pretending good humor when he pushed it back. "Okay, don't eat. More for us, and I'm starving. Maggie, you're not eating either?"

"I'm not very hungry at the moment. Maybe in a little bit."

"Why go out to dinner then?" Ben snapped at her. "It's a waste." He got up, dropped his napkin by the side of Doris's plate, and left the table.

Doris twirled her cup of tea. "Remind me to leave him at home next time." When she looked up, her face was skewed by a forced smile. "I'm sorry about Ben. I'm only married to him, you know. I don't actually work his controls. Sometimes he manages to do that by himself — and that's when all hell breaks loose."

"That's the truth about marriage, isn't it?" Milt put in wistfully. "My wife could really surprise me when she had a mood on, but it was usually because of something I did."

"So then don't apologize for Ben," Maggie said to Doris, more harshly than she'd intended. "He acts like an asshole all by himself. I don't understand why married people always feel they need to explain and make excuses for each other."

Doris gave her a look of gentle pity, as if to say how little her friend understood the way marriage works. Oh, I understand a lot, Maggie assured herself, I just find it a little suffocating. She turned, to see Dale at the front of the room, her body silhouetted against an enormous fish tank. Something yellow and blue swam behind her head, bubbles appeared like an effervescent scarf around her shoulders. Maggie waved her over.

"Sit next to me," she urged as Dale came to the table. She pressed herself against Milt, felt him hold his breath as the round of her ass met his hip. "Come on. Here."

Dale squeezed in next to Maggie, shook Milt's hand in front of her mother's face. "I saw Ben leaving. What's up with him? He said he was going to sit outside for a while but he wouldn't tell me why."

"We had an accident earlier in the car. Ben was driving, but it wasn't his fault," Maggie said, surprised at how quickly it came out, how it felt startlingly like a — married — excuse to her. She described the scene to Dale. Milt was silent next to her, unsure with all the crowded female presence. He sipped at his beer with concentration; tiny bubbles of froth burst on his lips.

"Other than that, the evening's been a great success," Doris added. Her lipstick had faded unevenly, as though she'd been made to eat something she couldn't stand. "Actually, Ben and I began the day fighting about Tina. It's only gone downhill from there." Maggie felt a rush of unfamiliar worry for her friend.

Doris began to talk about Tina, how she'd recently found out that the girl's older brother had been shot last year as he crossed a parking lot on his way home from work one night. Tina's mother had not spoken a word since, but stared for hours at nothing while relatives and social service workers hovered around her and waved their hands in her face. Tina had only recently stopped pulling her hair out in clumps; her scalp was embroidered with scabs. She liked Cray-Pas, and drew pictures of fields exploding with flowers. Doris shredded her napkin and scattered the petals on the table. She suspected Tina didn't always get enough to eat, which was why her teeth were streaked with brown near the gums and her hair looked singed.

"She's an amazing kid. I can tell what she's thinking just by the look on her face." Doris let out a thin, high laugh; the embarrassment of love, Maggie thought. "All these years of working with kids, and I've never felt this way about any of them. Oh, you know, I've loved a lot of them, felt sorry for them, hated others, and I can't explain this exactly except to say that I want Tina for myself. That's how she makes me feel. I want her to come live with us for a while, at least until things straighten out with her mother, which I'm not sure will ever happen. I can feed her, I can take care of her." She hesitated. "Is that terrible, coveting someone else's child?"

"I don't think so," Dale said, almost on cue. She picked at the flakes of an egg roll.

"So Ben's furious about it," Doris went on. "That's what this is really all about, why he's being so awful. He says we already have two kids, he's done with that sort of thing, he doesn't need anyone else's, or all the work, but you know what I say to that? Too fucking bad for him. Maybe *I'm* not done with that sort of thing. I've done things his way, and for him, forever. My turn now. He can take care of himself if he doesn't like it."

"Is that what he said? " Maggie asked.

"No, Maggie, that's what *I* said. But how would he take care of himself? It's disgusting how dependent he is — we both are — how I've let that happen."

"I wouldn't call it disgusting," Milt said softly. "That's marriage."

"Maybe he thinks it's too much," Maggie suggested. "With Aaron, his" — she stumbled on the word — "future. Maybe Ben feels he's the one who needs your attention now." Maggie wondered at her authority, when Ben hadn't said anything to her. But what was her friend doing, filling a hole left by pain and trouble with more of the same?

"I can't control the timing of these things." Doris glared at Maggie. "I thought you'd side with him — it's why I didn't say something to you before — and you're my best friend, for godssake. You're supposed to support me in this. And I have not forgotten about Aaron, not for a single fucking second, so don't you dare suggest that's what I'm doing."

Maggie sat back, slapped.

"Doris is right," Dale said, and turned to her mother. "It's not like she's replacing one child with another."

Slapped again, by her own daughter this time, who had always defended her. Maggie drew in a painful breath. She understood why Doris had asked Dale to be there with them; the evening and its storm had been inevitable, and she'd wanted Dale's ballast.

"I don't think that's what Maggie meant," Milt suggested, and then looked at Dale. "My wife died, but I can't —"

"Look, Milt, I'm really sorry about all this," Doris said, her voice thick with dismissal, "but I'm not sure you —"

"No, you're wrong. I do understand," he interrupted. "But it's okay." He spoke with awe, as though something were opening inside him for the first time. "You all have families. This is just what happens, isn't it?"

BEN and Doris sat in the car while Milt walked Maggie to her door. In the next yard over, Mary Wayland, in her lemon-yellow Keds and waxed legs that shone unnaturally in the dark, waited while her dog ran about on the lawn.

"Your grass could use a haircut," Milt said to Maggie, and touched his own buzzed hair. "I can come over with my mower, if you want. I'll just throw it in the back of the car."

Maggie felt a touch a dread when she looked at Milt. Why is it, she wondered, that I don't want what I can have, that I don't want what would be easy and uncomplicated? She didn't have the energy to give Milt anything just then, not even an answer about the grass. She didn't want his attention, because she wouldn't know what to do with it.

He jammed his hands in his pockets and looked back at the car. "Okay, whatever you decide, you let me know. Ben was in fine form tonight, hitting that guy, and then marching out during dinner. That was something, wasn't it? My wife never liked him, to tell the truth, said he thought too much of himself. We didn't see Ben and Doris at all socially. Now, though . . . Well, Doris has been very nice to me. The lonely bachelor and all."

He says bachelor, not widower, Maggie noted. "It's a hard time for Ben. His son is sick," she said. "He has skin cancer. They removed it, and he's had treatment, but no one knows what's going to happen."

"Well, yes, all over, a hard time for all of us," Milt answered. "The world is filled with terrible things, Maggie, and sadly for Ben, he's not spared by the element of surprise like some of us. My wife and I . . . I don't know, I just wanted to say that I think it's wonderful what you're doing for your daughter. I'm sorry she was hard on you, by the way. She didn't seem to understand what you were saying. Still, all this makes up for some of the bad stuff that goes on. I didn't get a chance to say it earlier, with everything happening there wasn't exactly a good moment. But you make me feel hopeful. Really, you do."

"Thank you." Hopeful — she felt levitated by the perfect fit of the word. "Do you have kids?" Maggie already knew the answer but she had an impulse to hear him speak it anyway.

"Nope, we never had any children. Got a couple of dogs, though." He looked up at the sky salted with stars. "She was the love of my life."

Milt moved Maggie out of reach of the porch light. She prayed he wouldn't throw his arms around her just then, or kneel and grab her around the waist, pressing his face into her, because she didn't know what she'd do. She might be tempted to embrace him in the dark and tell him things, though she barely knew him. A drop of sweat ran down from his temple and dropped on his shirt. He pulled out a handkerchief and wiped his face.

"Hopeful," he said again, as if he knew the word's effect on her.

When she kissed him on the cheek he moved so his lips brushed hers, surprisingly cool for such a hot night. Ben pressed his foot to the gas at that moment, and the car growled impatiently at the curb. Milt laughed, and though it might have been an accident, his hand brushed her belly as he backed down the stairs.

My God, Maggie thought, her knees weakening, *The love of his life.* Had she *ever* felt that way?

She closed her eyes and put her hands on her belly. She floated above her front steps, the singing grass, the fragrant boxwoods, the dog racing in blurry circles. She felt the baby move inside her. The flutter surfaced, beckoned her to touch not bone or skin but the pressure of water and reassurance. Before joints, before flex and extend, and long before the words — step, flee, trespass, Mother, hold me, release me. Just like a daughter, she thought.

MAGGIE had never expected to have a girl. Early on, she had predicted Dale would be a boy, curly-haired, firm-jawed, athletic, like Gordon — nothing like her. Maggie imagined that even as a tiny child, her son would stand with his legs hip distance apart and make pronouncements. She pictured asking herself, *Who is this little man I've given birth to?*

On the day Dale was born, Maggie was stunned by the femaleness of her baby. She blinked disbelievingly at the milky discharge winking from her infant's pale nipples, and at her vagina, swollen to the size of a fist. Dale was infused with Maggie's hormones; for that moment, they were twins. Maggie had done well, her mother, Virginia, had informed her, by having a girl. And then she'd added, with that particular ability of hers to claim responsibility for even the uncontrollable events in life, that all mothers were meant to have daughters. Gordon had wept at the birth, already in love with his daughter. In his pocket he had a list of people to call.

Until she was seven, Dale reveled in her body. She wrestled with her stuffed animals under the canopy of the white bed she'd been given by Gordon's parents, and when she rubbed the bears and bunnies between her legs and piled them onto her naked chest, her mouth opened wide in pleasure. In the bath, the wash-cloth became a snake twirling around her lovely round thighs, the soap a slippery fish between her legs, Dale's own fingers like flut-tering birds on the grin of her vagina. Water down her hair felt like hot chocolate, Dale said. She was fascinated by the names of her body parts, and by vomit, smells, blood, freckles, snot, the slither of blue veins up her arm, her father's penis glimpsed in an open robe.

And then by the time she turned nine, Dale was fat, and any pleasure in herself disappeared. Modesty locked doors and scram-bled under covers to undress. She turned the light out when she went into the bathroom. Even though Maggie had watched every inch of every move Dale had made, her daughter's transformation seemed overnight, a nasty, unfair surprise. Without warning, Dale had become one of those cherry-cheeked little girls with jelly-bean-shaped bodies. She painted her chewed fingernails bright red; her plastic beads bounced off her round chest, her lips receded in a pout, she hung back at birthday parties in tights that cut at the waist and bound her thighs. Kids hate fat kids, they're terrified of them — all their gluttonous worries stuffed into one unfortunate, cautionary body — and Dale, mystified and full of hate too, withdrew into a shape that wasn't really hers.

Those were the years of fighting with Gordon, and Maggie was convinced it was the sounds of discord and dissolution that Dale swallowed and couldn't shed. Maggie accused her fat, dead father too, and his fat-seeking genes. One summer when Dale was twelve they drove her, sulking and silent, to Camp Catalpa in Ver-mont. When Maggie saw the giant catalpa tree in front of the din-ing hall, its branches hung with desiccated beans that looked like the dry arms of thin women, she was sure she was dropping her daughter in hell. It was a fat farm, full of miserable teenage girls in ill-fitting, ugly clothes, whose thighs rubbed together and chafed in the heat. They all walked with a similar hunch of shame, their arms across their pudgy breasts.

The landscape was brutally, mockingly verdant, a deep jewel-green Maggie had never quite seen before, the surrounding gentle swells of land sliding languidly into a blue lake. This was perfect, sensuous nature; unlike the girls, who were anything but. The dissonance made her want to cry and steal her daughter back home. Over the summer, Dale wrote her parents on pink, scented stationery about the gnats that tortured her scalp, but also about the songs they sang at night, all with the words "beauty" or "inner" in their titles, and graceful outstretched arms in their choruses. They read *Our Bodies, Ourselves* on a regular basis, Dale reported. She loved Catalpa, she'd lost weight. She filled the pages with fat, happy exclamation points.

On her first day home from camp, Dale posed like the thin girl she was determined to become. Maggie had pulled her daughter's hair from her forehead and inhaled the scent of someone else's shampoo and damp pine. She was furiously happy to have Dale back, relieved to have her break the silence that had finally landed, spent, between herself and Gordon that summer, sending them both into their work for long, unreasonable hours. The thought that all Dale had needed was an escape from her parents filled Maggie with terrible regret. On that first day home, flush with information and buoyed by friendship, Dale wanted to know when she was going to get her period.

"Everybody is different. When you're ready, it will happen," Maggie said. She knew just how stiff she sounded, just like her mother, who had memorized the words from a pamphlet she'd written away for from a sanitary pad company. But her daughter's frankness had caught her off guard; she had never thought of her child as a woman until then. "And sometimes your periods change, or don't come at all, if you lose a lot of weight like you have. But your body knows when the right time is. You have to trust that."

And what did any of that mean, Maggie asked herself, and looked away. Could she explain, with Dale right there in front of her, that she herself hadn't been ready, that menstruation and responsibility were not at all related? The mind and the body were feuding sisters for life, but you couldn't say that to a child struggling to merge the two and hoping to emerge beautifully.

"Believe me, you'll wish you weren't in such a hurry," Maggie had said clumsily. "It's not so terrific." Her hands were lost in the depths of Dale's camp trunk, unpacking her things. Her daughter's clothes were damp from weeks in a cabin, and smelled unfamiliarly of smoke and something adult she couldn't name. She pressed a shirt to her nose.

Dale slowly ran her eyes up Maggie's face. "Yes, but when?"

"I don't know."

From then on, every time Maggie got her period she thought about her daughter still without hers. Gordon tried to reassure her in his way, but he was uncomfortable talking about it and in any case didn't think he should have to. Friends told her stories about cousins and co-workers, young women flooding bus seats and school chairs with sudden surges of blood, fainting in locker rooms, soaking mattresses. Maggie had heard that a taste for meat was a sign menstruation was imminent, so she packed the refrigerator with the best hamburger and marbled steaks and waited. But Dale, on her strict diet of rice cakes and tuna fish, wouldn't touch any of it. She was a vegetarian, she announced, and just looking at the meat made her sick.

"The body is not a Swiss train," Ben had told Maggie one day in the lab. "It doesn't always arrive when you expect it to."

He'd been pleased with his analogy, which she thought was idiotic and typically male, this image of a machine, huffing and smoking, emerging from between a woman's legs. Doris was concerned about Dale too, and whispered and hovered around her as if piling on the female presence would bring on the bleeding from sheer pressure. Maggie bought a Brazilian fertility doll at a flea market, with breasts made out of shells and hips covered with stiff hemp. She kept it hidden in her underwear drawer and touched the little puckered face for luck. The lips were a bean split in half. At times, when she was naked getting out of bed, or undressed in a store's changing room, she found her daughter examining her body, as if to understand that this is what a woman is, this is what I am meant to be.

Three months before she turned fifteen, Dale said she wanted to see a doctor. As the appointment approached, Maggie struggled to keep her fears to herself, knowing that they were vague and irrational and not to be shared with Doris or any of her other friends, certainly not with Gordon. Sometimes in the middle of the night, unable to sleep, she'd stand in the shower until the hot water ran out. With the mirrors fogged, her skin a shrieking pink, she was able to avoid seeing her breasts defined in any way, her pubic hair as anything more than a shadow, so she would not imagine Dale's body, pale and beautiful and mysteriously arrested. Boyish. Sick, maybe — yet what had Maggie done about it? When she reached into the drawer for her underwear, she felt for the doll again.

The appointment was with Maggie's gynecologist, Dr. Anderssen, a thin, white-haired man with a practice on Beacon Street. On the drive there, Dale's window was open slightly and the cold air hit her face so that her eyes teared and the tip of her nose turned red. She fiddled constantly with the radio, until Maggie barked at her to stop. With her fingernails, Dale carved lines on the cover of a school book she'd brought with her.

Maggie didn't know what to tell Dale about being touched by a doctor. She was not ambivalent about her own body; her discomfort had nothing to do with self-hate, as her friends were convinced it did. What was humiliating, she thought, was having to pretend it was normal and fine to have a man's face peering uninvited from between her raised knees while his hands probed and she rambled on about how difficult it had been to find a parking space. As it turned out, when Maggie finally began to talk in clinical terms about speculums and Pap smears, because that was all she could manage, Dale stopped her and said in a tone of pure adolescent disdain that Doris had already told her everything so she could stop now. Maggie felt something huge had been stolen from her, but also that she'd probably allowed it to happen.

"Dale is getting dressed," Dr. Anderssen said later, in his office after the exam. "She's a lovely girl, very bright. And I wouldn't worry about the weight. All girls her age are concerned about their looks at this stage. Anyway, Mrs. Crown, I thought we'd discuss an issue of some concern before we bring her back in."

From that second on, Maggie hated him, and knew her face showed it. There was something wrong with a man probing a mother *and* daughter, something so subversive about creating a whole family of women who didn't want to look him in the eye.

"This is a case of primary amenorrhea," the doctor said. He had a clipped accent she'd never noticed before, and she imagined he had been raised in an ice-cold chalet by an ice-cold aunt.

"Well, yes, I know that Dale hasn't menstruated," Maggie said impatiently. "That's why we're here." Out the window to the doctor's left, between the framed diplomas and certificates, the rain began. The day had suddenly turned gray in every way. "Now tell me why."

"It appears possibly, during examination — well, no, I'm quite sure, but we'll still want an MRI and other tests for confirmation — that your daughter does not have a uterus. I haven't seen many cases of this, so I looked it up while I had a minute." He read from a square of note paper. "Mayer-Rokitansky-Kuster-Hauser Syndrome. Congenital birth defect. No uterus."

Maggie felt the unmistakable weightlessness of terror blow through her body, the sensation just before death, she imagined. She knew she should be thinking of an emptiness, a hollow place in her daughter's body. Instead, she pictured something solid, filled up, a heaviness, a cement plug the size and shape of a smooth purple eggplant. She pictured a perversion rather than an absence, rather than the incomplete flower the doctor tried to illustrate, his hands held as though he were a priest imploring her to understand the ways of the world and her part in it. She thought of something dead even as he explained there was never anything there to die in the first place. My daughter without a womb, she mouthed. But Maggie did not wail, pull her hair, or pound her chest. Her hands moved to her neck and harshly twisted her necklace, then back to her lap to dig into the nap of her skirt, then to the flesh of her inner thighs, her crotch.

"From what I do know," the doctor said, "this is a congenital birth defect like, let's say, a cleft palate or clubfoot."

Maggie was too stunned to speak. The doctor questioned her about the pregnancy, her mother, Gordon. With his onyx pen holder and too-tight collar, he had asked about what was in her womb, but not about what was in her heart. He did not talk about how resentment and misgivings and fear can circulate in the bloodstream, but Maggie was certain that for her they had been as toxic and deforming as poison.

She only said, "I was young."

The doctor shook his head. "There's really no knowing why these things happen in most instances, a quirk, something that occurred during gestation." He looked down at his hands, examined his nails.

"She can't have children."

He nodded. "That is true. But the sex characteristics are present, breasts, pubic hair, ovaries, most likely normal hormone production. More tests are needed, as I said." He looked at Maggie. "I have no doubt that Dale can have a perfectly fulfilling sex life. She's an attractive girl."

The image of her daughter splayed and naked on the table, parts missing and accounted for, sickened Maggie. The doctor began to tap a pen on the palm of his hand.

"Your daughter is still a child in most respects," he said. "My feeling is that we wait a year or two to tell her. I'm really not sure she has the emotional maturity to understand how little this is going to mean during her whole lifetime."

"How little?" Maggie repeated. "Cleft palate and clubfoot?"

"Those were simply examples. I'm not suggesting —"

Maggie felt an urgent pressure build at the edge of her eyes, as though the man were shrinking right in front of her, narrowed in her scope of fury. He looked puny and bug-headed. "You've never had a child, you son of a bitch. How can you even *think* you know what this is like or what it means?"

"Technically, of course, you're right, but I *am* a father, nonetheless. Look, I know you're upset." The doctor had pushed his chair back from the desk. "You shouldn't feel inadequate because of this. We're not looking to place fault here."

"Mom?" Dale stuck her head around the door. A nurse passed back and forth behind her like a pendulum. "You done? Can we go now, please?"

In that morning's discovery, the life of her family changed forever. Maggie had cradled Dale after she told her, but in her daughter's reluctance to speak or ask questions she could detect only an incomplete understanding. And what could her daughter really understand about something she hadn't experienced, hadn't even thought about? What did babies mean to a girl who was much more interested in boys? Maggie felt she was comforting someone who wasn't even there.

During the day, Maggie's thoughts were rational and measured. She was clear and precise at the lab, which had become a refuge where she often stayed well into the evening, but at night, at home, she twisted herself up in magical thinking as binding as rope. I know the shape of science, she told herself, but I *believe* in the spirit of the body, and for a moment in my life, I did not want this child, Dale, who is sleeping just down the hall. I am to blame because I am my daughter and she is me. At times she could barely breathe; she pictured calling 911 but suffocating before the ambulance arrived. She hid in the bathroom, lost her appetite, refused to throw anything away or lock the front door. She could not tolerate the sound of Gordon's voice or his touch, and she knew she would finally let her marriage die.

Throughout the next year, Maggie watched as Dale shaped herself into something that denied her loss and hid her sorrow. Sexiness looked like confidence and invulnerability, her certainty like a future of limitless possibilities. Maggie knew this was every woman's most careful deceit, but it was Dale's religion. She took pleasure in torturing the boys who milled around at the corner of Benton Road. She walked with her chin up and a sway to her hips. She was proud of her body, her brains, and her circle of admiring friends. Maggie sometimes had the chilling sense, as she sat at her desk in the lab or worked with someone in the eye study, that Dale was having sex at that moment. Once, she had felt so certain of it she left work early, to find a boy humping her daughter under the white canopy of the princess bed. She saw the bare soles of her daughter's feet resting on the boy's baby-smooth back. Seduction was the power of Dale's body, and it was a body that had betrayed her when she became fat, and then again in its imperfection. So Maggie backed away that day and quietly shut the door to her daughter's bedroom.

In those years, if Maggie had ever suspected Gordon loved Dale more than he loved her — how much easier *that* was — she knew it was true then. Gordon bought Dale presents of cream-colored camisoles, rose-scented rinses for her hair, mysterious feminine items he somehow seemed to know about. He punched his fist into the air every time she succeeded at something, beat someone in a test or a competition, came out on top, looked more beautiful, was *more* than anyone else. Dale and her father talked for hours alone, sometimes sitting in the front seat of Gordon's gunmetal Saab. On her school vacations, he invited her to meet him downtown for lunch, and Dale excitedly discussed with Maggie what to wear.

A month before he asked Maggie for a divorce (though at that point it was just a matter of who would say the words first) Gordon took the family to Puerto Rico, where he had a conference. He held his daughter's hand as they ran into the ocean, and Maggie wondered, rubbing her eyes with sandy fingers, what serene place he'd finally discovered with her, while she and Dale were still struggling to find anything together. At dinner in a seafood restaurant decorated with lobster claws and stiff nets, Gordon ordered Dale a real drink and toasted them all, as though they were a winning team and not a family in the midst of disintegration. What he was really raising his glass to, Maggie knew at that moment, was his own escape from the impossible and unbreakable bond of mother and daughter.

THE summer heat gathered in Maggie's bedroom now and kicked at her to stay awake as it tumbled across her body, bounced on her bed. She thought of calling her mother in Florida, but Virginia would be out at the condo's pool with her boyfriend, Ricky, for a naked midnight swim among the blue beetles and the orchestra of air conditioners. In any case, her mother wouldn't try to hide her disapproval of this "baby-making escapade," as she referred to it, and Maggie didn't want to hear it. She thought of calling Dale, who in the past had sometimes phoned her at this late hour, infused with the occasional insomniac's need to talk away the loneliness. She might tell her daughter how she'd felt the baby shimmying around, how she was sure it was a girl. She might ask her what she'd had in mind when she showed up at dinner and then left so quickly afterward. But Maggie knew she'd only wake Dale and pull her away from the safety of Nate in bed next to her. In the formless dark space of her room, Maggie would lose her words and her direction.

She got out of bed, put on a bathrobe, and went downstairs. She wandered out, through the yard tarnished by moonlight, sat on a lawn chair, and let her feet cool in the water of the kiddie pool, which was dotted with shining leaves. She thought of Milt, how stunned he was by life and how his heart had been turned inside out. Her two cats glowered at her from under the low bowers of a white pine, wondering what she was doing trespassing in their time. At the sound of a snap they shot away, and Maggie froze in her chair. Who was tiptoeing through the vulnerably pretty neighborhood at this late hour, hoping for an unlocked back door, a window left open, a bathrobed woman alone in a lawn chair? Every horror scene played in Maggie's head, and she was taut with fear.

There was another snap, a rustle, light footsteps, an eager pant-ing, and the neighbor's dog trotted into her yard. She had left the gate open and he had come to drink from the pool. Like the man who'd been hit, tumbled over the car, and then miraculously walked away unsupported, Maggie suddenly felt electrified with new life.

5

ON the morning of the amniocentesis, they had decided
to get off the train at the St. Paul's Street stop and walk a few
blocks down Beacon Street to Dr. Gauld's office, but Maggie had
not counted on the heat being so brutal before noon, nor on the
muddling effect it was having on her mind. Her body at twenty-
two-weeks pregnant looked huge and comical in its shadow, like a
summer squash. They passed a synagogue, white and squat, its
dome glaring like the bowed head of a disappointed bald man.
When the traffic ebbed and the street was momentarily muted,
Maggie heard the ticking of the parking meters and the day passing in noted, ominous minutes.

"Let's stop for a second," she said. "Let me catch my breath."

Dale's face was red from the heat and a determination to keep
her mother moving. "Here? We're only a couple of blocks away.
We should at least try to be on time."

"Why? Have we ever had an appointment when we didn't end
up waiting for them? Look at that." Maggie pointed to a basement

window on her left, where a woman sat in a dentist's chair, her mouth wide open and foaming with cotton. Her hands clutched the arms, and her paper bib rose with every dry-tongued swallow. "Can you believe we actually agree to have that done? And we pay for it?"

"Yes, or lose all your teeth. She looks okay, though. Actually, I think she's asleep," Dale said, bending down to get a better view. The delicate ladder of her backbone pressing against the fabric of her dress made Maggie feel a little weak. "That's happened to me before. I shut my eyes and give in to it."

"I wish I could do that, just relax and give in to things. I have a feeling that I need to keep my eyes on those sharp instruments and those hands coming toward me." Maggie turned to her daughter. "I'm scared about this amnio. I'm in no hurry to get there."

A strong breeze whipped up, snaked between the buildings, and billowed Dale's dress with impatience. "I know you are, but you've already rescheduled twice —"

"I couldn't help that," said Maggie, cutting her off. "There were things at work I —"

Dale gave her a skeptical look, but wouldn't get into it. "Look, we're here now, and you don't need to be scared. That's all I'm saying."

Maggie waited for a rush of traffic and filthy air to pass before she spoke. "Aren't you worried that we'll find out something is wrong with the baby?"

"Not really." Dale touched Maggie's forearm, a prod to get her moving down the sidewalk. "All the other tests have been fine, and the risks here are so small. Anyway, being worried, being scared before the test — well, it doesn't change anything. There's no point. I'll wait and see what's what and go from there."

In the past she'd seen her daughter make herself dizzy with worry over nothing: a cat missing for half a day, a delayed flight, a cake rising unevenly in the oven. Now her words sounded forced and false. The woman in the dentist's chair suddenly snapped alert, as though she'd been stuck with a needle from behind. Her eyes met Maggie's through the basement window.

"No, I suppose there's never a *point* in being worried if you look at it in that light," Maggie said, wondering why Dale had made herself so impenetrable recently.

Months earlier, they had tried to talk about the bad possibilities in all this, the expectations, the changes of heart, of deformed hearts, of deformed children. They had gone to see a genetic counselor, who used the word "eventualities" often, as though it covered all unpredictabilities in the world. Out his window, Maggie had watched planes take off from Logan as he spoke, and thought how much flying, like what she and Dale and Nate were doing, was a matter of faith.

Later, the husband and wife team of psychologists, who wore matching olive-green clothes and who worked at home in a basement office, had also used the word. That time, the sharp and ominous sound of it worried her and only partially obscured what Maggie knew was the couple's disapproval of the situation. Above their heads, their young kids raced around as if to say, we have a normal life, yours is very strange.

All this discussion had taken place, and ended, well before the process of hormone boosting and shots in the thick flesh, before temperature tracking had even begun, before needle-nosed inseminations and bared white thighs in whiter rooms were routine, before the child was more than an idea, and ideas are always perfect, with happy futures and without "eventualities." She'd bought into it, too, and amazingly they had never talked about abortion. But now she'd felt this baby move inside her. It was entirely real to her, human and vulnerable, even if it wasn't to Dale.

"Do you remember Tiny Tasha at the Topsfield fair years ago? You must have been ten or eleven," Maggie asked Dale as they waited to cross Beacon Street. "I found her photograph last night in one of my drawers. 'Thank you for your contribution toward my motorized wheelchair. Here is my picture. God Bless You,' it says on the back. 'From the world's smallest woman.' Twenty-nine inches high, and all done up in a pink, frilly dress that looked like it was made out of plastic."

While Gordon and Dale had gone to see Angus, the world's largest bull, in the next tent, Maggie had paid a dollar to see Tiny Tasha. She sat in a child's chair set on a raised plywood stage so she would be eye level with those who circled around and giggled at her, their feet tripping in a bed of hay. The tent had reeked of Angus's world's largest shit. Through the canvas that separated the two freak shows, Maggie heard her husband and daughter and saw their uneven, bobbing shadows. She'd felt a chill of shame — for the way she gawked at Tiny Tasha, looking her over like she was an exhibit ("Potato That Most Resembles Human Face") in the 4-H barn — and the visceral thrill that comes with having done something forbidden.

"Just stop. Please," Dale said sharply. "This baby is not going to be Tiny Tasha or any other freak. Your mind always goes to the absolute worst-case scenario. Did you know that? It really must be a kind of talent you have. But could we just get there already?"

Dale had not swum in pure, amniotic bliss, so how could she be so sure this child did? Maggie saw the twinkling headlights of the Green Line train coming toward them from the left. In the heat and the prestorm light the tracks appeared to buckle like leather, and the shadows from the large elms waved across her face. Maggie didn't know how she would ever get across the street, her heart beating so desperately she thought it might fly out of her chest.

Dale stepped purposefully into the street. Maggie watched her daughter become the same color as the sky, so she seemed to melt into it as she crossed the wide river of concrete. For a moment Dale was entirely lost to her, part of the city's humid smear now. Maggie was suddenly slippery with sweat, on her thighs and the skin behind her knees, her eyelids, and she felt as though her body was filled with warm, seeping water. The train blasted an interminable sigh in her face, and she closed her eyes and waited for it to pass. When Maggie looked again, Dale was on the other side of the street.

"Are you all right?" Dale asked when she crossed back to her mother. Her anxious expression reflected Maggie's fear. "I thought you were with me, and when I turned to say something, you weren't there. What happened?"

Maggie shook her head; she couldn't explain what had just passed, this clearest understanding of life's loose grasp. What she did know was that her daughter's hand had slipped into hers as they crossed the street and stepped into the building's cool lobby. When they were in the elevator Maggie said, "Tell me what were you going to say before, when you were crossing the street."

Dale pulled her shoulders back, stood a little taller. "Just that this is going to be the most perfect baby ever born." Her smile was like an overly sweet offering. "You'll see."

"And if it's not?"

Dale hesitated. "I guess we'll, you know, deal with it. That's all I really meant about there being no point in being scared." She pressed the button for 5 so hard that Maggie saw the tip of her finger turn white. "We know what we'd do if something's wrong. I'm not saying it's easy, but it's why we're having an amnio in the first place, to give us the information if we need it. Otherwise why go through this at all?"

"That's exactly what I'm wondering."

The elevator bumped up, and when it stopped on the third floor it took on the odor of rubbing alcohol and reheated food. Two women, another mother and daughter pair, got on.

"Down?" the older woman asked. Her hand hovered protectively over a dot of bandage where blood had been taken from her arm.

"Yes, down." Maggie jabbed at the L button.

"Actually, we're going up." Dale pressed 5 again, but the elevator had already started its descent.

"Down," Maggie insisted.

The other women glanced sideways at each other and stepped to the front of the elevator, hurried out when it finally stopped on the ground floor. Dale pressed 5, Maggie pressed L. The elevator door wheezed open and shut, open and shut, and Maggie caught flashes of Beacon Street through the glass front door.

"You seem so certain about things," she said. "Did you ever think maybe you should talk to *me* about this? That I might have some say? I'm just curious now, where exactly do you draw the line?"

A blush spread from the wide plain of Dale's chest up to her face. It's as if, Maggie thought, she's listening to the unspoken question: *Where would you draw the line if your baby had no uterus?*

"Why are you twisting things around, making it sound as though I'm so heartless I'd abort this baby in a second if it wasn't perfect? I never said that." Dale shook her head in jerks of frustration. "And yes, we should have talked to you, it wasn't so thoughtful, but it would always come down to the same thing in the end."

"And what's that?"

"That this baby is mine — so the decision is mine, too."

This was not a discussion about perfect children, terminations, or drawn lines, Maggie suddenly understood, but about attachment. She loved the baby already, she realized, and she'd imagined its future. She'd given her body over to it, and she housed the heart of another person. But Dale still remained at a safe distance from her child, from her idea: safe, because pronouncements were easier to deliver when you were far away; safe, because the realm of love was always a dangerous, cloudy place.

"But this body is mine," Maggie said, stepping out of the elevator and into the lobby. The trees waved out on Beacon Street, and turned their leaves to the rain clouds that collected like fists. "I won't do it. I won't have the amnio."

LATER, at home, coldest water by the glassful left Maggie gratefully empty-headed and as blank as sheet metal, and she got into bed. But when she closed her eyes, she pictured the story of that morning running like a dog through the yards of everyone she knew, overturning garbage cans and littering lawns, shitting in the bushes, howling at back doors to be let in, scolded, fed. When she turned on the television for distraction, a man on a talk show was describing how he'd gotten a paper cut opening the electric bill, and how he'd ended up losing his arm because of it. The screen showed a picture of his pre-amputation, gangrenous fingers looking like charred hot dogs forgotten on the grill, then one of his wife holding up his wide, stumpy paw supportively, then a commercial for toothpaste. What disturbed Maggie most was not the simple and gruesome oddity of what had happened to the man, but his serene and accepting way of talking about it, as though the tragedy had been destined for him. For most of his life, he explained after the commercial, he'd done bad — his wife looked at the floor then, her feet flexing in their dull pumps — but he was doing right now. He had plaques and accomplishments to prove it. The audience looked subdued, as though momentarily concerned that if this was the way the world actually operated, bad visited upon bad, they were in big trouble.

"But it doesn't work like that!" Maggie yelled furiously. You could never explain why children got cancer, why a woman who had survived Auschwitz would die under the wheel of a bus in Brooklyn, or why the man lost his arm, except to say that bad luck simply, randomly, falls to some.

Still, hadn't she always held herself — her resentment and unhappiness at finding she was pregnant with Dale — responsible for her daughter's being born incomplete? Hadn't she seen Dale's lack as her fault, and as some sort of personal punishment and payback? But *this* child was not a trial to test her convictions or her goodwill. It was not recompense, revenge, or a visitation, but simply a gift to Dale. She'd been wrong to draw the line where she had, to act as if this baby should be born at any cost in order to teach her daughter a hard lesson about life. One which she already knew perfectly well.

For the first time since Dale was born, Maggie allowed the weight of her guilt to lift a little. She watched it float to the ceiling and hang above and around her like a delicate cloud.

When the doorbell rang Maggie remembered, half awake and making her way down the stairs, that Doris had planned to stop by and bring her some dinner. She didn't look forward to explaining to Doris what had happened. But it was Ben at the door, soaked from the rainwater that came down in straight, dark sheets from Maggie's clogged gutters. He was both completely familiar and unrecognizable at the same time, and for a moment she couldn't place him.

"Yes, I know you were expecting Doris," he said, and stepped in past her puzzlement. "But there was yet another crisis with Tina she had to deal with at the last minute. Dale called Doris crying, Doris called me saying I had to talk to you. So did Nate. I got the whole saga. 'Maggie flipped out, Maggie lost it in an elevator, Maggie refused to have an amnio, Maggie ran away,' they said. 'Go talk to Maggie.'" Ben looked down at his worn sneakers turned the color of stone.

"Funny," Maggie said, crossing her arms over her chest. "They must think you're the voice of persuasion."

Ben shrugged apologetically, though Maggie suspected he might believe in his own power. "I don't know about *that*. But I'd say the consensus out there is definitely not in your favor at the moment."

"I'm not surprised. No one likes an obstructionist." Maggie led the way back to the kitchen. "To tell you the truth though, I'm not sure I care very much."

"Don't give me that," Ben said, trailing her. "You care a lot, more than anyone I know, maybe. Sorry, I'm getting water all over the place."

He sat down at the table and began to take off his sneakers. His feet were wrinkled and white, as though he'd been standing in a puddle for a long time.

"You're right, I do care, but only because I doubt myself and need some sort of guide. It's a terrible way to be, actually, way too much work, and way too crowded."

"You don't doubt yourself very often."

"Do you know what I understood this morning? That this," Maggie said, circling her hands around her stomach, "is still an abstraction for Dale. A child is an idea for her. For me, well, I want to throw up almost every morning, my breasts ache and I can't sleep, and I *feel* the baby all the time. I know who she is — there's nothing abstract about her at all. The other day Dale and I were talking about work and she asked me why you and I are still trying to find a way to prevent cataracts when it's so simple to remove them. This is the same thing."

"But it's a fair question, isn't it?" Ben sat at the table and wiped his face with the damp edge of his shirt. "I wonder about it too, whether there's much point to what we're doing anymore. Sometimes I think we're starting from the wrong end of the problem. Science flip-flopped at some point."

"But there are still people in all this, histories, and feelings. Dale doesn't see the heart in anything anymore. Not even in this baby. That's what worries me."

"She has plenty of heart. But practicality, efficacy, efficiency — that's where it's at. The age of stories is over, Maggie." Ben sighed. "You can talk all you want, but here's the simple truth you don't want to accept: it doesn't matter. This is Dale's baby. This is her choice."

The words stunned her for the second time that day. Maggie swung around the kitchen, opening and shutting cabinets, slamming the refrigerator. "Hungry and nothing to eat, so fucking typical of my life."

"Calm down. Do you want me to go out and get you something? I will."

Maggie stopped and looked at Ben. "Is that really it? This is about ownership and I don't want to accept that the baby isn't mine? It can't be that simple. *I'm* not that simple or selfish." She shook her head. "What I feel has to count for something, doesn't it?"

Ben shrugged. "No, it really doesn't. Sorry, but you knew that going into this."

"Yes and no. How could I really know? How is it like anything else in life?" Maggie watched Ben push a bottle of vitamins back and forth across the table. "Funny now — I feel totally alone in this."

Ben gave her a sympathetic look. "You're just the body. The body doesn't have much of a mind."

Maggie tightened the belt of her bathrobe to slow a sense that the room was rocking. "The body suddenly doesn't feel so good. Maybe I'll lie down for a while."

"You look kind of tired. I should get back to the lab anyway." Ben leaned down to put on his sneakers. "You'll be okay?"

"No, probably not."

Maggie saw Ben's reluctance — to go or to stay, she didn't know which — in the curve of his back, in the way his hands stayed poised just above his damp shoelaces. "What do you want me to do?" He spoke with his head still down. "You decide."

It was suddenly clear to Maggie that Ben was her comfort, true and immutable, and always had been. To ask him to stay now was only to finally say this out loud. There was a sharp taste in her mouth, a rich mix of risk and expectation.

"Then forget about work for once," she said, and put one hand on Ben's back. "I don't know why you keep running away from me, why you avoid me these days, but I need you here now."

IN her bedroom Maggie watched Ben bend to smooth out the sheets. When he stood looking over her as she lay in bed, she saw that his mouth was open slightly, and his eyes narrowed as though he were thinking very hard about something.

"You don't have to stand," she offered.

Ben sat on the edge of the bed and slowly tipped back, so that he was lying next to her. Her feet under the blankets, and his on top, made a wall at the end. He looked around her bedroom and Maggie knew he was seeing a part of her he didn't know at all — clothes, evidence of every day's indecision draped over the back of a chair, underwear, photographs of Dale at various ages stuck in the corner of a mirror, the way she'd knotted the curtain. The room smelled of her perfume and unwrapped soaps hardening in drawers. There was an apple core and a single pearl earring on the bedside table, books open and piled.

"Your roof is leaking," he said. "Can you hear it?"

Maggie listened to the familiar steady drip and pointed up to navigate for him the tributaries of cracks that ran across her ceiling. "It's been leaking for years. You can pretty much tell where. I'll get to it one of these days, sooner rather than too late, I hope."

Ben began to dry off next to her, and as the dampness evaporated it somehow drew them closer together. The backs of their hands touched. Maggie felt the anxious presence of Doris in the room, and the need to acknowledge her. "I haven't seen Doris in a while. She's always in the middle of something when I call. We have dates, she breaks them, or she forgets. What's going on with her?"

"Well, there's the all-consuming Tina now," Ben said, with an edge of resignation. "She has the most beautiful face, luminous at times, and problems that never seem to end. She pees in her bed, she hits kids at school. She runs away from me — I guess I scare her in some way. It's the strangest thing to walk by Aaron's room in the middle of the night and see this black-haired girl sleeping in his bed." His voice had become tender and distant. "I have to remind myself where I am, what year it is. What year I'd like it to be."

"When I saw you at the door before," Maggie told him, "I thought you were Aaron for a minute. Remember the night he showed up here after a party, drunk and wet, and wouldn't go home?"

It had been almost midnight when Maggie brought Aaron, panicked and sloppy, inside. Dale, woken by the noise, had run to get something left by her father for him to change into — he or someone else had puked on his clothes. Maggie made him a bed on the couch. When she called Doris to say that Aaron was downstairs, her friend's relief was so strong, Maggie was sure she felt it blowing through the telephone. Long past midnight she heard Dale and Aaron, easy friends forever, talking, and she was proud of her daughter's kindness and ability to comfort this boy who'd seemed so undone.

When Maggie got up the next morning, she found Dale and Aaron kissing on the couch, a blanket thrown over their lower halves. The air was damp and sweet. Gordon's shirt hung from the edge of a chair, and Aaron's pale white chest practically throbbed. Strands of Dale's hair fell across it.

"You looked just like him today," Maggie said. "I had to remind myself where I was, too, for a moment, what year it was."

Ben rolled left and removed his wallet from his back pocket. It was worn, suggesting the shape of his body, and it seemed to Maggie more private than anything they'd said or shown to each other in a long time. She crossed her legs and tried not to feel the length of his thigh against hers. He opened his wallet to a folder of cards, and turned them until he found what he was looking for. Behind the yellowed plastic was a picture of his family. It had been taken against a swirled swimming-pool-blue background, posed in a department store studio, when the boys were bursting out of their bodies, their bones growing faster than their skin. Everything was tight and shiny.

"Aaron and I still look alike. Even more so these days. Sometimes, for just a second, illness looks exactly like aging," Ben said. He touched the picture again, resting a fingertip on Aaron's arm, as though to blot out the fearsome limb. "I miss my kids as boys, when I could stroke them and kiss them whenever I wanted, and they'd run to me. I remember once when I was driving home from the lab and I passed Doris in the car with the kids in the back seat going out somewhere, and they gave me such a look of longing through the window it made me cry. Really, I pulled over and wept. I thought a man like me had no business being a father, I was too crazy about the boys, it couldn't be good to love them so much. Now all they want to do is talk to me like adults. They want to have conversations, they want to shake hands, talk about money and sports. Aaron calls to ask me what I think of isolated limb perfusion, and after that we talk about the NBA. I swear, Maggie, it's horrifying." His laugh was shallow. "You should have had more — kids, I mean."

"Sure, that would have been just what Gordon and I needed. We probably would have ended up killing each other. We were never quite on the same page when it came to Dale, even when she was a baby. I was uncertain and he was too certain. A bad mix."

"Then with someone else. Jesus, Gordon wasn't the only man on the planet." Ben slapped his wallet shut. "You know, I never told Doris what happened between Aaron and Dale that night. She wouldn't have known what to do with it — or with you, either. She's funny that way, private. I think she'd call it discreet."

"Who knows what happened that night. They were only kissing when I saw them."

Ben laughed. "Dale was the first girl Aaron slept with. What were they, sixteen? I think he was both incredibly proud of himself and confused at the same time. He'd been seduced by the beautiful Dale, queen of desire. I'm not sure we'd even had the condom talk yet."

"She didn't seduce him," Maggie said, her defensiveness a familiar pang. "I was right upstairs. I heard them talking. I remember, because Gordon had left a couple weeks before and I'd been waking up at strange times, midnight, five in the morning."

"Oh, I think she did seduce him, Maggie. From what he told me, Dale started it, and in just the right way."

Dale had glanced up to see her mother halted on the stairs that morning. It was just beginning to get light out, but Maggie was able to detect her daughter's hand stirring under the blanket, which was tented with Aaron's erection. Maggie didn't move to go back upstairs until she saw Dale unfold from the couch, naked under her open robe, a defiant flash of breasts and pubic hair. Aaron had put his head back and opened his mouth. Even his Adam's apple bobbed.

"Our poor confused, groping babies," Ben said.

"I'm sure they did fine," Maggie said in a final concession. "I wasn't mother of the year, that's pretty obvious, letting my daughter screw boys on the living-room couch. What was I thinking?" She paused and let the past slam up against the present. It knocked her hard in the chest. "I should never have agreed to have her baby. It's no solution. Children never are."

"No, that's completely wrong. This baby is exactly what you both need, you to give and Dale to take. For both of you to move on, let go a little." Ben touched her cheek. "But I think that an act like this, well, let's just say that love creates problems of its own. There's no right place for Dale to be now, no way she can repay you, or even thank you. It's just too big, too much, so she steps back, she acts assured and chilly. What else can she do?" Maggie appreciated his gentle acceptance of her daughter. "Nobody really likes an altruist, after all. They ask for nothing in return, which isn't normal, and they make the rest of us look bad. But I love you more for it. Really, I do. You've amazed me."

Maggie shut her eyes, overcome by Ben's admission, wonderful and impossible at the same time. She was alerted by his fingers on her shoulder and his breath gusting on her skin as he talked. She felt a catch on her arm, a move to the field of skin below her chin, a touch as warm and encircling as pond water travel down to her breasts, her nipples, each rib, her stomach, the skin drawn tight, thin, and oversensitive.

The bed rocked as Ben rolled off it. "Are you awake?" he asked, but she didn't answer.

Maggie heard his bare feet slap the floor, and thought, good, he's leaving now, that's what he should do. And I'll pretend I'm asleep. I won't even turn around. She held her breath and heard the downing of his zipper, the distant toll of the parts of his belt buckle hitting each other, the gasp of cloth as his shirt lifted over his head. When she turned, she saw his penis erect, his nipples tiny pink dots hidden in graying curls, his chin lifted as though he were standing against a wind, but his eyes were on her. He was the man she hadn't seen like this for almost half her lifetime now, her lover once. She felt not the disappearance of the years, but their bittersweet intrusion.

Ben opened Maggie's bathrobe in the same breathless way she'd once unlayered tissue paper to reveal a bouquet of flowers. His hands rested on the rise of her belly. He pressed his face to the skin there and inched his hands under her. He put his lips to her breasts, and when Maggie touched his hair she was surprised at how soft and fine it was, when she'd remembered it differently, the coarser texture of a younger man. No scent of him, no taste of his mouth, brought her back to what they once were; this was new and older now. It was not her size that made making love difficult, it was both of them moving impatiently, as if they couldn't get enough of what they knew, and couldn't get what they didn't know fast enough. In all her life, no man had ever been so passionate for her, though many had been smoother, and she had never been so sweet-smelling and unreserved.

They didn't talk, and later, when they were lying still, the phone rang. Maggie had no intention of answering, but Ben reached over to pick it up, as though this were his usual place, in bed with her.

"Yes, it's me," Ben said softly. He sat up and turned his back to Maggie, his voice muffled against his chest. "Why? Because Maggie's asleep."

She heard the metallic tone of Doris pulse over and around Ben when he stood up with the phone, and she was seized by a sickening disbelief at what had just happened, what she'd just done. The room was oppressively hot and sour all of a sudden, crowded and chaotic, better to leave than ever fix, and she put her hands over her eyes.

"Doris is coming over later," Ben told Maggie after he'd hung up. He stood looking out the window, tensing the muscles in his shoulders. "She and Dale. They want to talk to you. I should go."

"Yes, you should." Maggie got up and put on her robe. She spoke quickly to erase what had happened. "We can't do this. You know that. I asked you up here, I was upset, but this isn't good. It isn't right."

"No, it isn't," Ben said, still turned away from her. "And I left my headlights on."

He tried to snap the wrinkles out of his still damp pants, but the cloth slapped weakly against itself. When he put his T-shirt on, Maggie saw several long strands of her hair glistening against the dark fabric. This is how we're caught, this is how we carry some of the other with us at all times, she thought, but did not remove them.

"Apparently, I was supposed to have picked up some flowers Milt left for you at home," Ben said, his voice automatic and flat. "They're already wilted, according to Doris. An enormous bunch of pink and white roses from his dead wife's garden. Dead now, obviously."

"They died as soon as they were cut."

Ben kneeled to retrieve his wallet, which had found its way under the bed. He didn't look at Maggie when he left the room. It was still raining and her windows were open. She heard him splash to his car, heard the first tentative click and cough of his engine, heard the sound of his caution as he sat for ten minutes recharging the battery.

Maggie knew she couldn't stop Dale and Doris from coming over. She took a shower, rushed to rinse the smells and touch of Ben down the drain. When she was done, powdered and in a robe, she waited by the open front door and pictured the women passing Ben on Commonwealth Avenue, each too focused on their destination ahead to notice. She watched Dale park in front of the house. She was wearing the black dress she'd had on that morning, but it looked twisted and pulled, which made Maggie sure that her daughter had missed another day at work and had instead spent hours in anxious restlessness. The hair at her forehead was damp and clumped and she pushed at it irritably, a gesture Maggie recognized as precisely her own. Doris came in just behind Dale, her lips pressed tightly together, her eyes averted from Maggie's. She had always been Dale's support, and today, Maggie thought, I can see her even more clearly; she is also my daughter's urging, the hand on her back, pushing her here. She was not ready to hear what they had to say, to face this phalanx of women.

"I want you to cut my hair," Maggie announced before either of them spoke. "Short, all off."

"Oh, no, you don't. I won't let you do it," Doris said, and gathered Maggie's hair in her hands. "It's too beautiful. You're just emotional today, and I know you like to change things — your clothes, your plans, everything — when you're upset."

Maggie stiffened at Doris's touch and drew away, her hair still caught in her friend's hands. She felt the tug at her scalp. "You're exactly right. Emotional is the best time, the truest time, the only time as far as I'm concerned. Otherwise, you over-think. Why would you discourage me, Doris?"

"Because I'd do anything to have hair like yours." Doris touched her tight curls, and Maggie recalled how Ben's hair had felt passing over her skin. "Tina has beautiful hair, like mink, and you and Dale — it's what makes you two look so alike." She turned to Dale, who shrugged. "Maybe you want to wait until tomorrow to decide, is what I'm saying."

"Shit, it's just hair," Maggie said angrily. "My hair. And it doesn't mean anything one way or the other, doesn't say anything about who I am."

"I guess she wants it off then," Dale said. "I actually think it will look better. And you'll be much cooler, too. You look so hot now, rubbed red. You're all sweaty." Dale scrutinized her mother, her eyes darkening in concentration, and Maggie had the familiar feeling that Dale understood something about her, even if she couldn't always name it. "I think a cool bath first. Then we'll do it."

Dale led the way upstairs and ran the water. She brought a chair into the bathroom, placed it by the claw-foot tub, and told Maggie to get in. Doris, who had been standing in the doorway, turned away discreetly as Maggie dropped the robe off her shoulders and stepped into the bath.

Dale held her hands out. "Lean back. Let me scrub."

Maggie was enthroned, sunken, attended to. She recognized it as the simplest of scenes. After all, women bathed babies, sick husbands, and friends. Dale had come over to bathe her a year earlier when she had the flu and could hardly get out of bed. She'd brought a new bar of verbena soap, had washed her, let her soak, read to her from the newspaper. With her head back now, Maggie allowed the water to flow over her face and thought about Doris. They had been friends forever, slept in the same bed, held each other's children. Now Maggie had also slept with Doris's husband. She stretched, revealing the line of faint hair that ran down from her belly button to her pubic hair, her veined breasts, her round stomach, her inner thighs, between her legs where Ben had kissed. Doris had moved into the bedroom. Would she see beyond a tumble of sheets and pillows, would she know what a just-vacated room smelled like?

There was Dale at her head. Do you understand I'm capable of passion too? Maggie wanted to ask. The water roared into the tub. Tilting, she let herself relax. She felt the thick disorder of her hair spill through her daughter's fingers in great ladlings. Dale tugged gently, but Maggie also sensed in her touch the temptation — and the resistance — to yank hard, to hurt her.

She heard the slow scrape of a chair being moved in her bedroom, swore she heard the sound of sheets snapped into place, clothes picked up, drawers shut. *Don't you want to close some of these windows so the floor doesn't get wet from the rain?* Doris yelled in to her. *Let me make your bed for you.* She is a woman who doesn't see anything, Maggie told herself, and if she can't see this, if she can't detect her husband's scent, or the shape of the space he'd taken up, then all this won't hurt her. Instantly, she knew the ugly falseness of her thinking, and was grateful for the sheet of water that fell over her face and made her swallow fast for air.

When Maggie was out of the tub, Dale sat her down in the kitchen, scissors poised. Doris leaned against the counter and watched, one eyelid pale where she'd wiped off her makeup with the back of her hand, giving her a lopsided, tired look. As each fan of wet hair fell to the floor, Maggie sensed her daughter gathering the strength to say something. Her cutting was no longer tentative but confident, and her breathing echoed the swish of the blades.

"When did you learn to cut hair?" Maggie asked.

"Nate taught me. I do his, he does mine."

"Where is he tonight anyway?"

"School. Where else is he, ever? A hundred students, a thousand problems, and what a miracle! He's the only one who has the answers." Her exasperation was tempered by a smile meant to deflect concern. "He should be home pretty soon."

"And what about our problems? Does he have an answer to them?" Maggie's words were absorbed by Dale's stomach pressed against her face, soaked up by her daughter's heat. She smelled faintly of rosemary.

"Done." Dale hadn't heard Maggie. Now she surveyed her work, snipping off a few stray hairs. Maggie touched the newly blunt ends and understood that what Dale now saw was not so much Maggie, but herself, altered.

"This is good," Dale said, though her expression was not as sure. "Nice. Nice job I did."

Maggie got up to examine herself in the hall mirror. Everything seemed lighter, the shape of her face revealed, after so many years, as balanced and open. She was someone she didn't entirely recognize, a woman who could fuck her best friend's husband so easily. In the mirror Maggie watched Doris put strawberries in a bowl, pinching the green stems, the red juice seeping under her nails. Doris looked up, and her eyes met Maggie's in the glass.

"I can say this because I love you," Doris said shakily, "but what you did today, when you decided not to have the amnio — well, that was wrong. I know I don't know what it's like to be in your position, but if nothing else, take it from me and avoid heartache whenever possible." She laughed unconvincingly and ate a strawberry. "With Aaron, I have more than enough to go around, and I'm sure I haven't seen anything yet." Tears dropped into the bowl of fruit. "Don't be crazy, okay? Have the test, see what's what — which will be nothing, by the way — and go from there."

Dale gave Doris an uneasy look, and Doris returned a slow nod of encouragement. "I rescheduled the amnio for tomorrow morning," Dale said. "Nate and I are going to be with you the whole time. The office said they understood about today, it happens all the time. It's just fear working on you, making you act — well, not like yourself."

Maggie smiled. "And you're the mother," she said, knowing that there was a peculiar power in this naming. Dale looked relieved and suddenly very tired. Doris ate another sweet strawberry.

6

SET at a remove from the party, the plastic lawn chair whined under Maggie's weight. At almost twenty-eight weeks pregnant, she was as awkward as a drunk, unbalanced, and still surprised by it. Doris, behind her, had offered herself as an eave of shade, an awning to block out Labor Day evening's harshest sun. But Maggie knew Doris would have liked to step back much farther and retreat into the deepest rhododendrons in the corner of the yard, where the old branches curved to form a cave, cool and smelling of dirt.

"The faces are different, but it's really just the same people every year," Doris said about the crowd of graduate students, neighbors, colleagues, and friends treading on her grass. Maggie heard ice cubes fall hard against Doris's teeth. "I used to like having this party. I actually looked forward to it because it made me think how big and generous and fascinating our life was. Now it only makes me feel a year older."

"Stop giving it then," Maggie suggested. "Make this your last year." Doris was no martyr, she told herself, just weighed down, slowing down. "You and Ben could go away instead, to the beach, the mountains, some foreign city."

"He never goes away, you know that," Doris said.

"I'd take care of things at work. Ben knows I would."

"What I should do is go away by myself, go visit Peter in London while he's still there. Look at Ben, he's completely in his element," she said, her tone not entirely kind. "And of course there's Aaron, who he'd never leave now — not even to visit Peter for a week."

As though he'd heard his wife, Ben, wavering behind greasy smoke from the barbecue, suddenly glanced toward their cool corner. An X left by dirty hands ran across his white shirt. Shelby and the others around him laughed loudly.

"Anyway," Doris continued, "I have a feeling these people expect it, and they would show up even if we weren't here. They'd just go ahead and have the party without us."

"Which wouldn't be so bad," Maggie added. "I kind of like the idea, actually. All the glory, but you wouldn't actually have to attend."

Doris looked at her curiously. Maggie remembered one year at the party sitting with Doris in the same corner of the yard, breast-feeding their babies. The trees were thin and newly planted then, and the fence, now peeled and settled, had been optimistically straight. Both babies had nursing blisters and a blissful trickle of milk on their chins. This Labor Day, Maggie had to dodge endless curious questions and stunningly blunt remarks about *this* situation and *this* baby. Dale stood alone by the food, one finger trolling a bowl of nuts for the cashews, and Doris watched the side gate for Aaron. Things had changed, but Maggie would have liked to tell her friend how amazing it was that their lives had managed to run on such a straight course for so many years.

The gunshot of a window slamming down startled Maggie and she looked up the back of the angled Victorian. Her eye caught Tina, a flash of pink and black behind the glass in what used to be

Aaron's room. Once, she'd seen Aaron, Peter, and Dale leaning out the same window blowing cigarette smoke into a winter night littered with stars. She'd been standing on the iced lawn for only a minute to escape the oppressive cheer of a dinner party inside, and saw the red glow pass between them, Dale in the center.

"Tina," Doris said familiarly, and stood in front of Maggie, blocking her view. "Sometimes she asks for attention in very strange ways. Anyway, I should check on her, see if she's okay. She was kind of upset about all these people being here."

Again, Maggie wanted to say something — now about leaving the girl alone, letting her breathe, giving her some room to be unhappy, or anxious, or whatever she claimed to know Tina was currently feeling — but stopped herself. In any case, Doris had already gone toward the house, cutting an oblivious path through her guests. Maggie forced herself to get up and move to the patio.

Three weeks earlier in Dr. Gauld's office, Dale had reacted to the results of the amnio — everything looked fine and the baby was a girl — with relief, not so much for what was, but for what wasn't. Even as they hugged, Maggie had sensed something troubling and unresolved in her daughter, but Dale had denied it and said simply that she was happy. Later, Dale had driven her mother back to the lab, and Maggie had felt gaping McDonald's boxes on the car floor scratch at her ankles. The air smelled of ancient onions and sugar, and the back seat was littered with gnawed paper cups and chewed straws. Anxiety, she had assured herself, took all different forms, and if her daughter wanted to eat and eat to calm herself, well, Maggie understood a woman's impulse to gorge, and this was probably not such a terrible thing. She remembered how the strap of Dale's bra had sneaked out from under her black shirt, how the whiteness of it had burned in her eye like a grain of sand, how she had not understood why that single detail took up so much space in her mind.

Now she reached into a cooler for a beer floating in an icy soup and held the bottle against her neck. She closed her eyes and allowed the chill to travel through her body.

"That looks like it feels good, " Nate said, appearing beside her. "It's beyond hot out here."

"It would feel a lot better if I could actually drink it." Maggie slipped Nate's beer out of his hand. She took a long gulp before handing it back. He hesitated, and then wiped the bottle with his shirt before he drank again.

Maggie laughed. "Don't worry, you can't get pregnant from a beer bottle, I promise."

"Maybe you should talk to my students sometime," Nate said, chagrined. "The pregnant ones look right at me and swear to God they never had sex. Did this happen, did that happen? Did he put his penis in you? I ask, because that sure sounds a whole lot like sex to me. But these girls talk about their bodies like they're not their own, like they're just renting the space. Like they're watching it happen. 'Well, maybe he did,' they say, 'but I don't really remember. ' "

Maggie pictured the thin-armed girls, their lips heavily outlined, flopped onto the futon in Nate's office, telling him everything about their lives while he nodded, his eyes as wide and eager as they were now. On other days, he'd driven kids to the emergency room, the clinic, the police station, to detox, or just around for hours. Dale had told her once how he sometimes brought a student home to sleep in the extra room, and how he wanted to make love to her those nights. Clearly, Nate was turned on by these kids.

"How *do* they explain it then?" she asked, slightly unsettled.

"Someone had sex with *them*." Nate finished off his beer, leaned his head back, stretching sensuously. She watched his throat rise and fall with the recollection of something delicious sliding down it.

"How do you think Dale's doing these days?" Maggie knew from Nate's distant stare that she'd caught him somewhere else, that his mind had been nowhere near his wife.

"Oh, she's pretty good," he said, and reached into the ice for another beer. "Working too hard, as usual. They're always asking her to do something more, and she never says no." When he leaned closer to Maggie, she thought he was about to say something else to her, something true or honest, but he put his hand on her belly instead. His lips were wet and a little slack. "Just checking."

"How about you check with me before you touch next time," she said, and removed his hand from her. Confusion lodged firmly in Nate's eyes. "I don't like it."

The sliding glass door hissed open then and Aaron and Dale stepped out onto the flagstones. Aaron, brittle and thin, shook hands with Nate and then moved to kiss Maggie. His face glowed white and ghostly, while his mouth in contrast was an alarming, false pink, as though he'd just finished a cherry pop. He wore huge baggy pants and a voluminous long-sleeved shirt, so that he looked like a little boy in his father's clothes. Thin hair escaped like smoke from under his baseball cap. He looked to Maggie as if he might suddenly shatter, and though she finally breezed her lips over his cheek, which smelled sadly like baby powder, she wanted to back away from him and weep instead. He looked like death.

"I know, I look like shit," he said, and rolled his eyes. He lifted up his shirt to reveal a sunken chest and stomach, a belly button like a poked-out eye. "Pretty buff, don't you think? My clothes feel like steel wool sometimes. They say my skin is as delicate as an infant's," he added with an exaggerated smirk. "Jealous?"

"Hey, you look better than most of the people here," Dale told him. With her finger, she traced the dark skin below his eyes, and then the sharp point of his chin. It was both an affectionate and a morbid gesture. Aaron's amused smile was half obscured by Dale's hand resting on his skin. Nate shifted uneasily and stared out at the party.

"You're looking pretty goddamn enormous, Mags," Aaron said.

"I feel like a minivan. Did you see your father yet?" she asked, her tone forced and tiny. Ben was gone from his spot in the smoke. A circle of people had ominously closed to take his place. "He was over there a minute ago."

"Yeah, I saw him, and that was a barrel of fun, believe me," Aaron told her. "I saw both of my lovely parents, actually, his and hers, hissing like cats. Hosts of the year. Peter's smart to live on another continent." He scratched his elbow, and the sound, like skin scraping concrete, turned Maggie's stomach. "I'm hungry, Dale. Come with me to find something to eat," Aaron said.

They walked not toward the food, but to the private corner where Maggie and Doris had been earlier. Maggie wondered what they were talking about with their heads so close together and Dale's arms wrapped across her chest. Maggie left Nate and wandered into the house, dark after the sunlight, and as she stood at the foot of the stairs, heard the smooth sounds of Doris soothing Tina above. We have each retreated into some quieter place, she thought, and sat down on the bottom step; life is getting a little too noisy for us all. For the first time, the house looked dingy and faded to her, unchanged forever, the telephone sitting on the thin-legged table stained with the rings left by sweating glasses, the walls crowded with watercolors in browns and mustards, tones of inertia. The beige rug lay like a woman who has stopped expecting to be noticed. There was water running in the bathroom off the hall, and when Maggie went to the open door she saw Ben bent far over the sink. Through the room's frosted window behind him, colors of the party drifted by.

"Hi," Maggie said. Ben didn't look up but continued to wash his hands, moving them through a violent tussle with each other and a bar of pink soap. Water and suds spilled onto his clothes, over the edge of the sink, onto his bare feet, and puddled on the floor. "You look like you're trying to drown something. You okay in there?" she asked.

"No, not particularly."

"Why don't you come out?" As Maggie reached into the room to turn off the water, she felt herself slipping, the imbalance of her body testing itself on the slick floor. She grasped the door frame and pulled herself back.

"For chrissake, Maggie, don't come in here. What do you want, anyway?"

"Nothing, really. I'll go." This isn't my business, she told herself, and turned to leave.

"Did you see Aaron?" Ben asked, and looked up. He'd been crying. So much water, Maggie thought.

"Yes, I saw him outside a few minutes ago."

"Doesn't he look awful?"

She hesitated. "Pale and too thin." She offered only half of the worst truth. "But he seemed in a good mood. Happy."

"Why does he want to show me, to throw it in my face? What is he trying to prove?"

"Jesus, Ben, this is not about you. Aaron's not doing anything to you, he's not throwing his sickness in your face," she said. "You asked him to come to the party. What's he supposed to do, lock himself in a dark room?"

"Maybe, and maybe I should just poke my fucking eyes out so I don't have to look at him."

"He's your son. I don't believe this," she said.

Ben slammed the soap down and its dish, a clunky clay thing one of Doris's students had made, flew off the edge of the sink and shattered on the floor. Maggie watched the shards dissolve earthy red in the water, and kneeled to clean them up.

"Goddamn Doris," Ben said above her. His anger pounded her back like fists. "She just informed me that I can't act like this over every little bump, every bruise, every fever he has, that I only make it harder for Aaron by being so upset and by showing it so much. I'm not like her, stoic and keeping it together — that's not normal all the time — and for what? What exactly are we trying to pretend isn't going on? Our son's dying and she wants me to smile and shake his hand, and act as though it's all fine. If I want to cry, she says, I should do it later, when he's not here. Our son's dying, and she hates *who* I am, and *how* I am while it's happening. *Now*, when I'm acting more like myself than I ever have, she hates me?"

Doris had told Maggie how Ben tracked Aaron's health — test results, colds and complaints, blood work, weight — on the kitchen calendar. At first she hadn't understood what the half-moons, stars, and cragged arrows were about, but once she'd decoded her husband's scribbles she'd been furious. It was gruesome, she'd said, to have it hanging over them as they ate their meals, spaghetti and scrambled eggs and take-out Chinese, gruesome to mark their son's time right along with Veteran's Day, dentist appointments, and the termite inspection. And why didn't he mark the good days instead? She'd like to see *that* with her bran muffin. One morning she tore the calendar down off its nail, walked outside in her nightgown, and waited for the six o'clock garbage truck so she could dump it in herself. Crisis had revealed both of them, the recorder and the denier.

"But this is killing her, too," Maggie said, and recalled her friend's weeping over the bowl of strawberries. "Doris doesn't want Aaron to think he's only about tragedy, for his life to look only like disease. He could live a very long time."

Ben gave her an indulgent look, as if he appreciated the gesture of her words even if he didn't believe them for a minute. "What are you doing on the floor? Will you get up, please?"

"Okay, but you'll have to help me." Maggie put out her hand. "I can't do it myself, I just discovered."

"Huge. And beautiful." His face was full of disappointment, his hands by his side. Her knees ground into the wet floor.

A month earlier they'd made love in her bed for a second time when Ben had driven Maggie home from the lab because she hadn't felt well. They hadn't touched since, had barely talked to each other, and Maggie had decided they wouldn't ever again. What they'd done would be absorbed and finally flushed out of them, like a drop of poison; ultimately nontoxic, though it would probably leave some small, private scarring somewhere inside. Ben grasped her hand and drew her off the floor. She rose slowly, and then leaned solidly against him. She didn't know if she'd moved to Ben, or Ben to her, or if it was perfect convergence. She gasped.

"Don't go," he said. "Stay with me. I need you."

"Look, you're upset. Take a deep breath." His mouth moved against her neck and she felt his breath on her skin. He reached past her to shut the door. The heat of his hand on her breast was like a squeeze on her heart, both painful and exhilarating, and it made her blood flow faster. Maggie unbuttoned his pants, lowered his zipper with the pinch of her forefinger and thumb, slipped her fingers down the silky, wide slope of his muscles. She held his erection, but he grasped her wrist and pulled her hand away. He sat down on the narrow bench in the room, knocking a storm of dusty dried flowers to the wet floor. Maggie sat on him, the bulk of her belly resting against him, and slid him inside her, the fullness of her dress hiked up to her waist. Over her own breathing and Ben's, she heard laughing, a plastic cup dropped on the patio, a sizzle of meat, a hush of Dale, a blue spark of Nate, a brittle breaking of Aaron, a sigh of Doris, a watery flip of the baby, and then her own body and Ben's clenching together. Colors still passed on the other side of the window, moving now in a single continuous loop.

When she slid off Ben and stood, her dress fell like a curtain down her sticky legs. She felt a tide of guilt rise behind her eyes. What have we done, and what are we doing? What if it was simply solace Ben sought from her, and solace that had drawn them together in the first place. What if it wasn't passion at all, though it certainly felt like it, but a quick, selfish relief of their sorrows and confusions?

But loss and love, Maggie knew from her own history — and she thought now of Dale, close once and now dangerously distant — were arcs on the same circle. It didn't matter which point you started from, you'd arrive at both eventually. She thought of Doris above her, curling her toes in the green shag of the bedroom carpet, the fine lines around her eyes deepening, and she felt a great, final sadness for her friend.

MAGGIE left by the front door and scanned the street for her car, but she could not remember where she'd parked it. Panic was a door shutting on any possible clues, and for a moment she considered walking home despite the watery feeling in her legs. When she turned, she saw Milt watching her from his side of the fence; she could not pretend otherwise. She hadn't returned any of his calls, and his messages on her machine had become less sure, until they'd almost become apologies, and then he'd stopped calling altogether. Milt's hair was slicked back and much darker than she'd remembered it, as though he'd colored it in preparation for his reentrance into the world. His eyes were vibrant, but he was looking at her coolly.

"My wife's pug," he told Maggie when she stood opposite him, the chest-high fence between them. He looked down, to where there was a scratching noise at his feet and a small cloud of dust rising in front of him. "The garden's dying. My fault, I discovered I don't like gardening. So I might as well let him go there now. It's all fertilizer of one sort or another." Sweat dotted his face and an aroma of shit wafted up as strong as his discomfort. "Your hair is different."

"Yours too." When Maggie touched the blunt ends of her hair she smelled Ben on her wrist. "Are you going to the party?"

"I'm no good at parties. I used to be." He glanced down again as the dog wheezed. "Not true, actually. I was never good at them. Looks like you're on your way out."

"I was just leaving. I'm not feeling so hot."

"No?" Milt raised his eyebrows. "Well, I'm sorry to hear that. Probably the heat. Tell me something before you go."

"Look, Milt, I'm sorry for not calling back," she broke in. Pinpoints throbbed on her body. "I'm not an awful person, and I don't have a good excuse, so I won't give you a bad one."

"No, that's fine. Anyway, that wasn't what I was going to ask. I've been thinking about something recently. I was curious to know what you've been doing all these years."

"At work? Can we talk about this some other time? I'll call you, I promise. We could have a sandwich in the park."

He shook his head. "My wife died — well, you know that of course, I told you already. No, what I mean is, after being together, being part of a couple, what you've done all these years when you've been *alone*."

The evening seemed to darken around her. "I can't be the first single person you've ever talked to. Lord, Milt, I don't know what I've been doing. I'm not sure I even know what you're asking." But she did know she could never describe all the shapes and hues of loneliness; being alone mostly meant you didn't have to describe anything. She felt trapped and unpredictable now. "Ask someone else. I really have to go."

"I've tried," he insisted, "but you know how it is. It's a little like hearing about someone who's sick. You say, I hope everyone's holding up, and let me know if I can do anything, bring over a roast chicken or rake your leaves. But if you're not actually the sick one, you really can't know what it's like, can you? Then when it *is* yours — and death is really like a disease because it gets better and worse, and anything, a smell, the weather, can set it off — it's too late. You haven't learned a thing from seeing others go through it. So I don't know about other people being alone, or what I'm supposed to do now. I'm asking you. You seem good at it."

Divorce had felt a little like dying, she had to admit. The way Gordon had taken his last pair of shoes from the closet, his desk lamp and set of knives, and then Dale on every Tuesday and Thursday and every other weekend and holidays, was a worsening disease of sorts. It never got better. But a heart attack in a swimming pool? The love of your life face down and wide-eyed at the blue tiles? Your twenty-four-year-old son dying in front of you? Milt was right — what had she ever learned from anyone else's pain?

"I know you won't always feel so sharply terrible," she said gently. "You'll find things that make you happy, you'll do things that really surprise you. You have to change some along the way, too, which isn't always the worst thing either."

Dale, who had been watching them from a distance, now came and stood at the fence next to Maggie.

"Everyone has kids, a lover, a spouse," Milt said, and directed himself to Dale as he grasped the pointed top of one of the posts. "Really, nothing else is truly acceptable, nothing else allows you to be *in* life, just on the edges of it. It's the way we work, it's human history, and don't believe the people who say they chose to be alone, because there's something else going on there they don't want to admit. So how do you live alone when you have nothing to love? That's my question — maybe not earth-shattering — about the human race, hatched over many plates of moo shoo shrimp."

"I know the feeling," Dale told him, and Maggie saw some understanding pass between them. "Like you're playing a game but you don't know the rules exactly, you don't have all the right equipment, and you're just a little too embarrassed to ask one more time."

"That's exactly it," Milt said.

It was the misaligned in the man that was so compelling, Maggie realized; it tried to drag her in with the sole challenge of righting things for him. But was this, she asked herself bitterly, and inevitably thought of Ben and what they'd just done, and what they were becoming, the nature of attraction in middle age? It was pathetic and sad and she didn't want anything to do with it.

"It would also help if you'd stop feeling so fucking sorry for yourself," she said, startled at the slash of her words and at who she'd become in one afternoon.

Milt's face fell. "Thanks for the advice," he said stiffly, and turned to walk back toward his house, dragging the dog behind him. He slipped into his white colonial and shut the door, blank against what little light was left.

"How could you say that to him?" Dale said, trailing Maggie out to the street. "That was incredibly cruel of you. Doris says he hasn't even cleaned out his wife's clothes yet. There's still a pair of her earrings by the bathroom sink, and you tell him he should stop feeling sorry for himself?"

"And you, talking like you'd been alone and unloved your whole life. You'd think Nate didn't even exist. What was that shit about?" Maggie looked up and down the street for her car. "Look, I know it was cruel. I'm not pleased about it. But I couldn't help myself."

"You could help it. You just didn't want to."

"He thinks everyone else has it so easy."

"Compared to him, maybe they do. I was trying to make him feel better, but you couldn't just give him a chance, could you? Yes, I know Milt's a downer at the moment, and I know he's not the sexiest man on earth, but he's a good guy — and he'd be good for you. He actually thinks about things instead of just spouting idiotic opinions.

"The fact is," Dale continued, "you can't stand anyone who's actually nice to you, instead of those shitheads you always pick, the ones who are unavailable or you don't even like very much. Milt is someone who would be right for a change. He's not wrong about needing someone to be with in life, you know."

"No, he isn't. But I have you. I'm not alone." As Maggie said the words, the untruth of them hit her hard. She had never felt further from Dale in her life.

Dale shook her head. "I've been thinking a lot about later on, how in a few months, I'm going to have this baby, and *I'll* be with *her*. And I just wonder, Mom, who will you be with?"

Her daughter had spoken with a peculiar insistence, and her words were draped with the warning of a last chance. The day had turned late, and Maggie watched a heavier dimness begin to roll into the neighborhood, heard it quiet the birds, blunt the sounds of kids playing in the driveway across the street and of the party behind her.

7

BLIND and eighty-eight, Forrest Corey had eyes like opals in a dish of milk. They reminded Maggie of a ring Gordon had given her for a birthday, and the way the stones pulsed under running water. Forrest's eyes teared all the time, from smoke and ragweed, perfume and wool, and now from frustration in the lab's interview room as he tried to describe the sound of his ninety-year-old nursing home roommate slipping on the slick linoleum floor when he came out of the bathroom.

"Like a wet rip," he told Maggie. "No, more like a melon split open with a machete. You know how the seeds pour out in a rush?"

Once, after she had just enrolled Forrest in the congenital cataract study fifteen years earlier, Maggie had watched his eyes, dense as white china in a diner even then, grow wet. It had been on that first day, in his slightly lisping New Hampshire accent, that he'd told her how his mother had rubella when she'd been pregnant with him. Maggie took notes dutifully, and asked the right questions, but she was unsettled by the way Forrest stared at her when he talked, when most others seemed to look just to the right or left of her. At five years old, Forrest had explained, he'd believed everyone saw visions like he did — glowing insects skimming the lake, fire around the sun and the truck's headlights, his sister with wings instead of braids — until his mother told him it wasn't true, that most people only saw dull, dirty life. She said it was the blessed who saw what he did. His mother never gave him the truth, he told Maggie another morning, even when he'd gone more or less blind by the time he was ten and he didn't feel the least bit blessed. His hands and knees were scarred from falling.

For forty-five years he'd taught music at the Perkins School for the Blind, and his only disappointment was that he had never discovered a prodigy among the fumblers and bangers. Now, in the afternoon light, Maggie saw him move his fingers, the backs of which were tufted with silver hair, over the imaginary piano that was the table's edge, and heard the dull taps and wooden trills fill the small room.

"Like a bungled piece," he said of the man's fall, "like a monkey's fist on the keys, if you know how that sounds." He paused and wet his dry lips. "What's wrong with you?"

"Nothing's wrong," Maggie said. "I'm fine, but your friend, is he okay?"

Forrest shrugged noncommittally and continued to play his imagined music. Maggie sat back in her chair.

There were simply days, and this was one of them, when everything threatened to push her body off balance. She was ruled by the appetites of her body, both for Ben and for food, and then was left sick afterward. Hours earlier she'd hurried to Ben's office, where they met most mornings before anyone else came in. She'd pressed up against him, eager, laughing at herself and her ridiculous size, and the giddy danger of their being together again. But the single tap of their teeth in a kiss reminded her of the fact of real, messy life unacknowledged but persistent on the other side of the door. She'd pushed away from Ben and retreated to her office, where she'd done nothing but stare out the window at the turning trees. An hour later, a whiff of Shelby's cold coffee in a cardboard cup forced her to stick her head out the window for a blast of cool fall air and the dusty scent of drying leaves.

"Not nothing. Something's different with you," Forrest said. "I think you're leaving this place. I can feel it."

Maggie laughed, and touched his powdery hand. His breath smelled of canned corn and soft rolls. "Forget it, Forrest. You know I don't believe in that feeling thing of yours. This isn't the movies."

But after years of this work, Maggie *did* believe in the special powers of the blind, though she didn't like to admit it, and she looked to find evidence of magic in strange physiology. It was true that the blind compensated miraculously at times; it was easy to be fooled by them. Could Forrest sense a different heat coming from her now? Could he feel the air change when she put her hands on her belly to calm the flipping baby, and wasn't this kind of sight worth a lifetime of study, too? A study without statistics, she told herself excitedly, or measurements, or cause and effect, but one simply made up of stories. This was what interested her now.

"Okay, then you're pregnant," he said.

Maggie laughed. "Not bad. Thirty-four weeks, actually."

"Don't you think you're a little old for that?"

"Look who's talking. Who told you?"

Forrest's white eyes lowered demurely, his hands crossed on the table in front of him. "Your assistant."

Maggie smiled. "Nice try, but I don't have an assistant."

"She said she was your assistant. The girl who brought me in, whatever you want to call her. The blond, pretty one. Nice figure."

"That's Shelby. She's working with us for a while. And she told you what she looks like. How kind of her."

"Nope," Forrest said proudly. "That much I knew all by myself."

As though their conversation had conjured her all of a sudden, Shelby appeared in the door's small window. A telephone call, she mimed to Maggie. Important, and she had to go now. When she stood, too fast, Maggie spilled a cup of water and watched it move toward Forrest. Was it the tiniest humidity released in air or the smallest sound that made him pull his hand away, and then his chair, so that the water missed him and poured to the floor?

"Go," Shelby urged her.

"I know you're here, Shelby," Maggie heard Forrest trill, as she hurried down the hall.

BY Nate's own description, spoken through broken lips, it had happened somewhere just past the gentle curve of North Harvard Street, past the stadium but before the storefront bicycle shop, on a side street, sometime just after three-thirty, when a fall afternoon in the city turns violet. Nate had been pulled from his moped, beaten, and robbed of everything, including his knapsack, which contained his students' journals and his own books. He had been dumped where the curb meets the street. Linden flowers that had fallen a season earlier tangled in his hair, pressed into his skin, hid in the corners of his mouth. In the emergency room at Mass General, they found a cigarette butt that had lodged in the fold of his arm when he'd reached up to shield his eyes.

Even after he'd been swabbed, stitched, and sedated, Nate continued to swipe at the flowers, which were no longer there. His eyelids were the bruised purple of an eggplant, and fluttered as he passed his hand back and forth across his face. Maggie left the curtained space, dizzy from the sight of him and the smells of dried blood and bleached floors. *Three-thirty in the afternoon? Where was everyone while this was happening?* That the story didn't entirely make sense nagged at her, but the police were talking to Nate now, and had boxed her out with their broad backs.

She had tried to reach Dale, who was in San Francisco for the wedding of a college friend. At the number she'd given Maggie there wasn't even a machine to leave a message on, and Maggie pictured a house flattened by an earthquake so recent it hadn't yet made the news that played on a television in the visitor's lounge. She knew this was dangerous thinking, but rubble seemed all around her.

"I knew something was happening when it was happening," Nate had told Maggie when she'd first arrived, minutes before he'd slumped again into a drugged nap. "But I don't know what that something was. I was thinking about my eighth birthday party. That was my best year, eight. We went bowling at the Hanover Bowladrome, had hot dogs and Hoodsie cups."

Didn't people talk like this when they were about to die? Maggie had been there when her father's heart had stopped and then been restarted long enough for him to imagine he was ten years old and in a camp rowboat on a lake in Maine. His eyes were wide open as he talked about the fish he was catching, and he described the sound of the oars grinding in the rusty oarlocks. He hadn't seen Maggie or her mother standing right there beside him. It was fitting for him, an essentially unhappy man, that in such a state he was thinking about who he'd once been and not who he'd become.

"Eight? That was years ago. Why is he looking so far back?" Maggie asked a nurse, grabbing her arm as she passed by.

The woman looked at Nate before answering. "After trauma, memory of what happened is usually repressed, at least for a while. His mind has to fill with something now, might as well be birthday parties." She touched a tiny teddy-bear pin on her lapel. "When are you due?"

"What?"

"Your baby. When?"

A doctor appeared. "You his wife?" Maggie shook her head. "Anyway, tests are back. No real damage. We'll watch him for a couple of hours and then you can take him home."

"Me?" Maggie asked.

"You're here, aren't you?"

Maggie wondered how she would be able to take care of this boy when she could barely get out of a chair by herself these days. She left the visitor's area and tried Dale again from the phone by the elevator, but still got no answer. Her daughter was probably sipping iced coffee in some outdoor café with her face to the sun, her hair pulled back, a tight smile affixed to her face. Even in the heat, she'd be wearing something bulky to hide the weight she'd gained. And if she thought of her mother, her baby, her husband, they would only be where they were meant to be. At least that was how Dale would paint her life to the circle of reconvened, shining friends, instead of giving them the real picture — of disarray, of growing strangeness, of days missed at work without explanation. These women, tipsy with possibility and youth, would never doubt her, never suspect that behind Dale's last-minute decision to go to California was the need to escape.

She next tried Ben, but he was out of his office. She thought of calling Doris, but remembered her late class. Maggie reached Gordon instead. The hospital corridor was intermittently quiet while she waited for him to arrive, fed like a river now and then by streams of sound that came from patients' rooms. By the windows that looked toward the Science Museum and its alienesque roof apparatus glowing in the dark, a man and a woman in tennis outfits talked intently — they too had been plucked from the middle of something by disaster. Pink pompoms on the back of the woman's socks bobbed up and down as she talked excitedly. Maggie twisted the beads of her necklace around her finger and walked back to the bench where she'd been sitting minutes earlier. From a distance she saw how the vinyl had been molded by her weight.

Twenty-five minutes later, Gordon turned the corner at the far end of the corridor. He had a slightly lopsided walk, with one leg jerky from a sports injury, but it was still a confident, affluent-looking stride. The way the hands were slipped into comfortable pockets, the gold watchband glinting, the head held high with a sure sense of belonging, the whole body as announcement, was instantly familiar. Maggie waved at him. The beads still wrapped around her finger suddenly snapped like a small explosion and began to bounce musically down the hall toward her ex-husband. They were everywhere, skittering away from her, tiny golden eyes one shade darker than the beige floor. She picked up what she could, but already it seemed pointless; there were hundreds more she'd never find.

"Hey, Maggie," Gordon said, watching her with a look of amusement on his ruddy face. As he bent down to help her, his knees popped loudly. "Thanks for calling me. Not the best circumstances, wouldn't you say? How's he doing?"

Maggie reached under the bench and came up with a fleck of tissue and several strands of hair, which she stared at for a second before waving them off her hand. "He looks awful, and he's pretty drugged up and out of it, but everything's okay."

"It's incredible. I don't know about this city anymore. Dale goes away, and the first day, this happens. . . . I don't know what to say, what to make of it." Gordon shook his head — of mostly gray, Maggie noted.

"I don't know that anything needs to be made of it. The man was mugged."

"And Nate, of all people. He's like a kid, isn't he?" Gordon said affectionately. "Never thinks anything bad is going to happen to him. A few people actually manage to make it through life that way, but the rest of them get taught a hard lesson. They get their asses kicked."

Gordon had not asked for any more details than what she'd given him briefly over the phone; his nature was not suspicious, unlike hers. Facts were generally enough for him to go on. He looked down at several beads rolling in the dip of his palm and then slipped them into his shirt pocket.

"Did I give you this necklace? It's kind of pretty."

"I don't remember," she said, though she knew he had. There had been times of tenderness, too.

Gordon stood, his knees protesting again. His sneakers were a brilliant white, like capped teeth, obviously expensive, but never played in. He had done well; that was always perfectly clear. Dale reported that he and May were very happy together. Their new house was bursting with compatibility and expensive furniture. Maggie pictured Gordon's wife: billowing hair, billowing breasts, a thick swab of lipstick across her generous, open mouth. Twice a week she put on comfortable shoes and a khaki flak jacket over her designer clothes and became a docent at the Franklin Park Zoo. She collected glass animals, Dale said.

"Wow." Gordon exhaled when Maggie got up. She recognized the slow, almost seductive sweep of his eyes, the double swing of his tongue over his front teeth. The way he could make her feel ashamed so easily, still. "My God, look at you. You're really enormous."

Maggie squinted with familiar irritation. "What did you expect, that I wasn't actually going to look pregnant?"

"Well, it is sort of shocking, Maggie, you have to admit, but for chrissake, don't get your back up. I wasn't trying to make you feel self-conscious."

"But you do," she said, and sat down on the bench. "You always have."

Gordon sat next to her and brushed the dust off his pants. "If that's true, then I'm sorry. Nate's asleep, right? I'll go see him in a few minutes. You look good, Maggie. That's what I really meant to say. You've always looked good pregnant. Some women don't — it looks all wrong on them, fat and uncomfortable — but not you. You look like you were made for it."

"Do you remember when I was pregnant with Dale?"

"What a question. Of course I do." He jiggled the keys in his pocket.

There had been times when she'd been so turned on that she'd been content to hike up her skirt, pull down his pants, even settle for just being touched by her husband. In bed she arched herself toward him. But instead of laughing and enjoying what was happening, Gordon was disturbed by it and openly wondered what was wrong with Maggie. In turn, she'd wondered how she could have married such a tight-assed prig, and she'd shut her legs and closed her robe. With his arms folded across his chest, he had shamed her, and shamed her for being pregnant. After all, it was not what they had planned — and understood to be, at heart, her fault.

"I wanted to fuck all the time," she said.

"*Fuck*, Maggie? Jesus," Gordon said, embarrassed. "Well, did we?"

They could always fight about anything, just as long as they were on opposite sides. But Gordon's face looked softer to her just now, and Maggie saw that he might be willing to remember the past differently, less harshly, and that she might be willing also. It might feel a little like relief.

"Sure. Endlessly. We fucked day and night."

"That's nice." After a minute, Gordon cleared his throat and sat up straight, as though suddenly remembering who they both were. "At the firm, you're something of a novelty, you know."

"Novelty? Like a Kewpie doll or a pair of Mickey Mouse ears?"

"In a way." Gordon checked his watch and peered down the hall, as if they were waiting for nothing more than their bus to arrive. Maggie recalled how cruelly provocative he could be at times, twisting her up in a fury which he then pretended to be puzzled by.

"You really can be quite an asshole, Gordon. I'd forgotten that for a couple of minutes."

"Oh, come on, Maggie. Don't be so sensitive," he said, and patted her knee. "I'm simply talking about the surrogacy thing. Legally, its implications are complex and virtually untested. Most states have no precedent for surrogacy cases, so it makes a really interesting, not to say problematic, hypothetical case. That's all I'm saying."

"There's nothing hypothetical about *this*." Maggie lifted her shirt to reveal the curve of the bottom of her breasts, and her white belly, which rested partially on her thighs. In the merciless hospital lights, her stretch marks flowed like tiny iridescent streams. "Touch it if you don't believe me."

"Thank you. I get the point. You can put your shirt down now."

"I just want you to see. I am it, a real live woman. Inside here is your grandchild. You will be a grandfather, Dale will be a mother. I'll write it down for you if it would help. I'll draw a diagram, too. Do you have a pen?"

"Really, I get it." He sighed, and then made a clicking, determined noise with his mouth. "Dale, a mother. I have to admit I'm
still getting used to that idea. I never imagined her . . ."

It had taken Maggie years of marriage to understand how literal
Gordon was. He could follow the most complicated directions for
assembling a bicycle but he couldn't imagine whether tomato and
basil would taste good together. He could wade through complex
legal matters, but couldn't imagine how nice it would feel to
skinny-dip at night, in spite of the sign forbidding it.

"Well, she certainly wants it very much," he added.

"Does she? I'm not so sure anymore." Maggie wanted to tell
Gordon how difficult it had become to talk to Dale, how she
seemed so withdrawn, but neither of them had ever allowed the
other an inch of uncertainty when it came to their daughter.

"Are you serious?" He looked at her, but his head was drawn
back. "Of course she does. I think she sees this baby as her
redemption."

"Redemption from what?"

"From failure. That's how she sees herself, you know, on some
level. She's told me this over and over. On the other hand, she
thinks *you* can do anything and everything."

"No, she doesn't. That's ridiculous. You should hear how critical
she is of me. I don't know why she'd tell you that."

"How about you having this baby for her? Did that *ever* occur to
you? It's evidence enough, I think. For Dale it certainly is."

But wasn't it also an excruciating reminder for Dale? How could
her daughter ever be with her and not want to run away at the
same time?

"Look how attached she is to you," Gordon added. His tone of
voice could not hide a touch of envy. He looked down and flexed
his feet in their shining sneakers. "She wishes she were just like
you, Maggie. I happen to think she's pretty great as herself. I tell
her that over and over, but it's hard to get the message through.
You know how she can be completely impenetrable at times."

The hospital roused for a minute, a distant bell went on and off,
telephones rang, a beeper sounded. Gordon checked his watch

again, snapped its band. "Change of shift," he announced. "May's probably wondering why I haven't called her yet."

"Maybe you should check on Nate first, so you'll actually have something to tell her."

"I suppose I should. You say he's okay? I'm not good at this sort of thing. The mother of one of my partners was killed in a car accident last week. And what did I do? I shook his hand and looked appropriately glum. I don't ever seem to know what to say."

It was amazing how men like Gordon, Maggie thought, were able to make their weaknesses sound like strengths. They thought admission brought them absolution, and most of the time it did.

"You're in luck then, because you don't have to say anything to him. He's asleep. He won't even know you were here," she said. Her ex-husband had always been a bit of a coward. Gordon nodded, took a deep breath, and walked down the hall to Nate's room.

Maggie waited, shivering against the cold air that had suddenly begun to billow from the vent above her. After the divorce she and Gordon had made decisions about Dale independent of each other, and hoped everything would fit nicely together. Neither of them had really believed this was the way it should be done — and Dale had never revealed, or admitted, how hard it was for her — but they were both clogged with self-righteousness. Their divorced friends handled themselves so much better, it seemed. They established rules, they sent letters to each other if they had to, paid negotiators by the hour. But Maggie was too angry to talk without also wanting to smash Gordon's face in. She had not been the one to start screwing someone else, after all.

When they were first married and Gordon was in law school, Maggie would stay up well past midnight waiting for him to come home from the library. They would make wordless love, and she allowed that he'd probably talked enough for one night already. Still, at times, she wondered what they would ever say to each other.

One evening, after an early exam, they had gone to dinner at the cheapest Mexican restaurant in the city and were home in time to have sex while it was still light out, while the tastes of cilantro and chiles were still in their mouths. The surprise of being able to see each other was a little intimidating, erotic; they were like strangers who'd picked each other up over drinks. In the back of Maggie's mind was the thought that she really should get up to put in her diaphragm, but the idea was like a telephone ringing too far away to answer in time, and Gordon's face pressed into her neck was too heavy.

Years later, on the day Maggie had taken Dale to the gynecologist, Gordon had sat on the edge of the bed taking off his black shoes, his limp socks. He had the serious pallor of someone who spent too much time under harsh light. Maggie had thought then that he'd really gotten everything he wanted in life, while what she'd wanted had faded away until she could hardly even define it anymore. It seemed impossible to her that they'd been married for sixteen years. That night, he'd hissed the tie out from his tight collar as she stood before him, her hands pressed into a pyramid of prayer, just as she'd seen the doctor do that afternoon. Dale didn't have a uterus, she explained. She used a lot of clinical terms, hoping to bully Gordon with them, and she watched his mouth go slack, his lips pale. He picked up his heavy shoe and weighed it in his hand.

She put her face up to his. "Do you even know what a uterus is, Gordon?" Down the hall, music pounded from behind Dale's door. "Go ahead, throw your shoe at me."

"Don't be an idiot." He let it drop to the floor and looked at her. Even then she couldn't divine what was true in his expression, if it was anger or pain. "Why would I want to do that?" he asked. "Is it your fault?"

As Gordon left the room to go see Dale, he bumped Maggie's shoulder and rocked her on her feet. Later he stood over her while she pretended to be asleep. He wants to kill me now, she thought, but Gordon crawled into bed, pressed himself against her and wept, while she lay frozen, unable to turn toward him. She was amazed that they'd stayed together for as long as they had, given how different they were and how much they didn't feel for each other anymore. But there had always been a certain comfort and a dulling of disappointment, she understood, in never having to ask for, or deliver, very much in her marriage. Now as Gordon returned from Nate's room, she thought how old and foolish he seemed, and if she'd ever really allowed him to have any grief over Dale. Why, she asked herself, had she always felt he wasn't entitled to it?

"Nate's asleep," he said. "He didn't see me. I should go. Are you sure you can handle this by yourself? I'll stay if you want."

"I'm fine by myself. I'll tell Nate you were here."

BY ten that night, Maggie had installed Nate in his bed at home. The remote control resting on his chest was like a cartouche. He had ESPN on without the sound, an amber bottle of Percodan, which glowed in the bedside light, ice water with a straw, his attentive nurse in Maggie. From the hospital, she had finally reached Dale and told her what happened. Her daughter was silent at first, and then wanted to speak to Nate, but he was asleep. Maggie didn't mention the drop of blood in the corner of his mouth, or the way he was curled around a pillow, his eyes sliding under bruised lids. Dale was booked on the morning flight back to Boston.

Nate flowed in and out of sleep, mumbling and unfocused. For a while Maggie talked about mindless things just to make noise, and from time to time he repeated a single word of hers, but by then it was without any meaning. When his eyes opened, it was only to gaze at the television, but the images — of flipping snowboarders, rolling bowling balls, flying men with basketballs — were meaningless too, but mesmerizing. Maggie dozed in the chair by the bed, and dreamed she'd watched an entire day pass over Nate in brightness and shadows. Once, when she woke, she couldn't detect any movement under Nate's eyelids, only movement *on* them, reflections from the television, a soaring golf ball. For a moment she imagined he might be dead, his body melting from within, his brain fissured and leaking like a split jug. She leaned over to touch him, and his mouth moved but made no sound.

"What did you want to say?" she asked, and stroked his face. His skin was amazingly soft.

Months ago, Dale's egg and Nate's sperm had embraced in a laboratory dish (which was how Maggie liked to think of it, non-technologically, romantically, when the doctor's language was full of terms like venture, campaign, and success rate). Her feet had been in stirrups, and Dale had held her hand. The doctor sighed a little too wearily for Maggie's comfort and reminded them again of the high likelihood of failure. She looked up at the huge light above until her eyes seared. Later, no one could believe conception had happened so quickly, but Maggie had been sure the first time she felt her head spin after climbing the stairs. Now, with her fingertips lingering on Nate's cheek, Maggie asked herself who he was to her, this man, but not her man, not her son or her husband, but Dale's husband, and the father of the child she was carrying. What, if anything, did she really know about him?

"What did you want to say?" she urged again, but he'd fallen back to sleep.

Maggie circled the room, trying to uncoil the fatigue that seemed to be wrapping itself around her. As she did, she stopped to examine things — the clothes inside Dale's closet that hung together like a black cloud, a glossy picture-book version of the Kamasutra she found on the table by the bed — trying to piece together some understanding of her daughter's life. But the room, like all the others in the apartment, was mostly in shades of unrevealing white. Nate, purplish, swollen, streaked as a sunset, was the only bruise of color.

"You know, Nate," she said, though she knew he was asleep, "I don't think you and I have ever spent this much time alone together. Can I ask, is this baby confusing for you, too? Or is it just me and Dale? Do you think it was the right thing to do?"

She picked up a tiny framed picture of Nate's mother, barely making out the woman's face cast in shadows under an elm tree. "Perfect. All mothers should be so small," she said, and put it back. "Especially in the bedroom."

She opened the top drawer of the bureau and sifted her hands through the silky contents of Dale's underwear. "I wish you could tell me what I'm looking for, Nate, so I wouldn't have to do this," she said. "Isn't this crazy? I'm just trying to understand things a little better." When she leaned over Nate he flinched as though he saw her insistence coming at him. It made her think of Forrest Corey, and how he'd simply known to draw back from the spill.

Sometime after midnight, Maggie lay down on the single bed in the room that would soon be turned into a nursery. The minute her body relaxed, the baby executed a series of kicks and punches, rousing her to worry about the swelling over Nate's eye as she had once worried about Dale, sick with croup, in her crib. She worried that it was a mistake to have let him have another pill when she did, worried about the house alarm going off two doors down. She thought of Doris standing at her bedroom window at that moment, maybe the bed behind her empty, and seeing Milt in his back yard with his dog. Maybe they would wave to each other. She thought of Ben, still at the lab. When they'd spoken earlier, he'd offered to come over, but she'd said no; she wouldn't know what to do with him in her daughter's house. Maggie knew he would probably end up sleeping in his office again, curled up on the vinyl sofa among the papers and spare parts, a scratchy camp blanket thrown over all but his feet. The odd hours of science would be his excuse to Doris, who no longer asked for details. He kept the radio on for company and the Exit sign in the hall was his night-light.

Hours later, Maggie heard Nate talking and something fall in soft thuds, like clods of snow from a tree. Nate was standing in front of the hall closet when she came out of her room, a pile of towels and sheets at his feet. His underwear hung damp on his hips and the sweet, stinging smell of urine rose off him. The very early morning light still had a siltiness to it that made Maggie rub her eyes.

"You all right?"

"Oh, Dale, it's you."

"No, it's Maggie. What are you doing?"

"Mags. Okay. I was just trying to find a sheet. I peed in the bed. Sorry."

Maggie led him back to the bedroom and sat him in a chair. She was aware of how he watched her with heavy eyes as she pulled off the damp sheets. She covered the wet mattress with a towel, and then put a clean pair of sheets on the bed. He apologized again.

"Don't worry about it," she said, and put the pillows back. "It's the pills. They make you feel neither here nor there."

"I dreamed I was peeing off the side of a boat." He giggled. "It was really great."

"I'm sure it was. You can get back in bed now."

"When's Dale coming back?"

"Today, this afternoon. In a few hours. Come on, get in."

"But my boxers," he said. "Wet too. I have to get rid of them."

It seemed to take forever with his languorous movements to grasp the waistband of his shorts, slide his knuckles against his skin and draw them down a single inch. Nate had forgotten the mechanics of undressing, and then the mechanics of inhibition as he reached in to pull his penis out through the fly. A sad, pink nub, Maggie thought, so unmajestic. He held on to himself, his face relaxed in private comfort.

"Good enough," Maggie said, and guided Nate back into bed. She leaned to pull the sheet over his chest.

"Dale," he moaned, and clasped her shoulders, pulling her down.

"No, it's me." Maggie struggled to right herself, but her weight had shifted so that she hovered over Nate, her arms on either side of him. Her legs muscles were as weak as water.

"I know it's you, Mags. Dale, I mean, she doesn't know what happened. I should tell her, don't you think? She's my wife. She should know."

"I already called her. She's on a plane now, coming home. I told you that. She'll be here later." His fingers dug painfully into her arms. "You can tell her then. Let go, Nate. Let me stand up. You're hurting me."

His hand fell heavily against his chest with an alarming thud. "I don't usually take that route home, it's not even the right direction. There's this girl at school, she's got some problems, she had an abortion last year that really fucked her up, and her parents are probably going to kick her out for good. She's spent the night here a few times. I try to help her."

Maggie felt the walls of the room begin to lurch toward her and she sat on the edge of the bed. "What were you going to do?"

Nate spoke with his eyes shut. "I was thinking she needed some company today, that's all, so I was going to see her, take her out for dinner maybe, see how she's doing. She's going through this terrible shit, and so we talk. About what's going on here, too, the baby, me and Dale. It hasn't been so easy. Dale just wants what she wants. She sucks all the air out of the room sometimes. Did you notice?" He hesitated, and one hand stirred under the sheets to hold himself again. Maggie saw the ridges of his knuckles outlined by the cloth. When he spoke again, his voice had taken on a dreamy tone. "Her name is Alison."

The way Nate said her name — as lush as a kiss, a tongue wandering over skin — made Maggie sick. A pounding began in her ears, pulsed in her lips and eyes. Alison, the student on the other side of the wall, the one who turned Nate on so high that he thrust himself into Dale until it hurt. Maggie was profoundly humiliated for her daughter.

"Don't say anything more." Maggie held up her hands and wouldn't look at him. She stood unsteadily. "I swear, I can't bear to hear it."

"But she's so beautiful. She has a spirit that makes you think of water."

"Spirit like water? What kind of bullshit is that? Is that how they talk at your school? You were going to sleep with her, weren't you. No, you already did. You fucked your student, your water spirit. A little girl. You're disgusting."

"She's not a little girl."

"My God. Don't even talk to me."

"She's seventeen."

"How could you do this to Dale? How could you do this *now?*"

"I'm trying to explain to you —"

"I'm her mother. Did you think I would understand, it would be okay, if you just explained it well enough?"

"Yes, you understand these things. I mean, look how you live. You do what you want, you love who you want. And you know what it's like, Maggie, how Dale can get you so confused that you can't figure out who you are and what you've done, how she gives and takes away, how she can be there and not be there at all? It can make you crazy."

"Don't make her responsible for what you've done." Maggie waved furiously in front of her face. "Does she know about this?" Nate shook his head. "Good. And do you know what? You deserved exactly what happened to you today. I wished they'd done more, in fact. I'm only staying with you now for Dale's sake, not for yours. But do it again and I'll kill you myself."

Nate called her name as she left the room and went into the bathroom. He was still talking, but it didn't matter to him that no one was listening now, he just wanted to tell someone, and she knew what that was like. She shut the door and tried to slow her breathing. Her body was painfully tense, but she was overcome with fatigue. For an instant she pictured herself asleep in her own bed, in a perfect room, a solid house, in another distant year.

Maggie had seen tension lodge itself between her daughter and Nate for months. She'd tried to ignore it. After all, things were not much clearer between Dale and herself. Maggie wondered how much her daughter suspected what Nate had done, how much she understood with her eyes averted. Was it why she'd been so evasive, so impenetrable, for months, afraid of what Maggie might say or do if she revealed the cracks in her life?

She recalled Gordon's words earlier, how this baby would become for Dale a kind of redemption for her loss, but which loss was it now, precisely? Where would a baby fit into a marriage that wasn't even there? Her daughter's life, she realized, was a well-balanced construction, but it was fragile, and any wind or tremor would collapse it. That it might always have been this way for Dale filled Maggie with heartache.

She turned on the shower and stepped in. She scrubbed herself with Dale's almond soap, shaved herself with Dale's razor, smoothed herself with Dale's lotion, and put on Dale's yellow nightgown which was hanging on the back of the door. In the fogged mirror, she couldn't see her face, and tried to imagine that she *was* Dale, holding the baby. She rocked the weightlessness of the steam and pressed it to her chest. When the room cleared and she saw the fullness of her body, the weight in her arms grew warm and surprisingly real, and hers to keep.

8

S HE should have seen it coming, Maggie scolded herself, but she was thirty-seven weeks pregnant, and her mind was full of other predictions and premonitions. Still, she had known it wasn't right to wake up with grit in her teeth and toxic talc sifting down from the widening crack in the ceiling. It was squirrels, forced into her attic by a serious October freeze a month earlier, who were responsible. Now their frantic jig across water-stained planks, their persistent digging into bags of old clothes and shards of toys, their knocking over books and boxes, was causing her house to shift and then to split apart. The accumulated force of the smallest movements amazed her.

At first Maggie hadn't known exactly what the scramble of noise above her was. Her cats were suddenly vicious and alert when it got dark, prowling over her chest and even her face. Furtive times with Ben were never so safe when she had to blow dust from his eyelashes and his hair before she sent him home to his wife. Later she would sweep bits of plaster along with the private flakes and bits left from sleep and sex off her sheets. When she'd shown Dale the ceiling one day, her daughter had said this was not one of those isolated problems that was going to get better if left alone; there were probably hundreds of catastrophes waiting to explode like a string of firecrackers, and maybe it was time for Maggie to think about moving. Maggie had waved away the suggestion.

Finally, one morning, Maggie pulled the attic hatch down by its greasy rope and climbed the ladder. With her eyes at floor level, the beam of her flashlight caught the pupils of a squirrel frozen on hind legs. It held an old stocking in its paws, and strands of nylon thread were wound in its fur. The animal looked like a tiny woman dressed up in cheap clothes. It's my mother, Maggie thought, always drawn to chiffon head scarves and bulbous plastic earrings. That the squirrels had found some way into the attic she didn't know about and couldn't see filled Maggie with a sense of almost total defeat about her house. She backed down the ladder, closed the hatch, and waited for the ceiling to fall.

Which it did on this Sunday, as Maggie was getting dressed for the baby shower at Gordon's that morning. She was already late, slowed by vague unease about the day and the sight of herself in the mirror. The bridge of her nose had widened, and her eyelids were purpled by tiny, burst capillaries. Her skin, prone to fleeting rashes for weeks — which she had attributed more to her state of mind than to her hormones — was unusually placid that morning. Faded, waterlogged, she thought, I'm hardly myself anymore; the baby has swallowed me. She ran some lipstick across her mouth and practiced a gracious grimace for her ex-husband, her lover, her lover's wife, her daughter, her friends, and for her mother, whom Gordon had flown in from Florida.

And at that moment, with her teeth bared, the cracks widened with a tiny moan and the plaster finally let go of the slats. It happened not with a single, rumbling splat as she'd imagined, but with a gentle, musical drumming of ceiling pieces onto her warm blankets. Just like disaster to sound so harmless that it catches you in reverie. When it was over, chunks bloomed like scattered carnations across the bed and the floor, and there was a hole in her ceiling the size of a small body, as though a child had tumbled from above. Through the stripped wood she saw pinpoints of smeared light where holes in the attic roof pressed against the sky. Clearly, the roof needed repair too. Momentarily, she thought it wouldn't be such a terrible thing to have those daytime stars always hanging above her. But she felt tendrils of cold air blow across her face and knew that the decay in her house, which had always seemed so tempered and thoughtful, was finally getting ahead of her. She finished getting ready for the party and shut her bedroom door with something like a final good-bye, dust still suspended in the air like a confession.

MAGGIE drove to Gordon's on blacktop so smooth she could hardly tell she was moving at all. The houses were set back from the road and far apart from each other; the sense was of unlimited space. She'd seen photographs in the Sunday paper's real estate section of these "executive estates" — this one was called High Ridge — and had been amazed at how clearly the bigger-is-obviously-better message came through even in grainy photographs the size of postage stamps. Of course, Dale had described her father's new house for her many times, but she'd only half listened, the details of his sparkling life best left unimagined. Now Maggie saw how each house also managed to look imposing on its low-rising, broad-chested plot. Sharply pitched rooflines skewered their precise allotment of clouds. Such order and ownership would please Gordon every time he pulled into his driveway in his fancy, purring car, one that would give him permission to regret nothing in life.

But elsewhere in High Ridge, Maggie noted, there were no angles. There were no citified street corners of stone, no worn edges of granite curb, no power lines crossing poles and gridding the sky with spikes of blackbirds, nothing planted in hard rows to mark property boundaries. Shrubs grew in clipped circles and perfect spheres and cones, ornamental trees were forced to bend over small outcroppings of scrubbed rock. Even the street signs were rounded, as if to insist that life in this most unnatural neighborhood flow naturally.

Maggie allowed herself to get casually lost. She could always say she'd tried to find the house and failed, that the silence was too disorienting. Then Maggie saw a sign of life so startling in its incongruity, it could only be one thing: Virginia, her tiny, tanned mother, in bright turquoise stretch pants, matching sweater, and blue high heels, shivering in the white November chill and smoking a cigarette on Gordon's sloping front lawn. She waved at Maggie and bent to grind her cigarette out in the grass, which was chemically plump and much too green for that time of year.

THOUGH Maggie tried to avoid it, Virginia maneuvered to kiss her on the lips. Still, the smell of menthols and oranges on her breath was reassuringly familiar. As Virginia pulled back to look at her daughter and remark on everything, including her size, her skin, and the fact that she was late, Maggie noticed her mother's eyes watering. For a moment she thought her mother was moved by the sight of her, beset by memory and affection, and that she'd become softer and less certain that all this "baby-making" was just asking for trouble. But the weepiness was only the result of recent cataract surgery — mentioned to Maggie after the fact — done in a Florida clinic in a strip mall. Virginia popped a threatening tear on her cheek with her nail, polished the same color as her clothes.

"Gordon's done okay for himself," she announced, and ticked her head back to indicate the house. "This thing must have cost a pretty big load. Personally, I wouldn't want to live here. Too new, too big. Real estate's version of a lobotomy. What's all this?" She touched Maggie's hair, and then rubbed her fingers together as though she'd found dirt on a windowsill. "Ashes?"

"Plaster dust."

Virginia shrugged, incurious. "I want you to know that all those people are inside waiting for you."

"I'm only twenty minutes late. That's hardly historic. I got lost."

"You have to be *looking* first to get lost, hon. Otherwise, it's just called avoiding. I saw you drive around the block twice."

Virginia clasped Maggie's forearm and turned to walk back toward the house. Her mother seemed to get younger every year — it was Florida, it was her big boyfriend Ricky, her face-lift, her midnight swims — but here was an awkward, sinking stride; the crumble of osteoporosis, the wobble of creaky hips, inevitable disintegration. Maggie had imagined her mother dead before, but dying was something different.

"Goddamn high heels," Virginia muttered, then brightened. "Look, I'm making holes in Gordon's grass! Don't tell him it was me."

Inside the seamless foyer, Maggie stopped as her mother strode on, and had a sudden sense that what was gathered and waiting for her in the next room was not simply a party, but something more pressing. Her body ached in an unfamiliar and discouraging way. In the living room, she saw Dale leaning against Gordon, her head bent against his shoulder, her eyes half shut. In her father's house, with his arm around her, Dale was a child allowed everything.

Dale wore a brilliant blue shirt — no black today — the color of forced happiness, of cartoons and vacation weather. She levered herself off her father when she saw Maggie. Gordon glanced quickly at her, then away again, and continued his conversation.

"I knew you should have come with us, like I suggested," Dale said to Maggie in the foyer. "What happened to you?"

At first Maggie thought she might offer Dale the bedroom's collapse as excuse, but the sight of Doris moving through the room with Ben a few steps behind, stopped her. "I overslept. I'm sorry. Looks like things are okay here."

"You look tired. A little dusty, even."

Dale led Maggie through small circles of people to an over-sized white couch. They sat down, sinking toward each other. Gathered on a low table in front of them was a pile of presents, the ribbons waving as an overhead fan turned slowly. She imagined a string of rooms above her, unoccupied but always ready for guests, perfectly decorated and spotless.

"When it's time for presents, you do the opening, okay?" Dale whispered. "I'm never sure what to say or how much of a fuss to make. I feel like I'm faking it even when I'm not."

Maggie felt the weight of her daughter and the full moon of her own belly threaten to submerge her in the cushions. "Actually," she said, and attempted to rise a little, "I think you and Nate should open the presents together. They're for you guys anyway." She looked at her daughter. "He's the one who should be sitting here, not me."

"But we already decided on the way over. It was Nate's idea to do it like this. He wanted you to feel like it's your party too."

"How sweet." Maggie bit off the final sound of the word and held it like a piece of glass in her mouth.

Dale sighed. "I know. These things make me really tense too. It was May's idea and she's unstoppable."

Maggie looked at her son-in-law then, standing behind the chair in which Virginia sat observing everything through narrowed, blue-shadowed eyes. In the overheated room the scar across Nate's chin was bright red, a reminder of his confession to her. He nodded almost imperceptibly at Maggie, a collusion, she decided, and she stared back icily, as if to say, we *don't* understand each other, your secret is *not* ours. High to his left on the mantelpiece, an enormous vase of white lilies exploded around his head. Gordon, his face ruddy with a host's munificence, slapped Nate's back.

May swept around the room, her arms open to herd people together, her voice like a fat velvet rope. She had bent over to kiss Maggie a minute earlier, revealing the depth of her cleavage, the handfuls of her sloppy, enthusiastic flesh. Maggie had always liked May simply for the unlikely fact that she was, and wanted to be, married to Gordon. Her ex-husband's wife was like the sword swallower or the woman who could walk on hot coals: amazing, but you wouldn't ever want to be her.

Guided by May now, the guests formed a half-circle in front of mother and daughter. Reflections in the smudgeless windows settled too, as if uninvited uglier doubles — the liars, the selfish, the cheaters, the deniers — had collected outside to watch. Because she could not make herself look at Ben's face, she watched his back in the glass. Nate moved behind the couch and put his hands on Dale's shoulders, as though he were trying to keep her from floating away.

As Dale opened presents, and Maggie rested a finger on the bow, and then the box, she noticed how the women in the room, their faces rounded with hungry expectancy, had gradually leaned in so close to her belly that their desires and their doubts, like their breath, mingled together. This woman wanted to be pregnant again, that woman was for the first time. Some missed their grown-up babies, others regretted that they'd ever begged their kids to leave them alone. For a few, no past moment they tried to recall was in focus without their children in it. Everyone ached for the exquisite and painful business of motherhood, and Maggie was no different. But for the first time, the enormity of what she was soon to give away — this baby, her baby — of what she was about to lose, hit her in the chest. Dale cooed at something pink and matching. Maggie's breath tripped with panic.

And then Milt, whom she hadn't noticed before, was in front of her and offering a package in a ceremony of small steps and nods. She stared at him dumbly.

"*You* have to open this," he said, "because it's actually for *you*."

She unwrapped the box of perfume. Milt eagerly urged her to smell it and pushed the bottle under her nose. The scent made her eyes sting and her throat tighten, and she had the feeling that his dead wife had liked perfume, and that this gift was in all ways about her. Love was the only reference point for Milt, she understood, exactly what it should be. Had it ever been this way for her?

A terrible pain rose suddenly and propelled Maggie forward. The glass bottle, still open, slipped from her hand to the floor, trailing behind it a stream of oily perfume. A fragrant golden blot grew on the white rug, and Maggie heard Gordon rustling, swearing, toward her, his face like an irritated sore. She needed some air, she said, and struggled to rise off the seat. It was her last, most necessary bit of effort that day, and a thoughtful hand — Dale's, she hoped — helped her up.

Maggie pushed through a swinging door and stood alone in the gleaming kitchen, trying to catch her breath. She ran her fingers across the cool expanse of counter. An open cabinet revealed can after can of SlimFast, another the chrome of new, unused appliances. A bowed picture window looked out onto a vast back yard that merged into a neighbor's. In one corner, there were two old trees, standing long before a developer had even thought of High Ridge.

"Gordon's a clean-freak and a prick," Doris said, coming to stand next to Maggie at the window. "I never liked him."

"He would have liked to have the party without me. Gordon never imagined me in his house."

"Maybe. Don't worry about his stupid rug. He can afford another."

Doris looked thin, her face tight from anxious days, and Maggie recalled a recent dinner with Aaron that Ben had told her about; the boy had left the table in the middle of the meal to throw up. Later, he'd fallen asleep on their couch. There was a time when she and Doris had talked on the phone every day. They'd led parallel lives; they had their children, their work, for a while their marriages, in common, their problems always in alternating moments so that neither was ever without comfort or understanding. Maggie began to cry. I shouldn't be weeping in front of this woman anymore, she told herself; nothing is the same. She turned her back to Doris.

"This was all you needed. Look, I know you're down these days," Doris said, placing a hand on Maggie's back. "We haven't talked much. You always withdraw from me when you're depressed. I know that you're going to miss being pregnant and you're afraid of being left out of things. But you won't be."

Doris hugged her from behind, and Maggie stiffened. She knew Doris was the best kind of friend, but lost to her. She knew that she herself was the worst, betraying and disloyal and should never be forgiven. She turned to face Doris.

"You don't know how I feel, so don't be so fucking understanding all the time. Don't be so nice to me when I'm so horrible to you. It's weak. It isn't normal. Don't let people do this to you."

Doris paled. "What?"

"Have *some* self-respect."

"You can be such a bitch sometimes. God, I hope you have this baby soon." Doris left the kitchen.

Maggie knew she couldn't go back to the other room now, where everyone was sitting and laughing and wondering about her, where Dale was still opening presents, where Doris was shaking as she stood next to Ben. Maggie went out the back door into the yard and sat down on the bench beneath the trees. When she looked back at the house, May was watching her through the window. Maggie was grateful for her small, waved acknowledgment and also for how she turned away. Ben appeared in her place.

Then he was walking across the grass, his hands in his pockets. He sat next to Maggie and bent to pick a twig, which he began to twist in his hands.

"Shit, it's cold out here," he said. "You're missing the cake, you know."

"I don't like cake."

"But you're supposed to — it's your party." Ben tossed the twig onto the grass. "What did you say to Doris? She was pretty upset."

He was so close and so real to her that Maggie thought she could feel his heart beat and his blood run under his skin. "Don't you think it's strange I say anything at all to her?" she said, furious now, "except maybe 'Your husband's fucking me?' "

Ben didn't look up, and his tone was measured. "How about 'I'm fucking your husband.' It goes both ways, Maggie, or so I thought."

"Maybe, but here's the difference between us. In a few weeks you'll go back to Doris and the way things were," she told him, "but I won't be able to do that. Everything will have changed for me. I will have had a baby and given it away and I'll be completely alone."

"Things won't be the same, that's true enough, but nothing will change with us."

"Nothing will change with you and *Doris*, is what you mean. What I understood today, finally — and I don't know why it took me so long to figure out why us after all these years — is that *this* is what you like. This is what's new." Maggie ran her hands down her belly. "This is what turns *me* on. It turns *me* on, turns us all on. Everything swollen, big brown nipples, the ripe smells, the *idea* of it. It's made us all lose our minds a bit. It's poison in the drinking water."

"I could ask *you*, too, why now after all this time."

"Because for you, it's been a nice diversion from the shit that's going on in your life, Ben, and for me too, but it's not permanent."

He gazed absently at the house, as though some better answer lay inside. "Doris may not like me very much these days," he said, "but she's never left me unloved, and that's really something. But I'm too old already. I think I turned old the minute we got married, the minute she started putting me first. I never wanted that."

"Yes, you did, everyone wants that. People do what they can to make others feel loved; that's not terrible or wrong. Don't put this on her."

Maggie saw Virginia by the side of the house then, looking out at the street, smoke coiling around her head. Her mother reached around herself to adjust her underwear, a signal meant for her daughter, but what would Virginia ever understand about any of this? Her mother's life had always been a straight, efficient line; love never had very much to do with it.

"But why do things — why do *I* have to stay the same my entire life?" Ben asked. "There's you, stormy, caught up in everything, independent and strong-willed, and you do what you want and you always have. When we first met, I was scared of you because you were so determined and impenetrable, and then when you slept with that other man, I thought, well, this is a woman who can take love or leave it.

"I see you like this," he went on excitedly, and touched her stomach, "and I think it's twenty-five years ago. I'm going back in time, reversing my life, I'm going to do it all over again, differently. You're looking at me like I'm crazy, Maggie, but I'm not. Listen, it's amazing how easy this could all be. No bad outcomes here. I'm tired of thinking of things that end badly. My son's going to die, for chrissake. We can do it over again, be together now, have a child of our own. You've changed. You want something different now, too. I know it."

Maggie looked at Ben's face, which was taut with expectation. It was easy to see how wanting something badly enough could turn deception into comfortable delusion, but she resisted now. "You're not mine, Ben," she said simply, shaking her head, "and this baby isn't either."

Dale was walking toward them now, her arms across her chest, always this attempt to hold herself like a little girl, and to protect against what she didn't want to see or hear.

"It's not very sociable to be out here," she scolded, and wedged herself between them on the bench. "Keep me warm, please. Sorry Dad was such a jerk. You know, his *things*. What's going on out here anyway?"

"Ask your mother," Ben snapped. He stood up and walked back to the house.

"Charming guy. How can Doris stand it when he's like that?" Dale asked. She smelled of the spilled perfume and vaguely of Gordon.

"I'm not sure she can, actually."

"You two looked so serious out here. Were you talking about me?"

"Yes and no." Maggie glanced at the searingly bright day and suddenly saw her rubbled house floating there, her pocked roof and crumbled ceiling, and the inaccessibility of her bed. Where should I imagine myself now? she wondered.

"God, I wasn't serious," Dale said. "Now you have me worried. What were you saying?"

"Ben and I are together."

"What do you mean?"

"I mean we're sleeping together."

"Sleeping together," Dale repeated. "You're joking."

"No, I'm not. But I want you to understand —"

"Understand what? that you're sleeping with your best friend's husband? No, this is too cheap, too unoriginal for you. I don't believe it." Dale examined her mother's face and saw that it was true. The realization drained the color from her skin. She forced herself to speak. "Did I make you do this?"

"What are you talking about?" Maggie tried to touch her, but Dale stood up and took a step back.

"Did you think that because you did something good, you had the right to do something bad?"

"It's so much more complicated than that."

"No, actually, I don't think it is," Dale said.

She was unhurried and unforgiving as she walked across the lawn and went back into her father's house.

MAGGIE left Gordon's and drove to the lab, where there was always work, the one thing she still had. She steered her car over every possible pothole and bump to keep herself alert. It was almost three o'clock by then and impossible to find a parking space near the Bain Building. But if everyone else had found one, then she would too, and she circled the Fenway again.

Finally she parked next to a hydrant. Without the usual noise of students and lab workers, the Bain was menacing, her shadows too big and oddly shaped, her footsteps cloddish as they took the stairs. In the bathroom, she peed with such relief she felt her eyes flutter. But her body felt insistent and cranky. She looked at the words and pictures scratched into the white paint of the stall, scribbled by various hands and future talents in the world of science.

Maggie left the bathroom and sat down at her desk, stalled by sudden indirection. Her work seemed flat and lifeless, like something in a museum she'd looked at every day but now didn't quite see the importance of. She gazed around her office, at its familiar clutter, the nagging piles of papers and blooming folders, the posters and pictures she hadn't changed in years. It was in this place she'd tried to exist as no one's mother for a part of every day. Sometimes it had seemed like a matter of self-preservation. She wondered now at that strange need, because the fact was she had always felt the presence of Dale in one way or another. She could truly say that she'd never thought like a woman without a child, and she was better and fuller for it.

Her lower back clenched and she stood up to shake off the pain. She'd felt this before, if not quite so strongly. She would lie down for a few minutes on Ben's couch, she told herself, just until her light-headedness passed. Then she'd find something to eat. She stumbled down the hall to his office, and by the time she got to the door a vise was tightening in her thighs. She was aware of the effort it was taking to pretend she didn't know what was going on.

"Ben?" Why was she calling for him when she knew he was back at Gordon's eating cake? Maggie turned on the light, and saw a woman, mostly naked, spring up from the couch. A man, pink, hairy-assed, and turned away from her, lay on his side. "Oops." She laughed.

"You all right?" Shelby asked.

"Sorry, but actually, I'm not so great." Maggie let herself collapse, knees folding beneath her in a way she thought was neat and efficient, something she'd like to remember for later use. From the floor, she watched Shelby twist her pants around her waist, pull her shirt down over her breasts. The man on the couch wriggled into his jeans. Sweet and lovely, Maggie thought, until a crash of pain made her gasp.

"She's having the baby," Shelby told the man. "Maggie, you're having the baby."

"Really? How did that happen?" she asked.

"Great, a joke." Shelby bent to help her up. "Pretty funny."

In the back seat of her boyfriend's car, Shelby held Maggie's hand on the way to the hospital and told her about being made to watch her mother give birth at home.

"There's something about your mother's dooty you just don't want to see," she said. "But my parents are old hippies, and they thought it was a good, womanly experience for me. I was only nine, and all I wanted in life was a Barbie doll with hot pants and a Ken doll she could make out with. It just scared the holy shit out of me."

IN the hospital, the sensation was one of smoothness under the pain, so that on the gurney Maggie imagined for a minute she was still looking for Gordon's house on the flawless blacktop. But the straight lines and angles were endless here, and her eyes followed the overhead lighting around corners, through wide-swinging, wheezing doors. She appreciated the order, the neatly aligned tiles, everything white. White is the color of the redeemed, she'd once read.

They have laid me flat, she told herself, and shot me full of something cold. She had been undressed, and her arms were strapped down, crucifixion style. Maggie knew she'd been cut open, and felt the slow gaping of her body. Eyes sliding above masks peered at her. There were voices, but none she recognized. Something was taken out of her body, a great heaviness had been lifted, and she wondered if she were floating. Her teeth chattered and she was desperately thirsty, dreaming of a tall glass of ginger ale with ice and a striped red straw.

But Maggie didn't hear any crying, and nothing appeared to her in the steamy light above. A doctor — not her own — said something she didn't understand and then disappeared. They have left me, she thought, and heard the soft retreat of rubber shoes catching on linoleum. It was the sound of death being passed from one set of arms to another and out of the room. What do we do now that the baby's dead? Who will tell me what I've done?

Another tug somewhere below stirred her awake, and then she felt a snap as something was taken from her again. With a dull and heavy body that really didn't seem like her own anymore, she could distantly feel people working to close her up again. *Good as new*, they said serenely. *Bikini time*. They must think the smeary ceiling light is the sun, my consolation, Maggie thought, to talk to me like this. And then a baby was placed next to her face, though she could not free her hands to touch it. They said it was a girl. She did not understand why they would torture her with something so final, except to show her what she'd done wrong. And then she felt a tiny gust of breath on her cheek . . . and she was delighted and perfectly happy.

postpartum

9

A RIPPING woke Maggie up. Constrained by sheets tucked in so brutally they flattened her breasts, she was unable to ease the pain that sliced her in half. Her head turned left and right, but her eyes were slow to catch up in the room's violet, grainy light. Outside, she saw that it was dark enough to be night. Primal is the word that came to mind, the earth still going its usual course, despite her captivity in bed. She heard muffled voices and traffic banging away on Longwood Avenue stories below. She thought she heard cattails in the Fenway shushing against each other, and recalled the way pieces of garbage tangled in them during the winter. Dale, as a little girl, had thought they were bright paper decorations, stars and flowers, put there on purpose.

A nurse came in to check on her. Primal too, she thought, that this woman had sensed she was awake and now poked around Maggie's midsection and checked the IV line that ran from the back of her hand. Her touch felt distant on a distant body.

"How you feeling?" The woman's accent was round and tripping, and half-offered, as if she was used to talking to people who
might not respond. "You're my special patient. You're our star
around here, our own very famous lady. There were some people
from the paper, but I shooed them away for you." She leaned
down close to Maggie. "I'd do it for my daughter too, if she ever
asked me. But we're not like that."

Maggie considered asking her to explain some things, starting
first with the time and the day. The woman's digital watch pulsed
a green 4:13, but it could still be either day or night, and Maggie
was seized with the idea that she absolutely had to know, that it
would be the first corrective step back to life.

"Morning or afternoon?" she asked. Her mouth was dry and
pasted at the corners.

The nurse looked at her and wrapped the blood pressure cuff
up into a neat Velcro sausage. "Morning, honey," she said. "Very,
very much morning. Believe me. Can I get you something?"

The morning — but finally, what difference did it make? "Is my
daughter here?"

Again the nurse looked at her, and began to tuck in the sheets, a
tic of organization. Her hair smelled of lemons. "In the nursery.
Where else would she be, on a date?" She laughed.

Something clicked in Maggie's chest. She had two daughters
now, and asking herself which one she'd just meant was a little like
trying to understand what time it was, impossible but probably
essential.

"I can get her for you if you want," the nurse offered. "The big
daughter went home."

Maggie wanted to say no, don't bring her, the baby wasn't hers
after all, and it might have been the other daughter she wanted.
But she couldn't hold on long enough to speak. Her eyes closed,
and there was that ripping, hissing noise again as a curtain was
pulled around her bed to create an even darker shade of early
morning.

*　　　*　　　*

LATER, a thin sigh across her face woke her. When Maggie looked to the left to meet what had to be just inches away, there was only the military stiffness of the pillow's corner, an expanse of crisp white sheet, the bronzed bars of the hospital bed. But as her eyes began to focus beyond, she saw the baby through the cloudy plastic of a hospital bassinet. Her head was smooth and proud, and her mouth was round, with a pinpoint of darkness in the center. Dale suddenly appeared between her mother and the baby. "Mom?" she asked tentatively. "Are you awake?"

The sudden noise and shifts in light hurt Maggie's head. She felt ripped open and weak, and finally alert enough to identify each precise sensation of pain, to identify this body as unmistakably her own. When she reached for Dale, her daughter offered a cool hand, but her tear ducts were as distinct and lustrous as seed pearls; crying had been done.

"Dale." Maggie sighed. "Is she all right?"

"She's fine, great," Dale said, and leaned into the bassinet to pick up the baby. "Let me show you." Maggie didn't know if it was the sharp angle of forearm and chest Dale held the baby in, or simply the sight of Dale with a baby at all that was so astonishing. "Her name is Lily."

Lily, Maggie repeated to herself. Blossom, the girl in California. Rose, Daisy, Petunia, Lily. Dale, a shaded respite. "She's lovely. Lily — there's a bouquet of baby in your arms. Isn't it amazing we did this, that everything worked out so perfectly?"

"You wouldn't listen to me, but I told you it would," Dale said, and sat on the edge of the bed, looking down at the baby. "Are you feeling okay?"

Maggie nodded.

"You know," Dale went on, "when you left Dad's without telling anyone, and then we couldn't find you, I think we — I — had some pretty crazy thoughts about what you were going to do."

"Like what?"

"I don't know, run away. Get on a plane and never come back."

"You were the one who walked away from me. You didn't let me explain."

"I don't really know what there is to explain. You pretty much told it like it is." Dale began to move around the room with tiny, clipped steps that matched the cool precision of her words. "What's left to say?"

Up against the bright window, her daughter's face was unreadable, but she formed the unmistakable silhouette of mother and child. Maggie had given her daughter a baby — you couldn't ever do much more than that in your life. After everything, there was simply that to consider, and she hoped some measure of calm would come with it. She couldn't and didn't want to offer her daughter an explanation or apology, just this: Lily.

"Only that we should look at what we have," Maggie said. "Isn't the baby enough? Can you be grateful for her, simply happy?"

"More than you know. There's no way I can thank you for Lily. But isn't she enough for you, too?"

"Let me hold her, please."

Reluctantly, Dale handed the baby to Maggie. Lily's head turned toward her breast immediately, and rooted in the folds of her hospital gown. Within seconds, Maggie felt her milk struggling to come in and her uterus cramping painfully. The pull was such a familiar and remarkable sensation, it seemed no time had passed at all, and she would have liked to tell Dale, but the pain was also cruel proof of her body's purpose and the function of her parts. She pressed her lips to the baby's head, soft and smelling of soap. Lily's face was delicate but determined. Maggie felt the suggestion of Lily's arms and legs under the tightly wound blankets, and then Dale reached in, used her hands like a sharp wedge, and took the baby back.

Later, when Dale had returned Lily to the nursery and gone home to Nate and Virginia, Maggie remembered how her daughter, first as a child and then as an adult, would often look longingly at the cat curled warmly on her mother. Without a word of warning, Dale would walk over and take the sleeping cat from Maggie's lap and force it to settle in her own.

*   *   *

"I WOULD have come earlier," Doris explained. She'd flown into the hospital room as though someone in the hall had given her a push. "But Tina had — Shit, well, you don't want to know about all that. Ben's parking the car. I won't go into *that*, either. Let's just say it's the usual chaos." She stood back and surveyed Maggie, her hands pinching her waist. "You look good. Tired, but good. Lily's perfect, wonderful. She looks just like Dale, don't you think?"

Doris flicked at a pink Mylar balloon which was tied to the end of the bed and bobbed in a draft of air like a bloated fish in a tank. It had simply appeared at one point, and Maggie didn't know who'd sent it.

"You had us pretty worried for a while," Doris went on. "It was totally irresponsible leaving the party like that. Poor Dale, she was frantic and crying. And I won't even tell you what Gordon was like, or Nate." She talked nervously, took off her jacket, and sat down on the edge of the bed. "Can you believe you had a baby? I'm so proud of you." Doris's mouth contorted, and Maggie saw her fight the urge to cry. "Do they have you all doped up? Did you know a nurse is giving Lily a bottle now? Breast-feeding is really the way to go, but I guess this makes sense, actually, and Dale's taking her home tomorrow, anyway. So where is everybody?" She looked around the room as though she'd just noticed there was no one else there.

"They went home." Maggie didn't think she'd ever seen Doris so manic and unfocused. Her blouse was askew on her shoulders.

"And left you? It's still visiting hours."

"They were tired. They had a lot to do, I guess."

"Really? I was over there a few days ago, and they seemed to have everything ready and waiting. You know how you set the table hours before people are going to come over? It was a little like that. I wasn't allowed to touch anything." Doris began to dig around in her huge shoulder bag. "I have something in here for you, if I can find it. So you feel okay? An emergency C-section — that must have been scary."

"I don't remember a whole lot of anything." Except, she thought, when I was sure that Lily was dead.

"Probably not such a bad thing, either. Here — just what you need." Doris held out a chocolate apple. In its royal blue foil, balanced in the palm of Doris's hand, it was a jewel.

"I'm sorry for what I said before."

"I don't even remember what you said. Go on, take the candy. You used to love these things, remember? Am I right, that it's your favorite?"

Maggie nodded. Not long ago, when Ben was out of town Maggie would sometimes spend the night with Doris. With everyone gone, Doris had explained, she missed the sound of sleep threading through the house. Maggie understood it was really about preparing for the future; what woman hadn't said *This is the sound of myself alone.*

They'd rented movies on those nights and eaten too much candy — marshmallow peanuts and gumdrops, and chocolate apples — and drunk wine instead of having dinner. In the morning they were hungover, in their nightgowns, their lips still raw from the sugar, as they drank coffee and made fun of the way they looked. Now, Maggie began to unwrap the candy, picking at the foil with her fingernails, determined to eat piece after piece.

"I said you shouldn't be so nice to me," she murmured.

"Okay, so I won't be anymore. Listen, I want you to stay with us for a few days," Doris announced, and took the apple back from Maggie. "Let me help you with that. Your hands are all shaky. Is it the painkillers?" She held a slice out to Maggie and ate one herself. "I know you're going to say that you can take care of yourself, you want to go back to your house and to work, and to those awful cats of yours, but I don't think it's a good time for you to be alone. Right now you might think you're fine, but your body's been through hell and this is still a loss for you, and if it doesn't hit you today, then it might tomorrow. Ben doesn't expect you back at the lab for a while, anyway. Look, it's completely normal stuff, but who wants to be alone? I've already cleared the next few days to be with you, so you can't say no. I can drive you over to Dale's whenever you want." Doris leaned toward the door and held up her hand as though it had been Maggie talking at high speed. "Hold on for a sec," she said, and left the room.

She came back and sat down on the bed again. Ben followed, looking dazed and defeated, his hands curled in his pockets.

"I don't know what's wrong with you, Ben. You could at least say congratulations," Doris scolded.

"Congratulations, Maggie," Ben said, looking past her. "The baby seems good."

"*Is* good. He was worried about you, Maggie, practically pulled out his hair, such as it is. Did you know he was out driving around looking for you? I don't think he ever worried about *me* that way." She pinched out a laugh and ate another piece of chocolate, glancing at Maggie and rolling her eyes.

In the past they had teased Ben together, made fun of his moods to deflate him, exaggerated his quirks, until they noticed the kids had started doing it too. But now Maggie could not help Doris ride the bumps of her marriage. Doris turned to Ben again, back to Maggie, back to Ben. Her face flushed, and then its tension slowly softened and fell away, like a silk scarf fluttering to the ground.

Doris's bag crashed to the floor with the long clatter of scattering pebbles. Her mouth opened slightly, lips salved with chocolate, and her hand traveled down to her throat, her fingers clutching either side of her neck and catching in a gold chain with a diamond star at its nadir, and finally to her heart. Maggie smelled a woman's acrid, salty fear, hers or Doris's, or maybe both.

"Oh, God!" Doris groaned, her skin blotching red. "Now I get it. He didn't want you to stay with us. I thought maybe it was because of Tina, or work, or . . . Jesus, I didn't know why exactly. He's been acting so strange." She turned to Maggie, her head at an angle. "I couldn't figure anything out. How completely dumb of me."

"Doris —" Maggie began.

"Oh, fuck you," Doris whipped back. "Fuck you both. I'm going to pick up my stuff, and then I'm going home."

She slid down until she was crouching on the floor, her back cut hard against the metal bed frame, her eyes fixed on Ben's feet. "If you'll move," she said, and slapped his legs with full force, making him rock. "Let me get my things. Just get out of my way."

Ben looked down and placed a hand on his wife's head, his fingers nesting in her curls. Doris let it rest there while she made a hasty pile of pens, a small box with a gold bow on it, crayons, cheap plastic trinkets she gave to her students, lollipops, her allergy pills and reading glasses, the stuff of her work and life in that one bag. When Doris stood up, Ben's hand fell dully by his side, and she knocked against the tray table. A pitcher of water spilled across the bed and bits of chocolate apple smeared brown against the hospital white. Doris watched the water spread, and tears hung on her jaw like beads on a wire. Maggie felt the cold begin to cover her body, as if she were slipping under a sheet of ice.

"I really hate you both," Doris announced. "Fuck both of you."

Maggie listened to her footsteps fade away down the hall as Ben bent and picked up what his wife had left behind. He put her tissues, a lipstick, a tiny pencil stub, her pennies into his pocket. He'll keep his wife's things safe, Maggie knew, he'll hold on to them forever, ready if she ever wants them back. She thought of Gordon slipping the beads of her necklace into the pocket over his heart, of Nate wearing Dale's silver bracelet. She thought of herself folding a discarded shirt of Dale's into her own drawer at home, as though it were a sachet.

"'This is the worst way it could have happened," Ben said. "Finding out in a hospital. She's spent too much time with Aaron in these places recently."

"Finding out anywhere, Ben." Maggie's throat tightened. "What have we done to her?"

Their voices were filled with a certain inevitability; there was real sadness for the woman they both loved, but not all regret. Even in this room, with the red toxic-disposal box on the wall, the television looming like a huge fruit on a branch, even with Doris retreating past babies wailing down the hall, even in this damp bed, Maggie felt drawn toward Ben and the way his hand rested on the mattress when he leaned down, the way he was drawn to her.

TWO days later, when she eased herself out of the cab, Maggie saw that no one had bothered to collect her newspapers or bring around her empty garbage cans, which rolled on the sidewalk like drunken sentries, though Shelby had driven her car home from the lab. She discovered, too, that she'd left the front door unlocked, and was struck by how empty and chilled the house was when she'd expected to find some comfort here. There was the hole in the ceiling of her bedroom, inviting cold air to fill the rooms. She was empty too, and chilled with loss and loneliness. Had I never once pictured, she asked herself, life without Lily?

A thunder of paws sounded from above, and in a second the two cats tumbled over each other down the stairs. Maggie caught her breath when she saw the animals, horrified that she'd forgotten about them, except in the vaguest way, as though they belonged to some other part of her life. They hadn't eaten in days and were feral and ugly, their skinny tails stiff and shivering. They butted her ankles, forced her against the wall. Even their tiny pink assholes winked nastily.

"These animals yours?" asked the cab driver, who had come to the front door. His tone suggested he was ready to get rid of the animals for her if she wanted.

"They're just hungry."

"I don't like cats." He brought the things Maggie had taken from the hospital, the last of the tired flowers brought by friends, the semideflated balloon, the pyramid of waxy apples from Gordon and May. "They don't belong in a house."

Maggie wished he would leave, but he leaned against the door and watched the cats braid themselves around her ankles. When he'd picked her up at the hospital entrance, he'd told her that the baby hospital was his favorite run. Except, he added, when he picked up people who'd left their sick or dead kids locked in plastic cribs. He sometimes drove them to church, sometimes to a bar. He had six boys, two already in college.

"And you?" he'd asked, adjusting his rearview mirror.

Maggie had seen his dark eyes set on her, but she didn't answer. She could have told him how Dale and Nate had come to take Lily home from the hospital. Doris and Virginia, they'd explained brusquely, were in the car waiting, double-parked. Without a baby then, Maggie felt like an impostor on the maternity floor, a faker and fraud, and when she shuffled down the hall in her gown and paper slippers, she thought she saw in the cautious smiles of the other bloated women an understanding that she wasn't really one of them. How much of *that* could a man who had made six sons understand?

And then, against Dr. Gauld's sober advice, Maggie checked herself out of the hospital, and signed the form releasing everyone of any or all responsibility when she hemorrhaged or fell into a vegetative state because of a raging infection. The nurses shook their heads at her insistence, handed her a prescription for the pills which would dry up her milk, and went back to what they'd been doing before she entered their lives. Could anyone under- stand that her body and brain felt split in half?

Pollen from the flowers sprinkled the floor, and the cab driver smeared it in with his shoe. He was not waiting for her story, Maggie suddenly realized, but for his fare, which she'd come inside to get. She remembered a twenty-dollar bill, used as a bookmark, somewhere in the living room.

"Listen," she said after she'd found it and paid him, "you take the flowers with you, the balloon too, and the fruit for your wife and your boys."

"You going away?" he asked, gathering the things. She nodded.

When he'd finally gone, Maggie fed the cats, who ate too fast, scattering their food and clicking their yellow teeth. She saw her slippers under the kitchen table, where she'd left them days ear- lier; the pink satin bathrobe her mother had sent had ended up there as well. It had been clawed at until it was fuzzed with snapped threads, and a yellow stain of cat piss radiated on one arm like a halo. On the table there was a plate licked clean except for a few crumbs, a newspaper open to the crossword puzzle, a pen. Maggie could not remember the woman who had left everything just sitting there, a woman who was so sure she'd be back at the end of the day to put it all away, to water the plants, which had browned and stiffened, to lock the door for the night.

She took the stairs slowly, avoiding her bedroom and the sheets of cold air that slipped out under the door like urgent letters. Tomorrow, she told herself, she would call someone to come fix the ceiling. She went into Dale's room and took off her stiff clothes, the same ones she'd been wearing the day of the party. She wanted to take a shower, but found that the cats had used the bathtub as a cat box. It was more than she could stand at the moment, and she turned the water on as hot as it would go. All that shit, she knew, would eventually wash down the drain, even if it took days. Clouds of foul-smelling steam floated toward her and she shut the door.

WHEN she went downstairs again, her mother was standing in the hall, her fingers at the knot of scarf under her chin. "I called the hospital. They said you left. You really should keep your door locked, you know," Virginia said. "You're just asking for it this way."

"Asking for what?" Maggie didn't know if she missed the last step, or intended the embrace, but she fell hard against her mother. Grateful for the heat and the balance, she held on, even when she felt her mother stiffen.

"Rapists, murderers, burglars."

"Why didn't you come see me in the hospital?"

"Goodness, Margaret. Are you actually crying?" Virginia asked, alarmed. "Stop that, for godssake. Dale needed help with the baby. You're perfectly okay." She straightened Maggie up by the shoulders and then fixed the twisted collar of her robe. "Well, maybe I don't exactly know why I didn't visit. You always want an answer and sometimes I just can't give it. That's life." Virginia

marched into the kitchen. "Got a cup of coffee for me, sweetheart? What's that smell? Something die while you were gone?"

"Cat shit."

"I'll say, cat shit." Virginia lit a cigarette and sat down at the
table. "This can't hurt then. Is this the present I sent you by any
chance?" She had hooked the pink satin on the pointed toe of her
shoe and lifted it up.

"No, of course not." Maggie sat next to her mother. "Give me
one of those cigarettes. I think I'll take up smoking. It's never too
late for a disgusting habit."

"I get the hint." Virginia dropped the pack back in her purse,
and put out the cigarette on the empty plate. "You know, I can't
even smoke inside in my own house anymore. Ricky, he's become
a fascist like the rest of those anti-smoking people. I smoke on the
balcony like I'm some criminal."

"You can smoke here."

Virginia gave her an impatient look. "Okay, Margaret, here's
the way it is. You'll hear it from me, because I believe in telling the
truth, as you know. By the way, have you eaten anything today?
You don't look so good."

"I was just coming down for something, anything. I'm not sure
what's here."

"You have to learn how to take care of yourself. How old are
you?" Virginia stood on her toes to rummage through the cabinets
with their disarray of cans and boxes. As she did, a coil of gold
bracelets slid down her arm with a musical collision, a sound Maggie remembered from her childhood; Virginia had spent most of
her life pointing at things. There had been times when Maggie
was sick and home from school and Virginia had brought her
along to her work. Maggie would be parked in a chair in the corner of Virginia's office — she was the bursar at a woman's junior
college — given a book, a roll of candies, a thermos of orange
juice her mother had added too much water to. Feverish and self-
conscious, Maggie was still mesmerized by the exact movements
of her mother: hand to file, file to desk, hand to telephone, fingers
to typewriter, a yank on the pantyhose, fist to stapler, water glass

to mouth, admonitions to girls in sweater sets, tongue to enve-
lope, lipstick to lips. Later, home to husband, to feed, to clean, to
sleep. When Virginia finally quit the bursar's office after more than
thirty years there, she simply explained that she'd had enough and
was ready to move to Florida, as though the offer had always been
on the table. As far as Maggie knew, her mother had never tried to
figure out what the work she'd done amounted to, or what it
meant; she'd never tried to extract some bigger meaning from it.

Virginia opened a can of tuna fish and stabbed at the meat with
a fork. "I think what you did with Ben was not at all a good thing.
Not terrific by any means. I know it takes two, but I pin this on
you because I can. Got any bread? I'll make you a sandwich."

Maggie pointed to the refrigerator. "That's not fair."

"Fair? See? You're stuck on fair, always have been. Here you go
and do this" — Virginia struggled to find the right word — "this
baby business for Dale, and then turn around and act like it gives
you the right to do anything you want because of it. Is *that* fair? I
always wanted you to be more normal, and that's only because
I thought it would be easier for you if you fit in. But I guess that's
not who you are, you still trip through your life like your father,
with your own strange ideas. He didn't understand a whole lot,
either. Let me give you some lettuce on that. A little green
wouldn't hurt."

The sandwich was better than anything Maggie had tasted in a
long time; it was like all those things you weren't supposed to eat
anymore. Her father had cooked hamburgers rare and fatty, so
that the grease oozed down her chin when she bit into one. He
didn't talk much — stunned mellow, Maggie realized at one
point, by the shape of his marriage and the shrillness of his
wife — but he shared candy bars with her on the back steps in the
dark, looking at the sky and pointing out the stars. She thought
that was the only place you were meant to eat Mars Bars and
Milky Ways, and that he had this essential understanding over
everyone else who just crammed the candy in and tossed the
wrappers on the ground. Now she wondered what her father's
own, secret satisfactions had been.

"You shouldn't stuff yourself." Virginia circled her finger through the bowl of tuna fish and sucked it clean. "You'll get cramps."

"This isn't about Dale, you know," Maggie said.

"Don't try to tell me it's about how you and Ben love each other." Her mother looked at her suspiciously.

"Maybe it is," Maggie offered. It was needy like love, and certainly painful enough, but had she ever said it? Had Ben?

"Love. Oh, so effing what," Virginia dismissed. She seemed surprised at Maggie's sudden, loud laugh. "I know just how these things happen, you get lonely, you want to be held by someone, so you do what you can do. And everyone else has it, so you think you should have it too, that you deserve it, that it's fair. *There's* your fair. Just don't expect people to love you for it, because that's not going to happen. That's why this kind of thing never really works. Dale thinks you did this *because* of her, that it's some kind of balancing act you're up to. She gets hers, and you get yours."

"That's ridiculous," Maggie said.

But what her mother said also sounded vaguely right, she had to admit. Dale had said the same thing, days before in Gordon's cold back yard. She wasn't selfless, and giving Dale a baby was not a selfless act, though life would have been so much simpler if it had been. There was, finally, no such thing as altruism for her. She had wanted something in return for what she gave, and she had allowed herself to take it.

"Between you and me, Dale's a little confused about who's doing what to who," Virginia said. "And you keep your mouth shut about Nate. You don't have to explain it to me, either. That boy has one guilty look on his face, and he's all over Dale, doesn't give her an inch to breathe. Pawing her like there's no tomorrow. I know what's going on. Dale's got enough on her mind now, with the baby, that she shouldn't be thinking about what her husband did or does. That's their business and they'll work it out."

Maggie sighed. "What a mess we've all made."

"Not all of us. And don't feel sorry for yourself, Margaret. Everybody's life is full of these things. It's the way people live, it's how they find out what they want in the end. You have to try all the flavors first." Virginia shook her head. "Your house always looks like —?"

"Like what?"

"Talk about a mess. I remember when it was such a cute little place, too. Gordon used to have good taste, before he became so compulsive and rich. Let me help you a bit here." Virginia twisted off her two tourmaline rings and put them on the counter by the sink. She whipped through the room with a sponge, wiping around Maggie in widening circles, talking about Florida, the egret she'd seen on the airport tarmac, about Ricky.

When she was done with the kitchen, they went upstairs and Virginia opened the bedroom door before Maggie could stop her.

"What the hell happened in here?" she asked.

The room was still and unchanged, but the wind poured past the bare slats. "Just a little collapse. Age."

"Apparently. You know, Margaret, you have to take care of things. No one's going to do it for you." Virginia went into the bathroom, where the shower was still running. "This is too much, even for me," she said, and shut the door again.

Maggie felt a clot of blood slip out of her, and her incision, breasts, and head traded throbs. She lay down on Dale's single bed and looked up at the yellowed canopy, wondering how the brown stain in the shape of Italy had gotten there. Distantly, she heard her mother moving around in some other part of the house. It had turned dark in the time Virginia had been there, but the hall light lit the room well enough for Maggie to see how unchanged and cut off from the rest of the house Dale's room was, and how she'd allowed it to stay that way. Glass animals, deep and dense, like old eyes, were set in some precise, untouchable order known only to her daughter. In grade school Dale and her friends had collected silk flowers; had Dale arranged visions of romance and sex and domestic life when she stuck the stems in old wine bottles and placed them around carefully? The room was a shrine, with its dusty, venerated objects.

Virginia stood in the doorway and cleared her throat. "It might surprise you to hear that I believe in fidelity, Margaret."

"Why would it? Everyone believes in fidelity." Maggie paused. "As a concept, at least."

"Not true at all. But sex is the least of it really, if you must know — it's the other person you kill when you screw around." Virginia picked up a glass animal, and then another, appraising each. "Your father did it to me, and so I know. Oh, don't act so shocked," she said without looking at Maggie. "You of all people, for godssake." She was angry now in her humiliation, and her face, when she turned around, finally revealed its carefully tended age. The skin at the base of her neck sagged in pleats, like a loose stocking, and her mouth disappeared in itself.

"I didn't know." I didn't know my father had it in him, Maggie wanted to add.

"Of course you didn't know," Virginia said sharply. "I don't consider it anyone's business but my own." She sat on the bed next to Maggie and gazed out into the hall. "I never even told Ricky and I never will. Why I told you — well, I'm not sure."

Once, in a heat wave that made her mother forget her rules, Maggie, nine years old, was allowed to spend the night on the porch glider to catch the breeze coming up from the low end of the street. But she couldn't fall asleep. The plastic couch cover, printed with sunflowers, was brittle and smelled like other people's basements, and the way the woman and her grown son across the street talked evenly to each other made Maggie restless and suddenly as desperate to be inside again as she'd wanted to be out.

I don't want you changing your mind, her mother had warned, but Maggie had, though she hardly felt she had any control over it. Inside, she saw her parents asleep, spread-eagled to greedily claim the entire arc of the fan. They were naked and shining, her father's large, hairy thigh thrown over one of Virginia's bony legs, pinning her down, while her other leg kicked toward the edge of the bed. Her mother's breasts slid to the sides of her chest. Maggie had stared at her father's penis, a thick, purplish curl of skin. In the corner of the room, her mother's parakeets were silent in their cage, covered and dumb for the night.

Maggie had run out to the porch again. The mother and son across the street had gone in by then, but the light behind their screen door stayed on. Her fingers dropped over the edge of the glider and caught in the laces of her father's licorice-colored work shoes, kept there on summer nights to catch the breeze. Deep in, the toes still felt warm, like his breath. Everything was in place, she'd understood then, except herself.

"Don't go," Maggie said now, and touched her mother's back.

For a moment Virginia didn't move, and Maggie wondered if she'd fallen asleep, sitting, her chin on her chest. But then her mother stood up and removed herself from Maggie's touch. She patted her hair, tugged on the right and then the left earring.

"I have an early flight home tomorrow, and Ricky's picking me up at the airport. I don't want to disappoint him." She had told Maggie how she and Ricky sometimes drove Route 1 at four in the morning without destination so they could pretend the landscape of golf courses and intercoastal waterways was untouched and all theirs. Her mother, Maggie understood now, was finally, exactly, where she wanted to be.

"But stay here tonight, that's all I'm asking." If only you'd ever say you loved me, Maggie thought. "I don't want to be alone." Her body longed to have Lily back.

For a moment Virginia looked as though she were considering the option. "I have to go," she said, shaking her head. "Look at your front, Margaret. You're soaking wet. Didn't they give you something to stop all that milk?"

There was something curiously warm in her mother's voice. It sounded just a little like sympathy. Maggie recalled the feel of the prescription paper; it had been in her hand at some point, sharp-edged and heartless, and she might have dropped it. She pressed the wet cloth to her chest, an embrace of memory.

10

THE East locked itself in a late November freeze the day after Virginia flew back to Florida, and showed no signs of letting up. There was a story on the news about waves in Newport that froze in mid arc, about fattened-up Thanksgiving turkeys in New Hampshire freezing to death before they could be plucked and stuffed. When Maggie managed to make it to the window early one morning, she saw Dr. Riesen's wife, her coat collar high up around her ears, sitting helplessly in her car as it slid on the drive-way's black ice toward the street. The car nicked shrubs and snapped off branches, finally lodging itself in the dip at the edge of the lawn.

It was not hard for Maggie to imagine, as she left the window and the sight of dazed Mrs. Riesen, that Dale had prayed for pre-cisely this sort of weather. It was still too cold, her daughter had explained on the phone just that morning, to bring Lily out. It was nature's fault, bad timing — what could *she* do about it? Also nature's fault and bad timing, Maggie thought, that she was still in too much pain to make the short trip herself. Dale had rushed to hang up anyway, cutting short the sound of Lily's wailing and Nate's voice, suddenly loud.

Later, AAA attempted to drag Mrs. Riesen's car from its retreat in the bushes. Sinewy Dr. Riesen came up behind his wife and crossed his arms over her chest. They seemed amused by what was happening, joked with the tow truck driver, and leaned into each other for warmth. There was life among the clouds of exhaust and white breath. Momentarily, Maggie was lifted by the hope of it and its proximity to her in the promise of Ben, of Lily, of Dale again, of what she might have too someday. But then she was quickly pulled down, as though she'd been dragged over the spikes of the ice-coated green that separated her property from the Riesens'. She hadn't heard from Ben since the hospital. The baby and Dale were out of reach for now. Ceiling plasterers had promised to come and were blocked by the ice. She couldn't get anyone to even talk about her roof in this weather. Maggie stood by the window, blood indifferently staining her thighs, while the Riesens' car refused to leave the ice.

THE next morning Maggie found an ice scraper stuffed in the back of a drawer. She supposed the long list of postsurgical precautions she'd been handed as she left the hospital not only included driving and lifting, especially just nine days after giving birth, but also the vigorous hacking she was doing to free her car from its glaze of ice. She was tentative at first (and unwilling to call another cab or ask a friend, which would require more explanation than she felt up to), and worried about her stitches splitting open and her body dumping opalescent female parts onto the ground. She pictured the neighbors finding her splayed and pallid, scraper in gloved hand. She was, and always had been, a mystery to them — husbandless, pregnant, babyless, strange — and so better left alone in this unforgiving suburb. They might just walk away.

But the cold and the exertion were also numbing, and her body didn't balk. Her defiance, though she wasn't sure who or what exactly she was defying except the stupor she'd been in for days, was pure energy, hot enough to melt the ice. After everything, she didn't want her life to go that way, mourning and curled on the kitchen floor instead of moving on. As she drove cautiously to Dale's, the ice on the street shattered thrillingly under her tires like small, satisfying acts of vandalism.

By Dale's front door, the left side of a two-family, there was a wooden tub, which months earlier had been full of flowers, Dale's first attempt at growing anything. In June, Maggie had helped her choose the flats and break the clods of soil. Now the tub held ice-coated begonias, vincas, felty geraniums, all frozen in full stature, like bodies caught in a photograph. Maggie loosened the scarf around her neck and looked in through the window at the side of the door. Clothes, infant paraphernalia, empty plates, and containers of take-out were scattered around the living room. The baby carriage was parked in the middle of the hall as if it had been wheeled through the apartment and abruptly stopped. Maggie recognized the cut-glass ashtray on the windowsill — Gordon's at one point — still full of her mother's half-smoked cigarettes, bent like fingers, ringed with Coral Nights lipstick. A garbage bag, heavy with wadded diapers, split at the seams.

Dale passed into the room, dodging the obstacles as if they'd always been there. The baby was draped like a swatch of pink cloth over one shoulder, while the other shoulder was hiked up holding a phone to her ear. It was an awkward, crazy balancing act and a fumble and a drop was probably not far off. Dale looked up at that moment, her face startled to see another face in the window. She said something into the phone, dropped it onto the couch, and left the room again. Frozen on the steps like the flowers, Maggie waited, and wondered if she'd simply imagined that Dale had seen her or if it was the voice on the phone that had caused her to look up. She rang the bell.

"You didn't drive over here by yourself, did you?" Dale asked a minute later at the door. She had pulled her hair back and rearranged Lily in her arms. "You aren't supposed to drive, you know, not for another week at least. I told you this morning I'd try to get over tomorrow if it warmed up."

"But you've been saying that forever, and who knows if it will ever warm up? They say this is going to last for days. Have you felt it out there?" Maggie shivered and resisted the temptation to reach for Lily immediately. She knew she'd have to wait for Dale to make the first move, and stuck her hands in her pockets.

"I haven't been out."

"Anyway, the roads are empty so the driving's not too bad, and I feel fine, really. Precautions aren't law, and they're always based on worst-case scenarios."

"Which don't apply to you, I guess."

"I hope not," Maggie said, forcing lightheartedness over her daughter's dark tone. "Is Nate at work?"

"They canceled school. He walked to the store. You should have stayed home."

Maggie shrugged off her coat. Her bones were as cold as metal, but her lower half was on fire. She couldn't stand to have Dale see her in pain now, and she tried to shake off the slow burn inching down her thighs.

"I wanted to see you and Lily, and I was tired of you putting me off."

"Putting you off? Now you're just being paranoid," Dale said. "I'm not responsible for this weather."

Maggie followed her daughter into the kitchen. Formula was sprinkled across the counter, and Dale ducked around the open cabinet doors as she struggled to hold the baby and scoop the powder into a bottle. Her black pants were undone at the waist, and her turtleneck was spotted with trails of spit-up. Pillows of puffiness blued the skin around her eyes. Even in its exhausted pose, her posture was still defensive.

"Why don't you let me hold Lily while you do that?" Maggie offered.

"I have to get used to it." Dale's mouth was tight in concentration, but her voice was diluted with helplessness. Her free hand shook as she poured water, and the bottle tipped and spilled. "The minute I put her down, she starts crying. She never stops."

"She's not crying now," Maggie pointed out, but instantly regretted it when Dale's grip on the baby tightened.

"That's because I'm holding her."

Dale's frustration was benign enough, and this was the normal chaos of a new baby, but it made Maggie want to weep. Women were confident they were up to the largest acts of loving and raising children, but it was always the endless minor details and idiotic difficulties that made them doubt themselves. It was never possible to be entirely comforted by what you knew you *could* do.

"It just takes a while to get the swing of this. Come on, let me hold her for a minute so you can finish." Maggie finally slipped Lily away from her daughter. "Everyone needs help."

The baby was warm in her arms, her head in the palm of Maggie's hand. Lily's face was not blurred like some infants', but was remarkably well-defined and alert. In it, Maggie detected the first strains of character, intelligent, agile, and questioning. I don't ever want to let her go, Maggie said to herself with sudden and fierce attachment. This was the one time in life that it was possible to hold another person tight without also squeezing. Resistance was what made an adult embrace so compelling, but also so complicated; Lily was simple to enfold.

"My ears throb when she cries," Dale complained, and swiped at the hair that had fallen across her face. "She wants to be fed and held constantly. My eyes sting. I'm so tired even my skin aches. She doesn't give me a break. Why didn't anyone tell me it was like this?"

"Would it have made any difference what anyone said?" Maggie asked. "No one ever believes it will be like that for them. The truth is, babies are always overwhelming." Maggie tried to be soothing, but she wondered why Dale made Lily sound like a surprise houseguest who'd shown up with an alarmingly big suitcase and no plans for the next eighteen years. "Having a baby is like living next to the Southeast Expressway. There's always traffic, sometimes more, sometimes less, sometimes an accident, but you get used to it. And then at some point you realize you can't go to sleep without it. Do you know what I mean, Dale? You can't imagine that there was ever a time when it wasn't there and you can't imagine life without it?"

Dale didn't respond, but seemed transfixed by the cream-colored puddle on the counter. An oily tension had stopped it from running off the edge. Maggie broke the surface with her finger and watched the liquid drain to the floor.

"Say something, Dale," she said, when Dale didn't move to stop it. "You're spooking me. Are you that out of it?"

Her daughter's head snapped up. "Where's Ben now? How come he didn't drive you over here?"

"I don't know where he is," Maggie admitted. She recalled the way he had rested his hand on Doris's head, how Doris hadn't shaken him off. "I haven't talked to him since I left the hospital."

Dale let out a hollow laugh and bent to wipe up the spill on the floor. "Now *there's* a good relationship. I guess it was all worth it then, for those few months of fun."

Maggie turned away from Dale, tempted now to simply walk out the door. A knot of anger formed in her chest. "Let me have a little bit of life, Dale. I'm just trying to figure out what I want."

"What you want? Doesn't that strike you as just a bit selfish? You can't take something that belongs to another person just because you want it. It's really that simple." Dale's voice was laced with self-righteousness. She threw the sponge into the sink.

"It's not simple at all. Ben doesn't belong to Doris any more than Nate belongs to you. That's not what marriage is."

"That's *exactly* what marriage is, Mom. Nate *does* belong to me," Dale insisted. "No wonder you got divorced. No wonder you've been alone. You don't get it at all."

"Maybe neither of us gets it," Maggie said. The pressure of what was unsaid, what was still hidden from Dale, built under her tongue. "I didn't take anything that wasn't also given."

She carried Lily into the other room and sat down. The baby began to cry and Maggie tried to dispel the idea that this child, with her intense, adult-like gaze, understood how she lived between the two women. She pressed Lily to her chest to quiet her. Maggie's nipples began to tingle painfully and the milk quickly appeared in hot, steady drops. She switched Lily to her shoulder, and frantically fanned her shirt away from her front so that Dale wouldn't see, but it was stained dark green now over her breasts where it had once been a light olive.

Dale came into the room and stood in front of her, the full bottle in her hand. A bead of formula sat on the end of her tongue before she drew it in and swallowed. "Tastes like chalk." She grimaced and looked at her mother. Whatever composure her daughter had forced herself to gather in the other room was gone. "Look at your shirt."

"I know. The crying triggered it."

"It just happens like that?"

Dale would never understand how the body responded on its own, how it didn't care at all what other arrangements had been made. She stood up and handed Lily to her daughter. "Yes, it just happens like that."

"This has got to be confusing for the baby, the way your milk smells and —." Dale's voice was sharp with challenge. "Dr. Gauld gave you some pills. Didn't you take them?"

"Well, they didn't work, did they," Maggie said furiously. She went into the bathroom and slammed the door.

With her shirt off, she cried and let her milk flow into the sink, encouraging the flow as she'd done for days at home. In the other room Dale turned the music on loud, and it kicked at the door. Maggie's thin milk dripped steadily over the globs of toothpaste on the bowl, over the stiff hairs tapped from a razor, the rust stains on their way to the drain. She felt the waste of it, the incongruity of her flesh on the cold porcelain, and the shame for what she'd done and what a part of her must have wanted Dale to see now. She pulled at herself impatiently. And why could she hear the baby still crying, even over the music? What the hell was Dale doing?

When the door opened behind her, she was sure it was her daughter and they would come to some sort of understanding, because they would have to, they had years ahead with Lily always between them. But when she looked in the mirror above the sink, she saw Nate instead.

"No!" She rushed to shut the door, one arm over her breasts. "Go away."

Nate stared, slack-jawed, and the door bounced off his foot and back again at Maggie. "Jesus. Sorry, I didn't know you were in here," he said, backing out. "Sorry."

Maggie sat on the edge of the tub and wondered if she could stay hidden in there forever. She looked down at her wet shirt balled on the floor, and finally took a T-shirt of Nate's from the back of the door. When she came out of the bathroom, the music was off and Dale was feeding Lily a bottle.

"Where is he?" Maggie asked.

"He's de-icing the front steps," Dale said without looking up.

"You might want to tell him to knock once in a while."

"You might want to lock the door." She hesitated. "It wasn't intentional, you know."

Maggie listened to Nate scatter salt crystals on the wooden porch. Dale's face lowered toward the baby, and Maggie thought she was witnessing some kind of love and fascination among the confusion and fighting. When Dale's head snapped up, Maggie realized she'd fallen asleep, one hand clutching the bottle, while the other one fanned forward like an open gate for Lily to roll out of.

"Dale," Maggie said sharply. "Watch the baby. Careful."

Dale's eyes opened, dark and unfocused. "I wasn't asleep."

"For a minute you were."

Dale stood up and shuffled into the bedroom. Maggie followed, and watched as her daughter didn't so much lay herself on the bed as she did release herself onto it, holding Lily up for Maggie to take, as though she knew her mother would always be there, despite everything. And isn't that true, Maggie asked herself, and took the baby. She pulled the blankets over Dale and sat next to her. The windows banged in the wind. With Lily warm on her chest, like a hand on her skin, Maggie lay back, her feet in their damp shoes rising off the floor. She thought she heard Nate, still out in the cold, shaking the ice off low-hanging branches, a pointless, hopeful chore.

If she'd planned it, Maggie would have given birth to Dale in the spring so that the two of them could lie on their backs and look up at the tiny umbrellas of the flowering dogwood tree above them. Instead, Dale had arrived in the grittiest part of winter, the day after an enormous fire in a Chelsea nightclub had killed eleven people and blown bony soot as far as Waltham. Mysterious drafts smelling of charred furniture and burned hair had blown dust across the floor. In any case, and in any season, there was no dogwood in the tiny yard and there never had been, but Maggie had managed to conjure one up, explode it into bloom on the day Dale was born. Lily, close to Maggie's face now, was just as fragrant. The ceiling hovered like a low, spring sky.

"Mags?" Nate whispered. He had Lily in his arms, and Maggie panicked, after the fact, at the emptiness on her chest. "I'm not kicking you out or anything, but Doris is coming over in an hour. You might not want to be here then, if you know what I mean. Your call completely."

Doris, a woman never deterred by ice or cold or her own problems, who would have made a better mother to Dale, it looked like. Maggie struggled to sit up. "Give me a second, okay? I'll be right out."

She touched her forehead and felt a fever march like insects under her skin. She'd probably end up back in the hospital now, stupid and negligent, her innards clotted like loose scrambled eggs. Dale, curved in sleep, snored lightly. Maggie went into the living room, her arms across her chest to still the shivering. The television was on, and Nate was eating from a bag of pretzels while the baby slept against his chest. He'd cleaned up the room by pushing things into the corners.

"Sorry about before," he said. "I swear I didn't know you were in the bathroom."

Lily's lips were pressed, like sweet fruit, against Nate's warmth. As unsure as Dale had been with the baby, Nate was relaxed, and he kissed her head. Nate wasn't wearing his baseball cap, and the thinning, twirling spot in his blond hair caught her by surprise. Absently, she touched the freckled skin on the top of his head.

"Really, what haven't either of us seen of the other at this point?" Maggie sat on the arm of his chair, and for a few minutes neither of them said anything.

Nate took a deep breath. "When it warms up, they'll open school again and I'll have to go back to work. It would be good if you'd help Dale in the mornings, maybe for a few days, until she feels a little more comfortable with the baby." He spoke stiffly, as though he'd been waiting for the right moment and then realized there wasn't going to be one.

Maggie stood up. "I don't know. Dale doesn't seem to want me here. I don't understand why she's so angry about this thing with Ben, what it has to do with her."

"She's just hurt. She feels like you lied to her, and now she's caught between you and Doris. You know how she is anyway, not so good at change or things out of order. She wants a perfect world. She'll get over it."

In the light of the television, Maggie watched a pulse beat under Lily's skin. Again, she felt enormously drawn to the baby, and their clean attachment, when everything with Dale was so cloudy.

"Will she get over it?" Maggie demanded, and felt herself begin to slip out of control. She didn't want to cry but thought this might finally break her. "What more can I possibly give her? I'm not going to force myself on her now, put myself in her face. I have some pride."

"So *I'm* asking you, not Dale, and I wouldn't if I didn't think she really needed it. She's nervous with the baby. It worries me, I have to admit." He hesitated. "Doris is going to come in some after-noons to help, but the mornings —"

"Doris? You asked her before you asked me?"

"Well, it was already planned before, you know" — Nate cleared his throat — "your thing."

"My thing," Maggie repeated, angry now that he would toss it over her like a net to tangle up in. "And what's your part in all this? How the hell is *your* thing?"

Nate picked at the piping on Lily's blanket. "I messed up, I know that, but it's not going to happen again. I'm not a total idiot. I know how much I have to lose." He looked quickly over his shoulder toward the room where his wife slept. "Just think about it, okay?"

The cold was so hungry that Maggie felt it blow through the wood of the front door and swarm around her fever. She put on her coat, as useless as tissue paper. She knew Dale wouldn't actually turn her away, wouldn't forcibly deny her the baby or herself; Dale lacked the cold determination to hurt Maggie that much. But she wouldn't give anything, either, and that might be just as bad.

"Think about it, okay?" Nate said, and averted his eyes so he wouldn't have to see Maggie grab what he was about to present to her. "I promised Dale I wouldn't tell you this. Doris kicked Ben out of the house three days ago. He's staying with Aaron."

MAGGIE had been to Aaron's apartment only once before, three years earlier, when she'd gone over with Doris. It had been on the day he'd moved in, and Doris had decided to surprise him with a plant, which stooped in the back seat like an uncomfortable passenger, one skinny branch stuck out the window. The First Baptist Church on Prospect Street, where Doris sometimes ran an after-school art program in the sour-smelling basement, was only blocks away from the apartment, but the streets with their unexpected jogs and name changes flummoxed her, and they'd driven around confused for a while. The car's sunroof was open, and Maggie had looked up at the dense city trees in July towering over them while Doris kept insisting they were almost there.

Lydia Place was a stump of a dead end, with four narrow, tilting wood houses in need of repair that stared at a wire fence brocaded with vines. The place charmed Maggie. Doris said it worried her, but Maggie knew it was the sight of Aaron's friends, whom she didn't know, calling up to his third-floor window, that made her pull the key from the ignition so deliberately. Doris heaved the ficus out of the car and walked into the crowd with it, her ankles wobbling.

"I shouldn't have brought him the plant. It was stupid and a cliché. I embarrassed him in front of his friends. I embarrassed myself," Doris said later when they were driving home. "A mother shouldn't see how her child lives, because there are basically only two options — rejection or reflection — and either way, it absolutely kills you."

Maggie parked at the mouth of Lydia Place and got out of her car. The vines on the fence had been whipped leafless and bronze by the bad weather and she could see through to other iced yards. When she looked up, Aaron's window was blue-gray, the same color as the sky. Three bells were arranged haphazardly on the door frame, with no names attached. Would Aaron's be the one at the top, or the farthest left? She rang the middle one, and within seconds a woman opened the door. She was about Dale's age, Maggie noticed, dark-haired, her full mouth smeary with purple lipstick.

"Yes?" the girl said suspiciously.

"I'm looking for Aaron. Is he here?"

"I wouldn't know." She stared blankly at Maggie. "Maybe you should try ringing *his* bell."

"Oh, sorry." Maggie laughed uncomfortably. "Which one is it?"

The girl twisted so that half of her remained protected behind the door while she leaned out and pressed one of the bells. Maggie heard it buzz somewhere above their heads.

"I don't know if he's there," the girl said, looking up the dark stairs. She gave the bell another jab. "I haven't seen him in a few days. Maybe he's at his girlfriend's. Go up if you want. I don't really care."

"Thanks. Maybe I'll just check."

The stairway twisted narrowly past the second-floor landing, and up to the third, which was lit by a small, dim bulb. Aaron's door was shut, the two locks emphatic and unfriendly. From the minute she'd left Dale's house, Maggie hadn't actually imagined she'd find Ben there. He wasn't at the lab when she'd called (Shelby had said he hadn't been in for days), and she pictured him watching a chess game in Harvard Square in the freezing wind, or reading for hours in the aisle of a bookstore, or sneaking from movie to movie while only paying once. Already, the climb pounded in her head like disappointment, and threatened to rouse the fever that had ebbed for the moment. She rested in the close space with her weight against the banister, wondering what to do next. Below, Maggie saw the dark head of the first-floor tenant move back into her apartment. The railing shifted forward and the sound of splintering wood screeched and tumbled down the stairs. Maggie's hands slipped off the railing's rounded top and pawed at the air. Her body hovered over the edge.

"*Never* lean on that," Ben said, and pulled her back abruptly by the arm. "It's hanging on by a nail. Couldn't you see?"

Maggie didn't know if it was surprise at seeing Ben or the picture of her falling that made her feel so hot all of a sudden. "How could I see? It's so dark in here."

"Just be careful," he said, as though finding her — and her clumsiness — were only what he'd expected. "This place is a shit hole. Don't lean on *anything*."

Ben led her into the apartment, and pulled a chair out from the table that filled half of the cluttered room. "Sit here," he ordered. "I'll make you some tea. You okay? You look flushed."

"It's just the climb." Maggie took off her coat and wiped the sweat from her upper lip with the front of Nate's T-shirt.

Ben, relaxed in worn clothes and bare feet, moved with slow and practiced movements from sink to stove, from tea bag to cup, from spoon to honey to plate. It seemed possible to Maggie that he'd been working solely on this smallest routine of domestic competence for days. *Do you want sugar instead of honey? milk, or lemon? How are you feeling? Let me turn the radio off. Are you hungry?*

Only the center of the apartment was lit, so that she could not make sense of the shape or size of the two rooms. Something about the place was deeply private, though, as if it were obscured by folds of heavy velvet, drawn back only for special guests. Hot air from a heater attached to the oven blew toward her with Ben's questions, dry and uncomfortable. There was an unreadable flatness to his expression when he sat down, and it struck Maggie that maybe he didn't want her there at all, that she was a reminder of his regrets and missteps. Hadn't Nate said Doris kicked him out, and not that he'd left?

"Yes, I'm starving," she said, trying to discern his mood. "I'll eat anything."

Ben put an open box of crackers on the table, and without talking they reached in turns for handfuls. Maggie ate to the point of choking dryness, and then she drank her tea, pleased by the efficiency of this filling and quenching. When they'd finished the crackers, Ben made more tea and brought out a loaf of bread. Maggie unzipped the crusts from several pieces and curled them into her mouth.

"You look good," Ben said.

Maggie smiled to show she knew it wasn't really true but appreciated his attempt. She could almost hear her skin flaking in the heater's dry assault. "Where's Aaron?" she asked. It had grown dark outside by then, and past the time for him to come home, if he'd intended to at all.

"He's staying with his friend Kate." Ben said. "Only one bedroom in this place anyway."

"I'm surprised he wanted you here at all, under the circumstances. Dale isn't nearly so forgiving."

"Aaron doesn't know the circumstances," Ben said. "He's under the impression, and so is his brother, that Doris kicked me out."

"Didn't she?"

Ben shook his head. "No, it didn't happen like that. I want you to know that it was a decision we made together." He paused, and stirred his tea in an oddly formal way. "Aaron thinks it's because I smacked Tina."

"Did you?"

"Yeah, I did once, actually." Finally he looked up, but past her, as though he were expecting someone at the door. "It sounds terrible, doesn't it? I was in the dark one night, way after midnight — I mean literally, sitting in the kitchen with the lights off, thinking about you and what we were doing — and she wandered in. God knows why she was up. It was one of those weirdly noisy and warm nights we had last month, or maybe she peed in her bed again. She must have been hiding for a while before she jumped up, shrieking. That was all I saw, the flash of her nightgown, and a shape coming at me. My heart went crazy." Ben opened his hands quickly in front of his face and then let them fall on the table. "I just struck out at what was there, a reflex. Slapped it away."

"What happened?" Maggie's stomach pounded. She put her hand over her mouth.

"Doris came running in and turned on the light, and there I was, naked and dumbstruck. Tina was on the floor. She wasn't hurt, only as scared as I was. She'd wet herself and was sitting in this terrible little yellow puddle, and I couldn't do anything. You can explain over and over why you hit someone, how you were only protecting yourself, how it's instinct in the dark, but it doesn't change the fact that you did it. Or why I didn't go to Tina after or even pick her up off the floor. Doris and I, well, we both had this need to tell people, the boys especially, what had happened. It was like a confession, for both of us."

"But what was Doris confessing?"

"You live with someone long enough, and you're always partly responsible for what they do, too. Maybe it's just how you looked at the other person one morning, or something you weren't even aware you said or did a while back, but all those things have their effect eventually. She's the one who brought Tina into our house and I'm the one who didn't want her there."

"It's a terrible story," Maggie said. "But now you'd rather have your boys believe you're an impulsive bully who hits little girls than believe that you're here because of me, because of what we did. I don't get it."

"Of course you get it. Look, I want them — I want *Aaron* to believe what he can," Ben said, suddenly angry. "The boy's sick, he gets thrown off balance too easily. Jesus, what else can I do? Tell him I'm fucking around on his mother?" He leaned back in his chair and looked at the ceiling. Disgust tightened his neck and thrust his jaw forward. "What do you want, Maggie? Why are you here?"

She walked over to the same window she'd gazed up at earlier. She could not have predicted its generous, glittering offering of the frozen Charles River and the city's skyline beyond. It was the single secret every home has, the blueberry bush by the driveway, the drawer in the back of a closet, the perch she chose in her bedroom window. A good view was like the future, so wide you couldn't take it all in at once, and she wondered how this one made Aaron feel.

"I wanted to tell you that I saw the baby and I'm fine," she told him. "I'm really okay."

"Terrific." Ben had been leaning back in his chair and now the front legs tapped down on the floor. "What are you talking about?"

"Just that these past months, I was so afraid I was disappearing, afraid that after the baby was born no one would see me. Who would need to anymore? Not Dale, and not you. I tried to tell you this at the party."

"And I told you that you were wrong, but you didn't believe me, so what could I do?" Ben began to clear the table.

"No, I didn't believe you. And I didn't hold you back from Doris in the hospital, either, and I didn't look for you or call you, and when I didn't hear from you, I knew I'd been right. I *was* gone. You were proof enough of that, and so was Dale. And I was relieved, to tell you the truth, because I knew that if I was invisible, then everything I'd done was invisible, too. We could just forget about all of it."

"Then I'm glad it's worked out so well," Ben said tightly. "How nice for you."

"But I wasn't right at all. There's the baby. *She* saw me, *she* knows who I am. I know who she is and what she's like. That's not something invisible, that's something real. I'm still very much here, and so are you and what we did. And I'd like to be with you still. That's what I wanted to say." Maggie put on her coat, and fingered her keys in the pocket. "But I have to go home now. I think I have a fever, and I'm so tired all of a sudden I'm not sure I can stand up any longer."

"That's because you shouldn't even be out. You just had a baby," Ben said. He followed her downstairs, and at the bottom he hesitated. He told her to wait, ran back upstairs, and in a minute returned wearing shoes and a jacket that was too small and thin and strained over his chest. "I'm driving you home. I remembered you're not supposed to."

"I got here by myself," she said, but with no energy behind the protest.

As they walked toward Maggie's car, the girl from the first floor turned into Lydia Place. She clutched the unmistakable brown bag heft of a dinner alone to her chest, a scarf wrapped across her mouth. Though Maggie and Ben were only inches away when they passed, the girl acted as if she hadn't seen them in the dark.

"Creative parking job," Ben said, when he saw the odd angle of Maggie's car against the sidewalk and how it was now blocked in by others. "What were you thinking?"

"That you weren't going to be here. That I'd be back in a second."

She got in while Ben started the car and inched it back and forth. The noise was like someone trying to clear his throat. The engine raced under Ben's foot, and his face was energized with determination. His profile, illuminated by the streetlight, looked very young. Maybe, she told herself, he believes we're just going to fly out of here.

The rocking was lulling though, the heat blasting, and a numbness began at her feet and traveled up through her body. A tiny muscle in her lip fluttered, and she imagined that this was what it was like to be under a spell, helpless and warm and unable to care very much. The car door slammed suddenly, and Maggie saw that they were in the middle of the street now, pulled out from the space, when she'd only shut her eyes for a second.

Ben was on the sidewalk. He picked up a metal garbage can and took off the lid. As though he were wielding a giant pepper mill, he sprinkled frozen garbage on the car in front, and then some on the one behind. Furtively, he looked to make sure no one had seen him, and then scrambled back into the car. The front of his jacket was wet and smelled like old beer.

"How good was *that?*" Ben asked. His eyes were wide with excitement. "That felt great."

"Spectacular." She laughed.

"I'd do anything for you, Maggie," he said, suddenly serious. "It's always been true. I don't know why you don't understand that."

Ten minutes later, Ben pulled into her driveway. The light in Dale's bedroom was on from earlier when she thought she'd only be gone for a little while. The curtains were parted to reveal the pink walls. It was like looking into an open mouth.

Inside, Ben smoothed the blankets on Dale's bed. He watched while Maggie undressed. Later, in the dark, under the canopy, she didn't open her eyes when he slipped in next to her. He ran his finger lightly across the raised line of her incision, as if teasing it to let him in.

11

BEN hated the cold, but liked that he could do something about it. On that first morning he'd woken up in Maggie's house, he turned the thermostat up so high that the walls, unaccustomed to such expensive luxury, creaked happily. He shivered under chilled sheets, wore socks to bed and later kicked them off and ran his hot feet up and down Maggie's legs. Awake in the middle of the night, crowded in the single bed in Dale's room, she wondered about his reflex to caress her, and hers to be thrilled by it.

He tried to unbutton her coat, but she'd just put it on, along with her boots stained wavy by salt, and her gloves rubbed slick. When Maggie left the house in the morning for a walk, he said he didn't understand why she wanted to go out into such bitter weather when it was so nice inside. She didn't tell him there was something necessary about the way the cold made her cheeks pinch and her body firm up, how she thought her head might be clearing some, too, only when she was alone in the cutting wind.

It wasn't easy going, and Maggie found herself spending more energy on not falling than on thinking straight about her life. From behind windows one morning, people up and down the street monitored her slipping progress as she made her way out onto Commonwealth Avenue, which was sheeted with graying ice. The houses were proud and flat-fronted there, and didn't so much face as stare coldly across the street's wide division at each other. This was a route Maggie hadn't taken in a long time.

She and Gordon had always walked, even in the most extreme weather. She'd liked the sound of their matching footsteps, which took the place of compatibility and conversation. Gordon had a game then, and later as he pushed Dale's carriage or carried her on his shoulders: He would pick the house where they were going to live in a few years. From the beginning, he'd wanted the biggest, the highest up on the broadest lot, the whitest, with the windows that sparkled the most, and he never doubted that his success would give him all this. Maggie had listened to him as though this was not her future being planned out in houses she couldn't stand. She wondered then not so much at Gordon's very American predictability, but if he shouldn't have wanted something different and not simply something *more*.

In fact, the house he'd firmly set his eye upon one June evening belonged to a Greek real estate developer, his partner-wife, and three daughters. Potted topiary twisted by the front door in brass planters. Six months later, on their annual flight to Athens, the plane had crashed and the entire family had been killed. Gordon, pale-faced and undone in a way Maggie had rarely seen him, had heard the news on his drive home that evening. Eradicated, was the word he'd used chillingly. It was not the brittle brown topiary still on the front stoop months later, but the sight of all those uncollected supermarket circulars and *Seventeen* magazines spilling out of the mail slot that broke Maggie. She'd finally stopped taking that route, and eventually the house had been sold to the Transcendental Meditation Society. Now, years later, she saw that the front door those three beautiful girls had sashayed through was an institutional two-sectioned glass-and-steel number, with a sign that said "Closed. Please Come Another Time." Eradicated was still, almost twenty years later, exactly the right word for what had happened. And she was still in the same place.

INSIDE again, she worked to take off her heavy clothes and to ignore a fact of convergence: freeze and Ben, Ben and freeze. Everything had come to a stop. She had not talked to Dale or seen the baby since she'd been there seven days earlier; she didn't see what was going to change that. Maggie pulled at her gloves, but they sucked at her fingers. Already her skin was splitting under the leather. She heard Ben on the phone upstairs, and the slightly giddy tone of a man on an indefinite vacation, not one who had just dislodged his entire life. It was Tuesday, a week since he'd moved into her house — and more than a week that he hadn't gone to work. After each call to the lab, he draped himself over the arm of the couch, or lay at the foot of the bed among the tangle of blankets, insisting that he was exactly where he wanted to be.

Maggie pulled uselessly at her uncooperative boots. Used, is what she decided her body had become, battle-worn, scarred, like the women she sometimes saw in the Y shower room with chunks of their chests missing and enormous, puckered scars at their hips. They never covered themselves, she'd noticed; turning away was for other people to do.

Ben loped into the room wearing a T-shirt and boxers. "Let me do that for you," he said, and kneeled in front of her.

He yanked off her boots and rolled down her mismatched socks until they lay balled up on the floor. One finger traced a vein that mapped her calf muscle and ran up her thigh. Ben said she was beautiful, even when she felt so disarranged and badly repaired. She wondered if this attraction were new, or if it had always been there and she'd spent years misreading his moods and looks — and her own. What part of her past, Dale included, was actually the way she thought it was? The question panicked her slightly. A shift in light came through the window over the sink and rested in a four-square grid on Ben's chest.

"How was your walk?" he asked.

"It's warming up. I actually felt the sun today." She wasn't sure why she was exaggerating — lying, really — and had to look away. "Maybe you should go to the lab later."

"Maybe. The plasterers are supposed to show up in an hour." Ben's hands were on her thighs now, a rolling movement inward, a prying apart, but Maggie resisted. "Maybe I'll stick around for them," he added.

"I'm perfectly capable of telling them what needs to be done," she said. It was, after all, her house and her problem.

He smiled. "I know you are. But I want to stay."

Ben reached for his coffee on the table. Maggie had discovered he drank it light and syrupy-thick with sugar in the early morning, black, bitter, and cold by afternoon. She knew she was collecting evidence of misalignment, but also of endearment and routine; in her mind she was seeing what the future might look like. Living together, even for such a short time, had already transformed him in her eyes. It was a slightly scary pleasure to realize that he was less familiar now than her imagination of him was.

Maggie took his cup and sipped from it, confirming an awful bitterness. "I'm just wondering, do we care about work at all anymore?"

"Of course, but I've decided something," he said excitedly. "That when you get old, going blind is not the worst thing that can happen to you, not by a long shot. Some people are probably just as happy not to have to see everything, their kids getting sick, the paint peeling everywhere, Kmarts every two feet, Monica in their face.

"I'm just slowing down a little. You've never seen me do this so you don't recognize it." Ben placed his hands on Maggie's knees and leaned toward her. "We've been working so hard for so many years, Maggie. Sometimes I think about all the things we could have been doing instead."

"Instead? We don't know how to do anything else." Maggie laughed. "We're completely unemployable."

"It's true. Neither of us actually knows how to do anything useful," Ben said. "We were always rushing, but I only wish we'd gotten here sooner."

"But this was always here in a way, don't you think?"

Maggie leaned down and they kissed. Pleasure hummed through his body and into hers, but something still held her back. She marveled at how Ben seemed to have added his losses and gains already and arrived at contentment, while nothing in her life, except this singular feeling of love for him, was so easy for her to measure.

LATER, Ben lay on the living-room rug for his morning exercises. From the doorway, Maggie watched him lift his leg up and down like a pair of scissors, flexing his foot. At night, he stood sideways in the mirror, checked the topography of his torso, and slapped his skin smartly. His vanity was surprising, as though this were all a long, sexy preen — but leading to what?

"Life — or whatever this is," she announced, "still goes on no matter how fast or slow you move through it." She wanted her house to herself, if only for an hour, to think with him not in it. "You can't stay here forever."

"Why not?" Ben rolled to his back for sit-ups.

"Because I can't. I'm so restless I'm going to tear my hair out."

"When I was in high school," Ben puffed between barely aspirated counting, "there was a girl I went out with a couple of times. I was thinking about her last night for some reason when you were asleep. Nina — that was her name. I was really in love with her. Anyway, I took her out one night to the movies, and afterward, I walked her back to her house and we sat in her yard."

He stopped and hugged his knees to his chest. "It was hot and pretty dark, but I could see the sweat on her neck and watched it run down under her shirt between her breasts. I remember that perfectly, the sweet little drops lit up by her father's porch light."

Ben stretched his legs out and grasped his toes. There had been other stories that began like this one, coming out of nowhere, scenes that took place under suburban boxwoods or in the basement of a friend's house, stories that described the tortured lowering of a pair of white panties, the spastic unhooking of a bra. He whispered them to her in the dark or spoke them loudly under the brightest light. It didn't matter; he was almost evangelical in his recounting.

"Does this have *anything* to do with what we were just talking about?" Maggie asked.

Ben turned on his side again. When he lifted his leg, Maggie saw how his balls rested on his thigh like fruits. "So there we were, sweating like crazy, and I put my hand under her shirt. It was incredible, a real discovery. I had her nipple under my forefinger."

Ben had been a fumbler, a hard-on in khaki pants, a boy to make you feel wonderful, while she'd been in the library or in her room trying too hard not to think about herself. Maggie felt the girl she was then long for him.

"Why do you tell me these stories?" she asked.

"It's the sensual details I'm after," he said, "not the intellectual ones for once. I'm remembering things I'd completely forgotten, that's all, remembering what it's like to discover something, to simply want something so much you can't think straight. You do that to me, make me see it's okay to look back and feel that way."

"How about looking forward, too?" Maggie said. His stories sometimes made her feel like she was drowning.

She knew that if Ben went back far enough and often enough, if he was careful enough with the intention of these stories, he'd arrive at the time when he didn't have a wife to betray and wound, or a son to mourn, or years of work to dismiss, anything to explain. He'd have her. In many ways, Maggie envied Ben's ability to fool himself. It was so easy to be dreamy and a little blind to what was real, and she supposed it's what people did all the time, how they justified themselves and how they got through the toughest parts of life. But for herself, she knew it could never work this way, because what was real was also true to her. And the truth was she couldn't have everything she wanted now: Lily *and* Dale, Ben *and* forgiveness all around, love without loss.

"What are we doing?" she asked.

Ben looked at her, and an understanding seemed to cross his face. "What do you want to do, Maggie?"

"I want to see my babies," she said with surprising certainty that this was where she would start.

Ben understood. He would like to see his babies, too.

BY the next morning, things had thawed enough so that the streets were black, passable and busy again. Maggie drove to Dale's with the car windows open. Nate was at the door as soon as she stepped onto the porch. He was holding Lily.

"Good, you're here," he said, and let out a long, tired breath.

Maggie pictured him standing in the exact spot since she'd called the day before, waiting for her to show up. When she took off her coat he handed Lily to her as though this instant pass-off was understood and already practiced. With his hands free, he tugged at the knot of his tie. He looked like a kid forced to dress up for a relative's wedding.

"Hate these fucking things," he muttered.

Fatigue had gathered under his eyes, thin etchings circled his lips like sloppy tracing, and his cheeks were irritated from an overly aggressive shave. And the tie, the pants with the creases, the focused irritation, the glances over her shoulder — Nate had become, for the moment, the kind of man who reassures himself that freedom is just on the other side of this. All it would take would be a step away, a drive in the other direction. She brought Lily up to her lips, and inhaled the sweet smell of the baby.

"She's a great kid," Nate said, watching her. "Smart, and don't you think she's beautiful?"

"Do you have something important going on this morning?" Maggie asked, barely able to move her mouth off the baby's skin. "I've never seen you so spiffed up."

"Yes, and I'm late already."

Nate was edgy as he ticked off instructions about Lily, and Maggie wondered as she listened whether what was ahead for him that morning was fallout from his affair. No, affair was definitely the wrong word, too loaded; it suggested romance and adults. And the girl, skinny in a cotton undershirt, could only understand that she didn't have Nate anymore — in her, on her, telling her she had a spirit like water. Yes, it was over, he'd assured Maggie the other day, but that didn't mean the girl's broken heart wasn't bleeding out the story of what had happened. Maybe, though, this was only about the baby.

"Is everything okay?" she asked, though her tone was without sympathy.

"Fine," he said, and shouted toward the kitchen. "Your mom's here." He turned back to Maggie. "Well, she doesn't exactly have it together."

"It takes some people a while to get used to this. I was no quick study either."

"Sure," he said. "Jesus, I'm so late. What's she doing?"

He led her to Dale almost apologetically, as you might lead someone to a nasty mess you've left for them to clean up. Dale, leaning over the kitchen counter, was wearing an oversized, stained T-shirt and looked as though she'd just gotten out of bed, or hadn't slept at all. Her face was smeared with fatigue.

"Okay, I *really* have to go now," Nate insisted.

"So go already," Dale told her husband, and then turned to Maggie. "He's been saying that for an hour. Like he couldn't leave me until you showed up." She had been eating a doughnut when Maggie came in, and there were several bites taken out of the ones still in the box. "Don't look at me like that, Nate. I'm hungry."

"It's just that you're going to feel bad if you eat another dough-nut," he said, "and I'm the one who's going to have to hear about it later." He paused, and Maggie saw tension flare at the base of his jaw. "Look, forget it, do what you want, eat what you want. I have to go."

Dale took another bite and Maggie watched her struggle with the dryness. She turned to drink from the faucet. Dale had always been off the mark with her defiance. As a kid, she would break one of her favorite toys when she was angry at Maggie. She would end up sobbing over the pieces at her feet, mystified by how it had happened.

"You look like you haven't slept at all," Maggie said when Nate had gone. She loved Lily's pale pink features, and the perfect fit of the baby in her arms.

"She was up four times last night. Finally I just shut her door and put a pillow over my head so I wouldn't have to listen anymore. I mean, I knew there was no way she could still be hungry. And then I couldn't fall asleep anyway after that. I feel like I'm crawling around in the dark." She took another bite of the doughnut.

It pained Maggie to think of Lily's crying going unanswered. She knew she could try to comfort Dale, slumped as she was with her doughnuts and self-pity. It was what she'd always done, but she was unwilling now, and felt submerged by what it would take.

"Go take a nap," Maggie told her.

Dale dragged herself to the bedroom and shut the door. It was that detail again, the closed door, that Maggie found so disturbing, for its isolation. She had never been able to sleep with the door shut; she imagined too much happening on the other side. Maggie began to collect things for the baby's bath. She remembered bathing Dale in the kitchen sink because that's what the books told her she should do. Maybe other women didn't have a sink full of dirty dishes all the time, but Maggie always had to first scrub out the bowl caked with last night's tomato sauce, Gordon's coffee mug, and then lift the pieces of lettuce and onion skin from the drain. Dale's sink sprouted pizza crusts, apple cores, and sour baby bottles, so Maggie ran a bath in the tub. Her green shirt was still balled in the corner of the room from days before.

Bathing Dale had never been easy. She'd been a squirmy baby, sensitive to noise and touch, and often difficult to calm. She had been pure, physical body then and always jerked at the first drop of water. Lily was no less alert, but more considered, and strangely thoughtful. She followed Maggie's movements with a careful eye.

In the tub, Maggie placed the baby on her chest. Lily was no bigger than the space that ran between her breasts, no longer than the arch where her ribs joined to the underside of her chin. It seemed the right and intended fit. With the cup of her hand, Maggie poured water over the baby's back, and then over her own face, soaking her with contentment. She felt unhurried, and for that small amount of time, perfectly happy. Some time later, when she opened her eyes, Dale was standing in the room. Her expression was wild and a little sad, her hair a stiff mess around her face.

"I couldn't sleep," she said.

"Jesus, you scared me, Dale." Maggie's heart beat furiously at this apparition, and at being caught in an act of serenity and pleasure that should have been Dale's. How long had she been dreaming? When she looked down at Lily, she saw the baby rise and fall with the pounding in her chest.

"That looks nice, what you're doing." Dale's gaze traveled over the baby and the watery distortion of her mother's nakedness.

Maggie wanted to cover herself but remained half submerged. "How long have you been watching me?"

"For a while. You were humming, you know." Dale closed the toilet lid and sat down. She rubbed her eyes. "I'm glad you're here. I appreciate it even if I don't show it."

"That's good, Dale. I'm glad I'm here too." Neither of them spoke for a few minutes. There was only the slow drip from the tub's faucet and Lily's slight snore, sounds Maggie hoped might bring them to a truce. She felt the water begin to give up its warmth.

Dale forced an alertness on herself. "Nate told me you asked Ben to move in with you."

"More or less. Something like that. I'm not sure it happened quite that neatly."

"I just don't want to know about it, and what you're doing, or what it's like, or how good it is, or any of that, all right? If I don't have to hear about it, then I don't have to think about it, either."

"And then it isn't happening," Maggie said.

Dale rested her elbows on her knees and her chin in her hands. Her eyelids drooped. "Something like that. Not knowing has always worked pretty well for me. You know that."

Maggie tried to detect in her daughter's expression the first tiny admission that her marriage was in trouble, but she couldn't; Dale's eyes were closed and her face was hidden by fatigue.

SOMETIMES Nate would still be there in the morning when she arrived. His voice settled the baby, while his comments never failed to rile Dale, who eyed him tensely. Other days, Nate had already been gone for hours by the time she rang the bell. On those mornings, Maggie would find the baby alone in her seat, or restless in her crib. She was wet or hungry or inconsolable, an angry bundle of what her daughter seemed incapable of talking about with more than a grunt or moan. Dale ran into the shower or into the bedroom, or she slipped out of the house listing the errands she had to do, the friend she was going to visit, a stop at her office. She couldn't escape fast enough, and was always late coming back. At those times, Lily was the last thing she'd look at.

When Dale had been a baby there had been times when, within minutes of Gordon walking through the door, Maggie would be flying around the house in a rage about something that had gone wrong. Dinner wasn't started or even thought about, and she could have turned to that for dull distraction, but it was as though her husband's presence released something in her. The more she doubted herself as a mother, the more she was out of control, and the more he was stone-faced.

"Why aren't I happy?" she'd asked one night. She was on her third glass of wine, and she knew she reeked of desperation. "I'm supposed to be. What's wrong with me?"

"You *are* happy," Gordon had insisted. He glanced quickly at her — she seemed actually to pain him. He was still in his coat, the mail in one hand slapping against the palm of the other. "You just don't know it."

Shouldn't I understand then what Dale's going through? Maggie asked herself one morning as Dale rushed out of the house. I'd wanted to escape just like she does now, and I always came back.

SOME nights when Ben returned to Maggie's after a day at the lab, he wouldn't come inside immediately, but sat in his car in the driveway. He was addicted to the small bits of radio news that came on at the top of the hour, and would wait to hear them. A splash of red light on the snow meant his foot still rested on the brake. Maggie knew these moments were when he missed his family the most, when he actually had second thoughts he didn't want to bring inside to her. For everyone, in every day, there was this moment, sometimes tiny, of personal despair. For her, as long as she could remember, it was when she first turned on the lights against the dark; now it was also when she handed Lily back to Dale.

From the kitchen window, she saw Ben finally move, but it was just to run the back of his hand across his forehead. When she turned away to pour another glass of wine, she heard his car door squeak open and shut, and then his key in the back door. He looked up and saw Maggie — he'd been looking at his feet on the mat, still thinking of something else — and then dove toward her, like a plane coming in for a landing. His arm caught around her waist, his head moving up under her chin forced hers back, his lips rested on the skin of her neck. She was surprised by how deep her passion for him was at those moments.

"Yes," he said one night, his voice muffled against her.

"Yes what? Speak." She kissed him. She wanted to drag him upstairs with her.

"Yes, that smell." He tapped Maggie's chest. She was sure he meant the wine on her breath, too many glasses of it. "Baby. Here. A little milky, a little powdery, very sweet."

She always knew, when he looked up at her excitedly, that his own moment of despair had passed.

At night in bed, Maggie would recount the day for Ben, who was hungry for details, while he'd give almost none of his day at the lab, though he was faithful in the delivery of her paycheck. Slowly at first, she began to pepper her stories with hints of Dale's indifferences or missteps with the baby, how Dale seemed deaf to the distress, annoyed at Lily's constant demands. How her leaving on errands looked like escape.

What she didn't tell him was that every day she saw signs that Doris had been there after her, and that Dale never mentioned it. In her mind, Maggie catalogued Doris's sneaky reorganization of items on a shelf, her pitcher of ice water with floating lemon slices in the refrigerator, the way she'd folded a blanket at the end of Lily's crib, her careful, correcting attention to things. She didn't tell Ben how she soon found herself undoing what his wife had done. She drank some of the water, poured the rest out, and left the lemon slices to curl in the sink's drain. She moved the crib away from the window, put the blanket under a bed. How in return, she left signs for Doris. With the baby against her chest, Maggie cooked, and she imagined Doris inhaling deeply, but cut off short, when she walked into the apartment at two o'clock, by the intimacy of the smells, the warmth of curries and bite of garlic. Maggie teased with odd concoctions — raisins in spaghetti sauce, a capon stuffed with apples, chocolate balls studded with orange peel. Dale never said anything about the food or who had eaten it, but it was always gone the following morning, the dirty pot or bowl left soaking in the sink for Maggie to wash and fill all over again.

Maggie did not tell Ben how she'd forgotten her scarf at Dale's one day, the one she'd worn for years. She expected it to have disappeared by the next morning, Doris made a little crazy by Maggie's familiar scent on the familiar silk, but there it was, just where she had left it, ratty and faded, hanging on the closet doorknob, hardly worth paying any attention to. Maggie would not wear it again — Doris had made the last move of indifference toward her — and she stuffed it in the back of Dale's closet. Still, she and Doris were both covering for Dale's troubles and incompetence with the baby. Their reasons were entirely different, though in many ways entirely the same.

One night, she described for Ben how the front door to Dale's had been wide open when she arrived in the morning. Unsure of what she might find inside, Maggie stood for a few minutes on the porch before going in. Lily, on a blanket, was an arm's length from the door. She slept alone in the living room, stilled by sunlight and cold air. Maggie heard Dale drop a bottle of shampoo in the shower, heard it bounce against the porcelain.

In the kitchen the toaster had been yanked out of the wall, where tongues of soot licked up the paint. The cord dangled near the full sink, in which floated two pieces of black toast. A window was open and a sheet of frigid air traveled from one end of the apartment to the other, whisking out the smoke. The place was a wind tunnel.

"I swear," Maggie said to Ben, "it was as if Dale wanted someone to steal Lily. Everything was set for it. I considered taking her just to see what would happen." Maggie noted how Ben watched her so closely, how he seemed to mouth her words as she spoke them. "And to scare Dale. You can't imagine how easy it would have been to grab her and walk out. When I said something to her, Dale said it was Nate's fault for not shutting the door when he left."

For a moment neither of them spoke, but listened to clumps of snow slide off the roof, which was still in need of repair. Maggie imagined the holes slowly widening. She looked at where the ceiling had been patched but not yet painted because the plaster was slow to dry in this weather. It hung above them like a water-logged country.

Maggie began to tell Ben how one afternoon, only weeks after moving into her house, she'd gone downstairs after putting Dale in for a nap, and for a moment hadn't known where or who she was.

"I had a terrible feeling," she said, turning so that she faced Ben on the pillow, "that a good mother never feels this way, that her baby is the only reference point she needs. It doesn't matter where she is or what she's doing, or what she wants, or even who she is. None of that is relevant. Why did I imagine that? Sometimes I thought of Doris and how she seemed to know what she was supposed to do and feel. She looked at the boys as though there was nothing else to see."

"She still does," Ben said.

"It was never that clear for me. I was always divided. Except for now. Lily is my reference point." She paused to let her admission catch up to her. "So that afternoon, the living room was streaming with light and dust, and piles of laundry were everywhere, on every piece of furniture, stuff I couldn't possibly have chosen. I really thought I might be losing my mind, berserk with motherhood. I had no business being a parent."

"You called the lab every day," he said, "just to ask if there was still a place for you."

"Well, I had to make sure. I was like a starving person, checking to see if there was going to be any food left by the time I finally got there."

With the windows uncurtained that afternoon, and the sound of car doors slamming as neighborhood children came home from school, she had knelt on the floor. Soon her head had been pressed against the rug, her hands jammed between her legs. She had thought, I've finally toppled. She didn't want sex, hadn't wanted it or Gordon in a long time, and felt nothing more than a cold hand, mechanical, smashed between her legs. She was rocking suddenly, and she had no idea how long her baby had been wailing upstairs, or why the sound didn't move her.

"It all looks a little too familiar now when I watch Dale with Lily. It's the cruelest thing to do to a child, to resent her so much that you can't see straight, can't see what you have, can't see that you're pinching, or screaming, or being cruel. But Dale *wanted* Lily — that's the real difference — and now she can't wait to hand her off to me. It doesn't make any sense."

"If you think the baby's in danger —"

"I think she's always in a little danger, but that's how mothers feel all the time. *That* part always came completely naturally to me."

"Maybe Lily would be better off here for a while," Ben suggested.

Maggie considered it every day, and at night she sometimes wondered how it could be that Lily wasn't there with her. But she knew she couldn't take a child that wasn't hers just because she wanted to, or because it was also what Ben wanted. He raised himself up on one elbow to look down at her, and Maggie thought how frightening and wonderful it was to have someone know what she was thinking.

12

ONE morning on her way to Dale's, as she was stopped at the corner of Mass Avenue and Prospect Street, Maggie saw Doris and Tina on the sidewalk waiting to cross with the light. They held hands, and Doris's head angled to the left to hear what Tina was saying. The girl wore a bright pink parka with pink snow boots, and a knapsack was strapped to her back. Doris had a purple watchman's cap pulled tightly on her head, and her green coat, the color of wet hay, was too big and rolled up at the wrists. The pockets were jowly from overstuffing. It was one of Ben's coats, and Doris looked tiny in it, the hem sweeping at her ankles. Doris struggled to carry a sheath of Day-Glo poster board under one arm.

Maggie's first impulse was to duck down in her seat, but she knew Doris would instantly recognize her car, with the rust spots Doris always said reminded her of dried blood on a bathroom floor. There was also the dent like a dimpled cheek on the hood, where a brick had landed one summer night over a year earlier when they had gone to the movies in Somerville. Doris had touched the wounded metal, still hot from the sun, which had set while they were in the theater, and insisted righteously that they call the police and report what had happened. It was their duty. The brick, old, eroded, lay innocently enough next to the car. They'd gone to the brink of an argument over this, at which point both women backed away from the subject and Maggie pulled into a self-serve Merit station. Their retreat had seemed particularly female and a little tired to her, as she pumped gas and looked through the waves of fumes at the Saturday-night traffic.

Tina had a long cut across her cheek, and Maggie recalled Doris's never-ending supply of horror stories about Tina's family, the drugged-up cousin, the man they called Unkie. Doris had probably been thankful for the chance to swab Tina's cheek, to kneel in the bathroom, a hand on the small of the girl's back. She always had all the right things in her medicine cabinet: Band-Aids, Mercurochrome, gauze, calamine lotion, Kaopectate, Tampax. In hers, Maggie had prescriptions she hadn't finished, lotions crusted with age, pieces of beach glass.

One summer when the kids were young, Doris, Ben, and their boys, and Maggie and her family had shared a house for a week on Lake Winnipesaukee in New Hampshire. Doris had spent time in the same house as a child, and often talked about sleeping shirtless on a camp cot in the splintery screened porch when it got too hot in the house. Her eyes brightened and flickered when she described it. As it turned out, the screened porch had been converted into a laundry/recycling room, with cold white ceramic tiles on the floor and easy-clean tilt-in windows. The kitchen with its tin sink was now slick with spotless Formica, and the path down to the water had been widened, packed hard as blacktop, studded with No Trespassing signs.

On the first day there, Dale, overweight, awkward, embarrassed in a bathing suit, tripped on the only exposed root on the path and tore the skin off the top of her big toe. Doris had taken immediate charge, and in the laundry room with the door shut, had bandaged Dale's foot. Later, Maggie saw where the blood had stained the pale grout pink. Every night that summer week, the air smelled like bayberries and blueberries. She and Gordon drank too much and made love more often and more hopefully during those seven days than they had in years, while Maggie had flashes in the dark of Ben in his blue-jean cutoffs, his ankles pale in the lake, shadowed by passing perch. Dale among the boys giggled in the attic.

As Doris and Tina stepped into the crosswalk now, a sudden gust of early-January air swept the poster boards out of Doris's hand. Day-Glo sheets floated and escaped like kites with their strings cut. The burst of color was the most beautiful thing Maggie had seen in a long time; in the almost five weeks she'd been going to Dale's, there had been no break in the gray weather, no color at all. The pink board was the same color as Tina's open mouth, vibrant and moist, the green a match for the trim on her parka. The driver behind Maggie leaned on his horn, and Doris watched the orange board flap down the street and out of sight. She mimicked the swoop with her hand, graceful and laughing. Maggie drove on unnoticed, past the woman who wasn't her friend anymore, who seemed so disturbingly surefooted without her.

The sighting left Maggie unsettled and only heightened her annoyance at Dale for making her wait on the porch. Her daughter didn't seem to hear the bell, or the tapping on the window. Dale had promised, more than once, that she'd make a copy of her keys, but it was just one more thing undelivered. Doris no doubt had her own key and probably had for years. The picture of her on the corner with Tina, thrilled by the colors, was one Maggie couldn't shake. She jabbed at the bell over and over, until Dale finally came to the door, without the baby.

"No wonder you didn't hear me," Maggie yelled. The bluegrass music sounded like a cage full of squawking birds and she turned it off. "My God, it's not like you weren't expecting me."

"The louder the better," Dale said in a flurry. "Shit. I have to find my skirt." She searched behind a chair, got down on her knees to peer under the couch. The skin on the backs of her thighs looked doughy.

"Lily asleep?" Maggie took a step back from her daughter's agitation.

"Have you seen it? The short black one?" Things flew, drawers banged. Nate was cursed for having put it somewhere. Finally she stopped and looked at her mother helplessly. "I give up."

"What's going on?"

Dale sat back on her heels. "Nothing. I don't know, I'm going to meet Nate, that's all. I wanted to wear that skirt. He says he wants to talk to me."

"What does he want to talk about that you can't do it here?" Maggie's mouth suddenly went dry.

"I have no idea. Maybe he's bought me a book on how to be the perfect mother." She snorted. "Where the hell is my skirt?"

A wave of dread for her daughter washed over Maggie and she left Dale still searching on the floor. On her way to Lily's room, Maggie's eye caught the familiar bright pattern of the baby seat perched on the kitchen table. From where she stood, the room partially obscured by the door frame, the seat seemed to be floating in midair. But Maggie knew that couldn't really be, that some combination of light and angle and her own uneasiness was producing the illusion of levitation, and she took a step into the room.

"Lily baby," she said softly.

"Found it," Dale declared, suddenly loud behind her.

At the sound of Dale's voice, Lily's head turned, the movement enough to tip the seat off the edge of the table. The room itself seemed to freeze as the seat began its fall to the floor. It was a long, slow drop, and Maggie saw every tragic possibility unfold — Lily face-first on the smudged floor, a cleaved forehead, a snapped neck, a dead child. The seat landed on its rounded plastic bottom with a smash, bounced up and down again on its side. Dale had not moved, the skirt draped over her arms like a pair of handcuffs. The back of the seat blocked Lily from view.

"Dale," Maggie said. "Dale."

For a single second, she gave her daughter the chance to move to the baby first, but Dale was motionless. Maggie felt the floor rise to slam against her knees as she reached for Lily. The baby jolted out of her shock and began to cry, a wail so full there was no noise for a moment. Maggie held her at arm's length to check the baby's color, her eyes, the health of her fury.

"How could you leave her on there?" Maggie demanded. Dale knelt down next to her, her hands jammed where her legs bent.

"But she's all right. I think she's just scared."

"How could you let this happen?"

Dale stood up slowly. Her head tipped to her right shoulder while one hand stayed caught at the back of her neck. Her pale eyes drifted over the baby. "But *nothing* happened. Look, she's moving and crying, and that's a good sign."

"But you let it *happen*," Maggie said again. "Where were you?"

"I was . . . Jesus, I can't watch her every second."

"Yes you can. You have to. What do you think a mother does? You could have killed her," Maggie accused, even as she understood that things like this sometimes happened to the most vigilant of parents. Once, as an infant, her daughter had slipped from her hands into the bathwater, while for a fraction of a moment Maggie had been thinking of something else. She berated her daughter now, even as she saw that Dale's crisis was like a giant rock, heavy and dangerous, and rolling toward them at terrible speed.

"What the hell is happening to you?" Months of Maggie's frustration slammed into Dale. "You're not fit to take care of this baby. You're not a mother at all."

Dale's arms dropped to her sides in defeat. She took a step forward.

"No, just go," Maggie said. "Get out of here. Just leave us alone."

By one o'clock Dale still hadn't returned or called, and Maggie could not reach Nate at school. She had spent the morning pacing furiously through the apartment with the baby. Lily was agitated, quick to cry, and wouldn't eat. At one point, Maggie went into Dale's bedroom. Clothes were thrown everywhere, and the skirt Dale had looked so hard for was on the bed, the zipper ripped out of the seam. At one-thirty Maggie decided she wouldn't wait anymore, not for Dale, not for Doris to show up.

The weather had warmed considerably and Maggie put the baby in the carriage and walked to Harvard Square. The women she passed looked at her, then down at the sleeping baby, then up at her again. She knew they were making their quick assessments: she was a grandmother, a sitter, not the real thing. In the hollow air of a covered walkway, she wanted to yell at them: *I am the mother of this kid.* She felt it was truer at that moment than ever before. Lily sighed shakily, and Maggie, tired of the walk and the looks, headed toward Lucy's.

Lucy's was one of the few places she and Gordon had been able to afford when they were first married. Sometimes after dinner, if Gordon didn't have too much studying, they would drive in to Harvard Square and order huge, overflowing sundaes. Gordon would hang the cherry above his mouth as though he were feeding himself peeled grapes, or imagining someone more exotic doing the job. She would wipe the inside of the glass cup with her index finger and lick it clean. Once, as they were ready to leave, Gordon told her she had some fudge sauce above her lip, and had touched his own mouth to show her where. Maggie waited for him to clean it off for her, but his hands were in his pockets as he stood looking for change and his car keys.

Lucy's had been renamed Sweetie's, but the tiny store still had the same octagonal floor tiles with their endless alternating patterns of dirty and less dirty, the solid oak display cases of waxy chocolates and candied fruit slices, and the counter with its deep-grained and sticky surface. Maggie wheeled the carriage in, ordered a bowl of chocolate ice cream, and sat at one of the marble-topped tables. Maggie noted her fellow company: a woman bent over a table talking to herself and reeking of piss, and an enormously fat man with a shimmer of whipped cream clinging to his mustache. A girl in a striped pink-and-white uniform sprayed the table next to Maggie's with Windex, and the thin blue mist wafted through the air, settling above Lily's head.

"That's a really nasty thing to do while I'm sitting here. Maybe you could do that later," she said, and pointed at the bottle.

The girl stared blankly at her and sprayed once more. "My shift's over in like a second."

When a gust of air blew in, Maggie looked up, to see May making her way to the candy counter. Her full-length fur coat rustled elegantly at her ankles and the chain of her bag clinked against the glass as she pointed to the candies she wanted. She laughed at something the kid behind the counter did.

"Well, screw it then," May said. Her voice bounced through the room. The fat man looked up from his bowl.

May was holding her wallet up to the boy. She offered a credit card, but he shook his head. He did the same when she offered a check. May argued with him for a few minutes, and then turned around, her heels clicking officiously on the tile.

"Maggie," she said, and came over to the table. "I thought I was the only one who knew about this stupid place. Can you believe it, cash only? What century is this?" She looked into the carriage and cooed at the baby, caught her breath to continue. "Is Dale here?"

"No. Just us two girls."

May nodded. "We were over at Dale's on Sunday night for dinner — well, if you want to call mediocre take-out dinner," she said. "Gordon thinks Lily's the best. Serious, he said. Anyway, he took one look at the situation, the mess and those long, long faces, and offered to pay for someone to come in and help. I told Gordy he'll spoil them. *I* never had help with my girls." May laughed. "Anyway, I think Dale took offense."

"I've been there every morning," Maggie told her, and recalled Monday morning's tower of white paper containers and crumpled napkins on the kitchen counter. "I *am* the help."

"Really? Is that right? Dale didn't tell me." May fixed her hair in a compact mirror, and then tugged at the pantyhose around her waist. "I would love a cup of coffee."

"So have one. Sit with me for a while," Maggie said, eager for the flow of friendship at the moment. "It's just me and my friend back there." Maggie nodded to the hunched woman behind her.

"Lord, she stinks. I don't have a single goddamn cent, Maggie. Not one."

Maggie handed May a few dollars. "This is on me, big spender that I am. And thanks for the party."

"That was some time, wasn't it? With a surprise ending, no less. You got our apples at the hospital? Forget about a thank-you note, by the way — an overrated convention. Just more paper for me to throw away." May folded the bills like a woman used to handling lots of them. "Gordy would get a kick out of this, you know, you buying me a cup of coffee."

"He was always pretty easy to amuse," Maggie said. "Give him a rawhide chew toy and he was happy for hours."

"Wait. You weren't making fun of him were you?" May laughed, full-throated, and slapped her purse. "Relax, I'm just kidding. Make fun of him all you want. I think you're a kick."

May trotted off to the counter for her coffee. Maggie felt slightly bad about choosing Gordon — Gordy? — as a target. He seemed too easy now. May sat down again and took a deep sip of her coffee, the liquid beading on her thick, carefully applied lipstick. Maggie ran her tongue over her chapped lips and wondered how long it had been since she'd taken that kind of care of herself. Her mother never failed to fix her makeup after a private cry or a sudden breeze.

"So what about you?" May asked. "I think about you a lot, about how you're doing, what you've been through. I could be jealous. Who knows? Wouldn't put it past me. Anyway, sometimes I think, what the hell, I'll just pick up the phone. We could go to the movies, or have a drink."

"I'd like that. If I can have a baby for my daughter, I can also go out drinking with my ex-husband's wife. This is a new era."

"Okay, then. I might actually call you one of these days. I suppose you're not high on Doris's list, speaking of friends. Ran into her the other day with that cute little Japanese girl she's got."

"Vietnamese."

"Whatever." May shrugged. "She had that big pale man with her, too, the one who came to the party. The one who spilled the perfume all over my white rug. Jackass. The place smells like a whorehouse."

"Milt." Maggie tried to picture his bland face, his presence as suffocating as the air in a greenhouse. He seemed a long time ago. "Anyway, I spilled it."

May waved her away, looked down at Lily, and rubbed the baby's chest. Lily offered a full smile. "Lord, babies make everyone go a little nuts. They're like the smell of sex. Aren't truffles supposed to smell like sex? You know how they say first comes a new house, then comes a new baby? I say, first a new baby, and then a new man." May rubbed the baby again. "And Ben — well, I always thought he was very sexy. Is that ice cream?" Maggie slid the dish toward May, who wiped the spoon clean on a napkin before she took a bite. "And this one. Well, she's a funny baby, don't you think?"

"What do you mean?" Maggie asked.

May took another spoonful of ice cream before pushing it back to Maggie. "Most babies are so blob-like when they're this age. She seems — I don't know — alert, smart? Like she's listening, thinking about things. Look at that smile. Maybe I'm just confusing her with you." She shrugged and sat back. "Nate's very sweet with her. Dale, on the other hand — someday she's going to leave Lily on the roof of the car and drive off like that man in the newspaper did with his baby. It's taking her a while to get into the swing of this mothering business. I told Gordon he should say something to her. Is this my business? She's your daughter."

Maggie nodded. "And Gordon said, 'I don't think it would be appropriate to get involved.'"

"Actually, he said we should hire them a nanny." May stopped, and her face widened. "That's the same thing, isn't it?"

"Sounds like it to me."

The baby began to cry, and despite Maggie's jiggling and patting, and May's soft singing, the noise soon escalated to an alarming pitch. The sound veered off the glass display cases, ricocheted off the floor tiles, slammed into the counters.

"Oh boy, here goes," May said, and looked up at the ceiling. "Good lungs. Why did this happen all of a sudden?"

Convinced she'd been too quick to assume Lily was fine after the fall, Maggie told May what had happened. Bombs, embolisms, internal bleeds, swelling on the brain — things could be detonating inside Lily's body at that moment. May handled Lily firmly, feeling her, turning her over.

"What a morning you've had. God, mothers and daughters have it hard, don't they?" she said, squinting as though she were thinking of her own children. "But this is only crying. Lily looks a little pissed off, but otherwise fine. I don't see anything wrong except that she's hungry. Hand me her bottle, I'll feed her. You take it easy for a second. Go get yourself some more ice cream. Strawberry, this time."

"I didn't bring a bottle."

May rolled her eyes. "That wasn't too smart, was it. Time to go home." She handed the baby back to Maggie.

With a movement she could not have forgotten even in twenty-four years, Maggie reached under her shirt.

"Okay," May said cautiously, when she realized what Maggie was doing. "I guess it won't hurt. But you know, babies won't take the tit after the bottle. At least I've never heard about one that would."

"Neither have I, but I don't have a choice, do I?"

"Well, you do, but hell, I have a feeling you're going to do what you want anyway."

Maggie held Lily up to her breast. The baby stopped crying for a second, stunned at the unfamiliarity. The heat coming from Maggie's body thawed her eyes open, but her mouth remained determinedly shut. Lily looked as though she were considering her options with that same ageless contemplation Maggie sometimes saw on the faces of blind people.

"I don't know, hon," May said, now forming a protective barrier for Maggie so that their knees touched. "It's too unfamiliar, probably. How old is she now?"

"Seven weeks." Maggie squeezed at her nipple, teased it across Lily's lips. She felt a pounding under her skin, like the sun insistent at the window. She looked at Lily and knew it wasn't so much to want to be fed, or simply comforted. She prayed for the baby to accept her now, even parched and milkless, but Lily turned her head resolutely. Alert with disappointment, Maggie moved the baby toward her again, and this time she felt the baby relax and open her mouth. In a minute, the rhythm of sucking had lulled her to sleep.

"Okay," May said, watching carefully. "Look at that. The human pacifier. What else was there to do, right?"

"It hurts." Maggie smiled.

"I'm sure it does." May laughed. "Look how I spent my afternoon."

"You can tell Gordon you went breast-feeding with the girls."

"I don't think I'll mention this to him, you know? I'm not so sure he'd understand. Listen, would you mind lending me twenty dollars?" Maggie handed May her wallet, told her to help herself. "Why I came in here in the first place is I have to buy a hostess present for one of Gordon's lawyer parties tonight. You remember what those wives are like? God forbid I should show up empty-handed. They'd treat me like I just shit on their oriental rug."

Later, May drove Maggie and Lily back to Dale's in her forest-green Lincoln. The inside smelled of the cherry air freshener hanging from the rearview mirror. May wanted to know what Maggie thought about the genuine leather seats, leaving Maggie wondering about the mystery of attachment, particularly this woman's to her car. In many ways, she could not imagine anyone more unlike herself than fur-coated May — who was stroking the leather like it was a pet — yet amazingly, they'd married the same man. Maggie too stroked the butter-soft seat now at May's urging.

"Let me take the baby inside," May said when she turned onto Dale's street. "You just stay here in the car."

But Dale's car was not in the driveway, and there were no lights on in the apartment. Still, May got out and rang the bell. In a minute she was back in the Lincoln. "Give me the key. I'll get a bottle."

"I don't have a key."

May looked at Maggie. "Are you kidding?" She shook her head. "Have you always been like this?"

"Like what?"

"Letting other people run your life. I couldn't stand it myself. Okay, so what's your plan now?"

It had started to rain lightly, and the afternoon turned dark and even warmer. In the pewter light Maggie could be decisive; there was nothing else she could see but what was right in front of her.

"I'm taking the baby home. If they care at all, they can come and find me."

May waited until Maggie had started her car before she flicked on her headlights and drove away with two long, confirming blasts of her horn.

WHEN Ben came in after five, he knew instantly that the baby was in the house, and he pushed past Maggie without a word. He looked like a dog on a scent, a wet dog, just in from the beating rain, following his nose into the living room, where Lily was sleeping on a pile of blankets. Maggie had bought formula on her way home; an almost empty bottle now dripped slowly on the rug.

"I knew it," he whispered, and knelt down. His finger touched Lily's cheek, and for several minutes, he stared at her. "She looks just like you. . . . " He faded off, and then his tone changed suddenly. "Is Dale here?"

"I don't know where Dale is," Maggie said, "or Nate, for that matter. They seem to have disappeared."

She sat on the couch and told Ben everything, from the moment she arrived at Dale's, to when she'd driven home with the baby. His eyes stayed focused on Lily as he listened, as though he were trying to figure something out. He was still wearing his wet coat, and his face flushed slightly with the dampness.

"Well, what could you have done then," he said, finally. "Actually, I'm wondering why it took you so long, what worse disaster you were waiting for."

"But what I said to her, about not being a mother. I shouldn't have."

"It was true, though."

Maggie found Ben's stillness unsettling, and the way his face was locked solid in certainty made her feel as though she'd lost all judgment of her own. Her hands fluttered in her lap and then through her hair. "I have to call her again. See if she's home now."

"Sure, fine, do that. And then what?" he challenged angrily. "You've brought Lily here. So now? You're going to let Dale run things? Have you always given in to her?" She'd seen him use this tactic for years with his students, his sons, Doris — he bullied out answers when he was sure he already knew them. "What exactly is your plan here?"

"I don't have one," she snapped. "I just did what I had to do. I didn't plan on this."

"Whatever you want." Ben shook his head. "I'm going up to change."

An hour later Ben was just coming back from the store, where he'd jogged through the rain to buy dinner, diapers, and three plastic-wrapped baby gowns — he'd been unsure of the right size, he later explained, so he'd bought multiples — when Lily began to wake up. He rushed to her, picked her up, and handed her to Maggie. Each time the phone rang, Maggie stiffened and Ben looked unsure, but there was no call from Dale or Nate. Later, when Ben changed Lily, he stared at her lying diaperless on a towel on the kitchen table.

"I've never had a girl baby, you know," he said. "Even at this age they're rounder than boys. Their shapes are different. Look at these thighs."

He laughed as he traced the creases of skin on Lily's legs and arms, the folds that encircled her wrists and neck. He rubbed his fingers along the translucent tips of her ears. She was a fat and irresistible baby, impossible not to touch over and over, and Ben already adored her.

B Y ten o'clock, Dale and Nate had still not called. Maggie and Ben avoided each other, focusing instead on Lily, whom they refused to put down, as though someone might take her away when they weren't looking. Maggie felt like Dale when she stood at the counter and picked at food to fight off her anxiety. Finally pronouncing this vigil ridiculous, Ben said he was taking the baby upstairs with him. It was time for bed.

"And if they haven't called by now," he said from the doorway, "they aren't going to call at all tonight. You're standing there like some criminal waiting for the police to burst in. But Maggie? You didn't do anything wrong."

Alone in the kitchen, Maggie drank two glasses of wine, which quickly went to her head. She realized she had not eaten a real meal all day. With her hands over her ears, she rested her forehead on the table. Somewhere, she imagined, Dale was wandering and a little lost.

Twenty years earlier, a woman named Mrs. Lewellen had lost her son in the men's department of Filene's while she was having a sweater gift-wrapped for her father-in-law. Just turned around, she said, and he was gone. The next morning the boy, whose second birthday was the following week, was found in the service corridor near the elevator, wedged between two giant canvas containers of hangers. He was alive but terrified, with a broken ankle and a foot that hung at a queer angle to his leg.

Mr. Lewellen had come to the house the night his boy had been found to talk to Gordon. Maggie could not stop staring at his red-rimmed eyes and the dough under his fingernails. He and his wife owned the neighborhood bakery. He wanted to sue the department store and wondered if Gordon could help, since Gordon was the only lawyer he liked. Gordon always talked with the man while the rye was being sliced, or while Dale's birthday cake was being festooned with roses. He asked about business and neighborhood news, and now, ever tactful, with a hand on Lewellen's shoulder, he said that he wasn't the right person, but he could offer some names.

Maggie had dug her fingernails into the couch where she sat next to her husband, and fought hard not to say what she thought, that it was Mrs. Lewellen who was the problem, and not the store. How can you let a baby out of your sight?

"Don't be so judgmental," Gordon had warned Maggie after Lewellen had gone. "This sort of thing could happen to anyone. It doesn't mean she's a bad mother."

"No, Gordon," she'd said. "That's exactly what it means."

She'd been harsh and unforgiving then, a collector of damning evidence. Now, years later, Dale had let Lily out of her sight, too. Wasn't that still evidence enough?

When Maggie lifted her head again, the room was dark, her only explanation that the overhead light had blown, and not that she'd fallen asleep. A sheet of light slipped out from the open refrigerator. She jumped when the phone rang.

The sound of the ocean tumbled in her ear. "It's me," Dale said. "I should have called earlier. I know, I know, I know."

Maggie heard rushing water behind her daughter, a bathtub, a dishwasher, the beach. "Where are you?"

Dale hesitated. "You'll watch Lily tonight?"

"It's a little late to ask me that, isn't it? Tell me where you are, what happened."

"I'm with Doris," she said. Maybe Doris was holding Dale right then, sympathetic and certainly more understanding. "What you said this morning, about me not being a mother. You're wrong, you know."

"If I'm wrong, then you'd be *here* now instead of there." Maggie hung up on her.

Ben and Lily were in bed when she went upstairs. The television was on to a basketball game without the sound and their faces glowed in the jumbled light. Lily was asleep, sucking Ben's pinkie. The room was full of unsettling contrasts: Ben's wallet and keys on Maggie's bureau, his shoes resting on the corner of her nightgown, his hand on the baby's cheek.

"That was Dale, I assume," he said, his eyes shifting toward her. "You don't look so good."

"I drank too much." Maggie leaned against the doorway. "She's at your house."

Ben's eyes shifted back to the screen. "What did she say?"

"Not much. I hung up on her."

"And what about Nate?"

"I have no idea. He didn't come up. It was a very short conversation."

"What strikes me as funny," Ben said, looking down at Lily, "is that no one really talks about the father here, no one mentions Nate very much. And isn't he just as involved as Dale is? Men are really on the periphery, I've decided. When it gets to the heart of things, it's always mother and child, never father and child. You work from the inside out, but we have to work from the outside in."

His boys hadn't talked to him since he'd told them he was moving in with Maggie. One day, on an afternoon he knew Aaron had a routine doctor's appointment, Ben had sat in his car in the parking lot, waiting for his son to come out. When Aaron finally pushed his way through the glass doors, squinting at the menacing sun, Doris was only a step behind, and Ben did nothing.

"Come on, lie down with us," he urged now. "You can't stay there all night."

She shook her head and locked her fingers around the door frame, as much to prevent the room from spinning as to resist his pull on her. It was hard to think when she was close to him. Finally, when she couldn't stand anymore, she sat on the floor. She watched the news come and go on the television, and listened to Ben and Lily snoring together. Later she squeezed onto the bed with them. It was impossibly small for three people, and Maggie knew it was time to rearrange some things in her house, and plan for some kind of permanence.

*   *   *

J U S T before six, Maggie heard a car pull up in front of the house, its motor running, and knew it was the paper being delivered. Outside it was just turning light, and from the bed Maggie saw a plastic shopping bag on a tree branch across the street, billowing and caught like an escaped balloon. She heard a door close, someone running up her driveway, the kitchen door being unlocked and then banging against the chain — which she never put on, but Ben did. She heard swearing, and pounding on the glass.

Maggie went downstairs. When she turned into the hall she saw Dale reach in and fumble to undo the chain, and she thought, this is how fathers end up shooting their children who sneak in, burglar-like, past midnight. This is how people end up getting killed in their own home.

"You can't undo it from there," Maggie said. Her eyes met Dale's, which were red-rimmed and alarming through the inch of open door. "That's kind of the idea."

"Please let me in."

When Maggie unhooked the chain, Dale didn't so much walk into the house as stumble. Her body seemed disconnected in her down coat as she wrapped her arms across her chest. Maggie wondered if her daughter were hurt, the way she bent over slightly from the waist and hid her face, if Nate had done something. She recalled Dale's talking about his temper over the years, the way he slammed doors, kicked cushions, swore at other drivers as he cut them off.

Dale inhaled shakily. "Can you get Lily for me? I want to go home."

"Sit down. Tell me what's going on, where you went. I think you can do that much after what happened yesterday."

"Nothing *happened*." Dale's voice rose and she stared at the ceiling, as though tracking Ben's tentative pacing above. The skin on her neck looked thin and vulnerable. "Can we do this later? I just want to go home now."

"That's not good enough. You have to talk to me!" Maggie grabbed Dale hard by the arm, but her daughter shook her off.

"I can't. Will you get the baby?"

Maggie watched the crystals of snow on Dale's jacket wink once more before they melted in the heat of the room and darkened the nylon. There is a time, she knew, when your child's pain is your own and you step up and take it all from her. But there are times when your child's distress looks like the sheerest, most dangerous drop-off, and you finally have to take a step back.

"No, Dale, you can't have Lily now. You're in no shape to take her."

Her daughter whimpered, a fluttering of disbelief and misery in one breath. For Maggie, everything she had done in the last day seemed only what she had to do because there were no other options — pick up Lily when she fell because Dale wouldn't, feed Lily because she was hungry, take her home because Dale wasn't around. Now it was not a matter of making up for her daughter's mistakes anymore. Keeping Lily was something with its own direction and reason, and it instantly felt like the only real decision she'd ever made in her life.

"You disappear with no explanation, and now you're either hysterical or catatonic, or both. Look at the way your hands are shaking. There's no way you can take her, no way I'd let her go with you now."

Dale turned and left the house. Through the window, Maggie watched her daughter's unsure footing on the icy driveway. When she slipped, Dale tried to right herself at first, but then gave up, and allowed her body to fall forward, hands and knees smacking hard. Maggie held her breath, and felt a wave of humiliation for them both. For a moment Dale didn't move or look back at the house. Finally she stood up and made her way to her car. In the early morning, the sound of the engine and smashing ice splintered the quiet of the street.

13

IN all the years she'd been working in Ben's lab, it had never struck Maggie before just how much the place was set up like a series of animal stalls. She stood in the door without moving and pulled at her sweater, too hot already, salmon-colored and overly bright, which she had chosen to counteract her gray mood.

Until today, when Ben finally insisted she get out after almost a week, Maggie had stayed in the house with the baby while he went to the lab. She was tired of wondering when she might hear from Dale and Nate, and about what they would offer as explanation. She was jumpy from imagining what they might do — enlist the police, a lawyer, Gordon, the papers, Virginia, Doris, and anyone else who wanted in. At night, she swore to Ben that she heard the sounds of shifting feet in the next room, forces gathering to attack, but he said it was just the wind whipping across the windows.

Maggie had no plan for what she would do beyond the next minute when Lily would need to be fed, walked, changed, held.

The hours passed, broken only by the incidental change from light to dark, and the baby's sudden careening from sleep to alertness. Maggie had always thought an infant's mind was full of silvery shifts, like a school of minnows changing directions a hundred times a minute, but now she wondered what preternatural understanding made Lily look so intently at her. In her enormous and shapeless regret and longing for Dale, Maggie knew she was falling in love with Lily. She was grateful for the passionate life that was lived in the space between herself and this baby.

Now she watched the lab techs and postdocs working and heard the familiar, repetitive movements of measuring, scribbling, scratching, swiveling on a stool, blue-jeaned leg rubbing against blue-jeaned leg. Again she thought of penned animals, this time at Slater Park Zoo, a foul-smelling place she'd taken Dale to on many afternoons. Once, a monkey had reached his wrinkled black hand through the bars of his cage and ripped off five-year-old Dale's blue plastic barrette, the one shaped like a propeller. The monkey was fascinated by the strands of hair he'd yanked out with it, played with them like taffy and stomped in his own turds while Dale howled with laughter. Not long after, the zoo was closed down, and a few of the animals, the ones still healthy enough, were "re-zooed" to Cincinnati. How many of the lab workers, herself included, could be "re-zooed" if this place were to shut down tomorrow? Ben's lack of urgency about it was mystifying.

A burning stench, like scorched eggs and bad cigars, jolted Maggie back to attention. It was the smell of inactive people, closed windows, flat soda, and something corrosive spilled on the floor. A year earlier, Maggie knew, she would have jumped to the smell, tracked it down, cleaned it up, filled out the requisite forms to submit in triplicate. Now she put the neck of her sweater up to her nose and breathed through it. She turned away from the lab, crossed the hallway, and unlocked her office door.

Someone had made an attempt to keep order in the room after so many weeks, so that the stacks of paper and mail were at least well-balanced. Maggie didn't have to worry about things falling, but the organization wiped out any sense of necessity she might have had about starting in. There was no way to figure out the importance or priority of things. The menu from the Chinese restaurant down the street, a folder of requisition forms from the accounting office, grant paperwork, and a catalogue from Bloomingdale's were just the first things she picked up and then put down again. It was all garbage anyway, and she was tempted to drag her arm through the stuff and sweep it into several large wastebaskets. It would be a way to start over, and who would ever know what was lost? Had she only imagined her role here was important, essential even? It was possible that Ben benevolently, selfishly too, hadn't let her know otherwise. He'd simply wanted her there.

A newspaper clipping had been left on her chair, and she knew immediately that it was an obituary. Its long narrowness and gentle fold was to her, unmistakably, the shape of death, and for a minute she wouldn't touch it. Since the beginning of the eye study, Maggie had cut out the obituaries of the participants and filed them in a folder marked "Dead." It had been a solitary, senti-mental business of her own.

Now she studied Forrest Corey's picture. It had been taken when he was in his fifties, but his eyes had always been the same, she noted with a surge of sadness, misty, milky, curious, frozen somewhere in childhood visions. He had died the day after Lily was born, and was buried in Mt. Auburn Cemetery across the river. She didn't cry until she stood by the window and looked at the startlingly beautiful day, bright, sharp, mistless.

"There was a rumor you were here," Shelby said, and walked into the room. "You crying?"

Maggie ineptly wiped the sleeve of her fuzzy sweater across her eyes, spreading the tears. Her muscles had a fluttery, useless feel to them. "Yes. No. Maybe."

"Are you sure about that, Grandma?"

"Grandma." She shook her head. "Is that really me? You should see her, Shelby. She's extraordinary."

Shelby nodded. She wore what looked like the blue zip-up uniform of a gas station attendant, this one somehow altered to hourglass at the waist. The name Nils was stitched in red over one breast pocket. "I'd kind of given up hope we'd ever see you here again." Shelby ran a fingernail up and down her jumpsuit zipper. "Ben asked me to keep *some* order in this room. I don't know that I did such a hot job at it."

"You're probably too young to remember, but there used to be a television commercial," Maggie said, and rested her hands on the stacks of paper in front of her, "for sponges, or dish liquid, I can't remember which, that showed a very happy woman at the sink, and behind her was stacked every plate, glass, pot, and piece of silverware she'd washed in a year, which reached from floor to ceiling. It was like some nightmare of a forest with towering trees of dessert plates and coffee cups, appalling but fascinating at the same time. That's kind of how all of this makes me feel."

Shelby nodded. "Like finding out how many pounds of sugar you eat a year, or hot dogs, or how much money you'll end up spending on tampons during your lifetime."

"Some things probably shouldn't be added up."

"So, does the fact that you're here actually mean you're back?" Shelby asked when she was finally finished relating every conflict, crisis, and piece of news that had happened in the lab since Maggie had been out. "Too many men is the bottom line. We need a girl around here."

"You're one, aren't you?"

"But *you* actually know what's going on," Shelby insisted. "It might be Ben's lab, but you run the place. Everyone knows that — and if they didn't before, they really do now. The place is a mess."

Shelby's stories had the dull pull of nostalgia. The girl *lived* the place, the work, her ambition; the outside world was only incidental. I was like her once, Maggie thought, but that was another time, and I can hardly remember it now. She examined all that was completely familiar, the chipped mug that held her pens, the metal pull on the filing cabinet, even the way her knees banged up against the desk drawer that had never sat flush on its runners.

The lab was an unreal place. It demanded and received such unreasonable devotion — and she'd given it. You were either in or out, there was no middling here, like motherhood. Still, she knew something so strong and single-minded couldn't just evaporate. It always reemerged in another form.

"Everyone already knows you're doing the boss, if that's what you're worried about," Shelby said, and rolled her eyes.

"Doing the boss and the boss is doing me." Maggie laughed. "It's more complicated than that, actually. The baby's living with me now. "

"What, is Dale sick or something?"

Maggie shook her head. "No, she's okay. And it might be for a while. I just can't say right now."

Shelby pulled her zipper up to just under her chin. "I guess I don't understand what you're saying, then. I mean, your daughter didn't give her to you, and you didn't just kidnap her."

It sounded too much like a plea from Shelby. The girl wanted to know that there were some rules out there if and when she entered the real world, but Maggie wouldn't reassure her. In any case, she didn't think she could. Whatever explanation she delivered in this tiny office would not cut to the heart of the problem.

Shelby squinted, her head at a cautious angle. "So what did Dale do?"

Maggie didn't say anything, and when Shelby left the room, a pile of papers slid off the desk, the gentle slap of a thousand pieces falling to the floor. Maggie didn't want to be there anymore, and it wasn't just a matter of that day, she knew, or the day after. It wasn't just a matter of making her way through the crap on her desk, or reorienting herself, or allowing herself the time to care about it again. She couldn't imagine ever wanting to stay.

AN hour later, Maggie couldn't get in through her back door. She couldn't get in through the front door either. She glared accusingly at her key, tried the back again, and finally realized that the dead bolts were turned from the inside. A week before he announced he was moving out, Gordon had — guiltily, she realized after the fact — installed the locks himself. She remembered how he'd worn his special tool belt, how he'd neatly arranged his screwdrivers and drill bits like dentist's implements on a cloth. It killed him when she tried to tighten a loose screw with a kitchen knife. In all the time she'd been alone and was supposed to have used the dead bolts in place of a man, she never once had.

Now she pounded the door with her fists, kicked at the wood, considered smashing the window with her elbow. She could see no movement inside, and thought of the man who comes home from work to find his house cleared out, his wife and children, his television and dog gone. She thought of the couple who drive to their beach house the day after a hurricane only to find it has been swept away. Would they look for it floating on the ocean or would they simply imagine they had come to the wrong place? She pounded again.

"Whoa," Ben yelled as he ran into the kitchen and undid the lock. "Take it easy. What's the problem? Ever heard of the doorbell?"

"My house. I can't even get into my own house," Maggie said, struggling to catch her breath. "What is this, Waco? What's going on?"

"All I did was lock the door." Ben turned the dead bolt again when she'd stepped in. "I didn't expect you back so soon, anyway. Didn't you say after lunch?" His exactitude was unusual, his voice unsympathetic. One hand massaged his chest through his damp T-shirt. His running pants clung to his thighs.

Maggie waved him away and opened the refrigerator. "That's what I said, but I'm allowed to change my mind without consulting you. This is my house, after all." She reached for a pot, lifted the lid and smelled yesterday's pea soup. She took a wooden spoon from the jar on the counter and began to eat it cold.

Ben watched the spoon rise, his mouth mimicking hers. "Don't you want to heat that up?"

Maggie shook her head. Tiny splinters from the spoon pricked her lips and she couldn't taste anything but the cold. It was like drinking liquid metal, she decided; she'd be better off having a glass of water, probably. Her locked-out panic was not ebbing as quickly as she would have liked. "Where's the baby?"

Lily was asleep in a three-wheeled triangular carriage parked in the hall — a baby jogger, Ben informed her, bought that morning. They had just tried it out, in fact. The treads of the thick black tires were peppered with sand and tiny pebbles. A fan of mud drops crept up the purple canvas back. Maggie couldn't resist pushing the carriage a few inches forward to feel the smoothness of the ride, but Ben grabbed her shoulder and pulled her back abruptly.

"What's with you?" she asked. "You had the doors locked, and the curtains closed. You're acting really strange."

"I just don't want you to wake her, that's all," Ben said, and started up the stairs. "You should just let me know what your plans are. So, if you're here — you're here now?— I'll go in to work. Someone should." She heard him stop to catch his breath at the landing.

Soon Maggie heard the shower running, and she went into the bathroom. Ben's hands were resting on the top of his head and his eyes were shut. He wasn't exactly humming, but making a noise that was something closer to a tuneless vibration. A steady stream of water arced off his penis, and if he knew Maggie was in the room with him, he didn't show it.

She remembered a day when she first started working in his lab, and how he'd stood with his back to the enormous window as he lectured exuberantly about procedures and protocols. It was June then, a record month of breathtaking, thrilling storms, and when gray wings of newspaper suddenly began to swirl and make whispery sounds against the glass behind him, Ben didn't notice. Maggie elbowed the person next to her and whispered that if a sudden eclipse occurred right then, Ben probably wouldn't notice that either. She'd wanted something to happen then — a crash, a fire, a naked woman running through the room — just to see what, if anything, would distract this man.

In a few weeks, Maggie had decided that he wasn't distractible. His work and ambition were the same thing, so she couldn't play one off the other. Back then, nothing pulled him away, while she already felt the nibbling of diversion, of attachments and choices. And when she first slept with him midsummer, it was not without a selfish satisfaction of conquest that she had finally made him veer, made him look away from his career for a moment, too. But Ben never thought he'd lost sight of things, even when he was making love to her. There would be days when she'd be lost in some doubting, swirling storm herself, just like those newspapers on the humid air, and he wouldn't understand that about her.

"You're going to think I'm losing my mind," Ben said suddenly, his eyes still shut in the shower.

"That's always a possibility. Take a chance."

"Nate was following me."

Maggie leaned out into the hall to listen to the quiet of the baby still asleep. "What are you talking about?"

Ben parted the curtain, and water dripped off his chin onto her feet. "Well, he was here first this morning, but I didn't want to answer the door. I think he saw me through the glass anyway.

"Later, Lily and I drove down to Marathon Sports where I'd seen those joggers in the window. We did our thing there, packed up the jogger, and came home."

"And you saw Nate in the store? That doesn't exactly qualify as following."

Ben stepped out of the shower and Maggie handed him a towel. He rubbed his face and then patted the rest of his body dry. His chest looked overinflated and scalded from the hot water. "I just had a feeling I can't explain precisely. It was like being watched, that's all."

"So you didn't actually see him." She spoke slowly.

"You're making me sound like a crazy person, Maggie. Just listen for a minute. I put the jogger together and got Lily all bundled up, and we went for a run. Not too much of one, because I wasn't sure about the thing and didn't want a wheel to fall off. Anyway, we went by that day-care center over on Valentine Street, and then around the park at the library where they're doing some construction, and then we started back. And that's when I turned around — before, I just told myself I was being paranoid and I really should control myself, I was getting to be like you, for chrissake — and there was a car, a banged-up Toyota or Mazda, something like that, hanging back."

"A Nissan."

"Yeah, maybe a Nissan. A Japanese something."

"But it really could have been anyone."

"Yes, it *could* have been anyone," he said condescendingly, "but this particular anyone followed me up Commonwealth. And when the car didn't come down this street, I thought, fine, it's nothing, but then it comes creeping around from the other end. So that's when I fell," he said, out of breath again, as though he were still running, and glanced down at his leg, which was red and scraped, the color showing beneath the dark of his hair. "I banged my shin on the back step when I was trying to unlock the door and maneuver the carriage inside. I'm lucky I didn't shit myself, too. It was Nate. He had that idiotic baseball cap on. What an asshole."

"Maybe we should call the police."

"And say what? That the guy whose baby we have — stolen? kidnapped? pick your felonious term — was driving in a menacing fashion? Shit, it's not against the law to ride around and look at people." Ben's tone had turned suddenly accusatory, as though he'd thrown all his ugly fear onto Maggie in the telling of the story. It was reflexive, she knew, but gutless of him. "It's not against the law to look at your own child," he added.

"You could have talked to him," she said.

"Why, so he could ask for Lily back? And then what?"

Maggie went into her bedroom. The place smelled of wet books and dust. Distantly, she heard Lily crying downstairs and Ben quieting her. From the window she could see the entire length of the street, and across the way, where the Riesens' three-year-old grandson in a snowsuit played with a fat cat on the front steps. Maggie saw her single lost glove in a patch of lawn, hidden in brown winter grass, undetectable from below but bright and forlorn from this high vantage. A car idled one house down, a Nissan with dull matte paint and rusty lesions. It was waiting for her neighbor's arthritic mother-in-law to come out of the house, waiting to take her for a checkup at the rheumatologist's. It was the water meter guy, eating his lunch off a piece of white waxed paper on his lap and listening to the radio.

But of course it was neither of those, and the car inched toward her house and finally stopped in front of it. Was Ben looking out the window too, Lily pressed to his chest? Was he slowly sneaking into the basement, hoping to find a baseball bat or metal pipe? She didn't think she had ever heard such a heavy silence in the house.

Nate got out of the car. There was nothing furtive about the way he swung his legs out or shut the door, nothing hesitant, threatening, or uneven about the way he walked up the stairs and rang the bell. For a moment Maggie considered going down to him, but something stopped her when he backed off the stairs, looked up, and their eyes met.

Standing at the closed window and peering at her son-in-law below, she recalled that sudden, unsettling sense she'd had when she'd looked at him lying in bed after he'd come home from the hospital. I don't really know you, she'd thought to herself then, I don't know what you're capable of, or how you think things through. But now she saw that he was someone, like Dale, who was set on what he wanted. Dale might be cautious and single-minded, but Nate was also reckless. He would demand Lily back; he'd grab her if he had to.

"Open up!" Nate yelled. Maggie shook her head, and for a minute he stood looking up at her, hands on hips and the collar of his sweatshirt mimicking the disbelieving droop of his open mouth. Again he went up the front steps, rang the bell, and banged the knocker, an ineffectual piece of brass-coated junk in the shape of an eagle. "Open the fucking door," he said.

There was a rustling as Nate hacked his way through the mountain laurel bushes that circled too close to the house and ate away at the foundation's mortar. Maggie ran to other rooms, following the sounds of his movements as they wrapped around the house. The back door rattled, and the blue glass disc hung above the kitchen window smacked the pane. Bungee cords that secured the tops of the garbage cans from prying raccoons sprung loose and whipped against the metal. One had snapped on her on a summer night, and now she touched the half-moon scar the red hook had left just below her collar bone. There was a scrape as the cans were dragged across the crumbling patio, and then one of her aluminum lawn chairs crashed against the side of the house, shattering a window. It was the noise of glittering, wet fear, and Maggie's legs weakened under her. The second hit came against the front door.

Maggie stood fully and provocatively in front of the window now and opened it. "Go away, Nate," she said. "Someone's going to call the police. You're out of control."

"Come on. I just want to talk to you," he urged.

"So talk. I can hear you."

"This is crazy. Open up, Mags. I'm not going to do anything." He had softened his tone to a plea, and gave her a pale smile, an offer of his old charm. "I know, I know. I'm sorry about the window."

"I don't want you here. You need to leave now," she said.

"Lily's not your kid," Nate said, suddenly looking old and beaten. "Do you get that part, Maggie?" He dismissed her with a sharp wave and turned to leave.

The cat from across the street was warming itself on the hood of his car, and Nate seemed to consider the animal for a moment. One swift bottled-up punch to the head would send it into the street, brain matter and eyes like pink and gray confetti on the asphalt. But Nate gently moved his arm against the cat to slide it off. The Riesens' grandson, wide-eyed, watched from the steps.

Maggie found Ben on the floor in the corner of the living room. His back was against the wall, and Lily was between his legs, her head resting on his thigh. He was pale and sweating, and squinted as though the light were too harsh.

"Holy shit," he said. "What happened? I thought he was going to kill us. Was that a gun?"

A chair hitting the house, a window shattering, could sound like a shot, a battering ram, a siege to a man holding a baby he needed to protect. But it was over now, she said. Couldn't he get up? Ben shook his head; he was still having trouble catching his breath, and his heart hurt.

She took a step back from this man and this child in her house, an astonishing sight, but what had happened to her life? How had she ever let it get to this crazy point?

WHEN she didn't find Dale at work or at home, it was easy enough to find her at Doris's. Maggie had only to go through the back gate and stand in the yard to see her daughter in the kitchen playing Life with Tina. Through the glass door she could hear the click of the spinner and the sharp tap of the pieces moving across the board. The remains of lunch, one sandwich half eaten, the other untouched, sat on the counter.

"Fifty thousand big ones." Dale sighed with dark, exaggerated misfortune. She looked sleepy and oddly self-possessed, but Maggie knew it was easy to confuse calm with grief.

Tina laughed, swung her bare feet under the table, and held out her hand. "Pay up."

Maggie glanced toward Milt's house; he had moved his indoor plants outside in the middle of winter and their leaves were oily black and gnarled. She knocked on the glass, and Tina jumped up to slide open the door. The girl gave Maggie a quick, exaggerated hug around her waist and then bounced back onto her chair. Tina's sullenness was gone; she radiated contentment and Doris's winning-formula touch.

"Go," she instructed Dale, intent on the game. "Your turn. Hurry up, I'm waiting."

Dale looked at her mother and then beyond, her face unreadable. "You're killing me here, you know," she told Tina. "I have no money left. I'm totally wiped out."

"Go anyway. I want to wipe you out some more."

"Pretend you're me for a couple of turns," Dale suggested as she got stiffly up from the table. "You move my piece and I'll be right back."

"I'll probably cheat," Tina warned. "I'll try not to, but I might anyway."

"I'll know if you do."

Dale gestured for Maggie to follow her out of the room, and she sat down on the stairs, her toes curled over the edge of the riser. Maggie was startled to be back in this house, and startled to see that nothing had changed.

"Doris is out teaching so I'm baby-sitting this afternoon," Dale said. "Pretty funny under the circumstances, don't you think?"

"Hilarious," Maggie said.

"Where's the baby?"

"She's at home, with Ben."

"I hope you trust him." Dale restlessly straightened her legs out in front of her. A powdery pink shaded her eyelids and the skin around her nose; she looked barely on the up side of recuperation. "I could take Lily back anytime I wanted, just so you know. I have every right and recourse. I am her mother."

Maggie heard Gordon's icy words on Dale's tongue. "Right and recourse. That makes you a mother? I don't think so."

Tina called for Dale to hurry up. "I'll be there in a minute," Dale yelled back. "Did you come here to tell me that? You could have called."

"Nate did something crazy," Maggie began. "He followed Ben this morning and then he came to the house. I want you to tell him that he can't —"

"I don't tell Nate what to do." Dale looked down at her hands. "Did you know he's going to lose his job, be fired or end up in jail at the very least? He thought it was time to tell me he'd fucked one of his students." Her words stumbled over one another, as though there were too many in her mouth to hold. "Some girl — one I've actually met, too. He said it was only three times, which I guess I'm supposed to think is better than fucking her four times, and much better than fucking her five times."

"I'm sorry," Maggie said. She felt something burn behind her eyes.

"The night I left Lily with you? I was with Nate. He drove me all the way to Provincetown and back just to tell me he'd screwed this girl three times. He said it didn't mean anything, so I wanted to know if he'd only figured that out on the third fuck."

"Dale —"

"No, listen. Seven hours, and we didn't even get out of the car. The morning after, he shows up here saying that I have to take Lily from you because she's his baby, too — our baby. But he was scaring me — he had this look, square-eyed and red, and his jaw locked forward like he was ready to bite — and I thought, I can't give the baby to him, and I can't take her either right now. So in your kitchen, when I left without Lily that morning, when I left her with you the night before? I *let* you keep her, it was my decision, because I thought that was the best thing." She nodded and ran her hands up and down her thighs. "It was the safest thing."

"But you weren't in any shape to take her, Dale," Maggie insisted. "And you haven't been in a long time — not just that morning, and not because of what Nate told you. God, you wanted this baby so much! I knew someone was going to get hurt soon, something bad was going to happen, and I couldn't let it. I still can't."

"Maybe things haven't been perfect with me and Nate for a while. Probably some part of me knew something was going on the whole time." Dale's voice began to rise. "But I was thinking of the baby, too."

In the kitchen, Tina smacked her game piece down on the board, making the others jump and fall to the floor. Dale shook with humiliation on the stairs, and tears collected on the rise of her cheekbones. Once, Maggie had looked at her four-year-old daughter who was possessed with misery, as she was now, and was terrified by the way her whole, tiny body vibrated with it. Her own distress at that moment had been like a metal ball shot right between her eyes, and she'd shut herself in her bedroom, leaving Dale screaming on the other side of the door. Maggie hated this daily campaign of wills that motherhood seemed to require, and she thought then how easy it would be to walk away. Dale would have her father, in any case, who was much more measured and patient. So she'd pulled her clothes off hangers and out of drawers until she realized that Dale was quiet, how even through a closed door her daughter had recognized the unmistakable sounds of escape. Maggie had held her damp, stunned child and hoped Dale wouldn't remember what she'd heard. Now Maggie moved toward Dale on the stairs to hold her again, but her daughter shot up, done with weeping.

"If you knew something was wrong, why didn't you tell me?" Maggie asked. "All this time, everything's been so hard."

"If *you* knew, why didn't you tell *me?*" Dale shot back angrily. "Don't look so surprised. Nate told me that you've known about him and that girl the whole time."

Maggie was light-headed, and had to grab on to the banister. In the other room, she saw Tina tilting back far in the chair, two legs balanced on their narrow points, her fingertips resting on the edge of the table. Her face was a scowl of impatience.

"Should I have told you, Dale?" Maggie asked. "What would you have done then? I thought it would all go away when Lily was born and you would never have to know. I thought it was the best thing to do."

"The best thing? For who?" Dale rose from the stairs. "For you? Wasn't it just more proof to you that I can't handle things, not marriage and not being a mother? More proof that you should keep Lily, that I am exactly as you see me, exactly as you think you know me?"

Dale went into the other room, where Tina had overturned the board. Maggie watched as the girl posed defiantly and then swiftly kicked a game piece across the floor.

14

MAGGIE didn't think she'd ever seen Ben so distracted. He mumbled as he changed into blue jeans and a white shirt, and when he went to the mirror he stood like a dazed commuter waiting for the subway doors to open. If he noticed Maggie next to him, naked and still damp from her shower, he didn't show it, and when she moved her arms around him and slipped her fingers down the front of his pants he seemed surprised, and then disappointed, to find them there. He pulled her hand out and patted it.

"The chicken," he whispered, and went downstairs.

Maggie told herself that birthdays made everyone strange, and more so the older you got. Doris had always pretended hers wasn't happening, and when Maggie gave her a present, or Ben invited people over to celebrate, she went along with the plan, but not without a startled, slightly irritated look. She overflowed glasses when she poured, she drank too much herself. On her own birthday, a month before Lily was born, Maggie had eaten nothing but candy until her mouth erupted in tiny sores and she'd been forced to gargle with hot water for hours.

That morning, Maggie had given Ben a bathrobe with a bad macho design of triangles and slashes slapped against a filter of dull brown haze. The robe, he commented, was just like one his father had worn when he'd been hospitalized with a raging episode of eczema. It was another of his odd memories, raw and unreadable. Ben had kissed her on the mouth to say thank you, but his breath was dull, like air caught in an empty room. He had a lot of things to do before Aaron came for dinner, he explained, even at that early hour, with stickiness in the corners of his eyes, and he put the robe on the unmade bed, where it still lay like a lazy guest.

Maggie had been braver with Ben when they weren't together, and wondered how it was that familiarity had made her so cautious. One year, she'd given him a gift certificate for a massage at an institute named after an herb. Later, Ben told her how funny it was to be naked in front of a woman he didn't know, how he'd had an erection he hid behind a towel. Now she might as well have given him a shroud; he thought never having worn a robe was evidence of eternal youth.

It was almost five and Maggie was still not dressed, and after almost three weeks with the baby in the house, she knew this was just the sort of moment — rushed but impossible to rush through — Lily could pick up on, even in her sleep. A baby could hurry or slow you through anything. If she'd ever had the time — glorious leisure — to eat *and* read the paper, now she ate what and when she could, one hand to her mouth, the other on Lily. In the past, she might have considered one or a thousand things as she took a bath or a walk or talked with a friend. She might have sighed at the chaos in her drawers, the burned-out bulb, the unpaid bills, but always with a vague, placating plan to get to it soon. Now she looked at all that was undone as inevitable and unfixable. There were days, too, when Maggie and Ben barely talked to each other; the baby was always between them. Their desire for each other was deep enough, but buried somewhere under their delight in Lily. At night they lay jammed together, their hands frozen with good intentions in mid-touch, talk of the baby still on their lips.

The day after Maggie had found her daughter at Doris's, and minutes after Ben had left for the lab, Dale had appeared. Maggie had just hauled the carriage out the back door and onto the sidewalk when she looked up and saw her daughter walking toward her with a slow, contained stride. She had a moment of panic, under siege again, and thought about turning around and going back inside, locking the doors. It is a terrible thing to be scared of your own child, she thought, and tightened her grip on the carriage handle.

Dale was wearing a coat Maggie recognized as Doris's, and one of Nate's baseball caps. The outfit was an odd and overt touch; she wore her allies. A few feet away, Dale glanced at the white January sky and then at her feet. She is trying to decide who she'll look at first, me or the baby, Maggie thought.

"You're going out?" Dale asked, gazing just over her mother's shoulder. "Can I walk with you?"

"That would be nice."

Dale's hand rested on the carriage, brushing Maggie's, while her eyes swept over the sleeping baby. Navigating the thin and buckled winter sidewalk was as awkward and cautious as their conversation. Dale asked about Lily, and she talked about Tina, whose mother wanted her home all of a sudden, and about a burst pipe in Doris's basement.

They had reached the tiny pond in front of the public library by then, the place to turn around and head back. Maggie wondered out loud about the party in the middle of winter that had left the pond's frozen surface studded with empty beer cans; Dale said it annoyed her to see the place ruined like that. She took off Nate's baseball cap, so that the glare off the building's arched window caught in her hair as she squatted by the edge of the pond to collect the garbage. A line of children slid across the icy parking lot and into the library.

Maggie saw in her daughter's careful attendance to things, to her mother, to this toxic pond with its cans and thin ice, the strain of composure. If Dale had been undone a day earlier, she was resolved now to control the hour and herself. Maggie was relieved to see and touch her daughter — the effects of proximity were undeniable. But she also knew that their mistrust of each other, which must always have been there, had finally been laid bare. They might try to work around it, but the baby blocked their way now, and it was unclear what they would do next.

But on the following morning, and the ones after that, Maggie let Dale into the house after Ben had left for the lab. Again, they didn't talk about Nate, or what would happen next with Lily, and Maggie thought, For the moment, maybe this is enough. When she told Ben it was, his face soured. Once, when Dale was unable to calm Lily, who had erupted in wails of unhappiness, she simply handed the baby to her mother. Maggie lay Lily across her lap and stroked the smooth dip between her shoulders in slow, widening circles and then back again, reversed. For every baby, and every man, Maggie knew, there was one touch that always lulled. It was just a matter of careful discovery. Later she thought about how her impulse had been to turn from Dale, how she'd been so stingy when she hid this secret from her.

Lily, in her crib, began to cry when something broke on the kitchen floor. Ben banged around cleaning it up. It could be the pan of potatoes he'd sliced so thin Maggie thought she might go crazy watching him, or the bowl of salad with its compulsively culled pieces of lettuce, or anything else he'd sifted his anxiety over during the day. He had been in a frenzy of detail for hours, and she'd left him alone, but now she felt the day's tension tighten around her like a knot. After weeks of Aaron's refusing to talk to his father at all, his appearance was being treated like a magnificent visitation now. Maggie imagined the way he would scrutinize her with his father's intense precision and his mother's acuity. Would he admit that he'd always doubted her and the sneaky look in her eye?

Maggie wondered what a woman was supposed to wear when her lover's son came to dinner. She could hear Virginia scolding,

In that silk blouse, without a brassiere, your nipples poke out, and how good an idea is that? And, Contrition is not zipped up with a pair of pants, Margaret. The boy's not going to love you no matter what you do.

The week before, instead of calling, Virginia had sent a picture of herself and Ricky in their matching fish-motif cover-ups by the pool in Florida. Ricky was a little too red, Maggie thought, his bald head a little too spotted with freckles. They had on matching rubber flip-flops with a single rubber flower impaled onto the Y between the toes. It was out of character for Virginia to have sent a picture at all, and on the back she'd written "Greetings from poolside." From the exaggerated slope of her mother's writing, Maggie had wondered what she'd *really* meant to say.

Lily was still crying, Ben was downstairs, calling over and over, and a headache had crept under Maggie's temples. She put on a shirt, but tore it when her fingers struggled to slip the buttons into buttonholes that seemed much too small. From the hall she saw Ben at the bottom of the stairs twisting his hands in a dish towel.

"If you don't stop calling me," she said flatly, "I'm going to lose my mind."

"What are you doing up there? I hear Lily crying. Aren't you going to get her?"

"In a minute. I'm wondering why you didn't just meet Aaron at a restaurant instead of here. In my house — it's not right."

Ben sighed. "Okay, Mags, but we've had this conversation a thousand times already. It's too late now anyway." He hesitated. "This is where I live now, and I don't want to hide you."

"Maybe I want to be hidden."

"I don't know, maybe you do." The lights of a passing car swept quickly across Ben's exasperation. "Are you planning on wearing something on the bottom half?"

Maggie glanced down at the white of her underwear peeking out from the bottom of the torn shirt, at her legs, silvery with winter skin. "Last time I looked, you were still married," she said. "What about that?"

"What about it? Last time I looked, you didn't like marriage."

"It's not that I don't like it. I just don't understand it."

Ben squeezed his eyes shut and shifted from foot to foot. "This is killing my neck, looking up at you. Would you please come down?"

"What do you think is going to happen tonight? Do you think Aaron is going to approve of what you've done? You just cook him up a nice chicken, pour us all some wine, and he'll understand?"

"I'm not asking for his approval. I don't need him to tell me what's right or wrong." Ben looked over his shoulder into the kitchen and then turned back to her. "You and me and Lily — isn't it what you want too?"

Ben was twisted in frustration. The afternoon before, she'd been in the kitchen with Dale. They'd been laughing about something when Ben pulled into the driveway and saw them. He couldn't stand it, backed the car up, and left. If Dale had noticed, she didn't say anything, and when Ben came back hours later he smelled of beer and impatience and worry, of a man who wants to go home but has to wait.

"Wanting Lily doesn't make me her mother," she said. "Or us her parents."

"No, but acting like it does."

Maggie went into the bedroom, and shut the door against Lily's crying. In many ways, she longed for her old life back, her strange, creaking privacy, her solitary pacts with herself, her imagined romances. She and Dale would eat breakfast together again, picking off each other's plates, picking at each other. She would still wonder about Dale's closeness to her and sometimes pull back from it. She would still wonder at her daughter's neediness and how she was the cause of it, how she hadn't been a great mother. She would smell Dale's skin as her daughter reached over to fix her scarf, and recall the scent during her day at work. Her daughter would have a baby someday, and Maggie would wait and hope then, as she always had, for Dale's confidence and contentment to grow roots around the child. But Lily existed now; there was no time for waiting or hoping or working things out. There was only Maggie's fierce attachment and her certainty that this baby should be entirely loved and always wanted.

She finally got dressed, picked up the baby, and went down-stairs. Already, she heard Ben straining to be funny and loose. Aaron was noncommittal, his thin body posed against the counter. Faded constellations on his skin, a bad reaction to a med-ication, made him look as though he'd been spattered with some-thing. His face showed that the years of perfect, blemish-free youth were long gone.

"There you are," Ben said, when he saw Maggie and the baby.

Aaron levered himself away from the counter with two hands and hiked his pants up. It was an exact gesture of his father's, a sign of self-assertion. "We thought you'd fallen asleep," he said. "Or ditched us, maybe."

There was an awkward bob left and right, and then right and left, as they moved to each other. Ben watched, and let out a thin laugh as Maggie's and Aaron's cheeks fell together in something short of a kiss. Aaron smelled medicinal.

"Let me have her," Aaron said, and slipped the baby away from Maggie. Ben handed him a bottle. "She looks just like Dale. A clone. It's almost creepy."

As Maggie watched him kiss the baby and feed her, her own lips tightened in mimic. "I'll have some wine, thanks," she said too loudly, and pushed toward the cluttered counter to pour herself a glass. Ben cleared his throat twice. Aaron looked up, his tongue sweeping over his front teeth. He abruptly passed Lily back to Maggie, who spilled her wine in the fumble to take the baby.

"So it's his birthday, and he's doing all the cooking," Aaron said, watching her mop the front of her shirt. "Impressive work, Mag-gie. I'd say you have him trained pretty well. And so quickly, too. You must be good at it."

"I'm an expert at training men." Maggie opened the back door to let out the smoke from the oven and Aaron's bitterness.

Ben's laugh was flat and forced. "I *like* to cook, Aaron. You know that. I used to make you dinner all the time. Meatloaf, you liked, and sloppy joes, and scrambled eggs. What else? . . . I think we can eat now."

Ben had set the table in the dining room and placed a bowl of apples and two candles in the center. The way he'd chosen a cloth and carefully folded the napkins, the way he'd baked himself a tilting pink birthday cake, stuck it with candles and put it on a side table, touched Maggie but also made her more heavy-hearted than she thought she could bear. She put Lily in the wind-up swing, sat down, and wondered how she was going to make it through the evening.

Ben served Aaron, his hands shaking. "You should have seen this place earlier. Maggie doesn't throw anything out," he told his son enthusiastically. "There were piles and piles of papers, junk, books. It was amazing. I swear, getting to this table was like unearthing an entire civilization. I was expecting to find fossils at the bottom." He laughed. "Evidence of another life."

Ben's desperate attempt to align with Aaron, who was stone-faced, turned Maggie's stomach. The chicken was slimy in her mouth and she had to force herself to swallow it. She knew another glass of wine wasn't going to help, though it could dull things, and that might be enough. She reached for the bottle and poured, lost in the promising sound of the liquid and her first gulp.

"Go easy with that stuff," Ben said, interrupting his story to pull the glass away from her mouth.

Maggie wanted to spit her mouthful at him. She couldn't stand how he was talking so much about nothing and taking the wine away from her like she was some kind of glassy-eyed dinner drunk. When she poured another glass, he didn't say anything more to her, but turned to ask Aaron a hundred questions. He was unaware of his son's irritation and how he was pushing his food around on his plate. It made her feel sorry for all of them. Ben tried to persuade his son to accept some money, a gift, no strings attached.

"Would you stop? First of all, I don't need any money. And second, it's Mom's money too," Aaron finally said. "You might want to ask her first before you start giving it away."

"I don't need to ask her."

Aaron shook his head. "I think she'd feel differently about that, actually."

Maggie stood up to rewind the baby swing, which had clicked to a stop. The wine rushed to her head and she leaned against the metal frame. Out the window, she saw birds darting across the back yard, yellowed in the light from the house. It made her long to be alone.

"I really hate those swings," Aaron said behind her. "Look at that baby, she's completely narcotized, an addict. She's dopey with it. It's obviously not good stimulation."

"Maybe not," Maggie said, and gave the knob an extra forceful wind for effect. Lily grew heavy-lidded as the swing started again. "But stimulation is overrated."

"Well, in that case, go right ahead."

"So I have your permission now," Maggie challenged. "Because I know you've had so much experience with babies, Aaron. Any more advice for me?"

"Yeah, how about giving Lily back to Dale, for starters. How's that for some novice advice?"

"Come on, stop it, Aaron. Maggie, sit down. Can we just have a nice dinner?" Ben opened his arms to the table. "Anyone want chicken?"

"I guess desperate situations call for desperate measures," Aaron added, and held his plate out to his father, though he hadn't eaten anything. "Oh yeah. Lots more for me."

Ben was pleased, unwilling to hear his son's taunt, and he piled the food on the plate. Maggie's heart beat too fast. She was flushed and felt the rumbling approach of something big.

"There's nothing desperate about any of this," she said to Aaron. She walked behind him and rested her hands on his shoulders. His body tensed under her fingers. His hair had a frailty about it, beautiful, soft, and without a future. It made her heart pinch. "We did what we had to do. Just so you understand that."

"Hey, I'm not saying I don't understand, Maggie. You do what you have to do when it comes to family. That sounds so good.

That's your theory of kinship. I don't really even blame you particularly."

"What are you talking about?" Ben asked irritably. "It's a stupid
baby swing, for godssake. Can we drop it?"

"Because I know what it feels like when you think you're going
to be left all alone very soon," Aaron said. He turned to his father,
who had gone pale, and let his hands fall to his lap. "There's this
picture — right, Dad? — where you're standing absolutely still
while everything around you is going at top speed. So then you
try to grab on to something that passes by you. It's like that
human whip we used to make at the skating rink. It's always a little
too scary to be on the end, but you're desperate to be included
even if it means you're ultimately going to get smashed into the
side. Am I right? So you just grab on?"

Maggie couldn't stand to see the fleck of potato caught in the
corner of Ben's mouth like he was an old man, or the way his eyes
moved back and forth so quickly. He looked lost, and then suddenly deflated, as though he knew it now. "Who are you talking
to?" he asked.

"I was talking to her."

"But you're looking at me," Ben said.

"Yes, because this isn't really about Maggie, although it was an
amazingly shitty thing she did to her best friend. Quite unoriginal, too. Look at it this way, Dad," Aaron went on. "Maggie
wanted someone to do this baby with."

"I'm not even following you anymore," Ben said. "What the hell
are you talking about?"

"Single-parenthood sucks. And really, who wouldn't want a
baby? They're great, and this one's pretty cute. And bang, there
you were, all set and eager to be a dad, and you decided that it was
better to leave Mom before she dumped you. Everything fit
together amazingly well. They say relationships are all about timing, and this one was timed perfectly."

"No, that's not right," Ben protested.

"Which part isn't?" Aaron asked.

Ben's face was alarmingly red, and something caught in his throat. "All of it."

"Stop," Maggie said. "Stop it, Aaron, leave him alone. Are you okay, Ben?"

Ben nodded, and his eyes clouded as he drank the water she handed him.

"But wasn't it like at least once a year you and Mom had 'the talk' about splitting up?" Aaron asked when his father put down the glass. "We always knew, because she'd get kind of weird for a while and you'd make this huge effort to come home from work early and be attentive to her and ask me and Pete if we wanted to play ball or Ping-Pong in the basement. You wouldn't leave us alone — didn't you wonder why we were always at a friend's house? And then you'd both forget about it, and we would too. I guess we didn't take it so seriously after a while."

Ben tapped at the skin below his throat. Sweat darkened his collar and he stared down at his hands on the table.

"Do you remember that time, Maggie, when I showed up here after a party completely shit-faced? I didn't want to go home that night because I thought that was it, my parents were going to split. And then I thought I might as well get laid in the bargain. Dale, the jumper cables of my auspicious sexual career."

A tingling worked its way through Maggie's body. Lily ticked back and forth in the swing like a doped referee. When had she and Ben passed the point when they loved each other's children simply because they loved each other? She was furious at Aaron and couldn't look at him.

"So you know what it's like then?" Ben asked Aaron, suddenly alert again but so desperate to find common ground that he hadn't even heard what his son had been saying. "You understand this feeling of losing that makes you just want to grab on to something?"

"But what were *you* losing? You had it good," Aaron told his father. "There was nothing wrong with the way your life was going, except that you were getting old and maybe bored, and you were getting scared, and what can anyone ever do about that?"

Ben rounded away from the table as he pushed his chair back and stood up. "My life wasn't going so great. I was losing *you*," he said. "I still am."

Aaron paused, his mouth slightly open. "Don't put this on *me*."

"No, *you* don't understand," Ben said, moving around the table. "There's nothing worse for a parent than losing a child. It is the very bottom, the absolute end of things, the end of life. It just stops there, because you never, ever recover. I know you're going to die and I can't stand it." Ben went to Lily, lifted her from the swing, and held her. He kissed her head.

A fresh and bitter understanding — that his father had pronounced him dead and was already holding a new child — passed across Aaron's face.

"Fuck you," he said, and stood up from the table. "I'm still here. I'm not nearly dead."

MAGGIE washed a few plates and dumped the untouched food into the garbage. Aaron had left by the back door, which was still open and let in curls of cool air. As she stood at the sink she had a sudden sense that Aaron was in the yard, waiting — for his father maybe, or the better fortune of a long life — but when she went out to look for him he wasn't there. She clenched her bare feet in the icy grass and wondered what she would have said if she'd found him on the steps or against the tree, hands in his pockets. Aaron had heard and seen something he should not have, and she hated Ben for it.

It was a bright night, with high, silver-etched clouds, and she could see the frozen silhouettes of birds in the trees, and beyond, the simple cutout shapes of her neighborhood. She sat on one of the lawn chairs, which was damp and cracked from the weather, and pulled her feet up under her. When she was still, the birds moved again, someone coughed next door, and there was a slight, salty breeze she hadn't noticed earlier. Behind her were Ben's sobs coming from the house, but they didn't move her.

Doris's complaints about Ben had always seemed so harmless and almost impersonal, what looked like the inevitable nicks acquired in a long, happy marriage. Wasn't it a betrayal that Doris had never once said to Maggie she didn't want to be with Ben, and Ben hadn't said anything either? Maggie had complained often enough about Gordon, but felt no qualms revealing what she now realized should have been private: that he was scared of black men, he sometimes cried when he came, he thought he was unattractive. It was a betrayal of him to have repeated these things to anyone, but she and Gordon were never any kind of reflection or protector of each other the way she thought happily married people were, the way Ben and Doris seemed to be.

Upstairs, Lily was awake in her crib and stared at the doorway as if she'd been waiting for Maggie all evening. Maggie leaned over the rail and tried to erase the tension from the baby's face. She wondered what had scared Lily, what she was thinking. Maggie wondered too, as she began to sing, how many other mothers actually crawled into the crib with their babies like she was, making themselves tiny enough to fit in this small, true place. Lily's face, so close to her own, appeared wise as a daughter's, as though she understood a mother's confusions.

Ben's face in the bedside light was pale but inflamed around the lips and nostrils. His shirt was soaked with sweat around the collar, and his hands were laced over his chest.

"Some happy birthday," Maggie said, and sat down next to him. "Are you all right? Don't do that with your hands, okay? You look like a corpse."

"That's what I feel like. Dead."

"Crying can do that to you. It empties you out."

"I haven't been crying. I feel like shit. I'm shaking, hot and cold, and I can't breathe. I don't know what I'm feeling." He took in a sharp breath and held it.

"I don't know what I'm feeling either, Ben. What you did, what you said to Aaron was wrong, about him dying. Being dead. You can't think of him that way."

Ben held up his hands, "I'm sick now, Maggie. I want to throw up."

"I'm sure you do."

"No, I have pains running from here to here." Ben struggled to speak through a fog and traced a line from shoulder to shoulder. "I can't get comfortable."

"Sit up," Maggie ordered, and when she saw he couldn't do it himself, she gave him a push. His body was alarmingly slack and slick with sweat. He smelled sour and frightened.

"Did you see the way Aaron looked at me?" he said. "It's a terrible thing to see that look from your kid. It could kill you, I swear to god." He shimmied his shoulders to throw her hands off. "No, this is worse. Let me lie down."

Ben rolled onto his side, and with his knees pulled up fell asleep almost immediately. During the night Maggie awoke to his sharp movement. His legs stiffened and bent, opened and closed, and Maggie listened to the awful sound of his anklebones smacking against each other. He ground his teeth and snapped his elbows. He shivered and sweated, moaned in bad dreams, and she knew he'd made himself sick.

In the morning Ben wasn't in bed, and Maggie was relieved he was up, and had let her sleep. She heard him moving around and talking to Lily in the kitchen. When she got up, she saw that the bathroom window was open; she wondered if Ben had leaned out to watch her sitting alone in the cold last night. In the yard to the left, her neighbor was on a stepladder trimming a bare cherry tree with a handsaw. He turned to look up at her.

Downstairs, Ben was walking the short length of the living room while he carried the baby. He was still in the clothes he'd slept in, and his head was bent at a sharp angle to the left, so that his ear was near his shoulder.

"What are you doing?" she asked.

"Oh, well," Ben said without raising his head or stopping. "Having a hard time getting comfortable. I feel a little better moving."

Maggie's fingertips turned cold. "How long have you been doing this?"

"I don't know. I don't know what time it is. I must have pulled something yesterday, lifting the . . ." His words trailed off. "Trying to walk it off, the strain, or . . . I gave the baby . . ." He struggled to finish the sentence. "Will you hold her?"

"Look at me," Maggie commanded as she took Lily from Ben. "Try to straighten your head. Can you look at me?"

He gave her an apologetic smile. His lips were blue against his teeth. "I can't really do that now. Have to keep tilted. If you want to talk —"

"I don't want to talk. I think you're having a heart attack."

Ben pushed past her. "Crazy. I run every day, great shape. I am not having a heart attack. Don't you think I would know?" He was trying to be forceful, but there was no force to his words. "Gas, maybe. That awful chicken. I'm not much of a cook. It will go away."

When Maggie caught Ben by the shoulders and put him in a chair, he didn't resist. "Don't get up," she warned, and called 911. "Don't move." His head flopped to one side.

As they waited and listened for the siren, Maggie kneeled on the floor and put Ben's sneakers on for him. His feet were cold, and his skin was tinged with purple. He put a weak hand on top of her head. She wanted to tell him that he couldn't die, that she loved him, that she understood how the fear of losing could make you want to give it all away first. She held on to his ankles and pressed her face to his shins. When she looked up, his eyes were wide and expectant.

"It's passing, I feel better now," he said, and smiled at his weak attempt.

The paramedics arrived, there was a flurry of tight activity around Ben, and Maggie was suddenly outside the circle created by the men and their equipment. She sat in the dining room and held Lily. In her fear, Maggie knew she was strangely focusing on details, how the cats had eaten off the plates during the night and pawed their way through the icing on Ben's birthday cake, leaving pink paw-prints everywhere. She saw how the white shirts strained over the backs of the paramedics as they bent over Ben, how these men were too bulky for the room. Ben was lost among them and she saw only his sneakered feet.

After they put Ben in the ambulance, Maggie got dressed. In the car she struggled to buckle the baby's seat, and pinched Lily in the process. The baby wailed. The car stalled when she put it in reverse, stalled again at the end of the driveway. Her feet moved heavily on their own, and wanted to be running, not driving. In the mirror she saw that a line of neighbors had collected to watch the morning's action. They stood on their swept steps and slick black driveways, next to rows of perfect hedges. The man with the handsaw had placed the toothed edge against his leg. On their faces was a look of speculation, part curiosity, part unease. Some were people Maggie knew; others she was sure she'd never seen before. In the unusual light of the morning, in the season's earliest shift, in the way the air pressed down on Benton Road, there were those who had finally emerged, but only for the gruesome sight of a man leaving by ambulance, and its precautionary lessons.

15

I T was an absolute rule, they insisted: no babies allowed. Somewhere beyond the massive, chest-high desk, beyond the blond woman who ignored Maggie bearing down on her and the thick, wheezing doors was Ben. Just once in all the bustle, she'd seen his face gray with fear.

"Do you know when someone dies back there?" Maggie demanded. "Do you feel any responsibility at all to tell us out here?"

The blond woman looked up from her computer but her fingers were still poised over the keyboard. She was only irritated by the interruption, not moved by the question. She's probably been called a bitch and a cunt, Maggie decided, and people have tried to reach over the desk — now she understood the reason for its height and heft — to slap her face, yank her gold chain with the filigreed cross right off her neck, bend her fingers back until she gave in and told them what they wanted to hear.

"No one's died," she said coolly. "So why don't you sit down."

"I can't. You see, I have this baby — I already told you that — but I also have to go in," Maggie insisted. She wanted to say that the problem really was that she didn't have enough arms to hold Ben *and* the baby, that it wasn't fair to make her choose. "So we have a problem with your rule."

"You're just going to have to hold on," the woman told her, and gazed at Lily. "Maybe you should call someone to come be with you. That's what most people do."

Maggie turned away from the desk and looked out into the waiting area. Half dressed and half forgotten was the room's code, and Maggie, disarranged and fluttery with anxiety, fit right in. Wasn't everyone imagining death in this place? Wasn't that why the building buzzed with a low roar of terror? No one, and not the nurse behind the desk, was going to make a sympathetic exception for her. A man in blue work pants hadn't had time to find his belt, and when he went to the desk to ask what was happening to his son — drug overdose, Maggie decided — he clutched at his waistband like he'd clutch a child's hand at a busy intersection. One woman shivered without her coat. Her shirt was a faded jade nightgown that clung to her thin breasts, and a smear of turquoise toothpaste was stuck in the corner of her mouth. A baby in filthy, footed Tasmanian Devil pajamas crawled around on the floor, dragging a bag of Cheez Doodles from the vending machine behind him. The place smelled of bad food and alcohol, and the swirled dust from a distant vacuum cleaner.

She went to the single working pay phone. The receiver was sticky and strangely warm in her hand, and Maggie thought about how much bad news had been sobbed into the thing. The ribbed metal cord was cracked like a twisted spine and too short; it was impossible to hold the phone and the sleeping baby without crouching. A sulky kid watched her with a smirk and went back to picking at his fingernails. Maggie called Dale at Doris's, but no one answered. On her second try, she left a message on the machine for anyone who picked it up: *Ben is in the hospital.*

Defeated, Maggie sat down on a plastic chair. It had been almost an hour since they'd brought Ben in, and now a stream of

better-looking people, ones who had waited to have their break-
fasts and showers, to drop the kids off at school or do a little
banking before coming in, filled the waiting area. They sat with
their legs out, ready for the long wait, undisturbed by gusts of
activity and stretches of calm. She lifted Lily from her stiff shoulder. The baby had a damp, shitty smell to her, and Maggie
moaned.

"What's up?" the woman next to her asked.

Maggie looked at the baby on her lap, at the man still on the
phone, and then at the woman, whose black skin and bleached
hair made such a contrast that she seemed to glow.

"I forgot a diaper, and everything else, if you can believe it."
Maggie's own laugh surprised her, but she heard weepier strains
hiding in its core.

"You weren't thinking, that's all." The woman lifted a huge can-
vas bag onto her lap and began to poke around in it. "My son?
He's four, and he doesn't wear Pampers anymore, but I always
keep a couple in here, you know, to remind me of when he did."
She held out a diaper and smoothed it like a piece of fine material.
"It's going to be kind of big for that little baby, though."

"Thanks. It's a lot better than nothing." Maggie put Lily down
on the chair, and the woman snapped a couple of baby wipes
from a plastic pack and handed them to her. "So is your son
here?" Maggie asked. The words felt too large, like teeth that
weren't hers.

The woman had been staring at Lily, her bent legs and her
folds of flesh, and she looked away quickly, as though she'd been
caught. "No, my mother. She fell out of bed this morning. She's
way too fat, and of course she has to call me to bring her." She
turned to watch the revolving door unload its steady catch, and
Maggie knew there was something deeply unsure about the
woman beside her. She could feel it making the row of seats
tremble. "Nope. Could have called anybody, but she calls me,
and now I miss work. Just fell out of bed, that's all."

The woman picked up a magazine and began to read as
though there had never been any conversation. The pages

flipped furiously. In front of them, on a spot on the floor, light from the window mixed with the light from overhead, like water on ice, like the pond by the library she and Dale had stood by almost three weeks earlier. It was the woman's son, six, or ten, or fifteen, Maggie suddenly realized, who was in the emergency room, now and probably all the time. And what could his mother do but sit out here and wait and offer other stories?

She looked up to see Nate standing a step inside the revolving door. The people who circled through banged into him, and he rocked forward but didn't move to get out of their way. His eyes met Maggie's, and he stumbled as he maneuvered between the seats toward her.

"Hey," he said, glancing from Lily to Maggie. His shoulders were hunched, his neck and head rounded downward as if he were standing in a punishing wind. "How's Ben doing?"

"You know, I'm not really sure." Maggie's voice was empty, but also hardened against him. "How did you know I was here?"

Nate sat opposite her, his hands jammed under his thighs. His face, like his clothes and body, was tired and loose. He had the look of someone who's had nowhere to go for a while. "I saw the ambulance."

The woman next to Maggie got up and dragged her bag, as though it were filled with stones, to another seat. Nate moved into her chair. Maggie felt the heat of his body move toward the baby.

"What do you mean you saw it?"

"Jesus, Maggie." Nate sighed, and looked away when he spoke. "I was on your street when it happened, when they took Ben out. Okay? I mean, I'm not proud of acting like a stalker, but I was there. I watch, to see what you're doing, see how the baby is. See what Ben's up to, how Dale is. I have a lot of free time these days." He forced an empty laugh. "I want to see that you're still there, I guess."

"You've been watching me?" Maggie was floating, her chair bobbing on water. "I can't believe you."

"I have a right, Maggie. And I could take Lily if I wanted."

"You have a right?" Her breath locked in her throat. "You know what? — fuck your right, Nate."

For a minute he stared at his hands splayed on his knees. The muscles in his neck throbbed. "Look, I'm not crazy. Maybe just out of my mind that one afternoon, but what the hell was I supposed to do?" he asked. "I told Dale what I've been up to."

Maggie shook her head. "No, she said she hasn't talked to you."

"Not true." Nate shrugged. He was not entirely uncomfortable letting Maggie know she'd been lied to by her daughter. "Sorry."

Dale had known, then, that Nate had been watching her. She'd performed in front of the window and stood posing with the baby for him. She had opened the back door so he could hear what she was saying. Was any of it — her attention to the baby, her act of confidence — real, then? Maggie's mind was thick with confusion.

Nate looked at her not unkindly, but she saw that he was not about to reveal to her the shape of his marriage. She understood that what he and Dale did and decided was theirs alone and always would be. It didn't need to make any sense to her.

"I think that nurse over there wants you," Nate said, and nodded to a woman who waved at Maggie. "You should go."

Maggie didn't like the straight line of the woman's mouth, the boyish narrowness of her hips, or the way she stuck out one heel of her white clog to hold the door open. Her crooked, beckoning finger filled Maggie with dread. The television sound blasted on suddenly, and the baby began to cry.

"I can't bring Lily in there," she explained. "They won't let me."

"I know," Nate said. "So I'll sit here with her and wait for you to come back. I told Dale, and she's on her way over. You have to go see Ben now. He's probably going out of his mind, wondering where you are." He looked quickly somewhere past Maggie. "I'm not bad, you know, just an idiot sometimes. And I'm sorry about everything." The nurse waved impatiently again. "I came in to help you, that's all."

"I don't trust you, you know."

"I'm sure you don't." Nate sighed. "But you used to love me, Maggie. I know that's true. And Ben — well, you just shouldn't leave him alone now. It isn't fair."

Maggie felt the weight of resignation, of acceptance of what was hers now, and she handed Lily to Nate and walked toward the doors that were still held open for her.

THEY were moving Ben upstairs to the Cardiac Care Unit, and Maggie was pressed against the wall by the sudden current of his gurney passing in front of her. She squeezed into the elevator with him, a transport man, and two women. Ben's face was slack but not relaxed. An IV, like a quill lodged under the skin on the back of his wrist, quivered slightly as the elevator bumped up. Maggie wanted to touch him, but stuffed her hands into her pockets.

"Heart attack probably." Ben's voice was breathy, as though a load rested on his chest. The black woman's bag of stones; it would squeeze the life out of him. "You called that one."

"Sure, I'm a real medical genius." Maggie could hardly look at him now, so anxious and scared, with a sky-colored Y of tubing up his nose. The floral designs on his gown gave him a soft, helpless look. "How do you feel?"

"They were going to give me a clot buster. That name — pure macho power, don't you think? Clot buster, ball buster, ghost buster."

"Dustbuster," Maggie added. She recalled the tendons of pain on his face the night before, and how she'd thought they were his punishment. "But do you hurt now?"

"No pain." Ben breathed in pinched, cautious puffs. He forced a smile, but it looked only like humiliation.

He was slipped into a capsule-shaped space enclosed on all sides by a curtain. Through the noise of alarms, beepers, and rubber soles across the floor, there was the high whistle of Ben's breathing and the halos of stains, blood, shit, vomit, on the

striped cloth that waved in a mysterious breeze. Not carnival
stripes, or the stripes of a party awning, but faded and badly colored, as in some disquieting dream.

Ben lay with his hands palms down. Flecks of parsley from last
night's dinner were still under his thumbnail, a detail that made
Maggie weak for its history and its part in her life. A nurse hovered over him, tugging, checking, adjusting, asking questions. She
stuck several round patches onto his bare chest, attached leads to
them, and switched on the monitor to the right of the bed. Ben's
heart rhythm etched itself across the screen, hopeful and beating
to show that all was well. His blood was drawn, rising startlingly,
richly, in a glass tube, and she remembered the last time they'd
made love, a week earlier, how a steady melancholy had risen in
her so that she couldn't even speak to say she loved him.

When the nurse left, Maggie stood up and began to move frantically around the tiny space. "I wish this room had a window," she
said, and tugged at the collar of her shirt. "A view of anything
would be better than this. And it's so loud in here," she went on.
"Maybe I can turn down the noise on one of these things." Maggie
faced a confusion of knobs and switches and steadied a shaking
hand with the other.

"Don't," Ben said. "Jesus, don't touch anything. What are you
doing? Talk to me. Where's Lily?"

"She's with Nate." There didn't seem to be any point now in not
telling him the truth, though she saw his look of surprise and pain.
"They wouldn't let me bring her up and he was there." Maggie
hugged herself. "It will be okay. I promise."

Ben nodded, too weak to disagree. His eyes closed and his
mouth moved to the amplified sound of his heartbeat. "I'm going
to be an old man after this, Mags, and you're going to leave me. I
need you, but why would you ever want me now?"

She looked at his bare, freckled shoulders, the droop of his
gown, his chalky skin, and the thin tear that slid down his cheek.
What he was asking was whether she loved him enough for this
trouble, for the unexpected and the unwelcome, which would

change their lives. The question terrified her and she couldn't answer. The cardiologist arrived then, blunt with interruption and noise as he pulled back the curtain. A heart attack, he confirmed, and explained that they wouldn't know the extent of damage, if there was any, for a while. They would keep Ben on a cardiac monitor and move him to an intermediary unit in twenty-four hours if there was no change.

The doctor delivered his words and moved his hands in careless, authoritative gestures, as though he were used to scattering futures in the air. Ben's mouth was so dry, his tongue caught on the roof of his mouth when he spoke. He's desiccated, Maggie thought, a brittle, ancient man in this repulsive tent. Is he mine now to take care of forever? Am I trapped by his illness? This is not Ben! she wanted to scream, this is not my man. Maggie had wanted to dance into love and maybe out of it, never be ensnared by it. She stumbled through the curtain, which clung to her face like a scolding.

The hall was momentarily quiet. The next patient room was empty, the bed flat and white, everything set for the man who was moving a too-heavy bookcase at that moment, the woman in the meeting whose skirt suddenly felt too tight, the wafer of an old lady in the nursing home choking on some memory. Maggie went into the tiny bathroom and locked the door. She touched the long cord dangling in front of her and the engraved plastic sign on the wall instructing to PULL IN CASE OF EMERGENCY. This was an emergency, but in the middle of it she was for shit, selfish, a coward. A better woman would rally and reassure instead of run away. A better woman would already be thinking of what to do next instead of wondering how it was that life, that someone else, had tied her down once again.

Hidden in the tight enclosure of the room, smeared chrome and white tile, Maggie heard water coursing through the hospital pipes, and when she leaned against the wall she felt it rushing through her like loss. It was all around her now, splashing and filling the room with the form of her round-faced father. At the beach once, when she was eight, he had pretended to drown, slipping away between the high, purplish waves. Virginia had fallen to her knees in the sand and pulled at her bathing suit. Her mother's silent, solitary collapse had frozen Maggie; she thought her heart had stopped beating. But when her father emerged just yards down the shore, full of his own joke and slapping his chest, it was already too late for him to take his death back from Virginia; she had already lived it and wouldn't ever truly forgive him for doing that to her. Maggie was simply grateful to have him back.

She had imagined Ben's death that morning; for a minute she'd seen her life without him. The truth was, she had never entirely wanted the obligation of love and everything it exacted, and so she'd held some part of herself back from it. But now it seemed that in the truest life, pain was part of happiness, responsibility was part of release; you couldn't ever have one without the other. Ben was hers, so was his fall. For a while she'd allowed herself to picture a different way — Lily for Dale, Ben for loneliness, dreaminess for reality — but life wasn't predictable or controllable like that. The picture suddenly seemed cruel and foolish, and Maggie was humiliated, a fool, and humiliated again.

THAT night after she left the hospital, Maggie swerved to avoid a dog crossing Commonwealth Avenue so lazily it was as though he had other things on his mind. When she turned onto her street, she saw Dale's car in the driveway behind Ben's. Though earlier Dale had come up to the hospital floor to say that she would take Lily back to Benton Road, Maggie hadn't been sure she really would. As she parked she had a flash of earlier, the bright sunlight, the man trimming the cherry tree with his handsaw in the wrong weather. It could have been years before. The cats, who were sitting on the steps waiting, came rushing in with her through the back door.

Though it was not even ten, the house was still, and Dale had left the light over the stove on, something Maggie never did. The kitchen had an unfamiliar smell and feel to it, larger, cleaner, more solid in the almost-dark. Other forgotten lights, the tiny one in the hall that only worked by turning the bulb, had been left on for her, illuminating angles and depths she'd never noticed before. It was how someone else might see the place. It was how she might see it if she didn't live alone anymore. She realized she had always looked at Ben's presence as something temporary — a box of unpacked books, a painting leaning up against a chair — something to move around, rather than move in. Upstairs, she looked into Lily's room. The baby was asleep, snoring lightly, her hands flat on either side of her head. Maggie dragged with fatigue.

"Dale?" she whispered when she stood outside her daughter's old room. She imagined Dale wide-eyed under the canopy, surrounded by the glass animals winking in the dark. "Are you awake?" When there was no answer, Maggie opened the door. A sweet, humid cloud hovered in the air. At first, as her eyes adjusted, she could barely make out the shape of the bed or her daughter asleep in it. The light from the street washed over Dale's cheekbones, the tip of her nose and forehead, her shoulders, the tops of her breasts, one nipple peeking above the blanket's edge.

And there, next to Dale, another shape shifted and pulled at the sheets. The same light caught the peak of Nate's nose, the thrust of his chin, the point where his collarbone met and dipped, and beat with his pulse. His hand brushed against Dale's arm, his fingers dragged along her skin and over her breast. And the sweetness in the air was suddenly, very clearly the smell of sex rising from the stirred bed. And why shouldn't she have expected it? It was the scent of feet touching under the covers, of lips pressed against hot eyelids, of heated bodies, of herself and Ben not too long ago. For a moment Maggie simply stared, and then she backed out of the room, her fingers pressed against her mouth.

WHEN Maggie got up in the morning, bruised and disarranged from bad sleep, Dale and Nate were in the kitchen. Nate, dressed in a jacket and tie, was watching Dale feed Lily a bottle. The baby hummed slightly as she pulled at the nipple. In the bright light, they looked like they'd always been there in this sunny pose; she was the one who had simply woken up out of place, in the wrong house, superfluous. She was tempted to grab Lily from her daughter and run. Dale stiffened when she saw Maggie.

"I would have woken you," she explained quickly, as though she sensed her mother's cold assessment of the scene, "but you were exhausted and I thought you could use a few more hours. I already called the hospital. Ben's doing fine."

Maggie pictured him, bare-chested and fixated on his heartbeat, and her mouth went salty. Nate handed her a cup of coffee.

"Where are you going?" she asked him. It wasn't what she wanted to know at all — What are you doing in my house, with my daughter, with this baby, was closer to it, but she couldn't form the words yet. She drank the coffee, hoping for its bitter, immediate jolt.

"He has an interview," Dale answered, as Nate ran a finger under the knot of his tie. "At Parkside Country Day. Tenth grade English, and boy's basketball."

"Teaching? " Maggie asked. Her face grew hot.

"These people at Willow," Nate explained, not looking at her, "they basically scare the pants off you. But they have no intention of telling anyone about what's happened because they think it would make them look pretty bad. So I'll get good recommendations from Willow and end up teaching somewhere else."

"My God," Maggie said, shaking her head.

Nate glanced at Dale, who had gotten up to walk the baby. She was bent toward Lily, her face hidden, and Maggie recognized the gesture as her own, one that said, I will hide in you so I don't have to think about what's happening here. It infuriated her.

Nate cleared his throat. "I guess I should get going."

"And what do *you* think about all this, Dale?" Maggie demanded. "It seems like a system that doesn't work very well. Too easy to walk away from it all — and walk into it again."

"Yes, you should go," Dale urged Nate. "I'll see you later."

When the noise of Nate's car had faded away, Dale turned to Maggie, who saw in her daughter's face just how thin the shell of her marriage still was.

"Leave him alone," Dale said angrily. "This is mine, between me and Nate. He's *my* husband. This has nothing to do with you, not your business. People fuck up, it happens. I forgive him."

"But what about what he did? You just forgive him if it gets *you* what you want?"

"Yes, if it gets me what I want," she said, holding the baby. Her eyes were the elegant color of platinum. "You don't forgive because you're generous. You forgive because you're selfish. You get to a point when you can't stand to think about what's happened anymore or what you've lost, because it doesn't get you anywhere. It just screws you up more. It's done. I have to deal with what I have left."

"What *do* you have left?" Maggie looked down at her bare feet, pale and entirely familiar on the scuffed floor, and asked herself the same question. Only this baby seemed clear at the moment.

Dale put Lily in her seat and poured herself a glass of water, which she finished in a long, leisurely sip. She wiped a single drop off her chin with the back of her hand and sat down. Her hair was pulled back tightly, to reveal the fine sculpture of her face. "I have Nate," she said finally, "and I have my marriage."

Maggie saw how much her daughter had changed in the weeks since she'd shown up at her back door, so undone and panicked, demanding Lily back. Dale was full of clear resolve now, salvaged from everything she'd known she was in danger of losing. It showed in the way she sat straight, crossed her long legs under her nightgown, and looked at her mother with a kind of cool, pitiless patience. It showed in the way she rested her fingers on the baby's head.

Maggie felt a sudden stab of pain behind her eyes, which made her shiver. "You want me to forget everything?" she asked. "Just like that?"

Dale nodded. "Something along those lines."

Maggie had never seen her daughter so self-assured in all her life, not swayed or blown around as she'd always been by her mother's stronger storms and louder winds. Not tethered to her mother at all anymore. Isn't this what she had always wanted for Dale, wasn't it remarkable strength? Maggie tried to rub the pain and the question from her head, and said she had to get to the hospital to see Ben.

16

MAGGIE hesitated in the lobby before going up to see him. She thought her sudden lightheadedness had to do with the fact that she hadn't eaten since the day before, and not that she'd rushed away from her house and Dale. The coffee Nate had given her earlier sat meanly in the bottom of her stomach. The gift shop was to the left of the bank of elevators, its windows filled with carnations, as red and bold as infarcted hearts. Inside, it offered carpeted distraction, with bobbing balloons, thick paperbacks and magazines, fuzzy slippers, and bleachers of candies. With candy, Maggie thought, there was no deciding what you *needed*, only what you wanted, a rare and welcome dilemma in a hospital.

"You still eat that shit? You're going to get so fat."

Maggie swung around and dropped the box of Raisinets at Doris's feet. Start at the shoes, she told herself as she bent to pick up the candy piece by piece, then look at the weave on her socks, the white horizontals and then the black verticals. Notice the stitches in the hem of her pants, the careful creases up the legs, buy some time to think. She struggled to stand up but it felt as though a load of cinder blocks were balanced on her back.

Doris's face was hard and startlingly clear, polished. Her eyes were bright, as if some sticky film of optimism had been washed away. Maggie wondered if this woman had always looked so vibrant, like the kind of person who goes to the cliff's edge for the best view, not the kind content to sit in the parking area and gaze through the windshield with the motor running. Maggie saw her in a new light; Doris was walking confidently on a dark street, singing out loud, laughing unselfconsciously, admiring herself in the mirror.

"I haven't been up to see him yet," Doris said. "And I don't know if I will, actually. I woke up this morning and decided I should see Ben if he's going to die, but now they say he's going to be fine. So what's the point, really?" Doris hoisted the strap of her bag higher up on her shoulder. "It's like he has the flu or a sprained ankle. I wouldn't come running for that anymore. Believe me."

"But you're here. You came."

"And I'm not sure why now."

"I was thinking," Maggie said, aware of how easily she fell into the old rhythms of their conversation, "how women always imagine they're going to die giving birth. I don't mean we dwell on the idea, or that we're even really aware of it, but it crosses our minds, maybe just for some fraction of a second, this possibility of explosion, destruction, of total body failure. We get close to it." Doris looked impatiently at Maggie, who continued: "I'm not sure men ever get so close to the idea, unless of course they're in a war. They don't picture dying, like we do. Ben was so scared, too scared to admit what was going on. He's still shocked that it could have happened to him at all."

Some picture of her husband played across Doris's face, but she let it pass, like a woman who's learned to live with the annoying interruptions of memory. "I never thought I was going to die when I had my babies," she told Maggie. "That was only you. Over-reacting." She paused. "Ben's going to be an invalid after this, you know. He might be okay physically, but the idea of getting old or sick terrifies him more than anything else. Have you noticed how vain he is? Does he do those idiotic exercises in front of you? He's a perpetual child, stuck somewhere at about eleven years old. He doesn't take his failings well, either, but you know that much about him. He's a sulker, a demander, he needs more babying than a baby. He'll nurse himself over this, and he'll expect you to nurse him too. So there's your future, Maggie, there's your brilliant lover and your new life. Your hands are really full now, but better you than me." She paused, took her sunglasses out of her bag and put them on. "You got everything you wanted, didn't you?"

Doris left the shop and Maggie followed her. They stood without talking on the semicircle of pavement that beached the hospital's entrance. A man carrying an enormous bouquet of flowers passed, and Maggie wanted to say something about how funny it was that his head was completely obscured by the dog-ear petals, so that he was a plant with legs, but she knew Doris wouldn't see it that way anymore, at least not with her.

"I'm sorry about how this happened," Maggie started.

"No, you're not." Doris waved away the apology. "I slept with Milt, you know. It was really pretty awful." She made a face and laughed uneasily. "Is this what you really want, someone who acts like Ben did? This is the part I don't understand, because I know you so well. Ben lied to me, he hurt me, he didn't think of me or the boys or anyone but himself when he decided to start sleeping with you. How do you pretend that's okay now all of a sudden? When it's about you, you simply change your mind? Are you that desperate that you don't see anything for what it is anymore?"

Maggie couldn't stand to hear Doris's words, which buzzed so close to her face. "Things weren't perfect with you and Ben," she said. "You'd been talking for years about splitting up. Be honest about that much."

"No one said perfect. What a crock of shit that is." Doris let out a derisive snort and then her face hardened. "But it was *ours*, Maggie, you weren't a part of it, so you can't ever know what our marriage was about. You don't understand the way people really are with each other, the push and pull, and you never have." She stepped one foot off the curb, but stopped as though she'd suddenly forgotten where she was headed. "I mean, look at you and Dale."

"What about me and Dale?"

Doris shook her head, amused but tired now of the conversation. She let a truck roar by before she spoke again. "You've always been invested in her failure. Did you ever make her tough times any easier? How about her tough times with Lily and Nate? Ever since she was a little girl you've held so much back from her.

"God, I remember what you were like when you found out she couldn't have kids. You disappeared, you were never home, and when you were, you weren't really there anyway. She came over to my house so often after school, and we'd play board games or talk or sometimes go shopping, and she'd end up crying a lot of the time. Gordon would come and pick her up. Sometimes he'd stay for a while and we'd have a beer. He was as miserable as Dale. I bet you never knew."

"No, I didn't." The picture made Maggie sick with regret.

"And then when you had the chance to give her a baby, you took it back from her. It's quite amazing, really. You can't stand to think she might not need you so much anymore." Doris began to walk away, but stopped to add, "I know I would never be so careless with my child."

SOMEONE had brought the pitted barbecue up from the basement and placed it on the grass. The night was oddly warm for January, hovering near a freakish 60; the air felt unsure, as though it had landed in the wrong place. Maggie looked at her house and knew that life was taking place there — she could feel its gentle pulse — but she didn't want to go inside. For a minute she stood and watched the coals blink and sigh in the dark. She hoped the day's tense inactivity, the hours sitting and waiting with Ben, would drain away, but she felt it clogged in the back of her throat. All day she'd ached to hold the baby.

Ben's new hospital room had a window which was partially blocked by the top of an enormous evergreen. The morning sun behind it had cast a green tint over his face. Even the light changing throughout the day had made his moroseness only look more mossy and sunken. His body had developed a mesmerizing tic, a nod to the predictable beep of the heart monitor, as though it was saying all he could stand to hear. He wouldn't ask about the baby. What words might throw his rhythm into an erratic pattern?

"Finally, there you are," a voice said through the open back door. "Oh damn, where are my slip-ons? So okay, no slip-ons. Oh, it's getting really cold out here, Margaret. Have to remember this isn't Florida." Virginia walked across the grass and placed her silky hands on Maggie's cheeks. "How are you, sweetheart? Things okay? My God, you look terrible."

"Thanks a lot." Maggie smiled, and touched the teased waves of her mother's hair. She imagined it was what a cocoon felt like, protective but soft. "I didn't know you were coming."

"Neither did I until last night." Virginia's sweatshirt was stunningly white, which made her face look bright and young even in the dark. "It was Dale's idea, so here we are. Nate," she whispered, and raised her eyebrows conspiratorially, "picked us up at the airport this afternoon. Sweating buckets, too. I like to see that in a guilty man. He was trying much too hard to make jokes and sounding like a jackass, so I told him to cut it out."

"I'm sure you did," Maggie said. Nate would stand too close, he would stare a little too intently, she knew. He'd touch a lot.

Ricky opened the back door. His sweatshirt was identical to Virginia's, though his strained across his broad chest. He said Maggie's name several times, and while one hand reached toward her, the other waved a long barbecue fork. Forty-five years on the Philadelphia Police Force; the man knew how to carry his weapon.

"Our prayers are with you," he said solemnly, and kissed her. His breath smelled freshly gargled, his smooth cheek liberally cologned.

"Lord, Ricky, he's not dead," Virginia said.

"I know that. How you doing, honey?" Ricky hiked up his green pants and put an arm across Virginia's shoulders. "You okay? How's the Professor doing?"

"Margaret doesn't look good," Virginia told him. "Old, don't you think? And you have a little rash." She touched Maggie's jawline.

"I'm just tired."

"Sure you are," Ricky said. "A lot's been going on." He pulled two kitchen chairs onto the grass. "Have a seat, girls, relax. You two talk. I'm just going to get those steaks and get dinner started. A barbecue in January. Do you love it?"

"He cooks," Virginia said. "Good thing, too, since I refuse to do it anymore. I did my years of kitchen duty."

Maggie remembered five years earlier when she met Ricky at the funeral of Virginia's only sister. At the time, he was just another one of Virginia's boyfriends, men with forced enthusiasms and awkward references to first wives and grown children, and Maggie didn't think she'd see him again after they'd eaten their fill of soggy food at the wake. But he told Maggie how he and Virginia had met at a coffee shop, even what they'd had to drink that day, and she saw how the tiny sandwich he held in the palm of his big hand trembled when he talked about her mother. Maggie swore she saw his lower lids fill, as though he might cry from pure joy in the form of Virginia. It had left her touched, hopeful, and oddly empty-feeling.

Virginia chatted about her flight from Florida and her troubles packing for such unpredictable weather, about the cleaning she'd done inside. Maggie saw only the highs of her mother's face illuminated by the stray lights of the neighborhood. She looked like a talking mask, with blank eye holes and mouth.

"Where's Lily?" Maggie asked.

"Dale's putting her to bed." Virginia held up a warning finger and then let it rest, with a dot of pressure, on Maggie's forearm. "Now you stay right here. She's doing fine, you don't need to butt in and tell her otherwise."

Maggie heard Ricky banging around in the kitchen and the low thud of the refrigerator door closing. "You can't come here and rearrange everything," she told her mother.

"Who's rearranging anything?" Virginia crossed her legs tightly. "Dale is Lily's mother, not you. You're the one who rearranges things when you don't like them the way they are."

Was it true, as Doris had said, that she was invested in Dale's failure? Maggie stood up and walked toward the house. Behind her, Virginia lit a cigarette and inhaled deeply, a backward sigh.

Upstairs, Maggie heard Dale and Nate with the baby, but slipped past them into her bedroom and shut the door. Smoke from the grill squeezed through cracks in the walls and around peeling window sashes, teasing and intrusive. She lay down on the bed and listened in the dark to sounds moving through her house. She could re-create the particular double-beat thump of Gordon carrying Dale upstairs, how his weight had always fallen twice on each step; he was extra cautious with his daughter in his arms. She knew the whispering sound of Dale wandering through the kitchen looking for Maggie, the groan of Gordon at the end of the day, the cool blue echo of the house with only herself in it. But what she heard now were movements she couldn't identify, except to say that they were of another time in this house, of people she didn't know very well, of different circumstances. They didn't include her and they didn't belong to her in any way. She was suddenly very cold, and got under the blankets.

BEN HAD BEEN sitting up waiting for her when she had finally gone back up to his room after encountering Doris in the gift shop. His hair was wild and bent from lying down and his eyes were focused on the spot where she appeared and then stopped. Maggie didn't know if his intensity came from a certainty that she would show up or his fear that she wouldn't. He simply stared at her, not at her eyes but something just below, as if she'd arrived to tell him something and now he couldn't understand what she was waiting for, why her mouth wasn't moving. Maggie walked to the window, and thought she saw Doris driving down Longwood Avenue at that moment. Could Ben smell his wife on her, or could he see Doris reflected in her face?

In the afternoon, the doctors had informed Ben of the extent of damage (mild), their recommendations (rest, a stress test in a few days, nothing more). This would not change his life, they told him; he could resume normal activity very soon. When they left, Ben let his head fall back against the pillow and asked Maggie, as though he'd become suddenly helpless, to find the control that would flatten the bed. His face levered away from hers and his eyes gazed toward the back wall, its metal plates, spigots, and buttons.

"But this is *good* news," Maggie said, standing over him. "Didn't you get that part? Good news, nothing more to be done. You'll take it easy for a while and that's it. This isn't going to change you."

"Of course it's going to change me," he said irritably, still looking away. "I always thought I could do anything. I thought I could have everything if I worked hard enough for it. But then something like this happens, and you realize that it's all out of your control. It has nothing to do with how much you want something."

What did I ever want so much? Maggie asked herself. There was Lily, but the more she tried to fix the baby in her mind, the more Lily floated out of reach, like a wonderful day you try too hard to remember in detail. What she had now, in real form, was Ben — pale, hooked-up — and something true about herself.

"That doesn't mean you should stop wanting," she said.

She brought his bed up again, and when he looked at her the tightness in his face began to relax, and she thought he finally understood she was there. "Are you surprised by me?" he asked.

"After all these years? Us? Yes, a little."

"Me too. We probably shouldn't be, though. It seems pretty right, as if it's always been there."

"Maybe we should go away. Just us," Maggie said, and then laughed. "We've been in the same place for so long. But what am I saying? You'll never do it."

"No, that's a good idea. When I'm out of here, in a little bit, after I talk to my boys, if Aaron's okay, we should take a trip. Someplace we can swim every day, float on our backs. Maybe learn an important new skill, like snorkeling."

"Someplace we can stay a really long time," Maggie added. Someplace far from what we've given up to get there, she thought.

MAGGIE listened to the sounds of Lily falling asleep in her crib, like a parade getting farther and farther away, and then she got out of bed. Virginia was still in her chair when Maggie went outside, but now she was wrapped in a jacket, with a blanket thrown over her shoulders. Ricky stabbed at the meat on the grill. His face was shiny with the fire's heat. Dale stood in front of Nate, who had his arms crossed over her chest. She looked uncomfortably cold but unwilling to admit it.

"Finally." Virginia glanced cautiously at her daughter. "Ricky, don't overdo it. No one likes leather."

"Ginny, honey," he said patiently, as though he were used to being treated as if he were slightly addled, "I have everything under control. Nate, why don't you go get Maggie a coat. Her teeth are chattering."

"I'm fine," Maggie said. "But why a freezing picnic anyway? You all look a little purple to me."

"Because this is so" — Dale groped for the right word — "unusual. I mean, who ever does this?" The enthusiasm in her voice was drawn, like a tight wire. "You'll get used to the cold."

"And the *night*," Ricky gushed. "A beauty. You don't see *this* in Florida."

Nate returned from inside with a coat, which he placed lightly over Maggie's shoulders. She could tell he was trying not to touch her or smooth the wool across her shoulders or flip the collar up against the cold. That morning's awkwardness, and the months of distrust, was like a tiny bird flapping, exhausted, between them, deciding where to land before it died.

As they ate dinner the legs of their chairs sank into the damp ground, until their knees and the plates resting on them rose higher and higher, until they were all similarly hunched. When they were done, and the plates tipped onto the grass, Dale leaned over onto Nate's lap. When her eyes met Maggie's, she shut them.

"That looks good," Virginia said, and rested her head on Ricky's wide thighs. "Keep me warm, honeypie."

"Certainly," he said, glancing at Maggie. "Tell us how the Professor's doing."

"He's a little blue." Maggie looked up at the stars. *He's mossy green.* She gave them the doctor's report. "He'll come home in a couple of days, I imagine."

The word "home" hung unclaimed above them.

"Men get depressed when something like this happens. I had a heart attack once, you know." Ricky tapped at his heart under his white sweatshirt, just as Ben had tapped his under the hospital gown earlier. Maggie felt her own blood turned into slush by the cold.

Virginia sat up abruptly. "You did?" Her voice was full of panic, as though it were happening in front of her that moment, and she moved to the far edge of her chair. "You never told me, Ricky."

"A small one. Went around for weeks — this was before your time, Ginny — thinking every little thing I did was going to kill me. Eat a cheeseburger — bang, I'm dead. Toss a football — I'm dust. Change the oil in my car — forget it. Sex — no way. What did I do? I didn't go to work for a couple of weeks. I just sat, and I didn't move, and I didn't want anyone near me because I wanted to be able to feel the next time my heart went on the blink. They shouldn't distract me in any way. I guess I wanted to feel what it was like to die. Don't ask me why — it wasn't going to do *me* any good, and I wasn't going to be able to pass it on and make a million bucks from it. And of course, no one wanted to be near me anyway after a while. I was a pain in the ass. Then one day I just got irritated at how I was thinking, so I got back on the job."

"Where you *really* could have been killed," Dale said, her eyes still shut. "That doesn't make a lot of sense, you know."

He laughed. "I figured that out a little late. And then I met Ginny and I didn't think about it anymore." Ricky tipped back in his chair. "Beautiful up there tonight. Amazing. Hey, Gin, you see these pink stars now?"

Virginia didn't answer, but sat with her head bent, her hands balled in her lap. She was making a low cooing noise, and Ricky put his hand on her back and moved it up and down her spine. He didn't say anything or try to hide her against him or tell her she should stop. He smiled indulgently, almost proudly. Sitting in the dark, Maggie allowed a bit of stubborn admiration for her mother, and what she'd finally arrived at, to warm her up.

Through the window, left open a crack, and over Ricky's voice detailing stories of his police days for Nate, who nodded in appreciation, Maggie could hear the baby cry. Dale's head was still in Nate's lap and he had arranged her hair so that it flowed over his knees like a blanket. Dale was looking directly at her, but Maggie was not sure what, if anything, Dale had heard.

Maggie concentrated on the sound, a series of whimpers easily mistaken for the whine of the chair under her, the cats nosing around their food bowl inside, the coals imploding in the grill. It was also like a pinpoint of numbness, tiny but impossible to ignore once you'd located it. Virginia, her head back on Ricky's lap, seemed to be asleep, her fingertips twitching as they hung down toward the ground. In the house next door someone glanced out the window and then shut off the light. Again, Maggie looked at Dale, who blinked slowly in return. A silver film of dew had settled on her daughter's face; that's how still she was, how unready she was to leave Nate at the moment.

"I'll be right back," Maggie said.

Inside, the house felt thickly warm after the hours of cold, and was painfully garish in all the bright light. Upstairs Lily was crying in her crib, and Maggie talked to her. The words sounded awkward, as though she knew someone was listening from the other room. She slipped her hands under the baby but could hardly feel the soft pressure on her skin. She brushed the baby's back where her gown had risen, and Lily suddenly tensed. Maggie felt her icy fingers begin to thaw against the warmth.

"It's okay, it's just cold hands," Maggie said, and waved them in front of the baby. "I must be half frozen and didn't even know it." But Lily was unsettled now, and Maggie held her tightly, pressing the baby's mouth against her neck to quiet her. She was desperate not to have Dale hear the crying, which was as pure and sharp as glass, or see Lily arching her back.

"Is she all right?" Dale stood in the doorway, a bottle in one hand.
"She's fine."

"Do you think maybe she's sick? She felt a little hot before."

Maggie began to walk the room, so that Dale was only a blur with the light behind her. "No, I think it was just a bad dream."

"I didn't know babies had nightmares. What would they be about if they did?"

Maggie shook her head, and noticed how Dale had chosen not to move into the room but stood leaning against the door frame. She understood at that moment why they'd stayed outside all evening: because Dale had finally decided this wasn't her house any longer. She didn't need it to be. It was not where her life was going to take place, not where she would imagine herself any-more.

"You'll take Lily tonight," Maggie told her daughter. It was a gift, a warning, and part of a question. A kind of sad relief poured through her. "Back to your house."

"Of course." Dale slipped the baby from Maggie's arms.

Dale went into her old bedroom, sat on the bed, and began to feed the baby. It was a startling sight, Dale so completely familiar in that spot, the bed's canopy over her like a light hand on a child's head, her girlish collections still in formation around her. But there was also the baby now, and Dale was so completely focused on her that she didn't even look up at her mother standing there. How it should be, Maggie told herself as she left the room.

*   *   *

HOURS later, Maggie awoke in the middle of the night to the sound of her mother and Ricky making love. They weren't loud or frenzied, but there was a rhythm and a rocking, as if they'd rolled into each other in their sleep and, confused about where they were, found this particular comfort. When they were done, Maggie stood in the dark of her room and saw her naked mother tiptoe down the hall to the bathroom. The skin on the back of Virginia's thighs drooped like expensive window treatments, her behind glowed white, her shoulders were dotted with luminescent spots. She held her hands up near her shoulders, like a young girl walking on her tiptoes.

SUNDAY-AFTERNOON airport traffic slid into the Callahan Tunnel like sludge, thick and dirty. Dale wasn't bothered by the cars bearing down around her, while Maggie, in the back with Ricky, the baby's car seat empty as a cupped hand between them, felt the pressure as though it were directly on her chest. She hated to think she was becoming one of those women who panic on bridges, sniff their food before nibbling it, catalogue their frailties, allergies, phobias, cramps. But even this packing-in was too much for her. The man in the next car was giving Dale the finger and licking his lips at the same time, the haze of the tunnel was blowing at them like this was some sort of noxious amusement park ride. The Tunnel of Love.

Dale gave the finger back to the man. "Fuck you too," she said.

"Oh my God, don't do that, Dale. What time is it now?" Virginia asked Ricky again. Tension ran through her body, and the thinnest line, a zipper from her recent face-lift, flushed pink.

"Plenty of time," Ricky assured her. "We will not miss our flight, and if we do, is that so terrible?" He looked over at Maggie and leaned his head toward her. "Your mother here always thinks we're going to miss our plane, our bus, even the movie we don't want to see very much. We're two hours early to everything."

"I'd rather wait than worry," Virginia said primly. "You're doing a good job, Dale honey. You just keep concentrating. But don't make any of these drivers mad, please. I read in the paper terrible stories about what they do." Ahead, a driver leaned on his horn, and Virginia slammed her hands on the dashboard. "Really, Margaret, if you hadn't insisted on coming, this never would have happened."

"No. This is Boston and the traffic would have happened without me." Maggie watched the left lane creep up beside them. Drifts of garbage, doughnut bags and paper cups, tumbled down the tunnel's gutter. It had been Dale who'd asked Maggie to come to the airport.

"Maybe an altercation up ahead," Ricky announced. He took off his seat belt, rolled down the window, and leaned out.

"For crying out loud, what are you going to do, arrest them?" Virginia asked. "And the fumes are killing us. Shut the window. We are definitely going to miss our flight now."

"You are definitely not," Dale said. "Just relax. God you're uptight."

Ricky fished around at his feet and found some old student papers of Nate's, which he began to read, his eyes widening. He cleared his throat and tried to cross his legs in the tiny space. Virginia bounced forward as he kneed the back of her seat. Maggie caught Dale's eye in the rearview mirror and looked away quickly. She couldn't get out of this tunnel and run if she wanted, but she could move over into someone else's car, slip in right next to them on the front seat. Take me wherever you're going, she'd say, though I'd love to see Provincetown because I haven't been there in years, or Gloucester, or Marblehead, so dramatic this time of year. I love the way the waves smack the brown, lined rocks. Drive me anywhere, but I have to be back tomorrow. I'm picking someone up at the hospital — and who knows what will happen beyond that.

"Don't come in with us," Ricky said when they'd finally reached the terminal's curb, "it will be easier this way." He motioned for a porter, then he leaned into the car. "You girls call Ginny tonight, okay? Or else she'll be miserable and I'll be hearing about it forever." He turned, to see Virginia pushing her way through the automatic doors, not looking back. "Gin's a worrier. She loves you both, just wants good things for you, Maggie, so be nice, okay? That's all," he added, and then hurried to catch up with Virginia, calling her name.

Dale drove, with Maggie still in the back seat. She maneuvered the car through East Boston to avoid the traffic and snaked into tight neighborhoods Maggie was surprised Dale knew her way through. The houses looked damp and split from a wet winter, all triple-deckers with sagging, soft porches anyone could fall through. She thought she could hear them splintering now in the cold sunlight. Dale slowed the car in front of a gray-shingled house that sat on the flat peak of a hill. Beyond it the city spread out like a brilliant stain.

"Why are we here?" Maggie asked. "Are you and Nate buying this place?"

"No, I just wanted you to see the view," Dale said. "We happened on it by accident last night after we left your house, and I thought you'd enjoy it."

Maggie wondered what Dale and Nate had been doing, what they'd been looking for when they found this place. And when they'd come upon it, why had Dale thought of her? In the cold, clear light, warehouse buildings fingered out into the harbor like hands resting on a bed. It would be beautiful and serene at night.

"It's a funny little city secret," Dale said. "There are still a few left, I guess." And then, as quickly as they'd come she drove them away again. "Where to now?" she asked.

"I need to pick up some things at the lab," Maggie told her. "I'm going back to work in a few days, when Ben's settled, so I should probably see what's going on before then."

"I'm in no hurry. Nate said he was going to take the baby for a walk and then put her down for a nap." Dale glanced at her mother. "I've decided not to go back to work. Dad and May have been really generous, so we don't have to worry about money for a while."

"That's nice for you."

"That's nice for Lily." Dale paused. "I know you think I shouldn't accept their help, but I'm going to."

"No, I think it's good you're taking it, it's the right thing."

Gordon had never wavered when it came to Dale. He was a true, good thing in her daughter's life . . . and so was she.

IT was always easy for Dale to find a parking spot, Maggie noted as they stopped in front of the Bain Building. When Dale got out, she looked up at the carved detail on the building's face just as she had when Maggie had brought her there as a child. Her calves pressed against the fabric of her blue jeans; she still had that slight girlish hyperextension in her knees.

"It's starting to rain," Dale said. "It's going to be a real mess."

The door was unlocked, and the two women walked down the dim hall. Nothing had changed, but it failed to move Maggie in any way. She imagined now that it was a place she could leave and never think about again.

"Do you know how long I've worked here?" she asked, her voice echoing in the stairwell as they climbed. "Longer than you've been alive."

"I can't imagine being so long in one place. Didn't you ever want to do something else?"

"Maybe I did sometimes, but mostly it didn't ever feel long to me. I always had an idea that things were changing and progressing, different every day, that I was working toward something, so how could I leave that? I thought it was mine in some way. And you can't leave what's yours. It's too scary."

"So, *is* any of it yours?" Dale asked.

They stopped to look through the window of the door to the lab. Shelby was on her stool, her feet wrapped around the rungs, her head bobbing slightly to the music on her headphones. She looked warm under the bright light.

"No, not really." Maggie hesitated. "What am I saying? No, not at all. This work is Ben's, every piece of it. He'll always come back, because he made it. It's like one of his children to him." She looked at Dale. "Maybe I won't come back to work here. I'm not even sure it will make any difference."

"That's bleak. To just walk away from it like that."

"Not bleak at all. I really feel like I could do anything now. If anyone had ever told me I'd feel this way about my work, I wouldn't have believed them. I started when I was younger than you are now. I was going to be a big success here. I had good ideas, like Ben. No — better even, smarter than his. Then I got married, had you, got divorced, and I still thought someday I'd start again where I got off track. And here I am now, forty-eight, and I'm not sure I want it anymore. The time passed, but my life moved only a little."

"I don't think raising a kid is little," Dale said. "Some people think it's big, that it's all that really matters. It's the only thing some of us — most of us — can say is really our own. Not work, but kids."

"I wish I'd understood that earlier. I wish I'd understood when you were born that you'd be my best work. I'd have done a better job with you."

"Maybe not. Maybe being a mother wasn't the job you wanted. Maybe you didn't want me at all, maybe you weren't ready. Motherhood isn't for everyone, you know." Dale was gentle in her speculation, but not forgiving. "Anyway, you're a slow learner."

Maggie looked at her daughter; a child who wasn't wanted can turn out to be loved entirely. It was an uplifting idea.

"The slowest," she said.

Maggie told Dale she wanted to get something from her office and that she'd meet her in the lounge down the hall. She went to the bathroom, and smelled the blood even before she sat down. She expected to find it flowing out of her, but there was only the tiniest red spot on her underwear. Maggie knew that after everything, she didn't understand her body any better now than before, its miracles and will. *I could have another baby all my own now* — the thought made her laugh.

A single fluorescent light blinked on the lounge ceiling. Dale was sitting on one of the black plastic couches, watching the pre-storm stir through the windows in front of her. In one corner of the overheated room the Coke machine hummed and dripped steadily, a sound as familiar to Maggie as her own voice for the innumerable hours she'd spent in that spot, looking at the same view. She sat down next to Dale, their shoulders inches apart. Past their twin reflections in the glass, Maggie was sure she saw the streak of an airplane pass into a gray cloud. She thought of her mother digging her fingernails into the seat's plastic armrest with each bounce of turbulence. There was a lot her mother longed to get home to.

"So Ben's getting out of the hospital tomorrow," Dale said.

"That's the plan. He's coming home with me. He's going to need some help for a while."

A student Maggie didn't recognize came in and bought a soda from the machine. He left without looking at either of them.

Dale shifted on the couch. "Aaron told me what happened that night at Ben's birthday dinner."

"Yes, it was awful for everyone," Maggie said. "Ben's heart broke."

The storm had exploded on the other side of the window, and Dale's voice was muted by the sound of rain hurling itself against the glass. "Look at that. It's your favorite kind of weather. Perfect timing."

Dale would be fine, Maggie knew at that moment. She had a clean place to lay out her life. A baby could change everything, and Dale had always known that better than she did. Nothing was ever perfect, there was always a loss for a gain; she'd lost some part of Dale and Lily now, but she'd gained something that was beginning to feel vaguely like serenity, like release. Maggie knew she couldn't give anything more to her daughter or the baby. This, finally, might be enough for the three of them.

*   *   *

WHEN Maggie looked out the kitchen window, she saw that the trees hung more heavily over the yard than they had the summer before. People claimed it was the result of a particularly icy winter and wet spring, but it seemed more than that to her. Everything was prone to fits of greedy growth followed by fatigue. Nothing knew when to slow down, and today, in the strong heat, the trees dozed and drooped under the weight of their own enthusiasm.

She and Ben hadn't gone away — this window's view was familiar but not in the least wearisome — though they still talked about the possibility. Maggie said she didn't think she could stand to miss another season's change, that a year ago her eyes were half closed all the time. Behind her, Ben was already well into a story, the remains of breakfast still on the table. These days, his stories often included his boys, Doris, the minutes of Aaron's day and the texture of his skin, the short time they'd had with Lily. Today the story was about Maggie, which made her realize how long she and Ben had been together, in one way or another. Sometimes she couldn't bear these reminiscences for how trapped they made her feel, how settled and decided it made their lives sound — how much like marriage it all was — and she'd tell him to stop.

But at other times, she knew things were going to be fine, she was ripe with happiness, and the truth of distance from Dale and Lily was not perfect but tolerable and probably right, and Maggie would let the cadence of Ben's voice carry her out into the back yard. Contentment was a wonderful drug, she'd discovered. Now she could still hear him talking, and though she'd drifted a little too far away to catch every word, it was good to know there was no urgency and she could always ask him what he'd said later on.

She looked admiringly up at her stoic house, then at the flats of faded flowers, which should have been planted already but were actually more beautiful as they faded. At moments like this, she couldn't help but imagine Dale in a yard in another part of the city. Her daughter would be wearing a shirt the sweet yellow of the pansies, shorts the color of leaves. The back door to her house would be open for the breeze. Lily would wander out on fat legs and bare feet, unsteady in the grass, to find Dale thinking of her mother. The child was Maggie's best work; both children were. Maybe they would all see each other in the late afternoon again, when it was a little cooler.

ACKNOWLEDGMENTS

In writing this book, I relied on the friendship and advice of many people. I would especially like to thank Judith McClain, Ann Harleman, Peter Kramer, Rachel Schwartz, Barbara Stevens, Elizabeth Keithline, Sandra Kunhardt Basile, Jill Schlesinger, Deb Norman, and the Providence Area Writers Group for their support and encouragement. I am enormously grateful to my editor, Sarah Burnes, for her insight and instinct, and to Jennifer Carlson, my agent. Thank you to Tobias and Alexander, who inspire me, and to Michael, my first and last reader and my heart.